I0669457

THE STEEL FIST

James K. Burk
writing as Rob Jackson

WolfSinger Publications ⟩ Brackettville, Texas

Copyright © 2023 by James K. Burk

Published by WolfSinger Publications

All rights reserved.
No part of this book may be used or reproduced in any manner whatsoever without the written permission of the copyright owner.

For permission requests, please contact WolfSinger Publications at editor@wolfsingerpubs.com

All characters and events in this book are fictitious.
Any resemblance to persons living or dead is strictly coincidental.

Cover Art copyright 2023 © Lee Ann Barlow

ISBN 978-1-944637-37-8

Printed and bound in the United States of America

DEDICATION

To Larry Ward and Doug "Redd" Ross,
who were there at the birthing.

CHAPTER 1

"Don't turn around—just drop the guns."

The voices came from only a few yards around the corner where Hasteen and Logan should be waiting. Reynaud caught his Mossberg bullpup by the foregrip and slung it to the ready position. His index finger tapped the safety off with only the faintest click. With the shotgun at his shoulder, he sprang to the side, clear of the corner. He pointed his weapon at the nearest of the five men who'd gotten the drop on his friends.

He shouted as he pulled the trigger. His target, a man with a rifle, was flung back, the rifle spinning through the air. A sound like a single, rolling explosion roared in his ears and three more of the ambushers tumbled backward, then Hasteen leapt after the leader's pistol. The fifth man's rifle still pointed at the ground and before he could swing the muzzle up, Logan whipped open his duster and touched off a burst from his Ingram. The spray of .45 bullets took the man in the upper chest and the body almost backflipped.

Hasteen snatched up the leader's pistol and sprawled among the bodies, scanning the buildings facing them. Reynaud pumped the shotgun's action and spun to make sure no one was behind him, then pressed himself against the wall and swung his weapon up as one of the sheets of plywood covering a second floor window swung open.

"You boys better get up here quick. I'm Norton."

A man concealed from Reynaud by the plywood tossed down a rope ladder, which quivered and clattered against the wall.

Sure he was safe for the moment, Hasteen thrust the dead man's pistol into his belt and reloaded his own weapon, a task his practiced hands completed in mere seconds. He dropped a cartridge case into the mouth of each of the men he'd killed.

Logan grinned up at the hidden figure. "You sure took long enough to answer your door. We catch you on the crapper?"

"I saw those boys lurking around. I hoped they'd just move on, but this'll work as well."

Hasteen gestured to Logan. "Go on up. I'll cover you."

Logan released the MAC-10 to let it hang by its makeshift sling and hauled himself quickly up the ladder. Reynaud followed as soon as Logan's body disappeared into the opening then crouched beside the open window, watching the streets as Hasteen clambered up. As soon as Hasteen was inside Norton hauled up the ladder, slammed the plywood shut, and slid shut a bolt. After glancing at the men, Norton turned and led the way out of the room behind the window, down a corridor, to another, smaller room. The second floor of the old OTASCO store had apparently been used as a warehouse, with a few smaller areas partitioned off to serve as offices.

Norton laid down his M-4 and gestured at a small camp stove beside an alcohol lamp. "T'isn't really coffee, but it's hot, black, and bitter. Help yourselves."

Finding half a dozen enameled metal cups, Reynaud chose one of the cleaner ones. After filling the mug with the fragrant liquid from the pot, he sipped at it cautiously. It was too hot to drink, but he recognized it as chicory. Sitting down on a box, he studied Norton while the others helped themselves to the brew. Norton was a big, burly man and, from the facial lines visible above a thicket of beard, a good-natured one.

"You must be Hasteen O'Ryan," Norton said, gesturing to the Colt single-action revolver in the plain buscadero rig. "You've got a good rep with that thing, but I'd heard you were rather dressier." Like everyone else in the room, Hasteen was wearing faded jeans. He also wore a denim work shirt that'd seen better days and a gray-green cloth around his head, on which he wore, Mexican-style, a black, flat-brimmed hat with a beaded hatband. The only other distinctive items were the ankle-length Navajo boots and a piece of leather tied around his left wrist to hide his ketoh, the bracelet derived from the bow-guard.

"That was Rennie's idea. He said that where we were going it might be better if I didn't flash as much."

"Good thinking." The beard was split by a grin and a hand the size of a ham was thrust toward Reynaud.

Reynaud took the hand and shook it. "Reynaud Dechaine. The other fellow is Logan Reid. He's an alumnus of the same Russ prison camp I graduated from."

"The more the merrier," Norton said, and shook hands with the other two. "Slattery recommended you pretty highly—all of you—but I've decided Reynaud will be running the show. I've got some other people you can use if you want 'em, so look 'em over first chance you get and decide whether to keep 'em or not."

Logan tipped back his charcoal-colored cowboy hat. "Were those gunnies outside part of the problem?"

"Them? Nah, they're just the usual third-rate scavengers who hang around the fringes of a herd. The opposition is a helluva lot more dangerous than that. Any of you ever hear of a group called The Steel Fist of the Lord's Righteous Fury?"

The others shook their heads.

"They're the usual fascist bastards that take names like that. The guy who started it was an ex-state department thug. We think he was tied to the CIA, but we can't prove it. After he left Foggy Bottom he put his thumbs into a lot of pies. He started out as a gunrunner and middleman, and eventually built himself quite a pile in Latin America. He found a friendly government down there and even started his own arms factories. At one time, he was equipping two or three of the nastiest bastards in the region.

"The arms operation got shut down when the asshole he was backing got shot, and he had to duck and run, but not before he'd shipped back a lot of ordnance and cash. He used the money to buy into a lot of businesses and prospered mightily, as the saying goes."

Norton poured chicory into a cup and watched the steam rise. "Benjamin Rutledge might've been crazier than a pet skunk, but he wasn't stupid. He apparently either anticipated the collapse or was worried about the possibility, and he set up cells in the Ozarks and on the left coast and a few in other places. The plague killed about as many of his nuts as it did anybody else, but they'd insulated themselves against the worst of the other problems— the food riots, the disasters, the sudden collapse of services—so they lost about fifty percent of their population instead of eighty to eighty-five percent—or higher, as in the major cities. And they were organized. They hit the National Guard armories where they could reach them and caught a lot of guardsmen trying to hold things together. When we and the Russians nuked each others' and everybody else's petroleum processing centers, the Steel Fist was barely touched, since they'd already squirrelled away massive fuel stocks.

"They've got troops, they've got armor, and they've even got some air cover. All their enclaves were situated for survival, but this base in the Ozarks is also well located for raiding, and I think they've got something a lot bigger planned."

Norton sipped at his chicory. "I hope to have more information for you in the next day or so. For now, you have some time off. Meet the other group, tell me who you like and who you don't."

Reynaud nodded. "By the way, we've got somebody else meeting us here. A fellow called 'the Deacon.'"

"Billy Joe McCluskey? Are you sure that's a good idea? I hear he's a little—"

"Crazy? Yeah, but he got crazy in the same Russ POW camp Logan and I were in. We've watched each other's backs before."

"Okay, you've got him. It's just that setting a fundamentalist to catch someone who talks the jargon seems a little dicey to me."

"Who've you got?" Logan asked.

"There's three of them, maybe four. Mario Petricelli is a big-city boy. He's medium height, medium build, black haired, so he more or less blends in. He was probably a 'mechanic' for somebody back east, but he's a good man at his specialties, and I think he can be trusted. Sally Thomas is a local girl, blonde, kinda short, with a figure that won't quit. She's a nurse, works for a traveling dentist named Charley O'Malley. He's iffy. He's balding, wears a suit and tie most of the time. Sally's got her own reasons for wanting to be in on this, and they're good ones."

"Personal, I presume." Reynaud downed his now-lukewarm chicory in one swallow.

"The biggest question-mark is a mean little dude who goes by Xuan or Deklay. Slattery heard about him; says he's supposed to be a fierce little mutha. He hates Army, isn't too crazy about Anglos, don't know how he feels about Cajuns."

Reynaud answered Norton's grin with one of his own. "Guess I'd better go find out. Where do we find these upstanding citizens?"

"They've been hanging out in a place called The Emergency Room." At the question in their eyes he grinned again. "It was a warehouse set up as a field hospital for the plague. Anybody can give you directions to the place. It's about five blocks north of here and two west." He nodded to Hasteen and Logan. "Why don't you boys go see if the coast is clear? Rennie and I will join you in a couple."

Hasteen had finished his chicory while Logan had sipped experimentally at his then ignored it. Both men got up without a word and left the room.

"Slattery gave you a real strong recommendation. If you're still alive after this is all over, how'd you like a permanent job?"

"Doing what?"

"The same thing I'm doing—helping rebuild. O'Ryan isn't the type. You only have to look at him to know he lives for the wire, the challenge. I've heard he's killed upwards of seventy men, but he doesn't even notch his guns."

Reynaud laughed. "He quit awhile back. Said his stocks looked like they'd been to a woodpecker convention and they were getting hard to hold onto. But he still keeps track. You probably didn't notice the string around his neck, but it has eighty-two beads on it."

"He doesn't care about the killing, Rennie; that's not why he does it. He keeps count because that's how many times he's been tested and passed the test. Someday he'll either fail or become an anachronism. Logan—I guess he's paying back for the time in the camp. When the fire in his belly goes out and he's built up some *dinero* he'll retire, probably open a bar or a whorehouse. But, according to Slattery, you're a regular crusader. You want to see things go well for people, and that's why you hate outfits like the Steel Fist."

Reynaud took out a twelve-gauge shell, checked to be sure it was 00 buck, and very carefully loaded it into the gun. "I'll talk to you about it after the party's over."

"Sorry, didn't mean to embarrass you." Norton stood, picked up his carbine. "There's a local, a fellow called 'The Colonel,' who's working for the Steel Fist. I'd like to have a chat with him; but wait until I give you the word. He's got a *pistolero* grafted to him and usually has four to six other bodyguards around. He's dangerous, and he's the only lead we have to the local chapter, so try not to attract his attention."

Reynaud stood and followed Norton back to the window. Logan was peering out through a crack. "Nobody there," he said.

"The bodies outside were stripped while we had our little chat. Looks like they even took the clothes that weren't all shot-up."

"They probably even took the cartridge cases I left in the mouths of the ones I killed," Hasteen grumbled.

Norton shot a look at Reynaud but opened the window without a comment and tossed down the rope ladder.

The three of them clambered down the ladder, then watched Norton draw it back inside and close the plywood.

"What was all that about?" Logan asked.

"Norton just wanted us to put the arm on someone, but that's for later. Right now, let's go find some friends."

~ * ~

The Emergency Room was doing a brisk business. The bar, made of planks and sections of plywood laid atop a double row of fifty-five-gallon drums, ran along the wall to the left of the door. Most of the rest of the large room was filled with mismatched tables and chairs occupied by locals, scavengers, travelers, and a few entrepreneurs.

As they approached the bar one of the bartenders leaned across the planks. "What's your pleasure?"

"Mostly sex," Logan said, "but you're not my type. What've you got?"

"'Shine, some tequila, jack, home brew, and some Vietnamese homebrew."

They ordered and Reynaud looked over the crowd. He found a party that looked like the group Norton had described. The dark-haired and dark-eyed man sitting with his back to the wall seemed to have noticed Reynaud and the other two from the moment they'd come through the door. To the man's right sat a blonde woman talking to a balding, cadaverous man who looked like an unemployed undertaker. The woman was plain, but she filled her jeans and peasant blouse nicely. The other man at the table was small and whipcord lean. His coarse, straight black hair was longer than Hasteen's, and he wore a cloth around his head and Apache boots. He was as dark as Hasteen, but his features were more refined, and his eyes seemed to have a trace more slant.

A glance told him Hasteen and Logan had also seen the group at the table. "Shall we go over and make our introductions?"

"Just a minute," Logan gasped after a sip at his drink. "I'll finish this and get another 'shine'."

Reynaud fished in his pocket and produced two of the new silver dollars, which he dropped on the bar.

The bartender looked closely at the coins. "You boys from Texas?" At Logan's nod, he refilled the glass. "We ain't got nothin' against the Republic here."

"Damn glad to hear that," Logan drawled, and grinned.

Before they'd stepped away from the bar they heard a voice, roaring over the din. "My ol' man usta call 'em zips. Said it was short for zipperheads. I never knew what he meant by that. I always called 'em dinks, 'cause they're all dinky little fuckers."

The source of the noise was a large man who'd just sat down at the table next to the group. "'Course, I guess you could call 'em dinks 'cause it rhymes with stinks, like that gawdawful fish-head beer they swill." The other three men at the table seemed to be enjoying their companion's attempt at wit.

"I think I'd like to kick a little dink ass tonight, and I think I see—"

The little man in the headband came out of his chair to his feet, and in the same fluid motion drew a large Bowie knife and drove it into the table in front of the big man. "Little boys brawl." His voice was surprisingly deep and rough. "Men use proper weapons to kill each other. If you'd rather, you can use this." He drew a roofing hatchet from his belt.

"Hey," the bartender bawled, "take it outside."

The big man grinned and pulled the knife out of the table. "I'm in the mood to do a little whittlin'." Watching the little man closely, he and his friends stalked to the door, followed by most of the crowd in the Emergency Room.

Logan put down his second drink. "Save this for me," he told the bartender, then smiled at Reynaud. "Looks like we'll get a chance to see the little guy present his credentials."

The three of them followed the crowd out to the dirt and gravel parking lot, where the circle of spectators and speculators closed in an area roughly bounded by two pickups and a burned-out hulk of a van. The circle was large enough for Reynaud and the others to easily find places to watch the action.

The two fighters squared off inside the circle. Reynaud heard

Hasteen bet five ROTdollars on the little man then he gave his attention to the two men in the center of the circle. The big man had peeled off a plaid flannel shirt and began working his muscular arms, loosening them.

The small man had removed his old army field jacket and taken off a large shoulder holster, which he handed to the blonde woman then he hefted the roofing hatchet.

"I'm gonna cut off your balls and feed 'em to you, dink," the big man roared.

As the little man moved forward, he slipped on a patch of mud and the big man, surprisingly fast, rushed him. The knife was a blur as it swept out and left a deep, bloody gash in the Viet's hip.

Almost instantly, the small man recovered and his good leg lashed out in a kick that left an angry welt beside the other man's left eye and, as the bigger man stumbled back, the hatchet swept out in its own arc and left a furrow on the enemy's left leg just above the knee.

"I'm really gonna hurt you for—"

Another kick, this time to the big man's uninjured leg, dropped him onto his back and the hatchet struck again, with a sound like a ball bat crashing through a picket fence.

Few of the spectators had expected the Viet to win, and almost none of them had expected the fight to be over so soon. The little man wrenched his hatchet free and walked around the body to pick up his knife. Almost negligently, he kicked the other man's head. The head recoiled from the kick then rolled back to its earlier position. If the big man weren't dead, he was certainly unconscious.

Without a backward glance, the Viet returned to the bar, limping slightly. Reynaud observed Hasteen collecting his bet and led the group back inside. By the time they'd reached the table, the Viet had put his shoulder holster back on and was donning the old olive field jacket.

"Lady and gentlemen," Reynaud said, "I'm Rennie Dechaine. A man named Norton said we could find you here. Do you have a place somewhat more discreet, where we can talk?"

The black-haired, dark-eyed man stood. "Charley's van is nearby. I'll get a bottle."

"My friend, Hasteen, here, has a few new dollars. He'll buy.

What're you drinking?"

A few minutes later, bottle in hand, they followed the dentist back to a van which held a dentist's chair and equipment. The Viet's limp was more pronounced, and leaving a blood trail. Charley pointed at the wound. "You're going to need some stitches. I'll boil some water."

Reynaud stared at the little man more closely. "What do we call you?"

"Xuan. Or Deklay." He stared back at Reynaud with expressionless black eyes. "My father was Apache, my mother Vietnamese. What is your pedigree?"

Reynaud grinned. "I'm Cajun. You go looking back far enough, you'll find French, Spanish, Black, and American Indian. If Xuan is fine with you, it's fine with me."

After a moment, Reynaud added, "I would suggest you keep your temper on a shorter leash."

The needles and gut had been sterilized and Xuan unzipped his jeans and slid them down, then lay down on the grass.

"I thought I showed great restraint. The man was looking for trouble and he wasn't going to leave until he found it. By challenging him directly, I excluded his friends from the fight." The dentist started on the first suture, but Xuan's face and voice revealed nothing. "I think he was still alive when I left him. I didn't finish him, which would've turned that crowd into a mob." He seemed to consider the matter another moment. "Yes, I think I showed restraint."

In spite of himself, Reynaud smiled. "You're very persuasive." He looked around at the others. "You must be Mario," he said to the Latin-looking man. "What're you doing here? It's a long way from the bright lights."

"It's been a long time now since there were many bright lights." The man's accent was northeastern. "Detroit might not've made it, even without the nuke. Nothing left to rebuild when all the power's gone and most of the tools besides. I've heard New York is even worse."

Finishing introductions, Reynaud said, "We're waiting for a friend, Billy Joe McCluskey, sometimes called 'the Deacon.' He can be obnoxious in a lot of ways, particularly with his religion, but he's a friend who's stood by us through trouble. Do any of you have any problems with that?"

This was answered by silence, and he looked into each of their eyes. If any of them had reservations, they were keeping their doubts to themselves. "Do you have any longarms?"

Charley poked his thumb in the direction of the van. Climbing inside, Reynaud picked up an Armalite AR-18 with a four-power scope. The AR-18 had been designed by the same company who'd produced the AR-15, but after they'd learned better. Its stock could be folded flat against the left side of the receiver, and the weapon could be fired with the stock folded.

A hardshell rifle case contained an L115A3 bolt-action rifle chambered for .338 Lapua Magnum, mounting a Redfield three-to-nine power scope. Ammunition for it would be hard to find but, short of a .50 caliber, there was no better tool for reaching out and touching someone when long distance was even better than being there.

He also found a Remington 870 twelve-gauge pump shotgun with a folding stock and, tucked down in the corner of the van, a little Armalite AR-7 survival rifle.

As he backed out of the van he glanced around and noticed the sun touching the tops of the pines. "Logan and Hasteen and I had better be moving if we're going to be out of town by curfew. I hear the local troops are a little trigger-happy. We'll meet you back here tomorrow, a little after noon."

Logan and Hasteen followed as he strode through the camp, threading his way around tents and makeshift shelters until they were clear of the place and making their way through forest and rugged rock gullies. They were careful to avoid ridges and open areas that would leave them silhouetted against the sunset. Twice they stopped, once when they heard movement in the brush ahead, and once to rest. While they rested, Reynaud sat and breathed deeply of the clean air, basking in the beauty of the sunset and the wooded country around them.

The sun had set and it was almost full dark before they reached the safe house. The propane tank was long empty, and Hasteen started a fire in the stone grill behind the house. While Reynaud cooked up skillet bread, jerky, and a pot of chicory, Hasteen drew water from the pump by the barn and filled the trough by the corral. Logan had already kicked a bale of hay from the loft and brought out two buckets of oats to the feed trough.

No one spoke until they'd eaten and Reynaud had shoveled dirt onto the fire. "I think," Hasteen said, "I'm going to put on the other gunbelt. I don't think a second gun will draw all that much attention, and I felt half naked today."

Reynaud thrust the shovel into the ground and sat on the end of a log. "What'd you think of the gang at the van?"

Logan sighed as he moved to a more comfortable position, his back resting against the same log. "The city boy didn't have much to say."

"He doesn't know where he's headed," Hasteen observed, "but he knows where he's been, and he didn't like it. He moves good and I think he'll be all right in the woods."

Reynaud nodded, although the others couldn't see it in the dark. "He's a steady hand, and he doesn't miss much. Xuan worries me a little. I think he's got a taste for blood."

"He's wound tight," Hasteen agreed, "but he looks to be a good man in a fight. He's got sand."

"The girl looks pretty able, too," Logan said, "but the dentist is no Doc Holliday. The first time there's trouble, he may burn a trail out."

"We'll see. We may get to find out how much nerve they have before we leave Springfield. Norton seems to have some work for us before we ever leave town."

Just inside the door they took up the kerosene lamps, lit them, and each of them took the room he'd claimed as his own. Whoever had once lived there had known how to live. The chest of drawers in Rennie's room was handmade of cedar, with bent muleshoes for handles. After leaning his shotgun against the wall beside the bed, he pulled off his jeans jacket and tossed it at the chair, then stripped off his gunbelt and placed it on the nightstand with the butt of the Smith and Wesson .45 within easy reach.

He finished undressing and blew out the lamp, then lay down on the bed with a grateful sigh. He hoped he wouldn't dream of the prison camp tonight. Those nightmares were less frequent now, but still unwelcome. To try to influence his dreams, he went to sleep visualizing the bayous he hadn't seen since he'd left for Creighton and the Air Force.

~ * ~

Hasteen woke to the sound of gunfire and tried to open his eyes. At first, there was only darkness, then he began to distinguish blurs; his eyes couldn't seem to focus, and his entire body felt as though the fever had burned him to nothing but ashes. When he'd passed out, fever-ridden, he'd slipped under consciousness to the sound of the Yei-be-Chai chant. Now he heard only the soft whisper of a light breeze and—there it was again—another gunshot.

His bones were hot, soft lead, and his muscles made of feathers, but he could at last see a jug holding water and dragged himself to it. Unable to lift the jug, he pulled it over. The water was warm and brackish, but it was life.

The water stung his cracked lips and he almost groaned as it reached his parched throat. When he thought he could stand it, he drank again.

His vision had gradually cleared, and he looked around the hogan. From the dim light, he guessed it was late afternoon. He seemed to be alone and wondered at that.

When the plague had struck and the doctors and hospitals proved worthless, many of the Dineh had gathered for a Blessingway outside Kayenta. They'd built hogans in the old way, all with doors facing east, and tried to retreat from the plague into the old ways of healing. He became aware of the stench of death, and realized the plague must've followed them. He felt panic, but passed out before he could crawl to the door.

The next time he woke he crawled back to the jug and drank again, but not so much his stomach would throw it back up. The hogan was darker and cooler; evening had come. He heard another gunshot, then a rough voice.

"Don't seem worth the trouble to shoot'em. They're all dead or dying, near dead anyways."

"You better not touch'em. Maybe they gotta different kinda plague."

Then Hasteen knew the only ones left in the village were the spirits and the enemies outside.

His eyes searched for a weapon then he saw his father's gunbelt. Rory O'Ryan had been a stuntman, following the camera crews. Hasteen could remember long visits when he was small but, as he grew older, the visits had become shorter and less frequent.

The only things Rory O'Ryan had left his half-Dineh son were the double-belt fast-draw rig, a pair of Colt single-action revolvers, and lessons on how to use them. He'd taught Hasteen fast-draw, how to point and shoot, knowing your bullet would find its mark, how to fan the gun and keep all the shots inside a target the size of a dinner plate at twenty-five feet, how to "roll" the gun, which was even faster than fanning, and just as accurate. He'd also taught him how to take the guns apart, how to tune the weapon so on half-cock the cylinder would turn at the lightest touch, with a tick like a fine watch. When his visits became less frequent, his mother's brother had continued the training, taking him to matches.

Now Hasteen needed the weapons and all the training he could recall. He already had the determination to kill.

Crawling to the gunbelts, he drew the guns and, in the dim light, checked them: they were empty. The cartridges in the belt loops were wax loads used for fast-draw matches and practice. Better than nothing, Hasteen decided. At close range, they could smash a brick, although they were useless at longer ranges.

After loading both pistols, he shoved one inside the waist band of his jeans and crawled to the edge of the door. It required all his will and energy to force himself up, to lean against the wall. He was bathed in sweat, and his knees trembled, but he was on his feet.

Within moments, he heard the whisper of boots in the sand outside and, very near, a voice saying, "Let's get this wrapped up. It's almost dark, and I don't relish the thoughta bein' here at night."

His thumb on the hammer, Hasteen pulled the trigger of the revolver, so there'd be no sound until the hammer was fully drawn and the bolt locked into the cylinder notch. A tall, thin man stepped through the open door. Thrusting the pistol to within inches of the man's ear, Hasteen snapped the hammer back and let it fall. The gun roared and the man, shot behind the ear, was flung against the other side of the doorframe and crumpled.

Even as he shot the first man, Hasteen fell into the hogan's doorway, already recocking, and before he'd hit the ground he'd fired two shots into the man outside. Everything seemed to occur with agonizing slowness. Hasteen had time to see the man's frightened face, pale in the shadows' gloom, then the bulky shape dropped its rifle and clutched at its middle. The body collapsed and the feet twitched in the sand.

On the ground, Hasteen dropped his revolver and clawed out the pistol from the holster of the first man he'd shot, then rolled and dragged himself away from the door.

He saw, to his left, a muzzle flash and heard the sharp report of a rifle. Pointing the pistol he'd taken at the muzzle flash; he snapped off a shot. A man screamed and fell, then was silent.

Rolling again, Hasteen slammed hard into the wall of another hogan and lay stunned for a moment. When his head cleared, he pulled himself deeper into the shadows and glanced down at the gun in his hand. It was another single-action, a replica, and, from the sound of the shot he'd fired and the recoil, he guessed it was a .357 Magnum.

He'd hardly caught his breath when a man ran past where he lay and Hasteen fanned two fast shots into the shape, which spun and fell.

"Burke! Sills! Steiner!" The last of the jackals was plainly nervous, his voice pitched higher by a throat pinched tight by fear. Staying in the shadows, Hasteen crawled toward the voice. "Patrey! Sills! What's happenin'?" The voice stopped as the man realized he was alone with the dead and one mortal enemy.

They stalked each other in the darkness.

Hasteen was almost overwhelmed by the stench and the horror of that scene. Often, he came upon bodies of friends or relatives, or people he didn't know but with whom he shared common bonds. Some of the bodies were marked only by the ravages of the plague, while others had plainly been shot. He thought one of the bodies he found was that of a niece, but he couldn't be sure; partly because of the darkness but also because her features had been distorted by the shot that'd caved in her face and blown away the back of her head.

Near midnight, the silence was broken by the crack of a rifle. Hasteen was sprayed by tissue and bone chips from a body a few feet away, and he fired back at the flash, and a second shot at the scream, then followed the sounds of moans and sobs to where the man knelt.

By the dim light of the moon, Hasteen could see the man

doubled over, with a moist darkness at his waist and a shattered right elbow. Cocking his pistol, he pressed the muzzle against the man's forehead then pulled the trigger. The hammer dropped on an empty chamber. The man he'd taken the gun from had loaded only five rounds into the cylinder.

With a snarl, Hasteen threw away the empty gun and drew the weapon from his waistband. The man was still conscious. He'd winced when the pistol clicked on the empty chamber, and he looked at Hasteen with fear-stricken eyes. Tears had left long, dark streaks in the dust on his face.

"Please—help me. For the love of God, please—"

Hasteen touched the man's left eyelid with the muzzle and pulled the trigger.

The body thrashed, then lay still.

Hasteen relived the two days in hell he spent clearing the village. He found the sand paintings and gave the sand back to the desert north of the camp. The bodies of the thieves and killers he dragged with a pole to the south of the camp and left them for the desert's scavengers, apologizing to the coyotes and the vultures for leaving them such foul meat. The bodies of the Dineh he covered with rocks or sand where they'd fallen, burying with them all the personal possessions he could find.

When he left the camp, he carried with him only his weapons, his few personal possessions, a few days' worth of supplies, and almost ten pounds of raw silver that hadn't yet been worked into jewelry, and he took a crooked trail away from the place of the dead, so the spirits couldn't follow him.

Hasteen woke, sweating and trembling with the memory of finding his mother and his mother's brother and all his family struck down by the plague or executed by the thieves who'd come to steal jewelry and turquoise from the dead. His hand closed on the butt of one of his revolvers and he levered himself up, then realized where he was: a cabin in Missouri. Releasing the pistol, he sank back onto the bed. He'd had this dream often enough that he no longer dreaded going back to sleep. Staring into the darkness, he heard a moan from Rennie's room. He wasn't the only one haunted by nightmares, although that was no consolation. Forcing himself to relax, he stared into the darkness until sleep came to close his eyes.

~ * ~

Norton reached the safe house at about nine the next morning, arriving as Hasteen was practicing his draw. After waving to Reynaud, Norton strode over to stand beside him. "Damn, he's good. I'd like to see what he could do with live ammo."

Hasteen heard the comment and faced Norton. "I thought you didn't want us to attract attention."

Norton gestured at the trees. "We're far enough from town."

Hasteen emptied the snap caps from the revolver and loaded it from a box at his feet, then slid the gun into its holster and picked up a piece of gravel from the driveway. Placing the pebble on the back of his right hand, he extended his arm. The Colt was in his hand, his left hand a blur over the hammer, and they all heard a single long explosion. Dirt geysered and glass from a discarded bottle sparkled in the sunlight, and in the sudden silence they heard the pebble hit the driveway.

After emptying the six spent cases and loading six more cartridges into the chambers, Hasteen spun the gun back into its holster.

Norton raised his eyebrows. "I guess that answers the question I had yesterday—why you wore that antique. Those antiques," he amended, noting Hasteen now wore two guns.

Hasteen strode toward them. "For the average man, the autoloading pistol is probably the best weapon because, in some ways, it's the simplest, but a good man can fire a double-action pistol faster than an autopistol can be fired: it takes a tenth of a second for an autoloader to cycle. And a man who's really good with his hands can fire a single-action even faster. And there's never been a handgun built with better balance, points more naturally or fits a man's hand nearly as well as Colonel Colt's old hogleg."

"Speaking of colonels, how'd you like to bag one?"

Logan, who'd come out onto the front porch, joined them. "Colonel of what?"

"It's what used to be called an 'honorary title.' This guy doesn't have a nodding acquaintance with honor. He's ex-army, and he seems to have some pull with the military governor's people, but he doesn't have any real rank."

"Okay," Logan said, "How do we grab him and how soon do

you want it done?"

"I'd like to have a little chat with him tomorrow. There's a rumor the Steel Fist has someone planted on the governor's staff. The Colonel will know who it is, and he'll also have information about the local cells that I'd give his right arm and at least one eye for. It's not gonna be easy; he always has four to six men with him, besides his private torpedo. There's another seven or eight men at the lodge he uses for a headquarters. What'll you need to do the job?"

"How about the Hundred and First Airborne?" Logan said.

"They're busy this week."

"One hell of a lot more information than we have now, for openers," Reynaud said. "Also, suppressed weapons for everybody, preferably .380 pistols or 9mm subguns with subsonic ammo, and explosives."

"That order is almost as tough as getting the Screamin' Eagles. The info I can get, and I'll get what I can in the way of tools. I'll meet you in town with the information and whatever equipment I can scrounge up."

Reynaud nodded. "Where in town?"

"You know the place. The fella running The Emergency Room is one of our people. There's a back room behind the bar. I'll let him know you boys will be coming to a private game."

"We'll see you then. Right now, we'd better be getting on the way. We're supposed to meet the rest of the crowd at noon. And we'd better leave a note for the Deacon."

"Don't bother. I'll leave word with the man watching the place. Oh, was there anybody you can't work with?"

Reynaud glanced at the other two then shook his head. "No, no problems with any of them."

~ * ~

There were, of course, numerous rumors about the origin of the plague, but the most commonly accepted was one of the variations of the theory the CIA and the FSB, each operating independently of their government, had started the plague. The theory had been given credence by the fact the temporary governments of both nations had, after the plague, been controlled by those secret organizations, until it'd become impossible for any country as large or as multicultural as Russia or the United States to maintain a national administration. The result, in both places, was a deep distrust in and disdain for the remnants of the brief puppet governments.

The plague and its aftermath had worked other, more basic changes. Many major cities and facilities had been bombed in the brief war following the outbreak and the problems of maintaining equipment to provide power and sanitary services had overwhelmed most of the survivors. Cities were complex, interdependent structures and, once they were unable to provide necessary services, became largely obsolete. People still inhabited some of them, but it was in a precarious, day-to-day survival in an almost unbearably hostile environment.

No new maps were being printed, but if they had been, they'd have borne no resemblance to the outlines of territories in the past. The United States no longer existed as an entity. In its place were half a dozen centers standing like islands of relative calm in a sea of anarchy. A few enclaves, most of them former military bases, continued largely as they had before the war, but most of what had been a nation had been reduced to a collection of third-world nations.

Texas was in turmoil, headed toward becoming a republic, as was northern California. Much of the southwest had been annexed by Mexico, then, when Mexico fractured into a collection of smaller states, the region declared its independence. The Great Plains held only a dozen or so centers of what passed for civilization, none of them controlling an area of more than about five hundred square miles. The northeast was pocked with vast graveyards, the skyscrapers serving as massive tombstones. The only other regions with any real identity were the southeast coast and Florida.

With the failure of the network by which goods and services were provided, most effort was bent toward simple survival, but the few attempts to deliver almost-forgotten amenities were generally successful.

When Reynaud, Hasteen, and Logan had found the other group they discovered someone who'd capitalized on the yearning for the greatest luxury of civilization; fantasy and escape. A deli van had been parked at one end of the campground and the sides raised to reveal a large-screen television. Two men busied themselves attaching tarps to the top and sides of the opening while another shouted to the crowd.

"The MOVIES are HERE! Get yourselves up here to see the flick. Choice seat holders get to vote on the giggly of THEIR CHOICE! First three rows go for two bits or trade, next five rows go for an ounce or trade."

Hasteen was one of the first to buy a "seat," paying two of his ROTdollars for a place on the front row. Other customers paid with silver or canned goods or ammunition. When the choice places were all taken, the hawker passed around "menus" and pencil stubs.

After the votes had been counted, the barker shouted for attention. "Awright, the first film's gonna be *Miracle on 34th Street* and the second one'll be *The Magnificent Seven.*"

The area nearest the screen was solid with men and women sitting on the grass, the crowd almost as dense back to the practical limit of the barely adequate speaker system. The crowd thinned, further back, although even Reynaud, his back against a battered VW van, paid two rounds of ammunition to stay within sight of the screen.

Reynaud stared at the people sitting on the grass or, further back, leaning against vehicles. They were like starving people at a diner. He hadn't been surprised at the choice of movies. *Miracle* was about love and faith and children and *The Magnificent Seven* was about ideals. All those things had largely vanished after the plague. Violence was now a daily fact of life, and sex was easily available almost everywhere except in the fundamentalist enclaves, so Hollywood's two biggest staples had been co-opted, but values and dreams and ideals had mostly been killed off, along with most of the children, by the plague and its aftermath.

Perhaps, Reynaud reflected, this yearning for beauty was part of human nature. He'd heard that, almost a century before, even the most rough-hewn sodbuster cabin had held, in some special place, a Maxfield Parrish print or some other piece of art.

More people arrived as word of the movie spread, each new patron paying some nominal amount for a view of the screen. Reynaud glanced at Mario, lounging against the side of a converted bus. The rest of the group had joined the crowd near enough to hear the speakers. He and Mario had elected to be the eyes in the back of the group's head.

The Magnificent Seven was almost half over when he saw two of the men who'd been at the table with the big man Xuan had probably killed. Uneasy, he gazed at the crowd, looking for the third man he'd seen at the table, edgy when he couldn't find him.

A glance at the two he saw was enough to let him know they'd spotted Xuan near the middle of the crowd. Mario caught his attention and signaled at the two, gesturing that he'd cover the man nearest his position. Reynaud nodded. The two men had split up, trying to flank the Viet.

Even as Reynaud stalked the near man he continued to search the crowd for the third man, but without success. Reaching down with his left hand, Reynaud slipped out his old KA-BAR fighting knife, slid it into his right hand, then, holding it discreetly against his leg, took the half-dozen steps that brought him only a pace behind his quarry. At the same time, he continued to examine the masses of faces, wishing for the sight of the third man.

"Repent, brother, and see the error of your ways." That quiet voice had come from behind him, near the van he'd left.

CHAPTER 2

As soon as he'd heard the voice, the man in front of Reynaud snatched for the revolver on his hip and Rennie slashed at the back of his hand.

The man he'd cut screamed and clutched at his hand. "Shhh," Reynaud whispered, "don't disturb the audience. As for the hand, that'll bleed a lot less if you hold it up high."

"Brother," the quiet voice spoke again, "that gun you're holding is a ticket out of this vale of tears and to a better world. Put the gun down or prepare for judgment."

Reynaud never turned, but he grinned broadly. The Deacon couldn't have chosen a better time to find them.

"Sorry about the noise," Reynaud murmured to the hostile men and women glaring at him and the other man. "We were just leaving."

The other man had fumbled a dirty handkerchief out of his pocket and wrapped it around his hand. "We can have a conversation behind that van," Reynaud whispered to him, indicating the vehicle with a nod of his head, "or a dissection right here. Your choice."

He and his prisoner had hardly gotten behind the van before they were joined by Mario and the Deacon, each with his own captive. Reynaud nodded to the new arrival.

"Hi, Deak. Awful nice timing."

The three locals stood together, staring at each other and glancing furtively at the armed men, obviously sure they were about to die.

"Take it easy," Reynaud told them. "It's apparent you boys aren't too bright, so I'm going to speak very slowly. I'm not fond of sore losers, but I'd hate to bother that bunch back there with loud noises." He looked from one to another. "You boys live near here?"

The sudden change of subject had left the prisoners mentally flat-footed. After staring at the others, the one he'd cut cleared his throat and nodded. "Not too far off, anyways."

"Well, I suggest you boys call it a weekend. I'll give you an hour to get what you need and get out of town, and if I see you packing iron in town again, I'll kill you where I find you. Is that straight enough for you?"

Nodding, they began to back away from Reynaud and his friends until they reached the cover of a tent, then spun and ran.

Mario leaned against the van and returned the .25 auto he'd been holding to its ankle holster.

"Good to see you again, Deak," Reynaud said around a grin. "What say we catch the rest of the movie?"

Billy Joe's face was as immobile as rock when he wasn't stump preaching, but he shrugged and turned back to where the crowd was engrossed, watching its fantasies flickering across the screen.

"Cheerful devil, isn't he?" Mario muttered as he fell into step with Reynaud.

"There wasn't much to laugh about, where we were," Reynaud said. "The only way the Deacon survived the POW camp was by going a little crazy, but he's always been handy when we needed help."

The three of them stood together, watching the movie. As the picture dissolved into a blizzard, Billy Joe strode to where the video-van's crew folded the tarps. Facing the crowd, the Deacon began to preach and, within moments, was serving up fire and brimstone to them. Some stalked away in disgust, a few slunk away in embarrassment, and more than a few edged closer, as absorbed in the sermon as they'd been in the movies. Reynaud watched a while, faintly amused by the occasional chorus of "amens" and "hallelujah's," until the sun began to edge its way toward the horizon.

Reynaud attracted the Deacon's attention and drew his forefinger across his throat. Billy Joe wrapped up the sermon with a prayer and marched toward the Cajun.

"Hate to break up the revival, but Norton's probably already at the Emergency Room and I'd rather not keep him and the rest waiting." He led the way to the bar. As usual, he was unable to read the expression on Billy Joe's gaunt face, but his manner expressed distaste. The bartender barely looked up as the three of them rounded the end of the bar and walked into the back room.

Norton stood behind a table littered with supplies and a quick survey of the room showed everyone was there but Charley. Norton must've read his thoughts.

"Somebody had to mind the store," he said. He waved at a second table, laden with food. "Have some dinner while we talk."

Picking up a plate, Reynaud loaded it with squirrel meat and gravy and greens then poured a tumbler of homemade wine. The Deacon helped himself to the food and, after sniffing at the pitcher, poured himself a glass of water.

Norton leaned over the table of equipment and picked up a silver-plated and exquisitely engraved Walther PPK, now equipped with a bulky silencer.

"It like to broke Donny's heart to have to chop up a beautiful little handgun like that, but it was the best we could do on short notice." He laid the weapon down beside a box of .380 auto ammunition, then added two boxes of .22 ammunition and a similarly suppressed Ruger Mark II semi-auto pistol.

Six brass shotshells lay beside a single-barrel shotgun cut to the length of a pistol. "We managed to scrounge up a few rounds of silent twelve-gauge and the gun. Those shells are pretty quiet, but they're only good up close."

Showing them five small blocks of what looked like modeling clay lying at the opposite end of the table from wires and detonators, he explained, "We also came up with a little plastique, if you decide to be more spectacular and you don't mind the noise."

The next item he held up looked like an aerosol can with a top like a hand grenade. "This vomit and tear gas is old police stock, but we think it's still good. There's three of these, and a couple of assault grenades."

"There must be a pony in there somewhere," Logan said.

"Sorry, girls and boys, but Christmas in August just isn't what it used to be. The other side's a damned sight better equipped. If you want some heavy stuff, you're going to have to take it from them."

"Speaking of the other side," Reynaud reminded him, "you were going to give us some idea of how to take the Colonel."

"Right. Tomorrow is Friday. That's the day the Colonel collects taxes." At Logan's raised eyebrows, he elaborated. "They tax air. If you want to keep breathing it, you pay. Tomorrow is also the first Friday of the month, which means the Colonel himself will be making the rounds. The Colonel puts great store by punctuality, so he'll be making his first stop within a minute or two of 9:20 AM, and at 2:00 he'll stop at Dorrie's Diner for a late lunch. He'll leave there at 2:25." He handed Reynaud a timetable of the route.

"If he's so predictable," Mario asked, "why hasn't somebody hit him before now?"

"A couple people tried. That's discouraged copy-cats. His car is armored for anything up to 7.62mm armor-piercing, and his escort is pretty trigger-happy. Also, he seems to have some heavy connections. For instance, the local militia leaves him alone, meaning he has at least one friend on the milgov's staff. That's one of the things we need to find out—who his buddy is, and how high up on the staff he is, to find out how deeply they've burrowed into the milgov's information.

"The Colonel almost certainly has files at his base." Norton tossed an old map of Springfield onto the table. "His base is here." He stabbed the map with a stiff forefinger. "It's an old estate northwest of town between Highway 160 and Melville Road. It has a brick fence, now topped with barbed wire, and he's added two guard stations just inside the gate. Those stations are always manned, and we think they're armed with LAW rockets."

Norton dropped a hand-drawn diagram on top of the map and pointed out an oval behind the large rectangle representing the house. "That's a root cellar. It's under at least four feet of dirt, with only a vent pipe or two, and a double door, so it stays cool, and it does it without using energy. The night shift guards probably sleep there, and I'd guess they also use it to keep items of value; maybe the files. As for the house, I'd bet a truckload of beer they've got a secure radio in there. It could be anyplace, including the attic or the basement."

Reynaud had finished his meal and had drunk as much of the wine as he could stand. The glass was over half full. "Where do you want us to take the Colonel after we've grabbed him?"

"Take him to the safe house you've been staying at."

Reynaud shoved the tumbler away. "From your description, you're going to need a damned good interrogator, someone really sharp, because this 'Colonel' sounds tough enough to take a lot of punishment and not give you his hat size."

"That'll be my problem. That's why I'd like to be able to get my hands on his correspondence."

"We'd better call it a night," Logan said. "Curfew is in twenty minutes."

Sally stood. "We've got enough extra blankets for you to stay in the camp."

"See you tomorrow, then," Norton said, and rose. He walked across the room and trudged up a flight of stairs.

The group gathered up the supplies in the packs Norton had left and returned to Charley's van. The dentist accepted the extra guests with ill grace, but Reynaud ignored the lack of warmth. Lying on a blanket, he stared up at the sky. The night was clear and, without the glare of city lights to obscure them, the stars were brilliant and seemed almost near enough to touch.

He'd already noticed tension in the atmosphere of the camp. Charley was brusque to the point of rudeness, and Xuan and Sally had the air of people sharing a private joke. Apparently, Xuan's social life had improved while Charley's had taken a turn for the worse. This could be the beginning of a major problem, which could interfere with the smooth functioning of the group. Considering the matter, he decided to give the problem time to resolve itself, knowing if the group's mutual reliability suffered, he'd have to take action.

Then he concentrated on his memory of the map and the diagram and tried to imagine the members of the group as chessmen, to be moved around to force the other king, the Colonel, into an impossible position. This had to be done with the least possible losses to his own chessmen. Sleep caught him still moving his men, not knowing how many he'd lose, or which ones.

~ * ~

The third stop on the Colonel's route, and the first inside the city, was a machine cooperative. Once it had been a machine shop: Now, it offered the services of a blacksmith, a gunsmith, and machine work that could be turned out on manually-operated machines.

As soon as Reynaud saw the Colonel's limousine with its smoked windows he discarded his previous plans. Hidden in the shadows of a shell of a house, he watched the drill. Two doors on the passengers' side opened and men carrying assault rifles or sub-machine guns took up positions, one at the front of the car on the driver's side, the other at the rear of the passengers' side. As soon as the first guards were in position two more men, both carrying shotguns, stalked into the building. Following them, after a ten-second interval, were two more men, one of them a stocky man with a square face and thinning white hair. He seemed to be unarmed, and Reynaud knew that must be the Colonel. The large man with him carried only a pistol in a shoulder holster. They were followed in another ten seconds by another gunnie with an M-16.

Reynaud guessed only the driver remained in the car, which continued to run until the procession returned to the limousine.

As soon as the car had gone, Rennie slipped out of cover and made his way back to Charley's van.

He'd worried about who should be allowed to carry a sup-pressed weapon. Hasteen was the best man in the group with a pistol, so Reynaud gave him the PPK. Mario took the single-shot shotgun and two of the silent rounds, while Reynaud loaded most of the rest into his bullpup. Logan had his own silenced weapon, a Russian Makarov with the suppresser built into the pistol.

Xuan had smiled grimly and gestured at his knife and hatchet. "I prefer my own silent weapons."

The suppressed .22 they gave to Sally, then he drilled the group on his new plan until he was sure each of them understood his or her role. The one person not briefed was Charley; taking him aside, Reynaud gave him directions to the safe house off Haseltine Road. He was to leave for there at 2:00 and wait for them at the house.

Reynaud dispatched the rest of the group to the diner in pairs or alone at five to seven minute intervals, until only he and the Deacon were left. Six minutes after Sally and Logan set out, Billy Joe and Reynaud started the walk.

Reynaud led the Deacon to the ruins of a service station across the street from the cafe, where the Deacon found a comfortable firing position that kept him in the building's shadows but gave him a good view out of a gaping hole that'd been a window. He checked the chamber of his FAL, then pumped open the grenade launcher mounted under the barrel and loaded it.

Glancing through the hole, Reynaud said, "Remember, Deak, don't fire if you don't have to. You're here in case someone fails to do his part. If worse comes to worst, the Colonel's party will probably try to use the limo for cover, so be ready to drop a grenade just on this side of it."

"I'll be ready."

Together, they watched silently until the limousine had pulled to a stop in front of the diner. Reynaud waited only to be sure the gunmen followed the same drill he'd seen earlier in the morning, except the car was turned off and the driver had rolled his window down. With a pat on the Deacon's shoulder, Reynaud slipped out the back of the building and circled the end of the block, to be on the opposite side of the street from the car and approaching it from its front.

Halting at the corner, he drew out tobacco and rolling paper and rolled a cigarette. He seldom smoked, but making and lighting a cigarette gave a man a chance to stop and study the situation without being obvious. He saw no one else in the group, and he could only hope they were all in position.

Hasteen and Xuan should be prepared to slip into the diner's back door. If things had gone according to plan, Mario should've slipped into the kitchen just before the place closed at two o'clock and unlatched the door or stuffed the lock. If that'd been noticed, Hasteen and Xuan would have to break in as quietly as possible.

Finished rolling the cigarette, Reynaud licked the paper then started down the street, pausing a half dozen paces from the guard at the nose of the limousine. Snapping a matchhead on his thumbnail, he sheltered the flame with his hands, drew a deep breath of smoke, then tossed the match to the street and resumed his walk to the car.

The guard had swung his weapon, a Ruger Mini-14, so the barrel was pointed at Reynaud's belt buckle.

Rennie tried to keep his hands steady and the nervousness out of his voice. He nodded at the man, then at the limousine. "Hell of a nice-looking car."

"Just keep moving." The guard seemed disinclined to conversation, so Reynaud kept moving, walking past the guard and alongside the limousine until he was beside the driver's window and no more than five feet away from it. His Mossberg was slung, barrel down, on his left shoulder.

Taking a half-turn to the left, he snatched the weapon and swung it into position. When the barrel was pointed into the window he fired, not even hearing the pop of the silenced round. Jacking the action, he turned again. The nose guard had lowered the Ruger's barrel and had been holding the weapon only by the pistol grip. Now he swung his weapon up. Reynaud saw the muzzle rise and swing toward him while he was bringing his own weapon to bear. Squeezing the trigger again, this time he clearly heard the muted explosion of the cartridge, then the guard fell backward, his upper chest and throat a mass of blood.

Again Reynaud pumped the action and flung himself down beside the car. From that position he heard a rapid, subdued popping and the guard at the back of the car fell behind the left rear tire, then Sally dashed for the car and threw herself down behind him.

Almost at the same instant they heard a shout from the diner —it sounded like Hasteen's voice—then the sounds of more suppressed gunfire and a single pop of a light-caliber weapon.

"Get his gun," Reynaud said to Sally, gesturing at the body of the man with the Mini-14, then he shoved himself up into a crouch and snatched open the driver's door.

The body of the driver lay sprawled across the front seat. Catching it by the belt, Reynaud hauled it out into the street, then he tried the second door, found it unlocked, and wrenched it open. Through the passenger's window he could see Logan, Hasteen, Mario, and Xuan racing for the car, Mario and Xuan dragging the Colonel. Hasteen sprang into the front seat, slid across, slammed the driver's door shut, and turned the engine over.

Logan stopped to retrieve the Uzi the rear guard had dropped then ducked into the car, taking the third seat behind Hasteen. Xuan and Mario flung the Colonel into the seat beside Logan then Xuan sprang inside. Sally sat to Reynaud's right, Mario to his left, so Rennie was sitting opposite their prisoner. Almost before Xuan and Mario had slammed their doors shut, the Deacon ran from across the street to join Hasteen in the front seat. Hasteen hit the accelerator and the car shot away from the curb.

"There's a CB up here," Hasteen announced. "Do you think they're supposed to call in after each stop?"

"How about it, Colonel?" Reynaud demanded.

The Colonel turned a rugged, tanned face with gunmetal gray eyes at Reynaud. He seemed to already be recovering from his initial shock and confusion. "If you know who I am," he snapped, "then you already know you're dead."

Reynaud glared back at him. "Is there a signal you're supposed to give your base before you return?"

"If there were, I wouldn't tell you. I suppose a concept like loyalty is too abstract for barbarians like you."

A sudden fury shot through Reynaud like a jolt of electricity and he leaned across to backhand the Colonel. The older man's head rocked with the blow, and blood shot from his nose.

"Don't talk to me about loyalty, you son of a bitch." Reynaud tried to stop himself, but the accusation had dug deep and things long left unsaid erupted from him. "Some goddam armchair Patton like you pushed the scramble button and I went. The fuckin' war was over, Colonel. It was a stupid, wasted mission, and it cost me six months in a Russian POW camp and a lot of friends. Bill Taylor didn't even get a grave. His plane blew, with Bill still in it. The bomber we were escorting might've gotten through to cause more grief, but the crew never came back." He lashed out again, slapping the Colonel on the side of the head. "Five good men dead, and me a prisoner. That's what your kind of loyalty got us." A line of blood ran from the Colonel's ear down to his collar, where it began to stain the cloth. "The armchair wonder that ordered the mission didn't risk his ass. So don't talk to me about loyalty or anything else you don't understand."

The Colonel spat a mouthful of blood at Reynaud.

Mario still held his little .25 auto. "This is getting us nowhere. Our employer only said he wanted the Colonel alive; he didn't say anything about the Colonel's walking to see him." He pointed the tiny weapon at the Colonel's right knee. "Do you know how painful it is to be kneecapped by one of these mouseguns?" Mario's tone left no doubt he was prepared to pull the trigger.

The Colonel's face paled and Reynaud realized the man finally understood the unthinkable had happened; he was now powerless and vulnerable.

"There's another little black box up here on the visor," Hasteen reported. "What is it?"

Reynaud studied the Colonel. Now that the shock of helplessness had passed, the man seemed to be preparing himself to endure whatever pain the group could inflict.

"Make it the left knee, Mario."

Mario thrust the little pistol at the Colonel's left leg.

"Hold it," the Colonel said. "That black box is a garage-door opener. It's wired to the front gate. We usually open the gate from the limo."

"Were you supposed to send a message before coming in?" Reynaud asked.

"No, no messages except in case of an emergency." The Colonel seemed oblivious to the irony.

"You just saved yourself a kneecap, Colonel," Mario said, putting the pistol away.

Leaning forward, Reynaud unbuckled the Colonel's belt and pulled it free then wrapped it around the prisoner's ankles and buckled it tight. His hands had already been secured behind his back.

For the first time, Reynaud realized the car's air conditioner was cooling the limousine. "Xuan, Logan, check your window controls."

They touched the switches on their armrests and the windows slid down with a faint whine, then they ran them back up.

Hasteen had turned right onto Highway 160, heading north and, minutes later, followed the curve to the northwest. To the southwest, they could see the remains of an airport.

"Keep alert for the driveway," Reynaud said. He pumped the action to clear and save the final silent round he carried, reloaded the tube magazine with buckshot rounds, pumped a round into the chamber then loaded another round of buckshot into the weapon.

"You'll never get away with this," the Colonel rasped.

"Colonel, you been watching too many late movies," Logan drawled. "All the cardboard villains say that, just before they get gut-shot. If you can't be original, just keep your fat chops shut."

"Help him with that, would you, Logan?" Reynaud took the bandanna from around his neck and handed it to Logan, who quickly tied it around the Colonel's mouth.

"Look sharp," Hasteen said, "I think we're coming up on the

driveway now." He turned the car onto an unpaved track. Just beyond a screen of trees they could see sections of a brick fence. Hasteen handed Xuan the PPK. Xuan loaded a fresh magazine into the weapon, while Logan did the same with his Makarov.

Hasteen slowed and pressed the button on the black box then they were beyond the screen of trees and moving toward an iron gate, slowly opening. Concrete guard stations flanked the gates and men with M-16s stood at "present arms" outside the posts.

"Now!" Reynaud shouted. "Take 'em!"

Xuan and Logan stabbed the window control buttons and as soon as the smoked glass had dropped far enough, opened fire. Inside the car, still largely enclosed, the concussion from the shots was a palpable hammering at the ears. The guards crumpled like paper dolls, then, with a curse, Logan tossed his Makarov on the floor. "Goddam jam!"

Hasteen continued along the drive, picking up a little speed.

"Time for the room broom," Logan muttered, and readied his MAC-10. Xuan flicked on the safety of the PPK and placed it on the floor, picked up and checked the Mini-14, then dug a vomit gas grenade out of a pocket of his field jacket. Sally took another gas grenade from her shoulder bag and handed it to Mario, who'd checked the Uzi.

"Hang on!" Hasteen shouted, as the car ran out of driveway and lurched around the corner of the garage.

"Sally," Reynaud said, "watch our guest. If anyone but one of us comes out the back door, kill the Colonel first."

The limousine skidded around the back of the garage and Hasteen brought it to a stop between the house and the root cellar. Mario and Xuan bailed out and ran to the vent pipe at the far end of the mound, while Hasteen and Logan pounded up the back porch stairs.

Reynaud was third up the stairs and, by the time he'd gained the porch, he heard the roar of a .45 inside the house. He scrambled into the kitchen just in time to see Logan disappearing down a set of stairs. The body of a man lay slumped against the base of the cupboard.

As soon as Reynaud glimpsed the Deacon at the door he moved to the door opposite the stairs the other two had taken to the basement. Crouching beside the door, he twisted the knob with his left hand then flung the door open hard enough to slam it against the garage wall. Beyond the open door, two steps led down to the garage floor. The nearest cover was the front end of a pickup, nearly five feet away. Chancing a quick look, he saw no one in the garage or the pickup, then jumped out and down, taking cover at the front of the vehicle. Another quick look, this one under the pickup, and he was sure the garage was clear. Besides the massive doors in the front of the garage, he'd entered through the only door. "Garage clear," he shouted, and moved back to the kitchen.

He'd just come up behind the Deacon, crouched by a doorway to what appeared to be a dining room when, from the basement, they heard the Ingram stutter out a question and a .45 bellowed its reply. As though afraid it'd be left out, a .223 barked four times in the backyard.

"Basement's cleared," Logan shouted. "We're on the way back up."

At that moment, a shotgun blast tore a chunk of wood out of the dining room doorway and showered Reynaud and the Deacon with splinters. Reynaud cursed in vivid Cajun French and ducked. Billy Joe tossed a grenade into the dining room, then sprang through the doorway and hammered off five fast shots.

Reynaud was right behind the Deacon, blasting at the room's other two doorways. A corpse lay huddled on the floor beside an opening to what looked like a living room, the body's limp hand resting beside the grenade Billy Joe had thrown, its pin unpulled. The other open door revealed a short section of a hallway and another open door, this one to a bathroom.

Hasteen and Logan had pounded up the stairs and joined the other two in the dining room. Taking in the situation at a glance, Hasteen gave directions to the others with hand signals. Logan swept the wall to the right of the hall doorway with two bursts from the Ingram, one at waist level, the other at knee level, while Hasteen fanned six shots into the wall to the left of the door, the holes at just above knee level and no more than six inches apart.

They all heard the thump of a body and the sharp clatter of a falling weapon as they hit the floor, then, a moment later they heard the crash of glass as someone threw himself out a window at the rear of the house.

The .223 outside spoke again.

Hasteen and Logan reloaded then Hasteen flung himself at the bathroom doorway. From his new cover, he fired another shot at the body in the hallway then glanced both ways along the corridor. Again he exchanged hand signals with Logan, and Logan leaped into the hallway, dumping a full magazine toward the front of the house while Hasteen darted toward the back end of the corridor, firing as he moved.

The Deacon nodded at Reynaud and began to fire random shots through the wall between the dining room and the living room.

Hasteen appeared at the hallway door. "Back room clear," he said then moved to join Logan.

The Deacon continued to fire into the living room until he'd emptied the magazine. While Billy Joe reloaded, Reynaud took a position beside the doorway. From this new vantage, he saw no movement in the living room, and little cover. He continued to swing the shotgun's muzzle in an arc until he saw a form crouched behind the couch. The force of his blast hurled the corpse out into the middle of the floor, where he could see the Deacon had shot the man through the wall. He finished the arc with his weapon until he was inside the room. "Living room clear," he shouted.

Almost instantly, Logan announced the front room was clear and stepped into the living room, where Reynaud and the Deacon were checking the body. Billy Joe looked up. "The wages of sin is death," he intoned.

Logan grinned. "I guess we're just here to enforce the minimum wage law." Staring around the shambles of the room, Logan observed most of the furnishings smashed by gunfire. "I won't arm-wrestle you to salvage rights for this place."

Hasteen joined them, guns holstered. "The radio room is in the basement, along with a dozen bunks and what looks to be a small arsenal. The front room here looks like it was used for an office; there's a desk and a file cabinet."

Reynaud slung his shotgun and strode to the front room. "There's a pickup in the garage. We can just chuck all the file drawers into it."

Xuan walked in from the kitchen. "The outside is secured." He helped them haul the drawers of files to the garage and they went through the rest of the house. The attic held nothing but old furniture and dust, while the back bedrooms yielded nothing of interest but a framed picture of a young man in a Marine uniform. After considering it a moment, Reynaud took the photograph.

Most of the military supplies seemed to be in the basement. Besides the radio, which they smashed, they found a rack holding five loaded M-16s and several unopened crates, as well as two crates of ammunition, which had been partly emptied. They added these to the files in the pickup.

Among the military equipment they found a dozen gas masks of various types. Xuan donned one, took another out to Mario, and the two of them entered the root cellar. While they were inside, Reynaud examined the corpses on the cellar stairs. After Xuan and Mario had wrenched off the vent cover and dropped the gas grenades, the men in the cellar, caught by surprise, hadn't been able to reach their gas masks until after they'd started vomiting. Apparently, these two had been desperate enough to try to break out and had been shot down.

Xuan thrust his head out the cellar door and looked up, the blank face of his gas mask gaping at them. "No files or masks down here." His voice was muffled and made hollow by the mask. "All they have down here are a few small arms. Some of them have been puked on, but we can bring them up."

Reynaud shouted for Logan, who was still in the kitchen. Logan came outside beaming and waving two three-pound coffee cans. "Hey, gang, these bastards had some real honest-to-God coffee!"

"Toss 'em in the pickup and get us a couple buckets of water. The hand pump in the kitchen should be working."

The weapons from the root cellar were rough-cleaned and loaded into the truck, along with all the other weapons they could find, including those of the gate guards. A tarp was thrown over the booty and Reynaud glanced at his watch. From the time they'd entered the gate, the entire operation had taken just a little more than thirty minutes.

"Logan, take the pickup and follow us. Hasteen, you drive the car again." Reynaud climbed back into the seat facing the Colonel. "He didn't give you any trouble, did he?" he asked Sally.

"He's been as meek as a lamb."

The rest of the team had scrambled back into the limousine and Hasteen hit the starter. With a roar, echoed by the pickup's engine, the limousine sped out of the gate.

"Mario, the Colonel might be feeling more conversational now. Why don't you take that bandanna out of his mouth and put it over his eyes?" Reynaud had no idea how Norton and his friends intended to question the Colonel, but saw no good reason for throwing away the lure of false hope. While Mario blindfolded the Colonel, Reynaud took the belt from around the prisoner's ankles then stared out the window.

Highway 160 had been an old road, even before the plague, and now it desperately needed maintenance it wouldn't receive for many more years, if ever. Hasteen took the turnoff onto 44 as fast as the road would allow, perhaps a little faster, and the trees along the road became thicker, with an occasional clump surrounding houses.

Another turn put them on Haseltine Road and Hasteen slowed to avoid raising a dust cloud. The limousine headed due south, the pickup following like an unrequited love. Hasteen found the driveway almost in time to slow the machine to a prudent speed. The heavy car leaned ominously then they were slowing even more on the gravel driveway.

As they cleared the trees they saw Norton and two other men standing in front of the house. As they stopped, Norton gestured at the pickup and shouted, "Took care of all your business at once, huh? Neat. Very tidy. I like that." He and the men with him helped unload the pickup then the shorter man got into the limousine.

"Logan, follow Donny in the pickup. He'll show you where to ditch the vehicles." Norton wiped sweat off his chin with the back of his hand. "You'll have to hoof it back, but you should be back here before full dark."

As the limousine, with its pet pickup, disappeared down the driveway Norton turned to the Colonel.

"Well, Colonel, I'd like to say this is a pleasure." He reached out and pulled off the blindfold. "I'd like you to meet an associate of mine, Bob Wilkes."

Wilkes was tall and angular, with a rugged face and coarse gray hair. He looked Lincolnesque, a perception he largely spoiled by wearing glasses that looked as though they'd been cut from the bottoms of Coke bottles.

"Nice to meet you, Colonel," Wilkes said. "I've been looking forward to this." He thrust out a hand then seemed to realize the Colonel's hands were bound behind his back. "Sorry about that, Colonel. I guess you weren't as eager for this get-together as I was. Well, let's get inside and get those off you." He put a large, bony hand on the Colonel's shoulder and gently steered him into the house.

As soon as they were out of sight, Reynaud handed Norton the picture he'd found. "At a guess, this might be his son. It may be some help."

"Thanks." Norton put the photo under his arm then helped them go through the crates. The first crate, marked with Asian ideographs, contained eight AK rifles with black plastic stocks and forearms. The stocks folded like that of the AR-18, and the plastic magazines filling the bottom of the crate were shallow arcs, meaning the weapons were chambered for .223.

The other crate with Asian markings held four M-79 grenade launchers with a loaded twelve-round bandolier for each launcher. "These are Thai-manufactured, I think," Norton said, "and the AKs look like they're Chinese-built."

Mario tore open the case with Arabic squiggles and laughed, holding up a machine gun that looked like the World War II German MG-42. After studying the stampings on the receiver a moment, he faced the others, grinning.

"These are new German MG-3s, modernized versions of the old 'Hitler's zipper.' They're better than M-60s. You can't reassemble parts backwards to make it a jammamatic, it isn't held together with wire, and you don't have to worry about it field-stripping itself while you're firing it if one of those damned wires pops."

"You seem to know the weapon pretty well," Norton said.

"I should. I spent a tour in Germany and had a chance to play with some of these. The crests on the receivers look like they might be old Iranian markings."

Most of the rest of the boxes contained ammunition; belts of it for the machine guns, hundreds of rounds of .223 and 9mm. Besides the crated weapons, they had an impressive array of looted equipment from the Steel Fist house—half a dozen handguns of various makes, the same number of shotguns, ten M-16s, two Mini-14s with folding stocks, five carbines and submachine guns in 9mm, five LAWs, and a small mountain of explosives.

"Det cord," Mario counted it off for them, "a couple more blocks of plastique, three sticks of dynamite, five gas grenades, and these—" he pointed to what looked like more gas grenades, "are thermite. They're usually used to destroy equipment or files. They'll burn right through a safe, but they don't explode; their effect is limited to a yard or so, so never throw one unless you can put it right on the money."

The contents of the last case puzzled them. It looked like an NBC suit. Norton was the one to provide the answer. "It's an anti-IR suit with starlight camouflage." He chuckled at the blank looks from the group. "It's used to hide from sensors that pick up infra-red—meaning heat—radiation, and it's camouflaged to also avoid being picked up by equipment using starlight or other light-enhancer equipment. It's a great little personal sauna. You could probably lose ten pounds in two hours wearing it. It keeps all the wearer's body heat in, along with telltales like the heat from the air you exhale. It has its uses, but it's also a helluva great way to smother yourself."

Reynaud gestured toward some of the other material they'd picked up, including a wide variety of canned goods. "At least it looks like we'll eat well tonight. They seemed to have pack-ratted away almost everything needed to fight a couple wars."

"That's probably just what they have in mind," Norton said. "I'm going to start going over that paperwork you brought me. 'Holler' when it's soup."

Mario began to field-strip an MG-3 and clean it of cosmo-line. The others had begun to break down their own weapons for cleaning and maintenance, leaving Sally, Charley, and Reynaud to themselves. Rennie took his shotgun to his room, returned with his rifle, glancing around, looking for the best position for keeping watch on the area.

Sally stepped up beside him and put her arm around his waist. "Ray, has anybody ever told you you're sexy when you're being bossy?"

Reynaud's chuckle was partly surprise. "Not lately." He chanced a look to where Charley stood, noting the dentist had turned a stiff back to the two of them. "Do you have a thing about getting fights started?" he asked her.

"With Charley? Nah, he's not the type. He just sulks a lot—when he's not pouting."

"Don't underestimate him. I'd hate to wake up some morning to find out he's given up filling cavities in peoples' mouths to put cavities in their heads."

"Are you afraid?"

"Not afraid, just cautious. I got stuck with leading this little war party and I'd prefer it go as smoothly as possible, meaning I don't want any unnecessary misunderstandings—like why I left you with the Colonel while the rest of the boys and I went to play hide-and-go-shoot with the homegrown Nazis back there. I didn't do it because you're a woman: I did it because I knew what the others can do. You're still an unknown quantity, and one that can give me as much trouble as help.

"I appreciate the compliment, but right now I'd feel a little more comfortable with a better view of what's around this place."

He started around a fold in the ground then looked back at her. "I'd appreciate it if you'd ask Hasteen to come spell me when he's finished with what he's doing. I'll be on the other side of that ridge." He pointed with his rifle then followed the line of the ridge to where it dipped into heavy underbrush. Making his way through the brush he trudged back along the ridge with the crest of the ridge between himself and the camp until he reached the shade of an old black walnut tree where he could watch the surrounding country without being exposed.

Still too keyed from the recent action to need to worry about dozing, he just sat and watched the breeze stroking the green countryside like a huge hand. He wondered if his nerves were just the result of the gun battle or if some sixth sense were ringing a subtle alarm. Whatever it was, he felt a very strong urge to be away from Springfield as soon as possible.

The sun was almost on the horizon when Hasteen rounded the ridge. Reynaud waved an "all clear" to him, then strode back to camp and started making dinner, starting a roux, preparing the rest of what he'd need to make a jambalaya. While the jambalaya was cooking he started a pot of coffee, reveling in the aroma of the fresh coffee grounds.

Looking back at the house, its outlines lost in the surrounding trees, he noticed the windows were all sealed against spilling lamplight.

A whistle from the ridge alerted him and he moved away from the fire to slip behind the woodpile. Within a few minutes, Logan and the man Norton called Donny approached the fire.

"You can come on out, Rennie," Logan said, "it's just us." He sank beside the fire with a sigh, found a cup, poured coffee into it. "Sorry it took so long to get back. I liked to never talked Donny into dumping the cars this side of the Kansas border." He poured coffee into a cup. "Jeez, I was wonderin' if I'd ever taste real coffee again."

Reynaud finished the jambalaya, filled two plates, and handed them to Logan and Donny. "You two sit and eat. I'll get the others." He filled two more plates and carried them into the house.

Mario opened the door at Rennie's kick at the frame. Seeing the plates, he said, "Wilkes and the Colonel are in the back room."

Reynaud delivered the dinners to the Colonel and his interrogator and returned to the fire as Norton arrived, his face creased by worry.

Logan finished chewing a mouthful and swallowed. "Norton, the last time I saw a look like that, a buddy of mine was called in to have his taxes audited back to nineteen ninety-six. The only good thing about the fall of civilization is that it took the IRS with it."

"Damn fine meal. My compliments to the chef," Norton said around a mouthful of food. He savored the taste before he spoke again. "I do hate to ruin a beautiful meal…but…well…what do you think of pulling another kidnapping, this one on a military base?"

CHAPTER 3

"I try not to think of it at all," Reynaud said. "What's this about?"

Norton finished another bite. "I got a lot of information out of the files. Now I know who the Steel Fist planted on General Meyer's staff; a man named Walter Davenport. He'd been in the Army before and got himself put in charge of intelligence. He oversees recon patrols, collates the information, and assembles reports to General Meyer. That means he can be choosey about where he looks for information, he can sit on or doctor what information comes his way—as well as pass on to the Steel Fist whatever he thinks they might like to know—and generally has a lock on the General's ear.

"We might be able to plant some of the more incriminating files we've found on him, but he might be able to lie his way out of it. Besides, that sort of thing takes too long. It's important we put the arm on Davenport as soon as possible. The files I've seen show he's pretty high in the Steel Fist's hierarchy.

"Donny, why don't you go spell Hasteen on guard duty as soon as you finish eating? I'd rather this whole crowd got it all at one time, and from the top."

Donny finished his dinner, then, with a rifle tucked under his arm, trudged off into the darkness. By the time Hasteen joined the party Norton had ended his meal and they were all starting on a second pot of coffee.

"Okay," Norton said. He picked at something caught between his teeth with a fingernail, then looked around, making sure he had everyone's attention. "The guy I was telling you about before, the founder of the Steel Fist, is a man named Benjamin Rutledge. Rutledge wasn't just another small-time bigot. He had friends in high places, pals with connections, and Rutledge himself was smart enough to be a damned good odds-player.

"The Steel Fist started out as a coordinating committee. Their job was to help a whole bunch of extremist organizations cooperate with each other. They included the Ku Klux Klan, the American

Nazi Party, the Aryan Nation, and a whole slew of other fascists. They also had contact with groups that were more respectable, or, at least, a lot less well-known.

"Rutledge used the committee to recruit members for his own group. It wasn't unusual for right-wing organizations to work together, or to have members in common. Rutledge's new wrinkle was selective recruitment and in gaining a degree of control, through proxies, over the various organizations he coordinated. If a group under his umbrella became too notorious, he kicked them out into the weather, and the next thing they knew most of their leaders were facing federal indictments. There were even supposed to have been murders and bombings carried out by Rutledge's core group, leaving evidence pointing to outfits opposing him.

Mario sipped at his coffee. "This Rutledge sounds like a very astute 'businessman.'" From his tone, it wasn't a compliment.

Norton grunted. "Yeah, a real credit to his race—whatever kind of reptile that is. Anyway, that was just the beginning. The next step was to set up cells. Rutledge picked the Ozarks as the base for his operations with smaller bands in other places; the Rockies around northern Colorado and southern Wyoming, the Appalachians around Tennessee, and the forests in Idaho and Washington state. Even a few in Kansas City and L.A.

"Rutledge himself disappeared at about the time of the collapse and some people believe he died of the plague, others thought he got into one power struggle too many and somebody under him bumped him off. I suppose there's always hope. While Rutledge might be gone, the bastard can't be forgotten. Before he disappeared, he came up with a basic program for the Steel Fist to follow. This wasn't a blueprint, with each detail written in indelible ink, it was more of an outline.

"The best guesses we can come up with are that in Arkansas almost seven thousand of the Steel Fist took up residence, some of them staying under cover to infiltrate, some of them moving into regions *en masse* to take over politically. At least three thousand of these survived the plague and recruited more members. We think they now number about five thousand."

"How the hell did they gain members," Logan asked. "Put an ad in the 'fascists wanted' section of the local papers?"

"I can answer that," Sally snapped, her voice hard and bitter.

"They claimed to be interested in maintaining law and order. Some of their crowd pulled a couple-three massacres, which they blamed on 'bandits,' then they attacked people who opposed them and planted 'evidence' on the bodies."

"That's one of the ways," Norton amended. "Another was to soft-pedal their racism. There are even a handful of Blacks, Viets, Hispanics, and Cajuns in the organization now, but not very high up the ladder. They're using them, essentially, for cannon-fodder and heavy labor, all but a few Judas goats, who get impressive titles and don't do anything but keep the minorities in line. It's some consolation that, if history repeats itself, the Judas goats will go first when they decide to purge the non-whites."

"All right," Reynaud said, "you've convinced us this clown is an organizational genius and Davenport is a major danger, but that doesn't necessarily mean we have to nail him on a base."

"I don't think you're going to have a hell of a lot of choice. With the Colonel in the bag and his radio base dead, we have only days, maybe hours, before Davenport may decide his cover is blown and skips. We've got to hit him where we can 'git' him."

Logan tossed a twig into the fire. "How about a woman? Horses' asses like that always seem to have a woman on the side. It's part of what passes for their style."

"You might be right. I've got dossiers on most of the milgov's staff, but they're in my office in town. At least I can check it."

"It's worth a look," Reynaud said, "but since we don't have enough information to plan, we'll make the plans when we get the info. After we've gotten this Davenport clown, then what? It sounds as though they've got the Ozarks region pretty well tied down. What, exactly, are we supposed to do?"

"Break up their plans. From what I can get out of the files, their headquarters are in Mountain Home, which is near Bull Shoals Dam. Bull Shoals gives them ample power with little maintenance, and they do have some big plan in the air. Maybe they think they can take over Springfield, or even Fort Leonard Wood. They might be able to grab Springfield, although they couldn't attack with anything near their full force without losing what they already have, and they could never hold a place like Springfield against good troops. I can't think of a richer target for them, but then I'm not much good at thinking like an asshole."

"You're doing pretty well so far," Logan said, and chortled.

Norton failed to see the humor in the remark. "Eat shit and die."

"You'd'a gotten your wish if I'd done the cookin'," Logan said with a grin. "Relax. Obviously, we don't have a guess in hell what their plans are, so we relax and play it by ear. You're gonna get an ulcer if you don't learn to lighten up a little."

"Logan's right," Reynaud said. "What you've just given us is mostly blue-sky. It's not enough to make plans on, so we get more information. There's got to be a way to get to Davenport, and that's our next step. Thinking too far past that is likely just going to make us desperate, make us jump at long shots instead of waiting for the right chance. Besides, I think we understand what kind of bastards we're fighting." He started pushing dirt on the fire with his boot.

Norton stood. "Maybe you're right, but I can tell you one more thing about the kind of bastards you're fighting. I've found out from the files they've set up prison camps, as nasty as anything the SS ran, even as ugly as the Russ camp you were in."

Reynaud felt the hair rise on the nape of his neck and the warm summer air seemed to have suddenly chilled. Glancing at Logan and the Deacon, he saw their haunted eyes. Forcing his voice to remain steady, he said, "Okay, we get the picture, but if we're going to do any good tomorrow, we'd better get some sleep tonight. Just be sure the Colonel sleeps sound and secure."

~ * ~

Reynaud slept fitfully; his rest disturbed by nightmares of being taken back to the prison camp. He woke feeling he'd marched a hundred miles carrying a ninety-pound pack. His eyes felt gritty and his mouth tasted like a locker room. When he saw them, Logan and Billy Joe were also red-eyed and unsteady.

"You boys going to be all right?" Norton asked at breakfast, the concern in his voice genuine.

"We'll make it."

The day was cut and tailored to their mood. The wind had risen during the night and thunder rolled through the hills. Chilling rain pelted them as though it had a personal grudge against them. The long trip back to Springfield seemed even longer than it had before, and the ex-POWs needed to stop and rest three times before they reached the boarded-up OTASCO building. Norton left them in an outer office while he studied files and didn't emerge again until almost nine, but then he wore a grin.

"You boys must live a pure life," he announced. "It's not going to be a cakewalk, but it's also not going to be as bad as I was afraid it'd be. Logan, you were right; Davenport has a woman on the side. Her name is Teri Watson, and he'll probably be seeing her today. He usually works until about noon on Saturday, then goes to see her."

Norton grinned. "She must be pretty good to be worth the kind of coin Davenport's shelling out for her apartment in a classy neighborhood. The place has plumbing that works and even has electricity from five-thirty to ten every night, courtesy of a generator. Most of the people there are civilians working on the milgov's staff." He laid another map of Springfield on his battered desk and marked a spot in pencil. "The apartment building is here. They have a large, landscaped area behind the building, with a chain-link fence around it on three sides.

"There's a little bit of a depression back of the fence with a few trees growing there, even have a couple inside the fence, but they've trimmed off any branches over the fence."

Reynaud examined the map. "How about just driving up and hitting the place from the front?"

"Touchy," Norton said, "very touchy. The building has security guards—two of them, each working a twelve-hour shift. The only way into the front of the building is through the lobby, which is where the guard is posted. As I said, it's a fairly classy neighborhood, so visitors are noticed, and because a lot of the milgov's staff lives there, it's pretty thoroughly patrolled by MPs."

Hasteen leaned over the map. "How about hitting from the front and the back at the same time? Is there some other way into the building?"

"As a matter of fact," Norton said, "there is. The place has balconies. Davenport's woman lives on the third floor and has a balcony on the east end of the back of the place. The bottom balconies—patios, really—have had their sliding doors covered by bars welded in place, but the balconies above them are still open."

Logan chuckled. "It should be a safe bet nobody will be out

sunning themselves today."

Hasteen slipped out one of his Colts and checked the chambers. "If I can get a windbreaker, some duct tape, and somebody who can pick locks, I think I see a way to get in from the back and grab Davenport. That just leaves the guards in the front and the getaway. We might be able to shoot our way out, if we have to, since we have the element of surprise."

"I can tickle a lock, and I climb well," Xuan said.

"As for the rest," Reynaud added, "Logan and I should be able to pull our weight. Logan, you take the guards downstairs; I'll handle the driver." He pored over the map a moment longer. "The biggest problem is having to take Grant back to Highway 160, going right through the middle of Springfield."

"In case you hadn't noticed," Norton said, "there isn't much traffic. I agree it's a lot easier to take someone someplace more secluded, but this looks like the best we can do."

Hasteen glanced at Xuan. "I've heard Apaches are deadly enemies, so an Apache and one of the Dineh ought to be able to handle about anybody." He unbuckled his gun belts and, after slipping the .45 he'd checked into the back of his waistband, handed the holsters and the other gun to Norton. Drawing the sawed-off shotgun from his belt, he broke the action to be sure it was loaded then shoved the weapon back into his belt. "Unfortunately, we're going to have to go in quiet and light. Leave everything here but a knife and that muffled PPK."

Xuan's face revealed nothing as he stripped off his shoulder holster and handed it and his roofing hatchet to Reynaud.

"We better hit the road," Logan said. "It's getting near ten, and Mr. Davenport is probably getting pretty horny about now."

~ * ~

From the concealment of a fir, Hasteen watched the backs of the apartments. The thunderstorm had stopped but the sky was still overcast and no one was outside but Xuan and he. The Apache strode purposefully toward the building. Most of the sliding doors showed drawn curtains, and Hasteen saw nothing to warn them Xuan had been seen. The little man reached the patio of the mistress' building and, using his left hand braced against the wall to help balance himself, stood on the wrought iron patio railing, caught the bottom of the railing of the second-floor balcony, and pulled himself up. Once on the balcony railing, he had to jump to catch the railing of the top balcony. Hasteen found himself holding his breath, but Xuan caught the railing and drew himself up. The tension gone, Hasteen almost chuckled as he observed how much the little man's progress resembled that of an inchworm.

As soon as Xuan reached the ledge he pressed himself against the wall and drew the PPK.

Hasteen released a deep breath and strode out of the concealment of the trees. All across the open area he felt as though he was being watched by thousands of pairs of eyes, and he had to fight an urge to run. Despite the chill, he found himself sweating and his hands felt shaky. He reached the balcony and copied Xuan's method, steadying himself against the wall. If his hands trembled before, it had spread to his legs and he almost fell as he stood on the railing. Standing to grasp the bars above him, he almost overbalanced. Pulling himself up, conscious of how helpless he was and how easy it'd be to fall, he felt as vulnerable as if he'd just gotten into a gunfight carrying only a cap gun He was sweating heavily by the time he reached the third-floor balcony.

Xuan's face was, as usual, expressionless but Hasteen felt as though the other man was controlling an urge to laugh. Nodding, Hasteen drew the shotgun. Slipping a plastic card out of his belt, Xuan worked at the lock and within moments they heard a faint click.

The curtains in the apartment had been drawn. Carefully, Xuan slid the door along its track, making only the faintest whisper of sound then drew the curtain away at the edge against the wall.

Xuan crept into the apartment, Hasteen at his heels. They'd let themselves into the kitchen, and an archway led to what must be the living room. Crossing the room like a wisp of smoke, Xuan glanced into the living room then slipped around the doorway. Hasteen, three steps behind the other man, saw him holding a blonde down on a couch, his right hand clamped over her mouth.

Hasteen drew the shotgun and pointed it at her, hearing her muffled screams.

"Just stay quiet, and you'll stay alive, y'hear me?" She stopped struggling and stared at him with frightened eyes. "My partner also has a gun. You make a peep, and they'll be burying you in all four states in this region. Put out your hands."

Tucking the shotgun into his belt, Hasteen took the duct tape from a pocket of his windbreaker and taped her hands together. Xuan made a gag of a scarf and Hasteen reinforced it with the tape, then they led her to the bedroom and bound her ankles together. Hasteen tugged at the bindings, making sure they were secure. "Your boyfriend sold out The Steel Fist of the Lord's Righteous Fury. We don't take kindly to that. It sets a bad example for the rest of the brethren."

Xuan played along with the gambit. "Are we going to have to kill her now, now that she knows?"

"No, the high command has decided it's better to become public and make examples of the Colonel and Davenport, and any other traitors who decide to set up their own games." He jerked a thumb at the bedroom door and stalked back into the living room, feeling satisfaction. Groups like the Steel Fist relied upon secrecy. He'd shattered their cover and, at the same time, laid the disappearance of two of their agents at their own front door.

The wait for Davenport was brief. Xuan stared through the front door fisheye when Hasteen heard footsteps on the stairs. Xuan held up three fingers, then signed that a guard remained at the stairway and the other had taken a position in the hallway opposite the door. Xuan had no sooner hidden himself behind the armchair than they heard a key turn in the lock and the door swung open.

A thin man with short-trimmed hair entered the room, closed the door, and turned to stare down the barrel of Hasteen's shotgun. In a low voice, almost a growl, Hasteen muttered, "Make a noise and you'll be wearing your head all over the ceiling." It took only moments to bind Davenport's hands and put a gag into his mouth.

Hasteen moved to the door, Xuan to his right. When Xuan nodded, Hasteen crouched and jerked the door open. The guard across the hallway barely had time to register shock before Hasteen fired and the man's face was replaced by a ragged red mask.

Xuan's pistol popped rapidly, three times, and the guard by the stairs fell to one knee then pitched forward onto his face. Xuan slipped out the door to pick up the dead men's weapons while Hasteen reloaded the shotgun and used the rest of the tape to attach the weapon to Davenport's head.

"If you try to run, or if you even stumble, this thing will take off your head with about as much noise as a popcorn fart."

Xuan added two more Uzis to their arsenal by the time Hasteen marched Davenport out the door. Moving carefully down the stairs, they'd reached the landing between the first and second floors when a door opened and a middle-aged woman, carrying a basket of laundry, stepped into the stairwell. Hasteen hardly had time to see her before the PPK spat twice.

Hasteen experienced a mixture of horror and grim humor. A small black spot appeared between her eyebrows and she pitched forward, still holding the basket, then, shrouded in wet laundry, tumbled down the stairs in a mad tangle of arms and legs and linen.

"That wasn't needed," Hasteen snapped at Xuan.

"Talk later," Xuan said. "We have to move now."

"Later," Hasteen agreed, and took the final set of stairs to the ground level. He shouted at the door, "Logan, we're coming through."

Logan stood from hiding the bodies behind the desk. "The coast is clear; let's get outta here." Clutching an M-16, he darted past them, ducked outside then stood beside the door. Xuan slipped out after him, scanning the street in the other direction. Hasteen prodded Davenport into a faster shuffle toward the car, which was already running, Reynaud at the wheel. Hasteen shoved Davenport through the open door to the back seat, pushed him down onto the floor, then put the shotgun down, its muzzle still against the back of Davenport's skull.

While Xuan and Logan dashed for the car, Hasteen ran around to the driver's door. "Scoot over," he shouted to Reynaud, "I'll drive." He'd once ridden a Jeep the Cajun drove and preferred to take his chances on being shot.

Reynaud slid across the seat, having to shove the driver's body to the floor. "Take it easy," Rennie said. "We don't want to attract attention by driving like a bat out of hell."

"Right. And you're telling me this?" Glancing down, Hasteen growled, "Damn stick shift!" Slamming his door shut, he waited only until he heard the back door close then the car sped away.

Hasteen kept the speed down, partly to be as inconspicuous as possible, but mostly in deference to the wet streets. They'd almost reached the intersection of Grant and Highway 160 and he'd begun to slow for the turn when a Jeep pulled around a corner ahead. The Jeep was moving too fast for the turn and swerved into their lane. Hasteen swung the steering wheel as quickly as the street would allow and the Jeep missed them by the thickness of a cigarette paper. Tires hissed as wet brakes failed to slow the Jeep, which slammed into a curb, then rolled over.

Hasteen took the corner, heading north then stepped on the accelerator as he saw, in the rearview mirror, another car, painted in olive drab, bearing down on them. "Discourage them, Logan," he shouted, and gripped the steering wheel tighter.

Rolling down his window, Logan shoved the M-16 out and dumped a full magazine of slugs into the pavement ahead of the other car. Bullets from the burst slammed into the street, then whined back up and ripped into the car's radiator and tires. The car seemed to shudder as the tires collapsed and began to disintegrate then started to swerve. The driver kept his nerve and the car slowed to a stop, steam rolling from under the hood.

Hasteen glanced back in the rearview. "Does that take care of it?"

Xuan stared out the rear window. "It's hard to tell, but I think there's another car about two blocks behind us."

A flatbed semi pulled into the intersection they'd just sped through and slowly pulled across the street, jumped the curb, and blocked the entire street.

Reynaud laughed. "That must be one of Norton's gang. That ought to take care of the problem."

"How did they get onto us so fast?" Logan demanded. "Was it maybe a leak?"

Reynaud shook his head. "If it'd been a leak, they'd have stopped us—"

"—Or shot us into fish bait," Hasteen suggested.

"Yeah." Reynaud paused a moment. "It must've been some alert citizen with a radio. It's about what we should've expected, hitting a place that caters to the military and civ employees."

"You might want to carefully detach the shotgun from the back of Davenport's head," Hasteen said, "but you'd better do it quickly. The corner to 44 is coming up fast."

By the time Xuan had freed the gun, Hasteen shouted a warning and put the car into a controlled skid that whipped them around the corner and into the middle of Highway 44. For the rest of the ride they watched for pursuit but saw nothing on the highway or in the air.

As soon as they reached the house Donny helped drag Davenport out of the car, then drove away, taking Mario and the Deacon to the head of the driveway to help hide the tracks in the wet ground.

Hasteen stared at Xuan then jerked his head in the direction of the barn. Without looking back, he strode across the yard and into the sweet hay-smelling darkness then turned to face Xuan.

"Killing that woman wasn't necessary."

"Are you sure? Maybe she had a radio. You can be sure she knew someone who did have one. We might not have gotten away if those soldiers had come just a minute or two earlier. Besides, if the girl believes the hints you dropped, the Steel Fist will be blamed for it."

"I'd feel better if I was sure it wasn't someone like the Steel Fist. There's a danger in becoming too much like your enemy."

"That's a philosophical point."

"You're right, it's a philosophical point, but my philosophy doesn't involve a taste for blood. We're going to have to work together closer than fingers in the same glove, and I need to respect the men I can work with. So do you. Do you want to have me watch your back, knowing I won't be as quick to kill?"

They studied each other in the dim barn, neither man moving. Finally, Xuan said, "You'll do."

Hasteen nodded. "Just remember, I'm trusting my back to you, but I'm also trusting you with my honor."

After a long pause, Xuan said, "We can work together."

The rest of the group tried not to stare at them as they emerged from the barn. It was Logan, glancing into the corral, who noticed the horses were gone and the corral now held mules.

"Hey, we had a kinky fairy godmother visit us. Any of you boys missin' a car in the punkin patch?"

Norton held up his hands. "Sorry, everybody, I should've told you. I figured you were going to have to go looking for the bad guys, and mules are better than horses for where you're going. They'll last all day on just a little water and food, they're more sure-footed than horses, and they don't spook as easy."

"Okay," Reynaud said, "we're convinced. Did your man get anything out of the Colonel?"

"The Colonel is a real conversationalist, once he gets going. Now, you see this fellow here?" He gestured at Davenport. "He doesn't look like much—looks like a corporate pirate to me, but Mr. Davenport here is third in command of the Steel Fist here in Missouri and Arkansas, so the chances are pretty good he knows all about targets and such. He also looks like the kind of fellow who'll listen to reason, because I think he'd wet his pants if we were to get really sharp with him." Taking the gag out of Davenport's mouth, he asked, "Would you like to get into the conversation, Walt?"

"I'm not telling you a goddam thing, asshole."

"Such language! I'm really sorry to hear that, Walt," Norton said, "because then you're going to have to put up with a whole lot of pain and die as unpleasantly as we can arrange, all for no good reason. Are you going to try to tell me you joined the Steel Fist to be a martyr? I won't buy that. You got into this racket because it gave you a chance to play 'great leader.' You're one of those arrogant bastards who thinks he'll never get caught, that he can get away with anything. Or, you think, if you get caught, you can either talk your way out of it or get your PhD in the prison library, write a book, and maybe run for office. Do you see any books out here, Walt? Do you want to see where we're going to bury you?"

Davenport barked a laugh. "If you're going to kill me anyway, why should I tell you squat?"

"Because you know the drill," Norton grated. "You've done this enough to other people, so you know how much it can hurt. You're not supposed to be afraid of dying—you're supposed to realize it can be the greatest relief you've ever known. If it helps, we've got all the information we really need to go after your bargain basement Nazis."

"Then why bother to question me? Shoot me and get it over with."

"You'd like that, wouldn't you?" Norton said. "No, there are some things I'm still curious about, and you've got the answers. Logan, why don't you take our guest inside? Take him to the front bedroom. While you're at it, let him drop in on the Colonel."

As soon as Logan and their prisoner had gone into the house, Reynaud took off his hat and wiped his forehead with his arm. "Is that such a hot idea? I don't think you're going to scare that guy."

"That's not what I'm after. The Colonel is in the pink of health. I want Davenport to think the Colonel's sold out; it might make him more eager to talk. What I said about the Colonel spilling his guts was a bluff. Everything I told Davenport came out of the files. We do have quite a bit, but I want to know the name of the number-one man in this neck of the woods. We also still need to find out what their next target is. I'll get back to you later."

Hasteen followed Norton into the house, found his equipment in the living room, and drew his carbine from its saddle scabbard; a replica of the 1892 Winchester lever-action, chambered for .45 Long Colt, so he could use the same cartridges in his revolvers. Working the lever just enough to see the brass cartridge case in the chamber, he lowered the hammer, swung the weapon over his shoulder, picked up his poncho, and strode back outside.

"I'll go keep watch."

Rounding the ridge, he found the place where he'd sat and watched yesterday. The ground was wet, but his poncho made a dry cushion. He sat and let his gaze roam, taking in the surrounding countryside and the clearing skies.

He had no sympathy for Davenport or the Colonel. From what he could understand, both men were cold-blooded killers, but taking part in this sort of operation left him feeling dirty. It was a little easier knowing the prisoners had no loyalty to each other or to anyone or anything else. If Hasteen appreciated any virtue, it was loyalty.

The sun came out and the light turned the hills around him a vivid green, while those further away emerged from the general dimness like faint blue memories. Birds began to chirp and he saw a red squirrel running along a tree limb. Donny appeared later in the afternoon and Hasteen was pleased to have seen him well out of range of most rifles. When Donny approached, Hasteen waved him on to the house.

After what he thought was another two hours his stomach began to grumble, and Hasteen debated with himself about returning to the house for something to eat when he heard two gunshots, muffled by distance and the foliage. Tossing his poncho over his shoulder, he stood and strode back, passing Donny on his way to take over the watch. Donny wore a grim look and barely nodded at him.

~ * ~

Reynaud tried to read the rest of his group. When Norton had gone inside to interrogate Davenport, Hasteen had gone to keep watch. Hasteen had never made any secret of his distaste for any aspects of their job other than being outdoors or stand-up gunfights. Xuan had set to work cleaning weapons, as unconcerned as if Norton had just gone to buy a gallon of ice cream. Logan, still exhausted from the same nightmares that had haunted Reynaud last night, had gone into the barn to try to get some sleep. Sally was nervous and irritable; he'd suspected she'd lost family to the Steel Fist and was now discovering revenge was bittersweet at best.

Suddenly he realized he hadn't seen Charley all day. "Sally, where's the Doc?"

"He's bottled up in his van. It's parked in the trees back of the barn."

Strolling to the corner of the barn, Reynaud saw the van through the trees, sauntered to the passenger's door, and rapped at the window. He was beginning to get a terrible suspicion. He'd forgotten to notice, when he'd seen the van before, whether it had a radio.

His knock was answered by a muffled voice which Reynaud took as "Come in."

Charley sat in a rear corner, hunched over his workbench. He only looked up to see who'd entered, then returned to what he was doing. Reynaud had to crouch to make his way back, noticing as he did that the van apparently didn't have a radio. When he reached where Charley sat he looked over the dentist's shoulder and saw the man was carving a lion out of paraffin. On a rack above him stood perhaps twenty more figures of animals, all carved of wax. Charley put the finishing touches on the figurine he was making then looked up. "What's up?"

"I was just wondering where you'd gotten off to. That's really nice work."

"Thanks. It's a hobby I picked up from a prof in dental school.

It helps relax me."

"Problems?"

"I just feel useless—like the proverbial fifth wheel." Charley put the finished figurine on the bottom shelf of the rack. "I'm no hero like you guys. Whenever there's gunfire I get so nervous I can barely see."

Reynaud laughed. "Is that what you think we are—heroes? Hell, we're just like you, just doing the best we can. Instead of a probe and a dental drill, we use guns."

"There's a pretty big difference. If I fail, somebody loses a tooth. If you fail, you wind up dead."

"We work at the odds. Nothing is a hundred percent, but we definitely play the odds. I didn't start wearing a gun to make it easier for someone else to kill me. Probably the only one of us who even comes close to giving the other guy an even break is Hasteen, and he's pretty careful. In some ways, you're a lot more important than we are—you're a civilized man. Civilization is worth fighting for. It's even worth having barbarians fight for it."

Charley snorted. "I wish Sally saw it your way."

"Maybe she will. That election's too close to call. I'd say she's got some problems she's still working on." He made his way back to the door. "Catch you later."

Returning to the rest of the group, Reynaud noticed Mario and the Deacon had returned. Mario had joined Xuan at cleaning weapons and the Deacon was just walking into the barn, probably for some needed sleep. Reynaud cleaned and reloaded his shotgun. He'd used the last of his silenced rounds on the driver of Davenport's car. His Johnson rifle was in the house and he had no desire to go looking for it. Drawing his Smith and Wesson and opening the crane, he dropped the six rounds of .45 Long Colt into his hand, then closed the cylinder and checked the action. The weapon appeared to be clean and the action, tuned by a first-rate pistol smith in Texas, worked like a fine watch. He reloaded the revolver and shoved it back into the holster on his hip.

He'd just stood and stretched some of the kinks out of his back and shoulders when Norton emerged from the house. Spotting Reynaud, Norton strode toward him. "I need two graves dug in the barn. They can be shallow. You know the other dimensions."

Reynaud walked to the barn with Mario and Xuan and they

worked in rotation until the graves were finished, then they woke Logan and the Deacon and began checking and cleaning the weapons they'd captured in the raid.

Late in the afternoon, Norton led Davenport and the Colonel out of the house, their hands tied behind their backs and their ankles secured by ropes with just enough slack to allow them to walk but not to run. Both men moved like sleepwalkers and Norton had to catch the Colonel as he stumbled and almost fell at the entrance to the barn.

Reynaud watched the others, noticed Sally also looking from face to face.

The first shot caused the mules to stiffen and look up. At the second report, a deep breath later, they began to mill. Sally had winced at both gunshots while everyone else seemed to ignore them.

After a few minutes Norton strode out of the barn, reloading his .45 automatic. "Rennie, you want to start chow? I'd like everybody else to start packing. I'll have a little bedtime story for you all."

By the time a pot-luck stew simmered in the big black kettle, daylight was beginning to fade and the eastern clouds had turned rose and gold. Norton waited until everyone had eaten and hauled a case of bottled beer from the well.

"It's kind of like telling ghost stories around the campfire, isn't it? This one should do a pretty good job of raising your hackles. The Steel Fist's target is Fayetteville. 'Why Fayetteville? they all rushed to ask.' Because, boys and girls, Fayetteville has a nuclear reactor, and the Steel Fist wants to make an A-bomb.'"

CHAPTER 4

"Wonderful," Logan said. "The world needs another atom bomb like I need a second set of armpits."

Norton scratched a mosquito bite on his neck. "We don't know how they intend to take Fayetteville, but we know they have bases as far west as Harrison. That's probably where they have their jump-off base."

"Why bother with Harrison?" Reynaud asked. "Isn't it mostly a resort community.?"

"Mostly, but back in ninety-seven or so, one of the big agri-businesses bought into the place for experimental farms and a lab station where they could refine formulas for insecticides and fertilizer."

"Fertilizer, huh?" Logan said. "That oughtta make those bastards as happy as pigs in shit."

"It's also got its practical side," Norton added. "It's one way to help feed a population. That's also where they have one of their prison camps. We think they're using slave labor to work the farms and to build an airstrip. They've got a Boeing Chinook 'copter and an OV-10 Bronco. Neither of those needs much of a strip, but their two C-47s need a lot of road for a running start when they're heavy-loaded."

"Damn!" Reynaud snapped his fingers. "I forgot about their goddam air force. Can we get stingers, or at least a fifty-cal?"

"I've told you before," Norton reminded him, "the other side has all the heavy weapons. Where you're going, it's thick forest, and they can't do much at night or in bad weather. I suggest you head south, swing around south of Springfield, and stay parallel to US 65. If you stay off the highway and avoid towns, you should be able to slip into Arkansas. According to the refugees, some towns south of what used to be the Missouri line have been burned out but, so far, they don't seem to have come north into Missouri. Just be careful, because they may have foot patrols out, and we don't know what towns they control in Arkansas."

"Do you want any of the weaponry we've collected from

around here?" Reynaud asked.

"Nah, we don't need many guns here. The Army keeps the lid on pretty well, and General Meyer isn't a tinhorn dictator type. You'll probably need them yourselves, if you find some people who want to fight back."

Norton stood and faced Charley. "That brings us to you. Are you going south with them?"

Charley savored a sip of coffee before he swallowed it. "If I go, what'll happen to my van?"

"I'm afraid we'll have to ditch it and burn it—make it look like you were hijacked. You can get the supplies you need out of it first, but the rest'll have to burn."

Reynaud saw the dentist pause and could guess he was visualizing his wax pets melting and turning into flaming puddles then the dentist got to his feet. "Guess I'd better go pack up what we'll need to take."

"Wait until tomorrow," Norton said. "I'd sooner we didn't show any lights tonight. Anything you want or need from the place —take it. We're abandoning the farm tomorrow. The military will find it sooner or later; if they haven't found it in about a week, we'll help them find it. We'll leave the Colonel's files here, so the troops will have some idea what to watch for."

Reynaud permitted himself a second beer and was feeling sentimental as he bedded down in the house for the last time. He'd felt as comfortable and secure here as anyplace he'd stayed since before the war. He only hoped the troops who found the place would treat it kindly.

Rising before first light, they started packing. They'd almost finished when Norton added an aluminum case to the last mule's load.

"It's a radio; in the odd event you need something I can provide and get to you, or, more likely, for you to call back information to me. It's a hand-crank unit, so you don't need to worry about batteries dying on you, just tennis elbow or whatever, because to broadcast you have to crank for about twenty minutes. You can send up to three minutes worth of message. You talk into the mike, then hit the transmit button. The machine does the rest, scrambling the signal and sending it in a 'squirt' that only lasts a few seconds, so the opposition can't get your position by triangulation."

By an hour after dawn they'd eaten and were following a track south, giving Springfield a wide berth. Jumping off on a Sunday was apparently a lucky accident, since old habits die hard and the local troops were performing only the most necessary duties and conducting the most perfunctory patrols. The group neither saw nor heard any aircraft.

Traffic on Highway 160, when they had to cross it, was also non-existent. By late afternoon they'd also crossed Highway 65 and saw the town of Ozark, growing, like the forest itself, on the sides of the mountain.

Five miles south of Ozark and within a hundred yards of the banks of a clear creek, they made camp, leaving themselves two hours of daylight to make a fire at the base of a large fir. They were careful to use dry wood and the fir branches broke up what little smoke the fire created.

While Reynaud made dinner the rest of the group scouted the area, noting a farmhouse, possibly abandoned, standing atop a knoll within half a mile of the camp.

The next day they halted near Bronson and that night crossed the bridge and holed up under an overhang between Hollister and Ridgedale.

Reynaud felt some urgency to move as quickly as possible, but the summer warmth, where even the bees seemed lazy, was taking a toll of the party's energy, and the nightly guard duty left them too little time to sleep. Reynaud had no desire to stumble into a Steel Fist patrol because someone on point was too exhausted to be alert.

When they set out again, a full day later, they slipped past Ridgedale by midmorning and within an hour saw blackened rubble on a hilltop. Logan peered at it through binoculars. "Looks like it used to be a farm. It's been burnt out. Wanta get closer for a better look-see?"

Reynaud shook his head. "If we stop for every sign of Steel Fist atrocities we'll become professional mourners and grave-diggers. The best thing we can do is hurry up to put a hydraulic whoa to this crap. Let's move."

They passed two more blackened shells of farms before they reached Omaha, Arkansas, and found nothing but fire-scaled timbers and ashes. Leaving the Deacon and Mario to guard their backs, the rest of the party crept to the edge of town. Logan, a dozen feet from Reynaud, pointed to where a burned area began.

"Looks like they napalmed the place from the air."

His shotgun at the ready, Reynaud dashed to the nearest ruin. Nothing moved. The house, if that's what it'd been, had collapsed with the fire, leaving nothing but a pile of charred wood and the stench of rotting flesh. Someone must've died inside the place and been buried by the rubble.

Hasteen strode into the town as though walking through a boring roadside park. Ignoring Reynaud and caution together, he walked to the highway and strode a little less than half his length, then knelt on one knee. After studying the street for several long minutes, he waved for Reynaud to join him.

Although reassured by Hasteen's confidence, Reynaud still felt terribly alone and exposed. As he approached, Reynaud saw what had caught Hasteen's attention. The pavement had been scored by gunfire, with holes gouged in the blacktop.

"It looks as though these were fired from the air," Hasteen said.

"Right, like somebody was strafing something, but there's no sign of what they were shooting at."

Hasteen nodded. "You can smell the dead, but there are none in sight. Did you also notice we haven't seen any cartridge cases?" He gestured at the wreckage around them. "Some of these places show signs of being raked with machine guns, but there are no shell cases on the ground, no empty magazines, and no bodies where they can easily be found."

Staring down the length of the street, Reynaud said, "Yeah, it looks like it was a real blitzkrieg, hitting this town from the air then sending in a clean-up squad. I hate to admit it, but these bastards seem very professional."

"It seems strange, though," Hasteen said, "for them to destroy the whole town and then hide all the bodies. If it was meant to be a threat or a warning, it would've been more terrifying to have left the bodies in the street and left some sort of calling card."

"Like your habit of leaving cartridge cases in the mouths of the men you kill?" Reynaud stared at what was left of a town. "No, it suits their purposes better this way. I think they want to create a dead zone. We'll have to watch for their patrols from here on. Beyond that, they used this to terrorize the people they wanted to—the people already under their thumbs. At the same time, if a recon patrol from Springfield came across the place and didn't take the time to really look over the area, they'd probably chalk it up to a marauding road gang."

Gazing at the blackened rubble around them, Reynaud said, "I'm starting a tab for those assholes. This is one they owe for. It's probably a dumb question, but do you think you could find a trail?"

"No good," Hasteen said. "This was done before the storm. See how some of the ashes are mixed with dirt? That was done by the rain. Besides, I think the trail would vanish into the air. Norton said they had a helicopter. How big would it be?"

"Yeah," Reynaud said, "the Chinook. It's a pretty big whirly-bird, probably carries twenty-five, thirty passengers."

Logan stalked from between the ashes of two buildings. "The Boeing can carry up to forty-four fully armed troops, a few less if you want to add a door-gunner with lots of ammo. Let's get out of here: this place gives me the creeps."

Reynaud emitted a loud whistle and, as the rest of the group appeared, waved them toward the hills to the east of town. He paused a moment longer, staring at the ashes, then Mario appeared at the far end of town and when Reynaud signaled for him to leave, signed back for Reynaud to meet him in the hills.

When Reynaud reached Mario, he snapped, "I thought you and Deak were supposed to watch our backs."

"I figured that'd include clearing the flank. While you were digging around down there, I circled around the east side of town. The area is clear, but as I was checking it out, I saw some likely fields of fire and saw where I'd set up a machine gun. I took a closer look at the place and found these." He held out his hand, showing rusted gray metal tabs and three discolored cartridge cases. "They couldn't take the time to hunt up all their links and cases.

"These links are off a disintegrating machine gun belt, proba-bly an M-60. The cases are 7.62 NATO, standard ammo for the '60. These aren't just slobs with heavy firepower; the people who did this probably have military training, or at least damn good paramilitary training."

"That inspires confidence," Reynaud said. "I guess the best

way to find out is to see for ourselves."

The way south was dotted with ruined farms, houses and barns burned, and occasional vehicles stripped and burned. Less than five miles from Omaha they found the ruins of Burlington.

Logan studied the scene through his binoculars then handed them to Reynaud. "Looks pretty much like Omaha, but they've left occupation troops. Notice the sandbags just to the left of what might've been a gas station? Looks like they've got a machine gun nest there. Wouldn't surprise me if they had other unpleasantness stashed around the place."

As Reynaud peered through the glasses, a man in military camouflage emerged from under a tarp and walked to the sandbag bunker. He turned the binoculars back to the canvas, which appeared to be stretched over a framework. The edges showed concrete and sandbags and he guessed it was pitched over a cellar. He could also guess the tarp covered a mortar pit.

"Y'know," Logan said, "I'd dearly love to give those assholes their ration of grief." He scratched the stubble on his cheek. "The Deacon is getting pretty good with that grenade launcher. Bet he could put that stuttergun into a nice suborbital parabola."

Reynaud shook his head. "As much as I, too, would like to walk on their heads, we'd better get out of here. If we hit this place, we may take casualties and we'd burn up ammo we might need later. Worse yet, we'd be blowing our chance to surprise them in Harrison. Let's back the hell out of here and pass the word to everybody to keep a sharp lookout. They may have patrols out."

The group slipped away through the trees cautiously. With Hasteen, Reynaud kept a rearguard. "If they do have patrols," Hasteen observed, "they're liable to find the mule tracks."

"I know," Reynaud said, "but there's nothing we can do about that except hope. We'll head straight east, but there's a town that way, Bergman, we'll want to miss. There's also a road through the area. From the map Norton gave us, it looks to be a gravel or blacktop road. Once we find the road, we keep it well to our left and slip past Bergman. We'll have to cross Arkansas 7, then get back into heavy timber. If we go south and a couple miles east of Bergman, we should hit US 62. I want to find a good base not too far from the highway, someplace secure enough for a rendezvous then a few of us will recon Harrison."

Logan spat. "Sounds like we might be stepping into more than we can scrape off."

"I'm hoping it'll be a little easier once we get inside their dead zone. Even with seven thousand people, they've got to be stretched thin in places. Don't worry, it'll get worse as we get closer to Mountain Home."

"How many miles to where you want the base camp?"

"As I recall the map, it's about ten miles to the road and maybe ten more to US 62. When we hit the road, we'll take a break and give Norton a call."

For over three hours they toiled over and around hills. Their appreciation for the scenery had been replaced by a grim determination to cover as much of that landscape as rapidly as possible. As they stopped for a rest, Hasteen took a sip from his canteen.

"I thought you said the road was ten miles off. That seems like two hundred miles ago."

"That's ten miles as the crow flies," Logan enlightened him. "Around here, if you wanta go ten miles as the crow flies, you better do what he does—grow wings and fly 'em. This state was cut on the bias. I wonder whether there's ten miles of level ground in the whole area."

"Silence," Xuan snapped. "Listen!"

For a moment Reynaud heard nothing then could distinguish the noise made by a light engine somewhere above them.

They all scurried for cover. Reynaud signaled to Logan and took the binoculars for a closer look, training the glasses on the top of the ridge ahead of them. What appeared, seconds later, was a gyroplane, something looking like the offspring of an uneasy marriage between a helicopter and an ultralight airplane. The pilot sat in an open framework in front of the engine and below the whirling blades. At the back end was a slab of tail like a flag.

"Hold your fire," Reynaud said, as loudly as he dared. Xuan and the Deacon had already brought their rifles to bear on the craft.

The gyroplane, apparently oblivious, clattered past and Reynaud waited until its noise had receded before he signaled for the rest of the party to move on.

"Be careful," Sally said. "Better stay to deep cover. There's a fire lookout tower on the mountain to the north, just on the other side of this ridge."

Reynaud grinned at Hasteen. "Looks like it's already gotten tougher."

"Scouting from the air with that little windmill seems sloppy to me," Hasteen said. "He's going to miss a lot a foot patrol would catch."

"It'd spot a group in vehicles, and it's cost efficient. Just one man and about as much gas as it'd take to mow a suburban lawn." Reynaud glanced at Logan and noticed he was still staring after the gyroplane. "Something wrong?"

"The question seemed to shake Logan out of a reverie. "No, just wondering if I'll ever get the chance to fly again."

"After this is over, maybe you can find a working airbase. Feel like you want to re-up?"

Logan slid his FN FAL back into the saddle boot. "Aw, mostly they're just flyin' the little stuff now. Being in the cockpit of something hot, like the Raptor, now that's like good sex."

"Yeah," Reynaud replied. "I flew one too, remember? But now we're flying these jug-headed beasts, so keep your eyes peeled."

As soon as they cleared the ridge they saw the road, running like a scar through the forest. Reynaud led them back across the ridge. "Knock off for a while." He glanced at the sun, then at the wristwatch he wore. "It'll take a while to warm up the radio. I figure we should let Norton know the latest poop, and bitch about his not letting us know they have a lot of light aviation. I'll crank first."

He dismounted and took the radio off the mule carrying it, slid the crank into its slot, and began to turn it. After his arm felt like it was ready to fall off and disown his body, he turned the chore over to the Deacon. By the time he'd composed the message he wanted to send, Logan was cranking the radio, and having to use real strength to turn it.

"It's stiffened up a lot," Logan said. Personally, I think it's a rip-off—all this cranking and no ice cream."

"You'd bitch if you were hung with a new rope," Reynaud said.

"Hey, I am hung, and nobody ever bitched."

Reynaud punched the mike button and reported the deadline south of the Missouri border, the massacres in Omaha and Burlington, and the fact the Steel Fist was using gyroplanes for patrolling.

"Anything else?" Reynaud asked the group.

"Yeah," Logan said, "tell Norton we all love him and hope his parents get married someday."

Deleting Logan's suggestion, Reynaud threw the switch to transmit then looked at the sky. "Sally, how well do you know the area around here?"

"Pretty well. I grew up in Bellefonte, about ten miles from here."

"Is there a place we can reach before sundown good enough to spend the night?"

Sally thought a moment. "I don't know of any caves that close, but there's an overhang two miles south and a little west. It's large enough to hold the mules, and we can make a fire there."

"Good. At least one hot meal a day helps." Reynaud gestured. "You lead."

When they'd reached the overhang and settled in for the night, Reynaud shared the first watch with Mario. They'd found a concealed position atop the overhang and spent the first two hours in alert silence before Reynaud's curiosity got the better of him.

"Mario?"

"Yeah?"

"How'd you get into the Army?"

"Joined up right out of high school."

"You know what I mean. If you don't want to talk about it, that's okay."

"My parents kept my nose clean when I was a kid. Helluva lot of good it did them. My father died of lung cancer when I was in junior year of high school. He'd worked in a garage all his life: doctors told him it was from the asbestos in the brakes he worked on, and the solvent fumes. The only things he left my mother were me and some bills. Fortunately, she had family. They took care of her, got her into a business college.

"That's when I learned what money can do. Not just shit like spiffy cars and big houses, but taking care of family. My father, he believed in honesty, but his honesty wouldn't even pay for his headstone: the family got that for him, too. That's when I learned about being a wage slave, and the price of the straight life." He was silent a long time before he continued.

"Anyway, I went into the Army." He laughed. "Join the Army and learn a trade; that's what I did. I was a first-rate sniper, though I never had to make a money shot. In my free time, I learned more about weapons and explosives than some Army specialists. I knew what I wanted. In the business I was going into, there's a lot of legit openings, but I didn't want to be somebody's accountant, and people with…singular skills…can just about write their own ticket.

"Also, in that line of work, a clean record is an asset, one I took care to preserve. You could run my prints through any police station in the country, they could be sent to the FBI, and all you'd get back would be my military record, complete with honorable discharge.

"I was coming back from a…business meeting in Nevada when the balloon went up. The plane I was taking had to land in Joplin, and I got stuck in the area. After I heard what'd happened back east, I decided not to try to get back."

"No family or friends?"

"No, my mother died while I was in the service. Got hit by a drunk driver. So much for the rewards of the straight life. As for friends, in my line of work, I learned not to get too close to anybody. It's safer for everyone."

"What about now?"

"Now," Mario said, "I'm not sure I remember how to get close to anyone."

~ * ~

By noon the following day, Sally had led them to a cave about a quarter of a mile north of the interstate. Reynaud was pleased to see it had at least three exits, one of them very well concealed. They stowed the weapons and staked out the mules, then Reynaud had to decide who'd be on the recon to Harrison.

His palms grew clammy when he thought of observing the Steel Fist prison camp, but he was the group's leader, and recon was partly his job. He'd have liked to leave Mario to help guard the cave; the sniper was more than competent, but he was also the best trained in infantry tactics in the group. Reynaud knew he wanted Hasteen with him: if they ran into a Steel Fist patrol, the action was probably going to be at close range and very brisk work, and Hasteen was better than a submachine gun. That meant the recon group could only take one more person.

"Hasteen, Mario, and I are going to scout out Bellefonte and Harrison. We've got one slot open, if someone else wants to come along."

"Aw, hell," Logan drawled, "if I stay, somebody'll want me to take a turn cooking, then half the group'll be down with the trots, or worse. I better go, for everybody's health."

"You sure?" Reynaud asked. "We'll be scoping out the prison camp."

"Yeah, I'm sure." Logan's usual grin was absent and Reynaud had seen that grim set to his jaw only rarely. He preferred not seeing it at all.

"All right, those of you who're staying here—I want you to keep an eye on the highway traffic. Try to find out if there are convoys and, if there are, if they have a schedule. Anything you can learn will help.

"Everybody who's going—light pack. Personal weapons, two canteens, spare ammo, a poncho, grub for two days—something you can eat raw. Logan, limit yourself to your rifle and one pistol or the MAC. I hate it when you clank when you walk."

"How about a little boomstuff?" Mario asked.

"Not this trip. I'd prefer they not even know there are hostiles in the neighborhood and, if they catch us, we probably won't have time to prepare anything anyway."

Hasteen loaded a pack with supplies then picked up his carbine. He considered a moment then decided not to carry it.

Logan was also facing a difficult decision. He'd taken off the MAC and its sling, unstrapped the .44 Magnum Ruger Super Redhawk in its shoulder holster, and unclipped the holster from the inside of his pants holding a Charter Arms .44 Bulldog. He kept the military holster and the silenced Makarov.

Mario selected an old leather military holster and a .45 Colt auto from the stock of captured equipment and ran his belt through the holster's loops. Reynaud considered whether to carry his rifle or his shotgun, decided he'd rather keep his pack lighter and his hands free, and left both weapons in the cave.

Sally looked up from a pattern she'd scratched in the dirt at the cave mouth. "Bellefonte, just a little northwest of where US 65 intersects with US 62, isn't much more than a wide spot in the road. Harrison, northwest of there, is a good-sized town. The Cargill operation, plant and farms, was just northwest of town; the airport was further out, in the same direction. The last I heard, the airport was closed. There was supposed to have been a crash there, and the runway got cratered pretty bad."

Reynaud studied the rough map. "I hate to take so many people along on a recon trip, but you know the area better than anyone else here. Grab and pack."

Sally looked smug. "Sometimes the best man for the job is a woman."

As soon as she'd gathered her gear Reynaud snapped, "Let's move."

With Sally leading, they set out, paralleling US 62. As much as possible, they tried to stay on the wooded slopes, avoiding the crests and the valleys choked with underbrush. A quarter of a mile from the cave they found a valley crossing their line of march. Sally led the group into the depression, Hasteen behind her.

A blur from the brush rushed them and Hasteen's Colt roared. Everyone sprang for cover, while Hasteen hurled himself to the side and rolled. The boar squealed as it was hit and tumbled to die in a thrashing heap. Hasteen glanced at Reynaud and shrugged, then reloaded the revolver, pocketing the empty cartridge cases. "Good thing it was coming toward me, or I might've missed."

"Yeah," Reynaud said, "real good thing." He studied the tusks, which looked like ivory scythes. He found three bullet holes: one high in the spine, one near the snout. The third hole was just over the wicked left eye of the dead wild pig. He looked up at Sally. "Is there anything close enough for someone to have heard the shots?"

"I don't think so. Sound doesn't travel too well in these woods and this underbrush, but we'd better get this carcass under some kind of cover before the buzzards find it and attract some walkin' buzzards, if you know what I mean."

Together they dragged the boar under some very dense brush then scaled the opposite ridge.

"Those things are fast as lightnin' and meaner'n the devil with a kink in his tail," Sally said, "and they don't like anybody or anything comin' into their territory."

"That makes me feel a lot better," Reynaud said. "Any other

little surprises?"

"Only snakes and bears. We don't want to stay too close to creeks for very long because of the water moccasins. And watch out for trees overhanging creeks. Cottonmouths like to get into the trees and sun themselves."

"Hey, Rennie," Logan said, "what's an ole Cajun boy like you doin' worryin' about a little wildlife? Hell, I thought you were raised to rassle gators and eat the snakes first."

"I went away to college," Reynaud said. "I got civilized. I didn't have your advantage of going to a college where the mascot was a particolored toucan who dressed like a hayseed."

"Oh, low blow, man." Logan chuckled. "My, we do get cranky when we get an adrenaline rush, don't we?"

Reaching the intersection of the highways, US 62 and US 65, at about three in the afternoon, they saw the Steel Fist had left a garrison at the crossroads. Three sandbag bunkers had been placed, one at the intersection, one further down each highway, and Reynaud, through binoculars, saw a flash of sunlight on the tin roof of a shack half-hidden in the trees.

As they watched, a convoy appeared, coming from the east. The lead vehicle, a Jeep with a mounted M-60, was followed by three trucks; a six-wheeler that looked like former National Guard property, and two battered five-ton trucks. It was impossible to see the cargo under the tarpaulins. The convoy slowed and the Jeep gunner waved to someone in the bunker at the intersection. The other man waved him past and the convoy, after slowing to turn onto the highway to Harrison, sped up again.

After watching a little longer, they retreated into heavier cover. "Well, what do you think?" Reynaud asked Mario.

"Not good. Anything moving through there is going to take a lot of damage. The bunker nearest the intersection has a .50, and the bunkers are too far apart to wipe out with just a couple of grenades. The shack in cover probably has a radio with enough kick to be heard at Harrison. At least it doesn't look as if they're patrolling aggressively."

Renaud nodded. "All right, now comes the fun part. We have to get a good vantage point near Harrison, and the Steel Fist has had time to find most of them, so be careful. They'll definitely have patrols out, and possibly booby traps, too. No talking unless it's necessary."

Slipping through the brush, they moved single-file. In less than a mile they saw Bellefonte, which had been reduced to rubble. Reynaud noticed, when Sally turned away from the town, her face was like stone.

Reynaud was glad to have a guide. It'd be all too easy to get lost in these woods. It seemed almost all the territory he'd seen was green and diagonal, with an occasional outcropping of stone to remind him he was in the mountains.

Sally had led them across country that looked untouched by man, at least, by white men. She seemed to be following game trails or, more often, no trail at all.

Again they had to dip into a valley and the game trail ran into another, wider, track. Sally waved the others back and they retreated up-slope and into heavy cover.

"That trail's been used a lot lately. Deer wouldn't wear it down that much," Sally whispered. "I think their patrols must be using it."

"Sloppy security," Logan murmured. "I like that in an enemy."

"Okay," Reynaud whispered, "is there another way around?"

"We'd better go wide around," Sally replied. "If they've followed this trail all the way around, it gives them a place to observe Arkansas 7, which we have to cross. We'll have to go further north than I'd intended, to get beyond a crook in the highway."

Sally again led the way, moving even more cautiously than before. Once or twice, through the trees, they could see buildings in the distance, but the view was so broken up by trees they couldn't even make out what section of town they were seeing.

For what seemed forever they climbed and crawled their way through brush, trying to leave no sign of their passage. It was early evening when they found Arkansas 7 and dashed across, one at a time. The crook in the highway was due to the curve of a mountain and they broke away from the highway to climb the western slope of the mountain.

Going through a thicket of evergreens, Sally almost set off a mine before she saw the tripwire. Mario crawled forward and disarmed the claymore. Reynaud gave the devil his due: the mine had been placed where it was unlikely to be set off by an animal, well away from game trails.

Sally made signs that a short distance ahead was a place to

observe the town. Reynaud, after glancing at the sky overhead, nodded. They should be able to study the setup for an hour, maybe two, if the binoculars had good light-gathering qualities.

Sally led them to an outcropping covered with brush, almost invisible from the town. The rock face below them fell off steeply for fifty feet then angled away. Eighty yards below them a trail snaked through the forest and within two hundred yards lay the beginning of a defense perimeter, stripped clean of brush and trees. The strip of land had been plowed and harrowed, but Reynaud doubted the enemy had either the equipment or the manpower to seed it with mines.

Mines probably weren't needed. The glasses centered on a tower made of telephone poles, cross-supported by railroad ties. The heavy structure was necessary because the tower it supported was a sandbagged bunker holding two troops with an M-60, with a canvas roof. Whatever other equipment it held was out of sight.

Lowering his glasses, he tried to get a general impression. The prison compound was a massive double square, enclosed and divided by a chain-link fence. The guard tower he'd seen was one of six around the perimeter of the compound, and just outside the fence. The areas nearest the dividing fence were bare earth, apparently where the prisoners were assembled. Most of the other three sides of each square were pole frameworks covered with corrugated tin, with canvas sides of various colors, presently rolled up and tied along the edges of the roofs. Between the rough barracks stood woven wire fences with barbed wire stretched along the top. Each compound had a shed serving as a latrine on the northern edge, and near the central fence stood a windmill and a large concrete trough of water.

A truck stood beside an armored personnel carrier near the middle of the southern fence, and, at the western corner, a tank crouched like some predatory beast, its deadly snout pointed out over green fields. As they watched, barefoot scarecrows trudged from the fields west of the compound, from a large building to the south, and from the section of road even further south, most of it hidden behind the building. Reynaud could guess that was the new airstrip.

The people being herded toward the compound were moving with the dragging shuffle of men—and women, too, Reynaud noticed—who'd been worked to exhaustion and beyond. Besides rifles, the guards also carried what looked like batons, but as Reynaud saw the careful way the prisoners avoided them, he realized the rods were cattle prods. A woman fell, and one of the guards jabbed her with the prod. They were too far away to hear the scream but saw her writhing in the dirt. Another woman tried to help the victim up and the guard thrust the prod at her, then kicked both women back to their feet and shoved them toward the compound.

Seeing the treatment of the prisoners snapped the last thread. Hatred and fury sprang up again, and his entire body trembled with suppressed rage. It was pain that brought him back, as he bit his lower lip until it bled. He glanced at Logan, then at the rest of the group. Logan's face was pale and his eyes almost feral. Sally scanned the prisoners with a fierce intensity. After tapping her on the shoulder with the binoculars, he handed them to her. Hasteen's eyes narrowed to slits, and looked hard enough to have been chipped from obsidian. Only Mario seemed to have kept his professional detachment.

Figures stepped out of the foliage below and trod along the trail. Reynaud, moving slowly, took the glasses from Sally to study the first Steel Fist soldiers he'd seen. These wore standard camouflaged Army uniforms and equipment, even to the Kevlar "Fritz" helmets, the only unusual markings being a green band around the helmet, and green armbands with the device of a gray fist gripping a yellow lightning bolt.

Reynaud watched the patrol until they were lost in the greenery and the evening gloom. Nothing about them had seemed outstanding. They'd seemed adequate troops but hadn't moved with the lethal elegance of born hunters.

Training his glasses on the prisoners again, he saw some of them had reached the back of the truck. They accepted bowls, then, walking carefully, not wanting to spill a drop of what passed for food, they returned to the compounds, where they sat and ate. The eastern compound was the men's. After the prisoners finished eating, they washed their bowls in the troughs, many of them drinking from the same cisterns.

He examined the whole area again, trying to memorize each detail and wanting to be sure he missed nothing that would upset the escape he was planning. The hatches of the APC and the tank were open and the crews seemed to be lounging in a shed behind the personnel carrier. Something bothered him, and he looked at the vehicle crews, counting them. There were too many for just one tank and an "ape." He scanned the area again and saw another APC parked at the end of the building. Examining the building more closely, he realized the east end was being used as a motor pool.

He looked past the compound and the other structures he'd studied. Beyond the airstrip stood another building, and beyond that, the town, sprawling over the rolling terrain, with only occasional signs of damage. He wondered if resistance to the Steel Fist had crumbled quickly, or been eaten out from the middle.

Daylight was rapidly fading, and he wanted to be far from this place before he rested.

He and the rest of the group flinched, as lights sprang on around the compound, most of them set to illuminate the area inside the fences, but one or two swept probing rays around the area. After waiting until his pulse rate returned to normal, Reynaud motioned to the others and Sally led them back the way they'd come. They crept back down the mountain and across the highway.

In the pitch darkness of the woods, relieved by only odd patches of faint starlight shimmering on stone outcroppings, their movement was reduced to a crawl. Each followed the sounds of the person ahead, and Sally, leading the way, seemed to follow some half-remembered internal map. Reynaud eventually realized they were headed down a gentle slope.

"We can camp here," Sally said. "We're in a little hollow, and about a mile from the highway."

Reynaud guessed they must've traveled for at least an hour and a half to cover that mile, and he badly needed a rest. Finding a stretch of grass, he sat down, rummaged in his pack, and began to chew a piece of jerky only slightly tougher than the heels of his boots. "Mario, what do you think is the best way to open up that camp?"

"The only way we can break in is to hit it hard and fast, using vehicles." Mario seemed to think for several minutes—or perhaps he was only trying to chew his own jerky. "We need to make the hit just about sundown, otherwise the prisoners will be too scattered. Also, hitting at late evening or just after dark will give us more time to try to get away; if we're lucky. It'll also keep their air power grounded. Whatever we do, we'll be going in with a fire-power disadvantage. I'm willing to bet the tower guards have gre-nade launchers as well as machine guns."

Reynaud chased the jerky with a sip of brackish water from his canteen and started on another piece of the dried meat. "Everybody relax. Logan and I will take first watch. That's okay with you, isn't it. Logan?"

"Just fine."

"Our little jaunt seems to have dampened your sense of humor, old buddy." Reynaud swallowed the jerky, which seemed to go down in a lump.

Logan also swallowed audibly, then said, "Just thinkin' of how some a' those guards would look with their cattle prods shoved up their asses."

"Keep a happy thought." Reynaud took another sip and put a few kernels of dried corn in his mouth. "Sally, are you okay?"

"Just eager to get in there and break the prisoners out."

"Who were you looking for?" The corn slowly softened from the moisture in his mouth.

"It doesn't matter. I didn't see him anyway."

"Just remember, once the party starts, we don't have time to play favorites, or do anything but get prisoners out and kill gunnies. Any extra time we have will have to be spent getting away or doing more damage to the Steel Fist." The corn finally softened enough so he chewed and swallowed it then took one more drink of water. "What was the building?"

"That was the Cargill factory," Sally said.

"Some of it's been converted," Mario observed. "The east side's now being used for a motor pool, and I think they've put barracks in, too. There was some guard traffic through the door while the prisoners were eating."

"You're bein' awful quiet, Chief," Logan said.

"I have nothing to say," Hasteen muttered, then, after a pause, "except, perhaps, it'd be good to turn enemies into friends."

"What're you talking about?" Reynaud asked.

"Just that I'd rather use those tanks on the Steel Fist than be shot at by them. If we strike quickly, we might be able to do that."

Mario chuckled. "Hot-wire an armored column. I like your style. Have you ever driven a track?"

"No," Hasteen said, "but I've driven a truck."

"In some ways, it's simpler. If you can get light enough to read by, it even has instructions printed inside."

Staring into the darkness, Reynaud decided he was unlikely to find a better place to keep watch than where he was. "Do you really think we could pull it off?"

"It won't be easy, but not much worse than anything else we might do. It'd help if we had more warm bodies on our side."

Reynaud sat motionless. Some of the old fire burned in him again, even after Texas. He was afraid to close his eyes, afraid he'd again see those prisoners being herded with cattle prods, or see other prisoners, from longer ago. An odd memory occurred to him then, and he wondered how Juho the Finn was faring; whether he'd made it back to Finland or if he'd stayed in Poland, or even if he were still alive.

He was too drained, emotionally, to sustain anger and so his mind turned away from it.

They'd need cars or, better, pickups or trucks to hit the prison camp. The best way to get inside those fences, certainly the quickest way past them, was to drive a truck through. Getting trucks shouldn't be too difficult, if the convoys ran on anything like a regular schedule, although timing their arrival at the prison camp would be much more difficult.

When he began to nod and his eyelids finally grew heavy he woke Hasteen and Mario then slept until dawn.

~ * ~

They'd returned to the cave by late morning and Reynaud sent Charley to bring in Xuan and the Deacon. Xuan had undoubtedly seen their arrival, and Billy Joe had been watching the highway.

Everyone gathered as Reynaud fixed some hot Cajun Spanish rice, adding some dried meat, and coffee. "Everybody get a good meal, because we're going to be busy for a long time, and I don't know when we'll have hot chow again." He looked at Xuan and the Deacon. "What kind of traffic have you seen?"

The Deacon accepted a plate of the rice and meat. "Yesterday, about fourteen forty-five, a Jeep and three trucks passed, going west."

"We know. We saw them."

The Deacon continued as though Reynaud hadn't interrupted him. "This morning, at oh nine twenty, another convoy passed, going east. It may have been the same Jeep, but at least two of the trucks were different. No other traffic."

Xuan looked up from his lunch. "That gyroplane, or another one like it, made a sweep to the north of here."

"We'd better keep a sharp watch for their air force," Reynaud agreed. "For now, eat and rest. We leave here at twelve thirty and we take all the weapons with us. We'll cache them near the highway, where we can pick them up after the hijacking. Be sure to cache everything we'll need later. Pack light for the ambush: I don't want us burdened with extra gear when we rush the trucks, and if the operation goes down the tubes, none of us will want to be carrying anything that'll slow us down. Now, we'd better make plans for what to do after the raid on Harrison."

CHAPTER 5

Hasteen supposed he should be flattered to be the only member of the team with a vehicle to himself, but he felt only the responsibility to cover Sally, who was lying on the highway in a patch of shade, her blouse ripped open.

He was beginning to worry. They'd expected the trucks earlier, between two thirty and three, and it was nearly four thirty. The delay made their timing for the raid easier, but he was beginning to fear there'd be no convoy that day, and they'd have to leave the prisoners in hell for another day, and he was afraid if they waited there'd be fewer prisoners alive to rescue.

Hearing the trucks before he saw them, he tightened his grip on his Colt, his left hand wrapped around his right, his left thumb set to stroke the hammer as soon as the first shot was out of the barrel. The sound grew louder then deepened as the vehicles slowed. He was ten yards up the road from Sally, sure they'd stop at least that far from her.

Glancing back at Sally, he saw she'd lurched to her feet and staggered a couple of steps into the sunlight.

A Humvee had drawn to a stop a yard or two past him and the muscles in his cheeks twitched, a silent curse. This would make a shot at the driver more difficult. The vehicle's noise changed in pitch as the driver shifted to neutral. The gunner said something to the driver and began swinging the gun around.

Hasteen fired and the gunner pitched forward, a hole in the back of his neck and his throat torn out. His second shot caught the driver at the base of the neck and the man shot forward, bounced off the steering wheel, and fell out of the Hummer.

Already bringing his pistol around to point at the first truck, another ten yards down the road, Hasteen sprang from cover. The man riding shotgun in the truck had dismounted from the cab when Hasteen opened fire, and Charley had opened up on him with a Mini-14. The man slumped against the truck and tried to raise the muzzle of his M-3 "greasegun" when Hasteen shot him in the face, smashing his lower jaw and blowing out the back of his head.

Reynaud had already killed the truck's driver with a blast from his shotgun and pulled the body from the cab.

The Deacon had hit the driver of the third truck and Xuan had killed the gunner and trotted to the back of the truck.

Hasteen dashed toward the back of the truck. The guard on the second truck had also climbed out and Logan had almost sawed him in two with the MAC then ducked behind the cover of the truck cab at an explosion of voices from the back of the third truck.

Xuan crouched beside the last truck, firing his .44 automag into the back of the bed.

Snatching the canvas cover of the opening of the bed of the first truck, Hasteen yanked it away. Nothing. He darted past Logan, who inserted a fresh magazine into his Ingram. Hasteen heard more clearly the babble of voices, loud and high-pitched with fear. Reaching the back of the third truck, he saw the crew of that vehicle were dead, and a man in the Steel Fist uniform lay huddled on the blacktop at the back of the second truck, twitching, a hole in the back of his shirt. Xuan stood beside the body, peering into the truck bed.

The back of the truck was open and Hasteen could barely make out a tangle of figures at the front of the truck bed. Tossing himself into the bed, he rolled to his feet.

"I've got his gun, I've got his gun!"

"Back away a little, let me get a piece of him!"

"Kill the sonofabitch!" All mixed with barely human screaming.

Realizing shouting in that din was futile, Hasteen fired a round through the roof.

In the sudden, ringing silence, the scrambling stopped and men, attached to each other by an ankle chain, fell away from another Steel Fist thug. Both his arms lay bent at unnatural angles and his face had been pounded into a red paste.

"Does he have the keys to those irons?" Hasteen demanded.

A prisoner, who'd kept more dignity than the rags he wore would seem to allow, shook his head. "The other guard had 'em."

Catching the guard by the collar of his shirt, Hasteen lifted the man's head from the floor. The guard moaned but seemed unable to raise his head. Dragging him to the tailgate, Hasteen shoved him out and shot him through the head as he lay on the blacktop.

Hopping down, Hasteen began to search the other guard's body for keys. He'd just found them when Reynaud, Xuan, and Logan joined him.

"What've you got?" Reynaud asked.

Glancing into the truck, Logan said, "Looks like recruits to me."

All four of them crawled into the truck and Hasteen began to try keys in the padlocks on the chain.

"Oh shit," one of the prisoners said, a thin man with a dirty bandage around his right hand. "Oh, shit, now we're dead."

Reynaud laughed. "Hello again, boys. You can unpucker your assholes and relax. You aren't in Springfield, you aren't armed, and you aren't enemies, unless you want to be. Who's in charge here?"

The prisoner who'd spoken with Hasteen glanced at the faces of the other prisoners, then at Reynaud.

"I guess that'd be me." He appeared to be an old man, with thinning white hair, aged past his years by recent maltreatment, but his voice and his eyes were still steady, and he had the aura of strength that marked him a natural leader.

Logan let his Mac hang by its sling. "We're on our way to Harrison to take out the prison camp there. Are you willing to get into the game? The ante can be a bitch."

"I can only speak for myself," the old man said, "but I'm ready to go." A general chorus of assent came from the others.

"If anybody wants out, now's the time to say so. We can leave you out here." Reynaud's offer was met by silence.

"Very good. Xuan, Logan, help get these bodies stashed in the greenery, and, while you're at it, grab as much of as many uniforms as we can use. And let's get this convoy on the road. Tell whoever's driving to head for the cache."

While the bodies were being hauled away, Reynaud and Hasteen took stock of the former prisoners and the equipment in this truck. There were ten ex-prisoners, three of them women. All looked thin and unkempt, but none of them had any major injuries. The guards' M-16s were still in the truck, and the second guard had carried a pistol. Reynaud watched the old man handle one of the M-16s and noticed he showed an easy familiarity with the weapon. "You a vet?"

"Two tours in the 'Nam, back in the early seventies."

"Know how to drive a truck?"

"That's one of the things I did there."

"I'm Reynaud Dechaine and this is Hasteen O'Ryan."

The old man extended a hand, shook hands firmly with Reynaud and Hasteen. "I'm Noel Taylor." He introduced the rest of the people in the trucks. "We didn't know what was happening when the trucks stopped, then we heard the shots. One of the guards was at the back of the truck, and when he raised his rifle, we figured it was either help or marauders. Anyway, Buford, there, hit the guard and then the little fellow behind the truck shot him. That's when the rest of us jumped the other bull."

"Are any of the rest of you vets?"

One of the women and four of the men had seen combat and all but one woman and three men had served in the military.

The truck started with a bellow, grumbled a moment then lurched forward.

In the ten minutes it took them to reach the cache, Noel explained to Hasteen how to operate an APC. When the truck stopped they all clambered out into the shade. All the vehicles had been parked under the cover of trees and separated from each other by at least fifty yards. Xuan and Mario took canteens and dried meat and climbed to positions from where they could watch the road while the rest of the group shared water and rations with their new allies.

Reynaud grinned at Charley. "You didn't do bad, but I'd appreciate it if you could keep your shots in your target. I had to duck a round or two when you opened up on that guard. You've got the enthusiasm down pat, now you need to work on accuracy."

"Aw, take it easy, Caje," Logan drawled, "you been needin' a little excitement. For a first fight, he done good. He's also a helluva good driver. Feel like drivin' into the compound at Harrison?"

Charley nodded. "I think I can handle that."

Reynaud winked at Logan, who'd just taken the least capable man with a gun out of a firefight where every shot might count and moved him into a role where he could be most help to the operation, and with the least chance of being hurt.

"Deak, what were the trucks hauling?"

"One was empty. The other had cutting tips for machine tools and electronic parts. Supplies for Satan's workshop." the

Deacon grumbled.

"They've been hauling something else, too," Logan added. "There's an ungodly stench to those truck beds. Smells like three hundred kids dumped their Mr. Wizard science sets in those trucks."

"Do you recognize the smell?"

"No, nothing I can put my finger on. Maybe they're shipping out fertilizers or something. Come to think of it, it does remind me a little of insecticide. Maybe the Steel Fist cockroaches are getting ready to suicide."

"Maybe. How many uniforms did you get?"

"If we clean 'em up, nine. I'm afraid I shot one into doll rags, along with the clown who was wearin' it."

"All right. We need to clean the uniforms and try to hide the worst damage to the trucks. It's a damn good thing the door was still open when you nuked the guard with that chatter gun of yours. I ought to make you ride in that truck and sit on the springs you blew loose."

"What can I say? I like song and dance, and I hadn't seen anybody do the 'funky chicken' for a while. As for the uniforms, we're gonna hafta promote some of our guests. If we're spotted any time before sunset, we're not gonna be able to pass off our redskins, or even you, as Steel Fisters, whether you guys wear their uniforms or dress like Canadian Mounties,"

Reynaud was aware his coffee-with-lots-of-cream complexion and tightly curled black hair would mark him, and he nodded at the remark. "I figured you'd replace the gunner on the Hummer. Pick your own driver. I'd like to be able to bluff our way past the checkpoint at the junction, but we'd better have a Plan B handy, just in case."

~ * ~

Hasteen had found a gap between the canvas cover and the sidewall of the first truck, and he peered out as the convoy slowed. A man by the hidden shack waved at the humvee ahead, then, arms raised, pointed to his watch. "You guys are runnin' awful late."

Logan's voice answered. "We took a couple hits from sniper fire and had engine trouble. Call home and tell 'em we're on our way."

For a moment the man paused and another man in fatigues, an M-16 slung over his shoulder, sauntered toward the truck. Hasteen's pistol was in his hand without his remembering he'd drawn it. The man stopped and eyed the truck, then shouted, "They shot you up pretty good. Anybody hit?"

"Nah, it was just a nuisance hit. We didn't even hear the shots. He must've been so far back from the road he was lucky to hit the truck."

Finally the man by the shack waved his arm in an arc as a signal to proceed. After another long moment, the truck lurched forward and Hasteen released a long-held breath.

At Bellefonte, a sullen man in a gun pit barely looked up as the convoy rolled past, and his wave was only to fan the dust of the trucks' passage away from his face.

At the first curve past the rubble of Bellefonte, the convoys stopped for what looked like a Chinese fire drill. Hasteen dashed to the Humvee, ducked his head into the helmet Charley handed him, then slid into the driver's seat. Mario took over the gunner's position and Xuan hid himself as best he could in the back of the Hummer. Noel and a .50 gunner took the first truck, while Charley and Logan moved back to the second truck.

Within seconds they were again speeding down the highway, nearing Harrison. Hasteen was relieved to be out of the back of the truck, and it was a pleasure to once again be behind a steering wheel. The pleasure palled as they noticed parked tanks, concealed until the convoy had passed them.

The road ahead forked and Hasteen hoped the right branch was the service road leading to the prison camp. The way they now followed was gravel-topped and rugged, and the Humvee became noticeably harder to control. Hasteen slowed, not wanting to pull ahead of the trucks. Reynaud had made it plain the success of the plan required all the vehicles to stay together until the instant the attack started. The town of Harrison lay to his left, close enough that even in the fading light he could see doors and windows of houses and could clearly distinguish a church steeple.

As they neared the airstrip he glanced out at the runway and cursed. A huge helicopter sat as though ready to pounce, and the cockpit seemed to glare balefully at him from under the drooping blades of the front rotor. They'd known there might be one or more aircraft at the field, and they'd even planned for the possibility, but it cut their margin for error much finer.

No time to think of that now. The Hummer was already passing the gaping opening to the motor pool and Hasteen noticed several trucks parked in the gloom. Gravel gave way to hard-packed dirt. Heeling the wheel hard over to run parallel to the compound fence, he drew his left-hand pistol, transferred it to his right, and hit the brakes as they drew abreast of the mess truck and, just beyond it and to his right, the shelter for the vehicle crews.

The Humvee skidded to a stop less than ten feet from the parked personnel carrier and the Hummer's fifty caliber machine gun, above and behind Hasteen, erupted in a rapid pounding.

Most of the crewmen were dead before they got to their feet. Two more were cut down by short bursts from Xuan's rifle then Hasteen flung himself out of the Humvee. One of the crewmen, wounded by the machine gun, tugged at the flap of his holster. Hasteen snapped off a shot and the man flew backward, shot through the heart.

"Hold fire!" Xuan shouted, and darted past Hasteen headed for the tank, thirty yards away.

Some sixth sense, honed in many gunfights, warned Hasteen and he spun to see one of the mess crew snatch at an M-16 leaning against the back of the truck. Hasteen fanned two fast rounds that tossed the body, kicking, into the dirt. Ducking then, he saw, from under the truck, a pair of legs in camouflaged pants, and pointed and fired. Dust flew from the man's boot, and, with a scream, he fell. As the wounded man went down, Hasteen placed the last two rounds in the man's body, shoved the empty Colt into his belt, and drew his right-hand gun.

A bullet tugged at his sleeve like Death trying to get his attention, and he whirled. A man with a rifle stood at the door of the building. Hasteen pointed and fired, watched the man's legs snap upward as he jackknifed in the air and fell to his knees, still doubled over.

Fanning the rest of the ammunition in the cylinder at the building windows, Hasteen saw one pane shatter then the heavy machine gun on the carrier opened fire. Thrusting the empty pistol back into its holster, he rushed into the carrier, crowding past Mario, and reached the driver's seat. Half-falling into the seat, he scanned the controls. An explosion just outside dazed him a moment, then he shook the fog out of his head and looked through the forward vision block. Xuan ran toward him, away from the tank. Dust geysered beside the running figure then Xuan seemed to dance sideways before rushing out of sight toward the carrier.

Hasteen was almost sure Xuan had been hit then Mario shouted, "He's in!"

Hasteen reached for the starter button, then something slammed into the back of the carrier and the world seemed to disappear in a brilliant flash.

~ * ~

As soon as he'd shot down the vehicle crews, Mario bailed off the Hummer and, in three strides, reached the personnel carrier. A belt was loaded into the .50 Browning, meaning the weapon had been at least half loaded. He hauled back on the retracting handle, released it, stabbed the bolt latch release with his thumb then swung the gun around to point it at the northwestern corner guard tower. The muzzle of the tower machine gun winked bright light in the dusk and dust leapt up from the hood of the Hummer. Mario pressed the butterfly trigger and the .50 roared to deafening life, throbbing, and sand flew from the tower's sandbags.

Ducking, he swung the weapon around to fire at the tower almost above him. Again the huge gun bellowed and bucked in his hands and the half-inch diameter bullets chewed up the heavy wood floor of the tower and caused the sandbags to explode.

Hasteen crowded past him on his way to the driver's station. Mario fired another burst into the nearest tower and saw a shattered, rag-like corpse drop from the bottom.

Suddenly he was almost deafened by a blast as a grenade slammed into the ground next to the "ape." The concussion hit him like a great fist, showering him with dust and clods of dirt. Wrestling the pintle around, he squeezed off a longer burst at the southeastern tower. The tower almost disappeared in a cloud of sand then the canvas roof collapsed onto the tower. If the crew wasn't dead, they were either badly wounded or seriously discouraged.

A bullet spanged into the side of the APC and another buzzed past him. Again he hauled the weapon around. Rifle barrels appeared in the windows of the building fifty yards away. He raked the middle of the building with machine gun fire, spraying it in concise bursts.

A flicker to his right caught his eye and he swiveled the gun around. Xuan was running back to the track from the tank, and the M-60 in the northwest tower was firing again. Mario held the gun on the tower and punched the trigger until he'd pounded the position to pieces. Seeing Xuan climb aboard, he shouted to Hasteen then a blast almost threw him out of the gun ring and a flash almost blinded him.

~ * ~

After Xuan had shot into the vehicle crews he slung his rifle and ran toward the tank, fumbling a thermite grenade out of his pocket. Reaching the tank, he hurled himself up, onto the hull. Using the limited cover offered by the bulge of the turret and the main gun itself, he pulled the grenade's pin and slammed it down on top of the turret just behind the mantlet, then leapt from the tank to hit the ground running. A truck had broken into the compound and men were tumbling out of the back. The cloud of dust around the truck grew rather than rolled away, as machine gun fire rained down on it. Ahead, the personnel carrier seemed a thousand miles away as his feet pounded the hard earth and his lungs pumped, drawing in air and dust.

Dirt danced up beside him and he broke stride to duck and twist, sidestepping to the other side of the line drawn by bullets. A bullet hit the fence beside him then he reached the cover of the carrier. Ducking down beside the boxy hull, he glanced back at the tank. Just as he was sure the grenade had failed to go off, it looked as though an invisible giant touched the roof of the turret with the tip of a massive welding rod. The light was so intense he had to avert his eyes. Still seeing an afterimage of the glare, he stumbled to the back of the APC and threw himself inside.

The rear door of the carrier was barely closed before the world seemed to have ended in a roar and a flash.

~ * ~

Logan's hands tightened on the Uzi. The truck cab was too cramped for him to use the FAL and he missed the extra firepower provided by the 7.62mm NATO cartridge. When the first truck turned toward the motor pool he braced himself for a wild ride. By the time Charley had turned the corner behind the humvee it had already stopped in a chatter of machine gun fire.

Ducking as the rear-view mirror on his side of the truck clipped one of the guard tower's legs, Logan caught at the armrest as Charley swung the wheel over and the truck slammed into the fence. Metal ground against metal as Charley followed the fence line, taking out a good twenty yards of chain-link then swerved to avoid the center tower.

Prisoners bolted for whatever cover they could find. He could almost see the gunners in their towers, suddenly aware they were being raided, jerking back the cocking lever handles of their guns.

Hitting the second fence almost directly from the side jolted the truck then it broke free. Logan reached over and killed the ignition while Charley was standing on the brakes and fighting the truck, trying to avoid prisoners frozen by fear or too weak to move quickly.

"Get out!" Logan screamed and shoved his door open as the truck stopped. He'd just hit the ground when a machine gun lashed the truck cab with a string of bullets. He could hear the windshield shatter and the slugs slapping into the sheet steel or pounding heavier pieces of metal. The last few rounds of the fusillade chewed up the front of the truck, and steam shot from under the hood.

Kneeling on one knee to make himself the smallest possible target, Logan fired a short burst at the nearest tower. He held down the trigger as he sprayed the northeastern tower, guiding the bullets up the sandbags, correcting by walking the puffs of dust and sand up to the gunner.

The gunner's head bobbed below the top of the sandbags and Logan wondered whether he'd hit the gunner or just made him duck, then the Uzi's bolt slammed forward on an empty chamber. Cursing, Logan squeezed the grip release to drop the empty magazine and pull another out of his belt. While running in the new magazine he looked back along the truck to see how the others were doing. Two of the former prisoners crouched, aiming grenade launchers at the east central tower and a third man, at the back of the truck, stood as though giving a demonstration of coolness under fire, aiming a LAW at the northeastern tower.

Logan could actually see the LAW rocket streak toward the tower, then it hit in a flash and a blast, and when the flash was gone most of the bunker had also disappeared.

The two grenade launchers went off almost simultaneously. One of them exploded inside the middle tower and one body was thrown backward out of the perch while the other bounced into the air and flopped onto the sandbags, the head and arms dangling.

Logan seated the magazine and yanked back the bolt handle just as a grenade sailed out of the last tower, hitting the ground between the man with the LAW and the men with the launchers.

The concussion from the grenade rocked Logan, and pieces of shrapnel clawed at his left arm and leg. Still dazed by the concussion, he saw two of the ex-prisoners lying motionless and the nearer man, covered with blood, lying on his side, trying to break his launcher open to reload it. Logan turned and swept the tower with fire, then hammered it with short, sharp bursts. The Uzi clacked on an empty chamber again just as he heard the hollow-tub report of the grenade launcher and watched the tower to see if it hit, then was stunned by a sudden glare.

~ * ~

Reynaud, in the back of the second truck, watched the first truck hurtle into the motor pool garage then was shoved first to one side, then the other, as Charley weaved past the tower. He felt the impact as the truck hit the fence, then the buffeting as it sped along the fence line, throwing a shower of sparks.

Stumbling, he had to catch at the tarp frame as Charley swerved again to miss the center guard tower, then was almost hurled to his back as Charley hit the fence dividing the compound. The truck had been slowed by the fences and lurched to a stop. Reynaud sprang out, landing on the wire mesh of the central fence. Prisoners were still scrambling for the illusion of safety provided by their primitive barracks.

The sounds of gunfire and explosions were all around him. He could clearly distinguish the heavy pounding of the fifty-calibers over the more high-pitched chatter of the lighter weapons, and he fervently hoped Mario or one of the others was using the heavy machine gun. Ducking behind the left rear of the truck, he planted the butt of the Johnson rifle firmly against his shoulder and began to squeeze off shots at the southeastern tower. From far away, it seemed, he heard the blast of a grenade and the sound of small arms fire striking the truck.

When he looked again at the tower the bunker seemed to be the center of a sandstorm and the canvas roof toppled, settled onto the sandbags spilling their contents in streams. Swinging his rifle around the corner of the truck, he shifted his aim to the southwest guard station. The twilight obscured the sights but he pointed the gun just above the sandbags and fired as rapidly as he could recover from the recoil of each shot. He lost track of the rounds he'd fired until he pulled the trigger and nothing happened.

Raising and turning the weapon in his hands, he saw the bolt locked open and fumbled in a belt pouch for a pair of stripper clips. The other truck had stopped in the men's compound and Sally and the Deacon were shouting at the prisoners and handing out weapons to them. Reynaud's hands were trembling so badly from nervous excitement he had trouble seating the clip in the guides, then he pressed on the cartridges and five of them disappeared into the loading gate.

"Stand clear." It was shouted by a calm voice from only a few feet away, then a tongue of flame licked past the back of the truck and he heard the sound of a LAW being fired. Moments later, he heard a series of explosions, one of them much further away. He cursed his own shaky fingers, then they inserted the second clip into the guides, shoved in the cartridges, and the rifle was loaded again. He tugged at the bolt handle then released it, chambering a round.

A blast just on the other side of the truck left his ears ringing and he peered around the corner. The northeastern tower was only a platform with part of the back wall still standing. Reynaud looked at where the voice had come from and saw a motionless body lying face-down in the dirt. The central tower was silent and a body lay draped over the sandbags. Looking back at the southwestern tower, he saw it still standing, then one of the bodies on the ground between the tower and himself moved and he heard the "crump" of an M-79. Suddenly he was flung to the ground, his ears ringing, a glare in his eyes.

~ * ~

Billy Joe had been helping Sally hand out weapons to the prisoners when he was abruptly thrown from the truck. He managed to tumble with the fall then scrambled to his feet just as the lights around the compound were switched on. Even as he searched for the source of the blast, he reached into the truck for his rifle. Atop the roof of the building west of the compound a puff of smoke dissipated in the evening breeze.

Flipping up the sights for the grenade launcher, he aimed just over the top of the wall and fired a grenade. For a moment he was afraid he'd missed, or the round had been a dud, then a flash shot up from the roof and a LAW launcher tumbled through the air.

He felt like a hunter who'd just flushed a pheasant, then heard the rude buzzing of a small engine, and a gyroplane began to rise from the roof. Billy Joe aimed in front of the mini-copter and fired his rifle as rapidly as he could squeeze the trigger. The body of the pilot pitched forward and the contraption slammed into the roof.

Opening the breach of the M-203, he shoved in a fresh grenade. The best way to keep the Satan-spawn at bay was to start the building afire, give them a taste of the hell for which they were bound. Aiming at an open window near the door, he was gratified to see, a moment after he fired, a flash. He lobbed three more grenades into the place and saw he'd managed to start another fire in addition to the one on the roof where the gyroplane had crashed.

Something between the building and the compound bellowed and moved and he readied another grenade before he realized it was a personnel carrier. The heavy machine gun on it opened fire and he could see the tracers streaking up and past him. O'Ryan and the others had done it!

Prisoners gathered around him, some shouting for weapons, some crawling into the truck, imploring for someone to get them out of this place. For the first time, he had a chance to actually see the prison camp.

As he stood and turned, gaping at the ruins of the fences and towers, his veins seemed filled with ice water, then with fire.

"No!" he screamed. "Not here! Not in America!" He staggered around the front of the truck as though drunk, unable to see where he moved, oblivious of the prisoners, looking only for one of the devils responsible for this outrage. He saw the legs of a tower, followed them up to a bunker with a body hanging over the side.

His own body had become a machine, and his control over it was failing. He could feel tears coursing down his face while his arms swung his rifle up. He fired, and the head shattered. Again and again he squeezed the trigger, poking new holes in the body until his rifle was empty, then his left forefinger crooked around the grenade launcher's trigger and he lobbed the grenade.

The grenade exploded against the sandbags beside the body and the evening air rained sand and body parts.

~ * ~

Mario found himself clinging desperately to the .50's spade grips. Using the gun to haul himself up, he staggered back to his feet. His ears rang and his head hurt. He raised his hand to feel for a wound and his fingers brushed against the side of the helmet he still wore. The Kevlar had been dented and scored. The crackle of flames and waves of heat drew his attention to the blazing wreckage of the Humvee and he realized then that someone firing a LAW had just missed them and the track had been hit by pieces of the Hummer. The APC's high sides had protected him from the worst of the blast. He also realized the sudden glare was from the compound lights being switched on.

Xuan, lying in the back of the "ape," began to move, and Mario saw no blood. He swung his foot up and kicked the back of the driver's seat. "C'mon, let's get outta here!" he shouted.

Mario scanned the compound, then the building, just as something exploded on the building's roof. The track lunged forward and he was almost thrown off his unsteady feet. The Southwestern tower still stood, although it was silent. Pointing the machine gun at the bunker, he hammered off three short bursts, ripping the guard post apart then ducked as the "ape" hit the fence. Wires whined and snapped, and some of the lights dimmed and expired. "Turn!" Mario screamed, "Hard right!" The APC just missed the truck still leaking steam and clattered toward the shambles of the dividing fence.

The prisoners who'd gathered around the truck in the men's

compound scattered again as the carrier lurched toward them like a drunken thing. One of the men ran toward it and it stopped. The man pounded on the front of the hull with his open hands.

"Get the hell outta there and let a man in who can drive that thing."

Hasteen crawled out of the driver's seat and made his way to the gunner's ring. "Take it, then," he shouted, and sprang over the side. Pausing only to reload his revolvers, he said, "I'm just glad to be out of that steel coffin. Has anybody seen Rennie or Logan or the Deacon?"

"We're here," Reynaud shouted. He and Logan carried a badly wounded man to the back of the undamaged truck and set him inside as gently as possible. "Get mattresses and blankets from the barracks," he snapped at an unwounded prisoner. "We've got wounded, and we've got to keep them warm. Sally! Medic!"

Sally appeared at the corner of the truck, pulling Billy Joe after her. His eyes were wide, staring at something months ago and thousands of miles away. Reynaud caught the Deacon by the front of his shirt.

"Billy Joe, we don't have time for this!" He shook the Deacon and Billy Joe's eyes seemed to focus for a moment. "Deak, for God's sake, snap out of it and help us! We've got wounded! We've got to get them out of here."

Billy Joe blinked, almost fell then caught himself. "What can I do to help?" He still seemed dazed, but at least he was responding.

"Follow me," Reynaud said, and strode toward the driver's door of the truck Charley had driven into the women's compound. He opened the door then caught Charley as he fell. The front of Charley's shirt was soaked with blood and a gash had laid open his right cheek. Reynaud lowered him gently to the ground then tore open the front of his shirt, finding a bullet hole in Charley's right upper chest that appeared to have broken the collarbone.

Logan unbuckled Charley's belt and pulled it free, then bound it around his chest and shoved Charley's right hand into his shirt.

"You get to play Napoleon for a while."

Charley's eyes fluttered open and he seemed to not realize where he was, then he looked up at Logan and tried to grin. He sought out Reynaud from the faces above him.

"Jeez, it hurts. Was anybody else hurt?"

"A few. Just take it easy. How's it feel, being a hero?"

"It hurts like hell, and I feel cold."

Reynaud, Logan, and the Deacon all lifted and carried him to the truck they'd use as an ambulance. Prisoners were already throwing thin pallets and blankets into the truck bed. Reynaud stayed long enough to be sure Charley was as comfortable as possible.

"You did well, man," he said. "You'll be all right. That hole in you is your ticket punched to get out of the war. You take it easy, you've earned a vacation."

Sally joined him. "Charley," she said, "You hadta get yourself shot up. I guess I'm just gonna hafta make sure you take better care of yourself after this." She stroked his cheek. "I gotta take care of some other people now. You'll be okay." As Charley closed his eyes, she jerked her head toward the back of the truck, and as soon as she and Reynaud were away from the truck she murmured, "The other guy in there is dead. You wanna haul the body out of the truck?"

Reynaud looked at the milling prisoners. "No, not unless we really need the space. If we take him out now, it'll look worse than if we leave him in." He studied her face a moment. "If you know some of these people, you might try to get them organized so we can get them all out. I don't want to leave anyone behind who can go or be moved."

He was interrupted by the second APC, which roared out of the motor pool and took up a blocking position in the road leading to the prison camp. As soon as the track had taken up its station, a truck pulled out of the garage and headed for the compound. Were the vehicles driven by the men Reynaud had sent to capture them?

Reynaud heard a sound that raised the hair on the back of his neck; the shriek of a turbine engine starting, then the chopping sound of huge rotor blades biting the air. The gunner of the second "ape" pointed his weapon at something out of sight and fired several short bursts. Tracers from at least one machine gun began to hit around the carrier. A few rounds actually hit the hull and shot upward, leaving wavering loops in the gloom.

The pitch of the aircraft engine and rotors continued to rise then settled to a steady racket, and a dark shape rose above the level of the building's roof. Both of the .50s on the APCs opened fire, weaving brilliant ropes of light reaching out to snare the helicopter and drag it out of the sky. A light machine gun near the tail of the copter, after a brief series of flashes, fell dark and silent.

Flickering light from the fire in the building splashed on the Chinook and Reynaud could see it slowly turning toward them. The .50s intensified their fire on the machine. Slowly, almost majestically, the nose dipped and Reynaud tensed, expecting a volley of rockets from the copter. Instead, it banked and began to sideslip. The bank steepened and the ship fell faster, dropping out of sight behind the building. A vast balloon of fire bobbed up and the noise of the crash and explosion was so loud he not only heard it, he felt it in his bones.

More trucks left the motor pool and Reynaud saw Mario frantically replacing the empty ammunition box on his machine gun with a fresh case and loading the new belt into the gun.

Either the fire had cut the lines to the lights, the generator had finally died, or someone in the building had finally realized the lights were aiding the rescuers and the escapees more than hindering them, for the last few compound lights died. In the darkness they could easily see a glowing hole in the roof of the tank.

An explosion blew two of the hatch covers away, a gout of flame shot out of the hatches, and the turret bounced, to lie awkwardly aslant on the hull.

The first truck from the garage had torn down another fence and prisoners were swarming into the back of it. Reynaud dashed to the APC and shouted to the driver, "Get up ahead. We're going to need you on point, but don't get too far ahead—"

Bullets whined over them and one of the men who'd climbed into the back of the track screamed and clutched his left elbow. Several of the prisoners in the mob around the trucks screamed and fell. Muzzle flashes flickered like evil fireflies on the hillside north of the compound and they heard the rattle of small arms fire. Reynaud hurled himself as far as possible from the muzzle blast of the .50. From the area around the truck he could hear grenade launchers sending their charges out. Mario "walked" his tracers up the ridge and fired almost a full belt into the site of the muzzle flashes while grenades began to blossom around the position. Reynaud knew that in darkness or near-darkness people tend to shoot high, but the volume of fire from the hill and from the camp meant enough bullets were fired to kill on both sides.

The firing from the hillside stopped, indicating the troops patrolling there were either dead, wounded, or searching for someplace safer. Springing to his feet, Reynaud raced toward the ambulance truck then almost fell over two women huddled on the ground. Trying to avoid stepping on them, he stumbled and fell, throwing himself clear and crawled back to them. One woman lay, badly wounded, wheezing from a hole in her upper chest. The other tried to reassure her, but with a voice that shook. Reynaud pressed his fingers to the wounded woman's throat, searching for a pulse. He finally located it, but the beat was so faint it was almost imperceptible. Dark blood ran from the corner of her mouth down her cheek, and her pale face was slack.

"It's a sucking chest wound," Reynaud said. "We can't move her; she'll die in the truck."

The other woman looked up, eyes wide, in a face as pale as that of the dying woman.

"No!" she screamed. "I'm not going to let her die, not here." She stroked the other woman's hair. "No, Stephie, I'm not going to let you die here." Panic and grief were mixed in her voice.

Reynaud considered seizing the woman and throwing her into the ambulance, or leaving her behind, so her hysteria couldn't infect the others. Instead, he shook her shoulder.

"Okay, help me lift her." When the woman stumbled trying to help lift her, he took the dying woman in his arms and carried her to the truck. After handing her to Hasteen and Logan, who laid her on a pallet, he caught the other woman around the waist and tossed her into the back of the truck.

"Hasteen, I want you to drive this truck out of here. Let one truck get between you and the track and stay in that position." Looking around, he observed all the wounded had been loaded and the other prisoners were boarding the other trucks. "Deacon, you ride shotgun on the first truck. Be sure you have your blooper loaded."

Reynaud had to run after the APC, shouting until the vehicle stopped. "Mario, watch out for their air force. We don't want them giving us a napalm enema. About five miles northwest of here is a little town called Bear Creek Springs. I don't know what they've got there, but the only way we're going to get through it is as fast as beets through a baby. And remember, they've probably got a mortar at Burlington. You may want to button up in the track and go like hell. If it's just a 60mm mortar they probably won't be able to hurt you in there."

"Unless they blow off a tread," Mario shouted back.

"Fucking eternal optimist," Reynaud grumbled. On his way back to the ambulance truck he drew his pistol and shot the wrecked truck's fuel tank, then kicked a burning sandbag into the puddle of gasoline. Not waiting to see the truck blaze, he ran to the back of the ambulance vehicle and climbed inside, feeling better knowing he was leaving nothing useful for the Steel Fist.

Finding a corner of the truck unoccupied, he sat and laid down his rifle. The adrenalin had largely been burned out of his system, leaving only bitter ashes and exhaustion. He should've assigned all the towers as targets before the raid, and should've remembered the patrols around the camp and tried to keep everyone down.

"Hey, boss," Sally's voice cut across his recrimination, "you gonna just sit there and feel sorry for yourself, or you wanna help?"

"Yeah, sure." He roused himself. "What can I do?"

"I've got some dressings left, some aspirin for pain, some zylocaine if the pain is really bad. If they're running a fever, let me know. I've got a little tetracycline and some penicillin. Mostly, just talk to them and hold a few hands. These are people who're sick or hurt, not beef carcasses."

The person nearest him was a man with his leg resting on a rolled blanket, raised above the level of his head.

"How you doing?" Reynaud asked, feeling awkward and stupid.

"I'll make it," the man said. "I took one in the knee. I don't think I'll be runnin' no footraces, but I'll get by. You got anything to drink? My mouth feels like it's drawin' boll weevils."

Reynaud felt around the pile of equipment that'd been shoved to the front of the truck until he found a canteen. He handed it to the man, who took a long pull, then handed it back with a sigh.

"Thanks. It's great to be out of that damned hole. Go ahead and help the others; I'll be okay."

Reynaud moved down the line. When he reached the woman he'd helped into the truck he reached out to take the wounded woman's pulse again, but the body was already beginning to cool.

In a flash, he realized where he'd seen the women before: they were the women the guard had tormented with a cattle prod the day before. He looked at the dead woman, then at the one silently crying.

"Your sister?" He knew how inane the question was, even as he asked it, but he also wanted to give the woman the relief of talking.

She nodded and looked up at him. Her eyes were startlingly dark in her pale face. "My younger sister. I was supposed to take care of her."

"You tried. Blame the Steel Fist. Or blame me for botching the rescue. Don't blame yourself. You tried."

The woman sobbed. He wanted to put his arm around her, to offer what little comfort he could give, but he sensed this was a private grief she didn't want to share. He moved on to the next victim.

He found two more dead, and held the hand of a man with a belly wound. The man asked for a drink, and Reynaud gave it to him. He knew better than to give liquids to someone with a wound in the stomach or abdomen, but the man was thirsty, and he was dying. The best he could do for these men and women was to offer reassurance and, in some cases, an easier death. No need to die thirsty.

The truck whined as Hasteen downshifted and it slowed to a stop. Over the sound of the truck he heard a rumble of distant explosions. With the first blast, he could see the truck following theirs and knew the enemy must've fired a flare. The explosions receded in the distance. The truck idled for almost two minutes then began to move forward again, slowly. The shifting of gears was accomplished with surprising smoothness, and Reynaud realized Hasteen was doing his best not to add to the pain of the wounded. They gradually picked up speed and the truck swayed and bounced on the neglected highway. Reynaud hadn't heard the heavy machine gun on the APC at the tail of the convoy, and he guessed any pursuit was still far behind them.

Moving to the next casualty, he realized it was Charley. "Doing all right?"

"Considering I've been shot, and I've got a broken collarbone, I'm doing great." There wasn't enough light to see Charley's face, but Reynaud could guess he was trying to grin.

"We're going to get out just past Omaha and send you guys on to Springfield, where you'll go straight to the med center; I've been told the Army still keeps it open. As soon as you can, get in touch with Norton and get him updated on what we found and what's been done so far. We're going to leave you with the trucks, the APCs and their guns, the M-16s, and one of the bloop tubes, just in case there are Steel Fist sympathizers in some of the Missouri towns on the route. You'll be taking everyone who doesn't volunteer to stay behind."

Sally joined them. "Do you want me to stay with you and the rest of the group?"

"No, these people are going to need medical care on the way to Springfield. We're bound to have one or two volunteers who have first aid training. If we get really lucky, we'll have a medic or a paramedic. And if the Steel Fist get their claws into us, we won't be needing doctors."

Reynaud paused a moment. "Did you find who you were looking for?"

"No, he's gone…" she forced the words out, "my father died two weeks ago."

"I'm sorry to hear that," Reynaud said. "For what it's worth, I recall someone once said, 'Living well is the best revenge.' Do that. We're going to break the Steel Fist, and you helped. Maybe we'll see you around."

The truck slowed again, and again Reynaud saw the light from the flare before he heard the sullen cough of mortar shells. The explosions walked away from them and they were left to wait.

This second stop made him more nervous than the first. His ears strained for the sound of aircraft. The trucks, parked in a row on the highway, were terribly vulnerable. A single pass by a plane, or two napalm bombs, and they'd all burn. He tried to concentrate on the ordeal of the men in the lead APC, bottled up in a tin can, rushing through explosions, wondering if the mortar crew might not get lucky and score a direct hit.

The mortar could fire a round about every two seconds, as long as its crew had bombs to lob, and the flare round that glared in the night sky had probably been fired from over a mile away. It took the APC about a minute and a half, going full out, to cover that distance, with the men inside fearing, every second, that a shell would hit near enough to damage a tread, or the vehicle would throw a track from the speed alone.

The explosions suddenly stopped, then, when Reynaud began to hope the mortar crew had run out of bombs, he heard a rapid series of blasts. The mortar crew had given up trying to hit the speeding "ape," and had decided instead to lock on a range setting and simply throw up a curtain of fire the track must run through.

The truck ahead roared then sped away. Either the APC had been hit or the men in the truck intended to be in on the assault. Either way, there were likely to be more wounded. If the mortar fired on the truck, even a near-miss could disable it, and the people inside, without the protection of armor, would be slaughtered. On the other hand, with the enemy using at least one machine gun to cover the mortar crew, the APC crew couldn't emerge from the track to use their guns.

Perhaps a minute—it felt like an hour—after the truck ahead had charged forward, Hasteen shifted gears and they moved again. They had to stop in Burlington to pick up three more men who'd been hit by shrapnel.

As they were loading the newly wounded into the "ambulance," Reynaud told the drivers to stop again two miles north of town.

When they halted again they shifted drivers and gunners, former prisoners taking over for Hasteen, Logan, and the Deacon, and a gunner was found to replace Mario at the .50. Of the ex-prisoners, nearly fifty volunteered to stay behind to either serve as guerillas under Reynaud or to go underground, to hide with friends or family and organize resistance to the Steel Fist. Reynaud looked over the volunteers and found only thirty of them fit to fight. He was arguing with one of them when Mario tapped his shoulder and pointed out the man who'd driven the lead APC out, a man about Noel's age. "I think we'd better keep that one. He's got some bad but important news you need to hear."

Reynaud followed Mario over to the track. Mario gestured at the Cajun. "Cal, tell this fellow what you said a little bit ago."

The man seemed embarrassed by the attention then looked sharply at Reynaud. "You're going to have to make another raid on Harrison."

CHAPTER 6

"What the hell do you mean?" Reynaud demanded.

"You know how they're going to hit Fayetteville? They've got—"

Missing pieces of the puzzle suddenly began to fall into place. Reynaud remembered the smell in the back of the trucks, the factory that produced fertilizers and insecticides, the apparent stupidity of attacking a well-defended town whose population vastly outnumbered the attackers—even if agents had been planted in advance.

"Chemical weapons!" Reynaud interrupted the man. "Those bastards are going to gas the city!"

Logan had overheard the conversation. "First things first: We'd better get the civilians out of the way. That truck," he indicated the first truck in the column, "isn't gonna make it much further. There's sacks of oxidizer in it. Do you wanna move 'em to another truck?"

"Don't bother," Mario said, "I'll move the truck." Claiming his pack from the "ambulance," he climbed into the cab of the disabled ten-wheeler and moved the truck off the road, parking it behind a stand of trees.

Reynaud joined in arming the men and women who'd stayed behind, and was surprised to see the dark-eyed blonde among the volunteers. She'd taken a pistol before he recognized her. "What the hell are you doing here?" he snapped.

"The same thing you are," she replied. "How does this thing work?"

Snatching the Beretta from her, he explained the working and showed her the operation of the de-cocking lever, handed it back to her on "safe." "Keep it that way," he growled. "I don't have time to teach you how to hit anything with it, and I don't need any more body orifices. You stay with us."

Some of the ex-prisoners were already disappearing into the trees, leaving only the dozen most lightly-armed to follow Hasteen and Xuan. Reynaud stayed at the tail of the file stumbling through the dark forest. Mario joined him. "The truck is now wired for sound, and the sound is 'boom.'"

"I didn't know oxider was an explosive," Reynaud said.

"It isn't, but the little bit of plastique and the stick of dynamite I left are, and oxidizer enhances explosives. I hope a lot of those goons are standing close by when they pop the door."

Reynaud tripped over a root and rubbed his hand raw on a tree branch, catching himself to keep from falling. "What else did you learn about the opposition on the ride away from the camp?"

"Those tanks we passed going in are mostly disabled; they're not much more than fixed artillery. Some of them have electric motors to turn the turrets, but most are operated by hand-crank. The engines, tracks, and even a lot of the wheels were cannibalized to keep the other tanks going. From what Cal says, the Steel Fist has about eight or ten working tanks. They're the old M-48A5s with 105mm guns. They've also got twenty-five or thirty APCs. According to one of the prisoners who'd been in the camp at Mountain Home, they've also got some artillery, old towed field pieces, eight 105s and four 155s. Be sure you never give them a target. They can hit you from miles away, and they could drop the roof of that cave right on top of us."

Reynaud groped his way up a slope, testing each place he rested a foot. When he'd estimated they'd covered seven hundred yards, he called a halt. "We're far enough from the highway they're not likely to find us right away. Any extra distance we gain in the darkness won't be worth the energy we'd have to burn to get there. I'll take first watch. How about you, Logan? Are you up to helping watch the back-trail for a couple hours?"

"As much as I hate losin' my beauty-sleep—"

"Forget it," Reynaud said, "you need it more than we need another guard. Hasteen, you and Xuan will take it for the next two hours, then Deak and Mario."

~ * ~

Mario shook Reynaud awake to a gray dawn. "I heard some trucks and tracked vehicles go by a few minutes ago. Some of them may have stopped, if they saw the truck we ditched."

Glancing at his watch, Reynaud saw by the dim light it was a little after five o'clock. Hauling himself to his feet, he discovered a few new aches and pangs.

"We didn't hear anything last night, so we can hope the rest of them made it to Missouri. Now, we'd better get a move on. Does anybody remember the way to the cave from here?"

Hasteen and Xuan both nodded, then started through the forest and the group followed. Reynaud kept them moving as quickly as caution and the weakness of the former prisoners would allow. They'd covered most of a mile when they heard an explosion behind them.

"Well, they found the truck," Mario said, with a grin.

During the march, constantly on the alert for patrols or light planes, Reynaud found himself playing with numbers in his mind. They'd killed or wounded at least thirty of the Steel Fist, perhaps as many as fifty, they'd knocked down a quarter of their heavy air force, taken trucks the Steel Fist could probably ill-afford to lose, and made off with two personnel carriers. They'd accomplished a lot, but still had much more to do.

When they stopped for a rest, he sat down beside Cal. "Why didn't they have more tanks around Harrison?"

Cal scratched at the beard on his chin. "Most of their tanks and carriers were either moving into position to attack Fayetteville, or had already gotten into attack positions. The same goes for most of their troops.

"They'd already charged a propane tank, one of the big ones off a farm, full of poison gas. They were going to have the big copter drop that. With the right wind, a tank of gas that size could easily wipe out half a city.

"They had a back-up plan, too. They'd found a crop-duster. The plane itself was pretty well junked, but they were going to pull the spray equipment off the duster and slap it on a light plane they have, a Bronco. They were going to use it to spray large areas with gas."

Reynaud considered the picture, found it left him feeling sick. "You seem to have a pretty good idea what's going on, Cal."

"I should," Cal said. He watched Reynaud take a tiny sip of water, then, when Reynaud handed him the canteen, forced himself to take only a sip when he clearly, desperately wanted to gulp. At Reynaud's gesture, he passed the canteen on. "I should," he repeated, "I was the Cargill plant manager."

"They made you work for them?"

"Same as everybody else. When they took over in Harrison, I burned the plant records. I knew what could be done with a plant like that. I'll always be sorry I didn't blow the place up, but I thought it'd be needed again someday, to help feed everyone. I tried to disappear into the blue-collar crowd so they couldn't force me to play Nazi scientist for them. It didn't matter: the man who took over the factory knew his chemistry. He was an arrogant son of a bitch. You know the type; short on hair, short on manners, long on ambition and self-assurance. He made it clear he knew who I was, but he didn't care—I was just another peon."

"It seems strange they didn't try to recruit you for the Steel Fist."

"They did try, before they ever moved on Harrison. They sent some little weasel around to try to blow smoke up my ass. He waved the flag while crapping on the principles it stands for. I served with the Black Ponies in the 'Nam. I didn't fight for something over there to sell it out back here. I chucked the little creep out of my office. And, yeah, I'd do it again."

Reynaud climbed to his feet. "Time to move again."

By late afternoon they'd slowed to a plodding shamble. Twice they'd had to take cover while a gyroplane passed overhead, and the rest breaks had become longer. The first time they reached a tiny, clear creek, Reynaud thought he'd have to physically beat the ex-prisoners away from the water. Their desperate thirst was hard to see, but Reynaud knew drinking untreated water from the stream was the quickest way to lose most of them to illness. Late in the afternoon, during another rest, he called Mario and Xuan to where he scratched a design in the dirt.

"I want you two to go on ahead to the cave. Make sure the area is clear then start a fire and boil as much water as you can. If you have enough time, kill one of the mules for the meat. These people need to eat and drink and rest."

"We'll do what we can," Mario said, and, slinging his rifle over his shoulder, set out at a fast walk, Xuan moving past him to take the lead.

As soon as the rest of them could rise again, they set out for the cave, faces bathed in sweat, tattered work shirts clinging to their bodies. Reynaud fell into step beside Cal, whose lips were set in a determined line. For the first time, Reynaud noticed the burns on his chest and cheeks.

"Are those marks from the cattle prods?" Reynaud asked.

"No, from questioning. They like to use cigarettes and stun guns, the kind that throw lots of volts."

"Why were they questioning you? I thought they didn't care who you were."

"As the others; we were all questioned. Maybe they were trying to suppress escape plans. More likely, they were just entertaining themselves. Sadists like to stay in shape, too. The women got it worst—most of the time."

"Do you think we put a stop to their plan to attack Fayetteville?"

"No, but you stalled them. I don't think they'll attack without the gas, but with the helicopter gone, they'll need to use the Bronco. Getting it ready will take them two, maybe three, days. We'll have to take out either the Bronco or the poison gas."

"Are they storing the gas at the factory?"

"No, that's too close to town. They turn out chemicals there then haul them to a cave further west, where they're mixed. They were using the copter to haul chemicals as practice for the delivery."

The blonde woman, walking just ahead of them seemed to wilt. Reynaud tried to catch her, but she was already down by the time he reached her. Rolling her over, he found her face ashen, she was cold to the touch, her hair was plastered to her skull by sweat, and her eyes seemed unfocussed. Grabbing at his canteen, he demanded, "Who are you? What's your name?"

She looked up at him and seemed to be trying to grasp the question, without success. She was obviously unable to understand the words or to find an answer in the mental fog in which she was lost. He poured a spoonful of water into her mouth.

Hasteen had run back from the point position. Staring down at the woman, he fumbled out a pill, handed it to Reynaud.

"It's a salt tab. Give it to her with a little water. There's another creek less than a quarter of a mile from here. We can get her and the rest of them into the water, cool them off, otherwise several of them are going to start dropping on us."

After putting the pill in the woman's mouth and giving her another swallow of water to help get it down, Reynaud took off his rifle and handed it to Hasteen. "Carry this for me, will you? It looks like I'm going to have to pack her."

Slinging the rifle over his shoulder, Hasteen helped Reynaud get the woman over his shoulder in a fireman's carry.

The woman hardly weighed a hundred pounds when Reynaud settled her on his shoulder and at least twenty times that when they finally reached the stream. Hasteen had gone upstream and the Deacon was watching downstream, both of them on the alert for cottonmouths. Reynaud laid the woman into the water, her head resting on the bank, and washed her face with handfuls of water until her color had improved and she actually seemed to see him before her. "What's your name?"

"Angie…Angela Carpenter. What's yours?"

He grinned. "Reynaud. It looks as though you're back." He handed her the canteen. "Take a little of this." As she sipped, he caught Hasteen's attention. "How far do we have to go?"

"Almost two miles, most of it fairly level—if the Steel Fist hasn't found the cave."

Reynaud took the canteen back. "Think you can hold onto my neck?" he asked Angela. "That fireman's carry can't be very comfortable for you."

"I can walk," Angela protested.

"If you try, you're liable to come down with something worse than heat exhaustion. We didn't spring you from the camp to kill you off on the way out."

Angela's eyes flooded with sudden tears at a memory. Reynaud gave her a few minutes of private grief then demanded she climb onto his back. With the end almost in sight, they set out for the final leg of the trip.

Reynaud himself was staggering, his lungs pumping in great gasps of the hot, muggy air, his throat parched, when they came within sight of the cave. Mario, atop the rock formation, waved an "all-clear" sign, but as soon as they entered the cave mouth they saw Xuan sitting on a ledge, his rifle pointing in the general direction of four men. Parked behind the men were trail bikes, their knobby tires worn almost smooth.

"Adam!" Angela shouted, "How did you find us?"

"We found these visitors here when we got back," Xuan said, in his gravelly voice. "They claim to be on our side."

"Angie," one of the men said, "are you all right?"

Reynaud set Angela down, then helped her sit and handed her a cup of water. "I'm all right," she said, and drank the water, "but Stephanie…" Tears came to her eyes and voice.

"I appreciate you rescuing my sister." The man who'd spoken stood. "I'm Adam Carpenter. We use this cave when we're in the area, but I guess you need it worse."

Carpenter was blond and pale-eyed, with a strong face and a slim but muscular build. He looked to be about Angela's age, maybe younger, although she was marked by the strain of the camp and the last twelve hours. Reynaud didn't like the coldness in Carpenter's eyes as he stared at the former prisoners and even when Carpenter made an attempt to be pleasant it was almost a visible effort, as though a streak of arrogance might be close under the surface. Reynaud made introductions for his group then gestured at the meat cooking. "There's enough for everybody. Join us."

Reynaud was tired but his mind was still clear, and working rapidly. Adam was obviously related to Angie, probably her brother, but his arrogance and the appearance of two of the men with him had roused Rennie's caution. One of the men, Ross, was nondescript, the kind of man one would never pick out of a crowd, but the other two were transparent. One of them reminded Reynaud of Cal's characterization of a representative of the Steel Fist as a weasel. This weasel's name was Steve, and Reynaud was sure nothing had escaped his furtive glances. The one who identified himself as Butch was heavy-set, with heavy-lidded eyes, and he gave the impression of massive strength, impressive stupidity, and probable brutality.

As they were eating, Reynaud suggested they join forces. Carpenter paused a moment, a chunk of meat halfway to his mouth. "I don't think so. We've been at this for almost a year, now, and we're doing pretty well." He tore off a piece of meat and began to chew.

"Who've you been doing well for, Carpenter?" Cal snapped. The older man's face seemed to glow like the embers of the fire, but with anger. "You sure as hell didn't do us any good. I remember you from when you worked at the plant. You weren't worth a tinker's damn then, and I don't see you've changed much."

Carpenter spat his mouthful into the fire, threw the piece of meat in his hand after it, and sprang to his feet. "I don't hafta take that kinda crap offa you or anybody. We'll just take my sister and leave."

"Your sister is in no shape to go anywhere without resting first," Reynaud said. "She stays. And, in case you hadn't noticed, it's dark now. I really don't think you want to go anywhere tonight."

Hasteen stood and stretched, then let his hands drop to within inches of his gun butts. "You don't want to go out there. Too many things slithering around in the darkness." He seemed faintly amused.

Carpenter seemed to suddenly realize he and his men were outnumbered and outflanked, and Reynaud's group was an unknown quantity. "You're right, maybe we should join you. I'll sleep on it." He took a bedroll from a frame on the back of one of the trail bikes. "Here, sis, this is something you can sleep on." He chose a flat place and lay down, making sure his M-16 and his holster with its Beretta pistol were within easy reach.

Reynaud stood. "I'll go spell Mario; he hasn't eaten yet." Stepping outside, he carefully felt his way up the rocks from where Mario kept watch on the surrounding area. "We're going to need two guards. Of the two, the one inside needs to be the more alert."

"You don't trust them, either." Mario hadn't asked it like a question, and the statement carried a note of approval. Patting his ankle holster, he said, "We can solve the problem with four little pops."

Reynaud grinned ruefully. "I wish it were that simple. We don't have anything to hang Carpenter or his pack on, and if we start dusting off people we don't like or don't trust we're going to lose the loyalty of people who do matter."

"Maybe you should've been a congressman," Mario said. "That's the same line of reasoning that kept my former associates out of stir. Personally, I think you're thinking with the head between your legs instead of the one on your shoulders. Look at it logically —only four guys, none of whom look famished. That smells like bandits to me. Also, if they've been at it for over a year, why are there only four of them? Is the Steel Fist really that popular?"

"Four is all we see. If he's very good at this kind of work, he may keep a larger force dispersed."

"If they're such a potent force, why haven't they hit Harrison before this?"

Reynaud sat staring at the stars, feeling the cool breeze that set the trees to whispering. Mario was probably right, even about Rennie's own motives, but he was determined not to kill Angie's brother out of hand. He was, however, also responsible for the people already with him. "All right, we pair off. During your waking hours you keep your eyes on 'Stevie the Weasel.' Hasteen can watch that side of beef with him. Logan shadows Ross. Carpenter's my worry. Go on down and let the others know what we've decided, and tell Hasteen to take over up here in a couple of hours.

"So, Carpenter's bunch is paid for?"

"If there's trouble, they're paid for."

After Mario had gone, Reynaud sat watching the forest around him. Mario was almost certainly right about his thinking with his gonads. Even tired, upset, and disheveled, Angie was an attractive woman, with her clear, fine skin and dark brown eyes. He also admitted to himself that her slim build and long legs made him realize what he'd cut himself off from, with the revenge fire burning in his belly and now with his responsibilities in this pocket-sized war.

Norton's offer to settle was becoming more attractive. Scanty meals of whatever was available, whenever it could be found, sleeping on rocks, and the constant companionship of other men had long since lost their charm. Now he wanted to build a life. Before he'd met Angie that'd been an abstract longing; now it was a sharp pang.

When Hasteen took over, Reynaud made his way into the cave. From the dim light of the campfire embers, everyone seemed to be asleep. Finding a patch of shadow from which he could watch Carpenter and his men, he almost bumped into Logan. "Sorry," he said.

"You know how it is," Logan drawled. "Too much excitement gives me insomnia."

Reynaud grinned. "Yeah, I know how it is." After spending almost an hour cleaning, oiling, and reloading his weapons, he kept watch while Logan maintained his arsenal. An hour after Logan had dropped off to noisy sleep, Reynaud woke Xuan then lay down himself.

Reynaud didn't wake until well past dawn and, once he began

to move around, felt rested, if slightly sore. Sitting down by the fire, he helped himself to a cup of coffee.

Carpenter sat down beside him. "I thought about what you said last night—about joining forces, and I talked it over with the others this morning, and it sounds good to us. With more help, we can really hurt these bastards, not just nibble at them with little raids."

"I'm glad to hear you sounding so ambitious," Reynaud said, sipping at his coffee, "because the area's probably going to be a hornets' nest for a while."

"We wondered what all the traffic was yesterday. Angie said you shot up the Harrison camp pretty good. Take many casualties?"

"A few." It occurred to Reynaud that Carpenter was asking a lot of questions the Steel Fist would like to have answers for. It couldn't hurt to mislead the conversation. "We sent a couple truckloads of people to Missouri for the military to take care of."

"You think the troops will come south; help clean up the mess down here?" Carpenter's manner was a little too casual for Reynaud to be comfortable.

"You never can tell; General Meyer might get a wild hair up his ass." Reynaud knew the Army at Springfield, undermanned and underequipped, wouldn't move more than a few bare miles south of Springfield, and then only to defend the city. This terrain favored defense too much for them to try to come after the Steel Fist, even if they understood the danger the organization represented. On the other hand, this terrain favored his guerillas even more. This place would be a Vietnam for the Steel Fist. He suspected Xuan would find the situation appealing and amusing, but saw no reason to let Carpenter in on the joke.

Carpenter stood. "I thought we might go out and do some scouting this afternoon."

"No percentage in it," Reynaud said. "They'll be moving forces around like crazy and beating the bushes. If you don't run into one of their patrols, whatever information you brought back would be worthless by tomorrow anyway. Most of my people need to rest another day. There is something you can do for us, though. We could use about a gallon of gasoline."

"Well," Carpenter said, "we don't have much—I guess we can spare a gallon."

As soon as he had the gasoline, Reynaud handed the can to Xuan. "There's always the chance they'll find our trail from Burlington and set dogs on the trail, and it's also possible they've got trackers. See if you can sprinkle a little of this on the trail as far away as you can get, then try to obscure any tracks we've left. Take Deak with you for backup."

Carpenter grunted. "That oughta make this place more secure."

"Don't you believe it. We're going to have to abandon this cave within the next day or two. There's been too much action around here, and the Steel Fist is bound to find the place before too long."

"What about our bikes?"

"If you know a good spot for it within a few hundred feet, hide 'em. Otherwise, fuck 'em up so the Steel Fist can't use them." For a moment, Carpenter looked as though he were going to argue. "We'll be going through rough country, so you can leave 'em behind or carry 'em; your choice."

Again Carpenter looked as though he was prepared to argue, then he stalked away.

Reynaud finished his coffee, stood, poured himself another cup, and sat beside Cal, the former Cargill manager, who was patting dirt, twigs, and stones into a miniature landscape. Reynaud leaned over for a better look. The center of the display was a mountain with a cave.

"It's where they keep the gas. I was taken there a couple times," Cal explained. "I talked to some of the others this morning to get more details, and to help a fuzzy memory or three. The only road to the place is the dirt road that runs west from between the p-camp and the factory. It's where, at the camp, they had the "ape" and the tank parked. Further west on the road they have a checkpoint with two APCs, about four hundred yards from the cave, and they keep a tank parked right in front of the cave mouth. Between the checkpoint and the tank they've parked seven or eight mobile homes, for the people who actually live out there —some guards and some techs.

"They've got a guard post on the mountain, near the peak, and I think they run at least one patrol, but the word is the place is mostly protected by booby traps."

"Is there any other way into the cave? Large fissures, maybe?"

"Not that I know of."

"This'll bear thinking on," Reynaud said, and studied the map, trying to find the weaknesses it must have then looked around for Mario and Logan. Mario was apparently outside, and Logan was just entering the cave. Most of the former prisoners were eating or sleeping. They'd had most of their reserves used up by the Steel Fist.

Cal had brushed his hands reasonably clean and poured a cup of coffee. "What're you going to do after this is all over?" he asked.

"I haven't thought that far ahead." Reynaud replied. "Settle down, if I'm lucky. I was trained as a mechanical engineer. That and a few years practice might make me a decent blacksmith."

Cal grinned. "Like my degree in chemistry ought to help me make some terrific lye soap. The rebuilding's going to take time."

Angie sat down next to Reynaud. "I couldn't help overhearing. My brother thought you might be trying to ruin the Steel Fist so you can take over."

Reynaud caught himself before suggesting the idea probably appealed to Adam Carpenter himself. "Is that what you think?"

She gave him a smile that left him feeling a little giddy. "It's awfully hard to think badly of someone who rescued you from Hell and saved you from heat stroke, but I really don't know you or the men with you, and it's intimidating to see men who seem to be part of their weapons."

"Necessity," Reynaud observed, "is a mother. We're not elite troops, or anything like that; we're more like a cadre. We pass on a little help and information to people fighting their way out from under barbarians, but we can't carry the whole fight, or even start it for them. We might add a little stiffening, but we can't give backbone transplants, and we're not so worried about job security that we want to see one barbarian replaced by another.

"The only kind of government worth a damn is self-government, and that can't be imposed from the top; it's got to grow from the roots up. First, you've got to have the will to fight for your freedom then be prepared to fight to keep it. In a way, the plague and the war were an opportunity—they bought us some time, and they opened some frontiers, and those are things we've needed for a long time."

Finishing his coffee, Reynaud reflected for a moment then chuckled. "If I'm going to lust after something, I'm not going to waste it on anything as cold and bloodless as money or power."

Logan sat beside Angie, opposite Reynaud. "You have to forgive him, ma'am. That Cajun boy sure knows how to lust, but he never learned to talk good English. He keeps leaving dangling propositions."

Reynaud laughed. "Angie, meet Logan Reid. He's our resident artificial Texan. He claims to be the last surviving descendant of the Lone Ranger. It took two weeks and threats of a shooting to break him of calling Hasteen 'Tonto.'"

"Hey," Logan cut in, "it was an honest mistake. He *is* our faithful Indian companion. And I'm also related to the Green Hornet. But I didn't come here to talk about my family tree, illustrious as it is. Rennie, I need to have a private word with you. It's about this outfit's pension plan."

Reynaud gulped down the rest of his coffee. "I'll chat with you again, later," he told Angie, then followed Logan outside. Logan clambered up the side of the mountain until they reached the lookout's position.

"We'll take over for a while," he told the woman, and they watched her sling her rifle and climb down to the cave mouth.

"I've been talkin' to Ross," Logan said. "He wants to join up with us. According to him, he's only been with Carpenter about three weeks. Ross was in the Army, at Fort Len Wood, but he used to live in Batesville, southeast of here. Anyway, he deserted and started headin' home, when he met Carpenter. He thought Carpenter and the guys with him were gonna blow him away, but he let it be known he was a helluva shade-tree mechanic and grew up on bikes, so they recruited him. He said the other three'd leave him a bike to work on while they went raidin'. He doesn't know where they went or who they hit, but he doesn't trust Carpenter much."

"Do you believe him? Your life's worth?"

"Yeah. I know it's funny, but I do. And did you notice he's the only one of the four who doesn't wear a pistol and carry his rifle around most of the time?"

Reynaud frowned. "Just remember, if he's playing a nice guy/bad guy routine with Carpenter, all our asses are on the line.

Be buddies with him if you want to, but keep watching him, and if he crosses the line, kill him."

"Count on it. By the way, I saw Carpenter lookin' like he had a raincloud buildin' in his bowels after he'd talked to you. Remember, he's your responsibility, sister or no sister." He paused a moment. "I gotta admit, that Angie's one prize filly."

Reynaud winced. It did no good to ask or tell Logan not to talk like a cowboy from a 1954 RKO western when the mood struck him. He searched the sky. "It seems to be clouding up. I'd appreciate it if you'd go down and find my poncho, if you can, and send it up with Mario. While he's up here, you can watch that shifty-eyed little bastard with Carpenter, and tell Hasteen to keep an eye on Carpenter as well as Butch. That shouldn't be too hard; the two of them are usually closer than Siamese twins."

"I'll do that. Butch is so dimwitted he probably couldn't get his pants on without Carpenter to tell him which leg to put in first. It's sad when brother and sister marry."

"I left my rifle below. Could I use your FN?"

Logan handed over the rifle and returned to camp. By the time Mario had reached the lookout point, the clouds had become more threatening, lightning flickered about the roiled dark masses, and thunder rolled its deep bass warning.

"Have you seen Cal's relief map?" Reynaud asked.

"I looked at it on the way up."

"What do you think is the best way to take the place out?"

Mario paused. "You're not going to like the answer."

"Try me."

"I think we should go around to hit it from the south."

"That'd add a good ten miles or more to the march."

"I know, and that's why I knew you wouldn't like it. It gets worse, in some respects. I think we should go in with no more than six or eight men. The rest of the people will make a quick attack on the junction south of Bellefonte then get the hell out. According to a couple of ex-prisoners, there's a town called Bruno, about ten miles south and ten east of here that we can use as a rendezvous. The town was cleared out by the Steel Fist, and they run a patrol through it once in a while, but not often because the road it's on has deteriorated pretty badly. The place has a shell of a service station still standing, so we have a place to find each other."

Reynaud started at a peal of thunder uncomfortably close. "It sounds okay so far. What're the problems, aside from distance?"

"We'll have to coordinate attacks over a long distance, but it won't need close timing. The attack on the junction—which has probably been reinforced—will just be tap-and-go. I'm hoping it'll loosen up the defense at Harrison, because they don't believe we can hit two places at once. The other biggest hassle is choosing who goes on the long trip."

"Who do you want?"

"I've got to go. I may be the only one who can rig a timed charge and know where to plant it for maximum effect."

"Couldn't you show one of us?"

"This is no time for on-the-job training. I want Hasteen, and I'd like Xuan along. Hasteen's fast, and Xuan won't hesitate to kill, and he may be the best at recon. Then we're going to have to take Carpenter and at least one of his men, maybe two."

"That's risky; worse than on-the-job training."

"That's the other thing I figured you wouldn't like, but it's better than trusting them with the other group. Think it over and decide whether the risks are worth it."

The wind had risen. Looking at the approaching storm, Mario said, "I'm going down. If it gets much worse, you'd better come down, too. Even the Steel Fist won't be out in this stuff."

Minutes after Mario had gone, Reynaud saw two figures approaching from the north. Raising the binoculars the other guard had left, he recognized Xuan and the Deacon, running toward the cave. Playing the binoculars on the trees behind them, he saw nothing, and when he found Xuan again the little man waved an all clear. The sound of rain pounding the trees could be heard over the wind, and lightning was striking much closer.

A mountaintop in a thunderstorm, Reynaud decided, was no place for a prudent man, and he made his way, as carefully as possible, down the trail to the cave. The rain caught him halfway down the mountain and he descended even more cautiously, but still slid the last fifteen feet.

The cave had been stocked with firewood, and Reynaud felt better just seeing the blaze. Sitting near the fire, he stripped Logan's rifle, dried it with a rag, oiled it lightly, and reassembled it, then nibbled at some meat and pan bread, washed down with hot coffee. For a time, he just enjoyed the sensation of contentment then braced himself for the work ahead. He needed to send a message to Norton tonight, to warn him about the poison gas, in case they failed to destroy it.

They had to make the raid, and it was time to announce it. He stood and faced the group huddled around the fire or scattered through the cave.

"We have to make a couple of raids, and the more important one will be on the poison gas dump. Volunteers for that raid are Mario, Steve, Xuan, Hasteen, Butch, Adam Carpenter, and myself. Logan, you take the rest of this crowd and make a hit on the junction west of here."

"Wait a minute," Carpenter said. "One of my men or I should lead one of the raids."

"You'll be my second in command, and Ross will back Logan."

Carpenter and Butch rose, and so did the tension. "Ross is a new man: he follows," Carpenter rasped, "he doesn't lead. Why don't I lead the other group?"

"Why, because I want the best men for the jobs," Reynaud replied. "I thought you'd want to be in on the big raid."

Hasteen, who'd been leaning against the cave wall, stepped toward the fire. "The way Rennie has it planned, two of your men can be in on the big one."

"Two?" Carpenter still faced Reynaud. "He named three of us."

"Well," Hasteen said, "there's you, and there's Steve and Butch. Steve has a brain of sorts, and Butch has the muscle. Between the three of you, that makes two men."

Carpenter didn't move, but Butch whirled, head lowered like an angry bull, to face Hasteen. "You're beginnin' to piss me off, 'Little Beaver.' Whatsa matter, didn't you learn to play cowboys and injuns right when you was a kid? I'm gonna come over there in a minute and whup on you."

Hasteen seemed amused. "You take a step toward me, and you're dead. If you think a man with a gun should let an ape beat him to death, you've got a funny notion of what's fair. What's the matter, don't you want to go on a raid where there aren't any old men to threaten, and no women or little boys to rape?"

Butch had been clutching his M-16 and swung the barrel

toward Hasteen. It'd covered less than half the arc when Hasteen drew and his Colt bellowed its familiar long roar. The first bullet slammed into Butch's chest and his heart exploded, the second tore through his throat and ripped apart his upper spine and the spinal cord. The third bullet left a black hole beside his nose and blew the base of his brain out the back of his head.

A "pop," painfully loud in the closed space of the cave, came almost as an echo, and Steve's right eye had a new pupil. The ferret-faced little man rolled onto his side and the snubby revolver he'd palmed fell to the floor.

Butch stood a moment longer, as though not realizing he was dead, then his legs folded and he hit the floor in a heap.

Hasteen's faint air of amusement never changed as he ejected the three spent cases, dropped one of the shells in Butch's gaping mouth, reloaded the six-gun, and twirled it back into its holster.

"Well, Mario," he said, and he bent over the corpse and stripped it of its weapons, "I guess it's up to each of us to haul his own trash." He finished by pulling off the dead man's boots and dragging the body out of the cave.

"Even heathens should have a few words from the Book said over them," the Deacon said, and followed the corpses out of the cave.

"It looks like Butch didn't take Hasteen seriously," Reynaud said in a soft voice. "Some mistakes are final."

Carpenter's glare at Reynaud was poison and ice, but he said nothing, just stalked to his bedroll.

"Sorry about that, Cal," Reynaud said. "Your people didn't need any more jolts."

The older man looked out into the rain where Hasteen and Mario were burying the dead men under rocks, and the Deacon was reciting a psalm. "That's all right. Even with the ringing in my ears, the show was worth the price of admission." Lowering his voice so only Reynaud could hear him, he said, "I think your boys stopped shooting too soon: the biggest snake is still alive. Carpenter couldn't be trusted before, but now he's sure he has to kill you."

Glancing to where Carpenter sat on his bedroll, Reynaud replied, "He won't try anything as long as we watch him, and once the raid starts, he knows if he screws up, he'll die first."

Turning at the sound of a light footstep, Reynaud saw Angie standing over him. "Do you want to ask why I'm frightened of men with guns? Your faithful friend started that fight, and he enjoyed it. I have to hope you destroy the gas, and I do hope you get back alive, but then I never want to see you again."

Reynaud stared up at her. Her mind was made up, and she had no intention of being swayed by facts. He watched her walk, stiff-backed, to the rear of the cave. It all seemed to be turning to dust and, suddenly, he was beginning to get a bad feeling about the raid.

CHAPTER 7

The next morning carried foreboding on the gray, dismal dawn. The group to raid Harrison had added the Deacon to their number. That left the other group three "bloop tubes," and Reynaud had decided he wanted a man along who could use a grenade launcher.

Even with the sun hiding itself behind clouds, the morning was warm and humid, and the footing treacherous. Before they'd covered a mile they had to tie themselves together with ropes and move in relays. Fresh mud stuck to their boots until they left tracks like bigfoot. As much as possible, they tried to hide the signs of their passage, but by midafternoon the sun had appeared and the humidity soared, and the party needed to use all its energy just to travel through what seemed a diagonal swamp.

The weather reminded Reynaud of the bayou, where he'd been born, and the hot, moist air felt as though he could grab a fistful of air and wring out a pint of water.

They halted just before dark and Xuan pointed to the east and a little north. "Harrison is about four miles that way."

Xuan, Mario, Reynaud, and Hasteen split the watch that night, and they were again on their way by first light of a day that threatened to be clear and hot.

Within two hours, Mario had found the first booby trap, a hand grenade, its pin pulled, in a tin can, with a wire running to a tree trunk on the opposite side of the trail. A tug on the wire would pull the grenade from the can, allowing the "spoon" to fly loose and arm the grenade. Mario carefully detached the wire then put the wire and the grenade in its can inside his pack.

"The wind is coming from the northwest," Reynaud said. "How fast is it moving?"

Looking at the treetops, Xuan said, "About twenty, twenty-five miles an hour."

"Good. We want to come in on the dump with the wind at our backs. We should come in on the place at just the right time, too."

By nine that morning they'd found ten more traps, some of

them ingenious, like a hidden board which, when stepped on, drove a shotgun shell against a nail. Some of the others were simply rusty nails driven through planks hidden in the detritus of the forest floor. Mario moved and reprimed most of the traps, and picked up another grenade and a claymore mine.

"Remember to look carefully at the backtrail," Mario said softly. "You'll want to come back out this same way, and a trail out here looks completely different when seen from another direction. Also remember we'll be coming out in a big hurry."

Reynaud hoped the Steel Fist had no dogs at the cave; coming in with the wind at their backs was a certain way to be detected by dogs. At least, most of the ground they covered had dried out. Later in the morning they crossed a small creek and cleaned the Steel Fist uniforms they all wore.

Rounding a hillside, they gazed down at a tank, mobile homes, two semis with flatbeds, and further away, two APCs. The cave itself was invisible from their position but they could see, slightly above them and to their left, a guard post, a log block-house, which dominated the hillside. An area of roughly a hundred yards around the blockhouse had been cleared of trees and brush, and the only openings they could see were firing ports, although a much-used path led to the back of the building.

"Deacon," Mario asked, "do you think you could get above that place and, if there's trouble, put a grenade through the back door? Watch out for traps, though; they'll be all around the place."

"His will be done," Billy Joe said, crawling away through the underbrush.

Alert for traps or any signs of a patrol, they descended the mountain, taking a route that kept them in heavy cover. Mario motioned them to halt a hundred yards from the tank, which had a tarp attached to its side to serve as a shelter for the crew. Mario pointed out a depression running from the brush to a boulder, then took the LAW Hasteen had carried, opened it, and showed Xuan how it was fired.

"The thinnest armor on a tank," he murmured, "is on the top. If there's trouble, try to put the rocket right beside the commander's cupola. If you do have to fire, get down that depression to heavy cover as quickly as you can, because that thing'll give away your position. If we're separated, get back to where we left the Deacon. If you can't do that, head for Bruno and we'll link up there.

"One more thing—we're going to need that silenced PPK."

Xuan handed over the weapon and Mario passed it on to Hasteen, who tested the pointing and the chamber to be sure it was loaded and the safety was off.

"You and Carpenter go first when we get down there. Wait until about ten past noon. I'm hoping they'll break for lunch before then."

The last sixty yards down to the cave were the most dangerous. They'd covered a little over a third of the distance when they heard careless footsteps above and behind them. The party froze, then, slowly, sank into denser cover. Nine men, wearing Steel Fist uniforms, strode past. Reynaud's breath caught in his throat. If one of them got suspicious... He breathed slowly through his mouth and was disturbingly aware of the sound of his own rapid heartbeat.

The patrol, passing only a few feet from them, was armed with a wide assortment of weapons, although all the assault rifles seemed to be chambered for .223 and the shotguns were uniformly twelve gauge. The third man in the row carried a cut-down grenade launcher in addition to his rifle, and the man at the head of the column wore a green beret. To Reynaud, they looked like professionals who'd gone soft on garrison duty, too safe for too long. He followed the line of men with his eyes until they marched into the camp.

Even before their pulses had slowed, they heard the wail of a siren. The tank crew scrambled out from under the tarp and clambered into the M-48, while men in blue work uniforms dashed out of the cave and toward a slit trench Reynaud hadn't noticed earlier. The patrol, which had gone into one of the mobile homes, practically exploded from both doors and took up positions around the perimeter of the base.

The tank commander looked like some nightmarish modern centaur, his head, arms, and torso jutting out of the cupola, looking part man and part machine. After peering through binoculars toward Harrison, he bent down, probably listening to one of his crewmen. He said something to someone below, listened to the answer then hoisted himself back out of the tank.

At the same time, a loudspeaker mounted on one of the APCs crackled to life then a voice, distorted by the speaker system, blared, "All clear. Minor trouble on the far side of Harrison. You may as well all break a little early for lunch."

The troops and technicians slowly left their defenses and gathered in the mobile homes, which must've been air-conditioned, for lunch. Only the vehicles' crews remained outside, and they huddled again under their tarps.

Mario gave everyone in camp a few minutes to settle down and Reynaud used the time to try to get his blood pressure nearer to normal.

Then Mario gestured, and Hasteen and Carpenter stood and walked toward the cave. This, with the escape, were the two most dangerous times for the raiders. Mario strode after the first two, and Reynaud admired his nerve, then it was his turn. He forced himself to his feet and concentrated on simply pacing to the cave. Two popping noises, only a split-second apart, almost brought him to a halt, but he managed to keep moving until the mouth of the cave had swallowed him and he was walking in shade.

Bodies of two guards lay just inside the cave; both had been shot in the head. Mario gestured at the corpses.

"Carpenter, you and Rennie replace these guards. Hasteen, go deeper into the cave to make sure there isn't still some tech around who didn't hear the alert." He stood, gazing at the tanks and piping for the chemicals, trying to make sense of the plumbing, and saw what he was looking for another thirty feet deeper in the cavern.

Reynaud slung his shotgun and picked up the dead guard's rifle, a Mini-14 in a bullpup stock. After stripping the ammo pouches from the body, he dragged the corpse deeper into the shadows then stood at the guard's post.

Approaching the propane tank, Mario rapped along it with his knuckles. "It's still full. I think it's a solid form of hydrogen cyanide, like the Zyclon B the Nazis used." He examined a unit mounted on the end of the tank. "Thank you, thank you, thank you; they've done most of my work for me. This stuff is a liquid and a solid, separated by a seal. They've got a charge in place to blow the seal, and they've even got it hooked to a timing device. All I need do is activate it and jury-rig a tamper-proof—something to set it off if someone tries to disarm it."

He made some operations on the unit while Reynaud watched for any sign of activity in the camp. Mario had just finished his work on the detonator when Hasteen returned from his survey of the cave.

"Nobody home."

Mario then set the dynamite and plastique he'd brought so the first blast would trigger a series of explosions destroying the equipment in the cave, then rigged the claymore he'd taken to a wire stretched across the floor a few feet from the propane tank. Taking the grenade in its can from his pack, he carefully placed it, upside-down, on the timing mechanism so anyone trying to reach the timer would knock over the can and arm the grenade. Finally, he dragged one of the guards' bodies out of the shadows, rolled the body onto its face to hide the bullet hole in the forehead, and shoved the other grenade under the corpse's arm, making sure the arm was pressed against the body.

"If they try to roll him over, they're going to get one hell of a nasty surprise," he said. "Now, let's get out of here. Hasteen, you go first, then Carpenter, then Reynaud."

"Wrong," Reynaud said. "You can provide better cover than Carpenter or I when you get to cover. My job is to make sure everyone who came in also goes out."

"This is no time to be a hero," Mario said. "We'll do it your way."

Hasteen strode out the cave with the confidence of a soldier with orders to carry out. Mario followed him then Reynaud gestured at Carpenter. "Your turn."

Carpenter's face was pale but he walked out behind Mario. When Carpenter was halfway to cover, Reynaud started walking. He could guess his face was almost as pale as Carpenter's, and he could feel the sweat running down his back, but the mission was almost complete. Carpenter had slowed as he approached the bushes and suddenly, just as he reached them, he tripped.

The sudden movement attracted the attention of a tank crewman. "Hey, Phil, what're you doin' away from your post?"

Reynaud was still six feet from the brush, although it suddenly seemed six miles. "I gotta take a leak," he shouted back to the tanker, and kept walking. Carpenter was now concealed by the brush and moving up-slope.

"Hey, you ain't Phil," the crewman shouted, then Reynaud heard a "pop," and the man screamed. Reynaud made a dive for the brush and scrambled after the rest of his men. He heard the sound of the LAW being fired, heard and felt the concussion as it hit something. Small arms barked and chattered, and bullets clipped the bushes around him. He felt a tug, as though he'd caught a pants leg on a thorn. From far above he heard a blast like a grenade exploding.

The rocket must've missed the tank, he thought, then he was momentarily deafened and tossed into the air as the ammunition inside the tank blew up. He glanced back. The tank was standing as it had been, the hatch covers open, but smoke gushed from the hatches and flames were leaping from the engine compartment. Pointing the Ruger at the space under the falling tarp, he squeezed off a short burst.

The camp resembled a disturbed anthill as men leapt out of the mobile homes and raced frantically for whatever cover they could find. The man with the green beret sprang out a door and rolled, then Mario's rifle bellowed and the man's beret flew off as his head exploded. A second shot rang out, and the man with the grenade launcher crumpled.

Reynaud concentrated on moving as fast as possible and staying in cover. The small arms fire seemed to slacken then, as they went up the hill, he heard the hammering of the .50s on the APCs. Mario fired twice more and the .50s were silent again.

Going up the hill was harder than coming down, and Reynaud sometimes had to clutch at roots and heavy branches of shrubs to pull himself up the steep slope.

He'd just reached a ledge and turned to see the camp when one of the troops below made a dash for the cave. Reynaud fired. At the first burst the man forced himself into a dead run. The second burst kicked up miniature dust devils around the running figure and the man's right leg folded under him, tossing him face-down into the dirt. At the third burst the man seemed to suffer a seizure, then lay motionless.

Reynaud's gunfire attracted return fire and he hugged the ground as bullets churned up the earth around him. From above him, an automatic weapon rattled and the fire lessened as a few of the enemy were hit and most of the rest of them opened fire on the blockhouse.

A few feet away, Reynaud saw the depression where Xuan had hidden. Mario crouched there now, his rifle resting on the lip of the depression. He touched off two fast shots then crawled like a lizard along the depression and up the escape route.

Waiting until Mario passed him, Reynaud continued climbing. The blockhouse was silent and Reynaud fervently hoped the Deacon had found some way out of the place before the troops below had shot the place to kindling. He looked back at the camp. Dust billowed up from the road from Harrison as reinforcements were rushed to the battle. He wondered why they hadn't used the remaining tanks, some of which were probably in the relief column, as artillery, then remembered what was in the cave. The troops below were still firing, but most of their shots were directed either below him, where he'd been minutes before, or at the blockhouse above.

He reached the place where they'd left Billy Joe. Just a few more yards and he'd be around the curve of the hill, sheltered from the worst of the fire from below.

A grenade exploded in the brush, twenty yards behind him, sending shrapnel whining through the shrubbery then heard the cough of a launcher a few yards above him. Billy Joe was still alive, and covering the retreat.

Turning to fire a last burst, Reynaud found the Ruger was empty. Reaching cover behind the hill, he released the empty magazine and threw it away, drew a fresh magazine from the pouch he'd taken from the dead guard, then reloaded and recharged the weapon. As he drew the bolt back the Deacon joined the party, holding the side of his head and with blood running between his fingers.

"Let's move, before they can outflank us," Mario said, tying a field dressing to Billy Joe's head. The Deacon's long face was streaked with blood. Mario must've seen the concern on Reynaud's face. "Just a scalp cut," he said. "It bled a lot, but it's not serious."

"I want Xuan in the lead, now," Reynaud said, "then the Deacon, Hasteen, Mario, then Carpenter. I'll be tail-end Charley."

He'd hardly finished speaking before Xuan was trotting away. Mario paused a moment to test the wind direction. "Good. The wind is still moving from us to Harrison. If you smell bitter almonds, assume the prescribed position."

"What's that?" Reynaud asked.

"Put your head between your knees and kiss your ass good-bye," Mario said, and followed Hasteen.

After giving Carpenter a few yards' head start, Reynaud got to his feet and loped after the others, heading for thicker tree cover in the valley below. He was still trotting downslope when he heard the irritating racket of light engines behind him. Spinning, he raised his rifle just as a gyroplane bobbed up and around the curve of the hill, followed immediately by a second gyroplane. Over the sound of the engine and the blades he heard pistol shots. The little machines were bobbing and weaving like boxers, but he decided to test the principle that if you put enough lead into the air, they just might run into some. Pointing the rifle at the nearer machine, he held down the trigger, emptying the magazine.

The gyroplane lurched into what looked like an evasive maneuver, then the blades brushed the hillside and the ultralight cartwheeled into the mountain. The distinctive sharp report of Mario's .338 Winchester Magnum sounded once and the second gyroplane tumbled in the air, the pilot's body sagging against its safety harness, then fell and crashed into the ground thirty yards from Reynaud.

Dumping the empty magazine, Reynaud inserted the last magazine into the rifle, recharged it, then turned and trotted after the others. A valley lay before him and he pushed himself to reach the denser forest. His lungs burned, as did his leg where he'd snagged it on the thorn. The air was hot, and he couldn't seem to get enough of it. Safety seemed to retreat from him, as though he were running backward. He heard a shot from far behind him, and the reply of the .338.

Then he was in unbroken shade. He stumbled on until he tripped over a root as big as his calf. He tried to keep up with his legs but, after two awkward steps, he fell.

For a moment, he could only lie on the ground and gasp for air, then he checked the rifle to be sure he hadn't plugged the barrel with dirt or pine needles. The gun appeared to be clear.

Mario appeared from behind a tree. "Are you able to get up?"

"In a minute."

"Better make it a quick minute. We're still less than a mile from the cave, and that timer charge is going to go off any minute now." He stepped toward Reynaud then looked down at his leg. "What's the matter with your calf?"

"I think I cut it on a rock or thorn."

Mario carefully leaned his rifle against a tree trunk, then knelt and pulled Reynaud's pants leg out of the top of his boot, and Reynaud suddenly realized the cloth was wet.

"No," Mario replied, "you've been nicked. Let me dress that."

Reynaud twisted so Mario could dig the bandage out of his pack then watched as Mario applied the dressing to his lower leg. His throat felt as though it were coated with dust. Pulling out his canteen, he discovered it was almost empty, and the plastic flask had a round hole in it near the bottom.

Mario noticed it too, and grinned. "Have you ever thought of going into faith healing? You seem to have the miracle touch."

"You've been hanging around the Deacon too much," Reynaud grunted. He drank the little water left in the canteen, then tossed it away. "Was anyone else hit?"

"No, you and the Deacon were the only ones kissed, but if we stick around here any longer, we're all going to be fucked. The nick on your leg wasn't a bad one." Rising, he extended a hand. Reynaud accepted the assistance and, with Mario's help, hauled himself to his feet.

At that moment they heard an explosion from the direction of the cave. "Do we run?" Reynaud asked.

"It wouldn't do much good," Mario replied. "Our best bet is to get across this valley and up the next mountain as soon as possible. The gas is a vapor, heavier than air, and the blast in the cave and the wind should send it in the direction of Harrison. We're upwind of it, so we should be safe. With a little luck, the stuff should dissipate in less than half an hour."

As they began to trot toward the mountain, Reynaud glanced at Mario. "How many of them do you think we got?" he panted.

"Not many. Not enough. They had lots of time to get their gas masks on. The best we can hope for is that some of their techs were in the cave trying to disarm the charge when it blew. The explosions might've killed a few of them."

They'd crossed the valley and were climbing the slope of the next mountain when they heard a buzzing that sounded like a giant bumblebee. Mario had gone ahead to his position in the file and Carpenter was almost out of sight ahead. Looking up, Reynaud tried to find the source of the humming, and his breath caught in his throat; the Steel Fist had called out some of their heavy air-power. He recognized the trim fuselage and twin-boom tail of the Bronco. "Take cover!" he screamed and threw himself behind a stunted tree.

The Bronco made a lazy circle and Reynaud strained to see if it were carrying the crop-duster's sprayer, but saw nothing but two tanks under the wings. As the circle was closed, the buzzing rose to a higher pitch, the nose dipped, then the plane seemed to be rushing straight at him. The gun muzzles in the winglet at the bottom of the fuselage winked flame. Leaves and branches from the tree showered down onto him as bullets slashed into the foliage. The machine swept past him, still firing, and the air seemed to rain cartridge cases.

Looking up the slope, he saw no one; the rest of the group had also apparently gone to ground.

The Bronco finished its firing pass with a steep climb, flicked over onto a wingtip to bank sharply, and curved around in a slashing turn. This time, the plane came in from the side, but its guns remained silent. Instead, the two tanks under the wings dropped, tumbling like silver footballs. Hunching down, Reynaud tried to protect his face with his arms. If he thought he could've done it, he'd have tried to crawl up his own asshole. He heard the tanks hit and the "whump" as the napalm ignited, then waves of heat battered him.

Something crashed through the bushes above him and Carpenter slid down an embankment. Reynaud grabbed him and hauled him behind the tree, not sure from which direction the Bronco would strike next. The plane had turned again, but the pilot seemed wary of the disturbed air currents above and around the fire. The machine circled the area once more then was gone.

"Are you all right?" Reynaud fumbled out his other canteen and handed it to Carpenter, who drank, then handed it back. Carpenter nodded.

"Did the others get away?" Reynaud asked.

"I don't know."

"We have to move—now," Reynaud said. "The wind is sending the fire toward us."

A sudden fury appeared in Carpenter's eyes. "You son of a bitch, you got me into this."

Reynaud caught up his rifle, biting back a retort. This wasn't the place for a bootless argument. "We've got to move," he said again. "There are troops behind us and a fire in front of us. We've got to turn south soon, anyway. Just be careful of booby traps; we haven't cleared this area."

They scrambled across fifty yards of almost open ground before they cleared the flames. As he ducked and dodged from one scrap of cover to another, Reynaud flipped the switch on the Ruger to semiautomatic, and when he'd reached the shelter of a fallen log he dropped behind it and rested the weapon's forearm on the trunk. "Keep moving for at least another hundred yards," he told Carpenter.

He needed rest. His arms and legs trembled with fatigue, his lungs ached, and his stomach was beginning to knot with hunger. Finding a little jerky in his pack, he gnawed it ravenously then swallowed a mouthful of water to help choke down the dried meat. Noting a flicker of movement in the distance, he covered that area with his rifle. Again he saw movement and made out a man, two hundred yards away, moving between two trees. He pointed the rifle, but the sights, instead of remaining steady, seemed to dance and jiggle. Taking a deep breath, he let half of it out before squeezing the trigger.

The man fell to his knees, clutching at his belly with both hands.

Reynaud ducked behind the log. Gunfire crashed and rattled, and bullets whined overhead or slapped into the log. The men below were firing without a target, wasting ammunition, and Reynaud found himself grinning. Apparently, they considered his corpse worth more than its weight in ammunition and napalm.

The grin vanished when he realized the soldiers after him were undoubtedly fresh and well-armed, while he was exhausted, hungry, and running low of everything, including luck. Why the hell didn't those bastards just give up the trail? They were going to lose more men before they took him—if they took him. He'd make sure of that. But he knew they were as determined as he was, and they were relatively rested.

Slipping into the gully that angled from the log to a stand of trees, he again attacked the slope. Occasional shots were fired but they were all wide, as he again took advantage of the curve of the hill.

He found a ledge curving back which, near its top, had a lip that would give him cover and an escape route. He toiled up the ledge. When he reached a place offering cover and a good vantage of the backtrail, he looked down over the lip. The ground dropped almost straight down for six or eight feet, then angled away for another thirty feet, most of it covered by hardy brush, ending about forty feet down in a broad, nearly level area. A sound above him alerted him and he spun and ducked. Carpenter was less than fifty yards away, his rifle raised and pointed at Reynaud. Reynaud saw the flash, then something crashed into his head, his neck was twisted, and he was aware of falling.

~ * ~

For the sixth time in as many minutes, Logan rubbed his moist palms on the legs of his pants and checked his weapons. He was, by temperament and training, a fighter pilot and a lone wolf, and now he had to lead a rag-tag collection of men and women into battle. If Rennie could do it, he decided, so could he, but it wasn't a job he'd envied or wanted. The day before, he'd taught those without military training how to load and fire their weapons —fortunately, most of them had some acquaintanceship with guns—but most of them were still a long way from being even mediocre soldiers.

He just hoped he'd given them enough clues about what to look for so no one set off a booby trap.

He glanced down at the watch on his wrist. The second hand was still moving, although it showed only a couple of minutes had passed since the last time he'd looked.

He'd reconnoitered the place and had observed the stiffening of defenses and the placement of reinforcements since their raid on Harrison. They'd moved in a personnel carrier and parked it beside the bunker with the Browning .50. The APC didn't mount a gun, but he thought he could see the end of a mortar tube protruding from the gunner's hatch. He'd also found what passed as a barracks, a collection of tents pitched in the trees behind the radio hut. A crude latrine had been constructed beyond the tents.

Ross and Cal should've had plenty of time to move their troops into position, even though Ross and his men had stopped to booby-trap the road from Bellefonte to the junction.

Logan glanced again at his watch; 11:40. Crawling the short distance to the outhouse, he stood, opened and shut the latrine door, then, as he strolled toward the camp, pretended to zip up his fly.

Logan knew the risks, but his Steel fist uniform was as clean as it could be washed in a stream, and the bullet holes in it were small ones. He only hoped these assholes didn't keep a count of who went into the can and who came out.

He'd loaned out the FN. For what he was planning he needed something devastating at close range. As he neared the shack he reached up and adjusted his helmet, then, when his hand dropped, it fell only to the butt of the MAC. He thrust out his left hand, shoving the rickety door aside, and swept the subgun up, spraying fire into the gloom. Sparks flew from shattered radio equipment and the two men were mangled by the hail of .45 bullets, and one was hurled through the opposite wall.

He'd hardly stopped firing before the camp behind him erupted with the staccato barking of rifles and the screams of men in mortal pain. Most of Logan's band fired one shot at a time, but even so they were rapidly cutting down the lounging soldiers.

Dumping the helmet, Logan pulled on a blue baseball cap from under his shirt, hoping everyone on his side would notice the cap before shooting at him.

Grenades exploded in the camp and, further away, Logan heard explosions from launched grenades and the insistent chatter of light machine guns, overlaid with the heavy pounding of the .50. He'd dropped the Ingram to let it hang by its sling and drawn the big Super Redhawk. One of the Steel Fist troops near him had taken cover from the incoming fire behind a tree. In his best Hollywood hero snarl, Logan shouted, "Anytime you're feelin' lucky, asshole!"

The man froze then spun. Logan seemed to see it all in slow motion; the man turning to face him, the big Ruger's front sight moving up to just under the man's left breast pocket. The .44

Magnum roared like an outraged bear and bucked in his hand. The 240-grain slug blew the man's heart and left lung apart. The old fury began to course through Logan's veins.

Another trooper staggered to his feet, his right elbow shattered, holding his rifle aloft in his left hand. "Here!" Logan bellowed, and when the man turned, he shot him in the face. The soldier's helmet flew off, with most of the back of his head still in it.

More grenades exploded at the junction, and with the cessation of the throbbing of the .50, the fire from the Steel Fist soldiers stopped. Logan glanced at his watch again. Reynaud had said they'd wear out their welcome in no more than three minutes, that they should get away before reinforcements could reach the junction.

"Blue light special!" Logan roared. "You have two minutes to plunder," then stepped back into the shed that'd served as a radio command post.

Smoke billowed from the smashed and bullet-riddled electronics gear. One box still hissed and threw sparks, and Logan heard the faint crackle of a small fire. Only one piece seemed to have survived the destruction; a large, leather cased portable radio. "Listenin' to rock 'n' roll on company time, huh?" he asked the corpse. Catching up the radio, he ducked into the strap then noticed an M-1 carbine leaning against the makeshift desk. It'd be a perfect weapon for one of the women. Picking up the carbine, he slung it over his shoulder.

The body lying on its side in a pool of gore wore a holstered pistol. Unhooking the pistol belt and pulling it free, he observed it had a loaded magazine pouch for the carbine. The corpse also wore a pair of very good hiking boots. Most of the people outside were barefooted. He tugged at the laces until he could pull off the boots then stepped through the hole in the wall.

The cadaver outside, barefooted and unarmed, had already been stripped. Logan walked around the shed, watched the ragged men and women pulling off boots and taking what clothing they could find in the camp. Others were shoving supplies into backpacks. "Be sure to get all the weapons," he reminded them, "even the damaged ones. Those are the only spare parts we'll find."

He looked at his watch again. "Check-out time for this fleabag is in thirty seconds," he announced, then dashed across the highway to the armored personnel carrier. As much as he'd like to take the vehicle, there'd be no way of getting it to Bruno without bringing along the Steel Fist's whole air force and most of their army.

"We've run a rope of diesel-soaked rags to the fuel tank," Cal said. "If you've got a match, we'll touch it off before we go."

Someone brought the mules up and packed the light machine guns and the heavy Browning, along with its tripod, onto the stronger of the two. The few bodies in the area had been stripped of their sidearms and boots and some were missing their shirts as well. That reminded Logan of the shirt he wore, and he ripped the armbands off the sleeves and threw them to the ground.

The people who'd attacked the camp began to stream across the highway and into the trees.

"Remember," Logan shouted, "east by southeast until we're out of sight of the place. We've got to get a move on. Cal, you and Noel take the lead. Ross, pick two other men to stay here with you and I for a rearguard."

The rearguard took cover among the trees southeast of the junction. Almost immediately, the APC began to burn, tossing up great clouds of oily black smoke. When the last of their group was out of sight among the trees, the rearguard began to withdraw, taking a little time to obscure the trail left by the others. They were almost out of sight of the junction before a battered truck rolled up the road and came to a stop by the shack. Logan could hardly see the soldiers who climbed out of the back. He grinned. The booby traps had delayed the reinforcements, who were most likely garrison troops without much enthusiasm for pursuit and the possibility of being shot at.

As the rearguard continued its unhurried retreat, a C-47 appeared from the northeast, flew around the camp in a broad circle, banked steeply, then flew back the way it'd come. An autogyro swept the area but was too high for any reliable observation. Either the pilot was also reluctant to draw fire or he was afraid of the air currents in the mountains, which could be treacherous.

By early evening the party was halfway to Bruno and had stopped for the night. After making sure guards were posted, Logan stopped by the campfire for a cup of coffee and a bowl of mightbe stew, so called because there might be anything in the stew. Logan hoped they'd taken the shoes off the mule before throwing it into the pot. Some of the people in this group might consider it a way to get iron in their diet. After a couple of bites, Logan decided it "might be" edible.

Someone sat beside him and he turned to face Angie Carpenter. After nodding to her, he continued eating. She tossed a dry twig into the fire. "How much farther to where we're going?" she asked.

"We're about halfway there, accordin' to a couple men who know the area. We'll probably get there tomorrow."

"How long before the others get there?" She had another stick in her hand and was digging the point into the ground.

"They've got a lot farther to go, and they may have to duck people followin' 'em. I'd say, no sooner'n afternoon of the day after."

"How long have you known him?" The stick stopped moving.

"Known who?"

"The Cajun."

"Rennie?" Logan sipped at his coffee, totting up the time. "We were both in a Russian prison camp for a good six months. Or a real bad six months. It took another two months to make it back to what's left of the states, another four—maybe five— months in Texas and on the trail north. I guess that makes about a year, give or take a decade. Every minute you're in fear of your life is worth about a year. Make it a century or so."

"What kind of man was he—before he got so cold?"

Logan laughed. "Rennie? Cold? You got the wrong man. He's soft as puddin' on the inside. He's one a' the very few men I like and trust behind me when I need a friend."

"Is a man you like different from a man you trust?" Angie asked.

Logan finished his coffee. "There's a big difference. There's lots of people I like. They know how to laugh and mean it, they're quick with a laugh or a punchline, but if trouble comes to call, they're not home. There's other men I trust and respect, like the Deacon, though I can't really say I like him much."

"And my brother—"

"—isn't someone I like or trust."

"How can you say that? You hardly know him."

"That's right, ma'am. I didn't grow up around him, I didn't

know him as a little boy who strapped on his cap guns and played cowboy, I never got scared when he hurt himself, I don't know his favorite music or food or color. All I know is I never had to make excuses for him, either. And I don't take any excuse for lookin' at the people with us like they were filthy animals to be preyed on, or who leaves his sisters in a prison camp 'cause he can't help organize a raid to spring 'em—"

"Freeze! And drop the gun!" It was one of the sentries, shouting out into the twilight. Logan kicked dirt on the fire and caught up his FN.

"Get down—get to cover," he hissed to the people sitting in a group. Crawling up the slope, he shouted, "How many do you see?"

"Just one," the sentry shouted back.

Logan motioned to Ross. "Take the guard's place and have him bring the prisoner in."

A few minutes later the guard escorted a man wearing a frayed work shirt and overalls. It was hard to guess the man's age. Maybe thirty-six going on sixty. The stranger peered around at the people in the dimness, then his face was split by a gap-toothed grin. "Josh! Ya got away!"

Facing the man the prisoner was grinning at, one of the men who'd been rescued from the camp at Harrison, Logan asked, "You know this guy?"

Josh was grinning, too, and he nodded. "That's my cousin, Andy. How the hell you doin', Hoss?"

"The happy family reunion can wait," Logan snapped. "What're you doin' here, Andy?"

"I came to warn ya. Them home-grown Nazis are runnin' a lotta troops into this area. Ya gotta get out."

CHAPTER 8

"Hey, this guy is still alive."

Reynaud heard the words but, for a few moments, the words made no sense. His fingertips fumbled at his head and touched wet hair, but he felt nothing like a real wound. He realized then the helmet he'd worn was gone.

Something hard probed at his belly. "Get up."

He opened his eyes. Six men in camouflaged battledress with "Fritz" helmets and Steel Fist armbands had formed a half-circle around him. Carpenter was another three paces away, with another man pointing a rifle at him. Carpenter was unarmed but his hands were free, then Reynaud remembered Carpenter had shot at him.

"I said, get up," the man shouted, shoving the barrel of his M-16 toward Reynaud's face.

Reynaud struggled to his feet, extricating himself from the large patch of brush into which he'd fallen. As he stood, he discovered his body was covered with scrapes, scratches, and bruises. Looking up, he saw the marks of his fall on the side of the bluff. The helmet he'd worn was stuck in a bush almost halfway up the slope.

"We oughta kill 'im right here," one of the men snarled.

"The cap'n wants all the live prisoners we can get," the man who seemed in command of the squad said.

"The cap'n don't know how hard it is to catch these bastards," the first man said. "Now, this guy, he just took one helluva fall." His voice rose on the last syllable as his fist plunged toward Reynaud's belly. Reynaud was able to scream to flex his stomach muscles and get most of the air out of his lungs before he was hit, but he was still doubled over and almost knocked off his weak legs. A fist slammed against the side of his face, cutting his face at the cheekbone, and his legs collapsed. He curled into a fetal position, trying to protect himself as best he could. A heavy boot landed a kick in his ribs and, for a few seconds of panic, he couldn't breathe.

"Knock it off, Jack. We don't wanna hafta carry him back."

Someone unbuckled Reynaud's pistol belt and when he could finally stand up again, he was frisked by rough hands, his wrists were tied together behind his back, and then he was shoved in the direction of the cave. "Don't worry about gettin' even, Jack," one of the guards said, "Cap'n Miller'll make him pay. The cap'n can make a brick wall sing, and this asshole will sing like an opera star. A soprano opera star, probably."

Reynaud could hardly believe he'd covered so much ground so quickly when now, aching in every muscle and joint, ravaged by thirst and exhaustion, he felt as though he were walking to Canada. As they walked, they were joined by more Steel Fist soldiers, and he guessed they'd sent nearly a hundred men after him and the rest of the team. Twice he saw bodies, and four or five men were being carried.

It might've been a heroic gesture to resist or laugh at the sight of their dead and wounded, but Reynaud was too weak to do more than put one plodding foot in front of the other. Until he had the means to resist, he could only endure.

When they rounded the mountain Reynaud looked at the cave, which seemed somehow blacker than it'd been before. The fire in the tank had been extinguished but the vehicle was a wreck, and he saw a line of bodies waiting to be carried off.

The squad escorting Reynaud halted at the back of a truck, where a man with black bars on his uniform's shoulders was directing the clean-up. "Two prisoners for Captain Miller, sir." The man in charge of the squad threw a perfunctory salute, which was negligently returned by the officer.

"Any more of them out there?"

"This one," the squad leader jerked his thumb in Carpenter's direction, "says there were four more of them, but he thinks maybe they got taken out by the napalm."

The officer drew a .45 automatic, cocked it, and pointed it at Reynaud. "Get in the truck."

As Reynaud climbed into the back of the truck, his mind was working frantically to gather facts and develop a plan to escape. The officer wasn't much respected by the men under him, and his show with the pistol had been more to convince himself he was dangerous than to menace Reynaud, who'd just walked over a mile with M-16s pointed at his back.

Carpenter crawled into the truck behind Reynaud and sat on the bench opposite him. Reynaud stared coldly at him but said nothing; nothing need be said. Carpenter already knew if Reynaud ever got the chance, he'd kill him. Three soldiers climbed in, followed by the officer. The soldiers sat well away from the prisoners, and on Carpenter's side, where they'd have a better shot at Reynaud. The officer sat on the bench on Reynaud's side, but well out of reach.

"What else did he—" the officer pointed at Carpenter, "tell you?"

"He claimed the other guy was the leader. Said he was told to go on the raid or he'd be killed. He also says he knows a lot about where the bunch that hit near Bellefonte was hidin'. He's real eager to cooperate; says he'll tell us everything." Looking sidelong at Carpenter, the squad leader snapped, "Hey, Judas, do you wear jockey shorts or boxers?"

"That's enough, Sergeant," the officer barked. "Does he know anything about Fayetteville?"

"What about Fayetteville?" the sergeant asked. "Nobody's said anything about it to me or the boys."

Pausing, the officer apparently decided the bad news was going to make the rounds soon enough. "The people in Fayetteville must've found out what we were plannin', and they attacked before we were ready."

"With what?" the sergeant asked. "High command said they didn't have anything bigger than mortars."

"That's what they used. They laid a heavy smoke barrage and hit our troops from out of the smoke. Tanks aren't much good if they can't see, and they had us outnumbered. They overran most of what we had there."

"Are we gonna be transferred there?" It was impossible to tell from the sergeant's tone how reluctant he might be to being sent into combat.

"No, we're pullin' back what we've got left and leavin' a garrison in Huntsville. The rest of the troops and equipment will be sent southeast."

The sergeant set his rifle across his knees and rolled himself a cigarette. "They shoulda gone for the munitions plants in the first place, instead of all this diddlin' around."

The officer stiffened. "It isn't up to you to question orders. If we'd been able to use the gas on Fayetteville, we woulda had the bomb. We coulda nuked Fort Leonard Wood, taken Springfield, and in no time at all we would've had the whole region."

"And if the dog hadn't stopped to take a shit, he'd'a caught the rabbit," the sergeant added.

"That comes close to insubordination," the officer snapped.

"Yes, sir, Lieutenant."

Most of the rest of the ride was in stony silence except for the growling and complaining of the truck. Reynaud watched the sergeant smoke his cigarette. He still hoped to find a way to escape, and now he had information to carry with him. Besides the losses in men and equipment, the Steel Fist was also suffering from poor morale and worse military discipline. Unfortunately, they were likely to take out their frustration on prisoners: that meant him. One of the soldiers had taken out a canteen and drank from it. Reynaud reflexively licked his parched lips.

Seeing it, the sergeant took out a canteen and tossed it to Reynaud.

"Sergeant!" the lieutenant bellowed, and shot to his feet, then, as the truck swerved, lurched and fell back onto his bench.

Reynaud took a long pull at the canteen. Even warm and brackish, it was water. It was life. Replacing the cap, he tossed the flask back to the sergeant, noticing the troops trying to hide grins at the lieutenant's humiliation. "Thanks, sergeant. If I ever get the chance, I'll do the same for you."

"Sergeant!" the lieutenant raged. "You're not to give the prisoners anything without my approval. Is that clear? You're on report, soldier."

"Yessir," the sergeant growled.

After a long ten minutes the truck pulled into a gravel driveway and slowed to a stop. Reynaud waited for the soldiers to jump from the truck before he trudged to the back of the bed and climbed down. They stood before a big white house with columns and green shutters in a style Reynaud would call pseudo-colonial. The lieutenant waved his pistol at a side door. "Move, you two."

Reynaud was disappointed in his hope the officer would try to escort Carpenter and himself alone. Two of the soldiers followed them as they were herded through the door, past a desk, behind which sat a hard-faced woman in a dark blue uniform, down a flight of stairs, and through a door flanked by sentries wearing more of the dark blue uniforms. To Reynaud, the uniforms had a strongly Nazi appearance, and the rifles they held were the Chinese-built AKs. The large room behind the door was furnished only with a desk at one end, a map of Arkansas and southern Missouri covering much of the wall behind the desk, and two chairs in the middle of the room. The chairs were plain, but heavily built, with stout straps on the arms and front legs.

A heavy-set man with a face turned scarlet by fury sat behind the desk, shouting into a radio telephone.

"Use your tanks," he roared. "Get them into blocking positions on the road to Huntsville. Hold the APCs in reserve. When you've got the defenses set up, withdraw the tanks and apes and send 'em here."

The man paused a few seconds, listening, then snapped, "Put out a directive: any deserters will be hanged, and anyone who surrenders will be considered a deserter." He slammed down the phone with a muffled "incompetent bastards," and glared at Reynaud and Carpenter, then turned his glower on the lieutenant. "What've you got?"

"Two prisoners, sir. This one gave himself up," indicating Carpenter. "He says the other one led the raid."

"You needed half a company and the use of most of the local air force for two men?" His rage was like a fire, eating everything within reach that would feed it. Reynaud guessed if the man wasn't already psychotic, frustration was driving him in that direction.

"No sir," the lieutenant said. "The other four were killed by the napalm."

"That's all of them?"

"Yes sir."

"Then recall the troops, you fool. Haven't you figured out it costs more than we can afford to beat the bushes looking for dead men? Use my phone."

"Yes sir!" As the lieutenant practically scampered around the desk, he added, "He also said he knows where the group that hit the junction is headed."

"Is that so?" The captain's voice was steadier. He rose and walked around the desk to stand before Carpenter. "All right, where are they going?"

"My sister's with them," Carpenter said. "I'd like to be sure she'll be taken alive."

"We'll do our best. What's she look like?"

"She's tall, pretty thin, has blonde hair and brown eyes."

"Got it. Now, where are they going?"

"Bruno."

Reynaud seethed, aching to tear Carpenter apart with his bare hands, but he knew the soldiers in the room would cut him to pieces with their rifles if he moved.

Taking two steps, the captain turned to confront Reynaud. "What've you got to say?"

"It's a good thing for you most of your troops are better than the dumbfuck lieutenant who points a pistol with an empty chamber at a prisoner." He remembered the lieutenant cocking the weapon but not racking back the slide, and he doubted the man had been carrying the piece with the hammer down on a loaded chamber.

The lieutenant had just finished his call.

The captain spun and faced him. "Hand me your sidearm." The captain hadn't raised his voice, but the command was as sharp as a pistol shot and the vein in his temple was throbbing.

The lieutenant seemed stunned by the demand but handed over the weapon. Holding the weapon less than a foot from Reynaud's face, the captain pointed it between Reynaud's eyes. He cocked the gun and asked, "Are you willing to bet your life on it?"

Reynaud paused. It was impossible to be sure. If he were wrong, perhaps it'd be better to get it over with as quickly as possible. Evidently, the captain was a vicious madman. "Yeah."

The captain pulled the trigger and the hammer snapped, driving the firing pin into an empty chamber. The lieutenant, now standing between the prisoners, looked stricken.

The captain laughed at Reynaud, then glared at the lieutenant.

"This is how you load the .45 Colt automatic pistol," he snarled, and drew back the slide, dropped it, chambering a round. He raised the pistol again toward Reynaud's face, then spun and shot the lieutenant behind the ear. Blood and brains erupted and the body jumped then fell, as jointless as a rag doll.

"Remember that well," the captain snarled at the prisoners.

"I'll kill you even quicker than that, at the least annoyance." Facing Carpenter, he pointed the pistol at his forehead. "Where did you say they'd be?"

Carpenter had gone white with terror. "Bruno."

Wheeling, the captain studied his map. "Makes sense," he said, and strode to the radio phone. "Captain Miller here. I want Delta Company to secure Bruno and set up an ambush outside the perimeter of the town. Have Epsilon Company split up and move into the areas along US-62 and US-65. Have them dismount their trucks and start moving toward Bruno. Keep the first two platoons of Gamma Company at the junction in reserve. They're to respond to any attempt to break out." Replacing the receiver on the cradle, he studied the prisoners. "Have a seat, gentlemen."

His mobile face underwent another transformation as he stared down in disgust at the body of the lieutenant. "Guards."

The door guards stepped into the room, assault rifles at the ready. "Watch these two," he told them, then gestured for the regular troops to pick up the body. "You, soldiers, get this piece of shit out of my sight. Tell your senior sergeant he's just won a battlefield commission."

While the troops dragged the corpse from the room, Carpenter and Reynaud reluctantly trod to the chairs and sat. Captain Miller drew his own chair from behind the desk, placing it facing the other two chairs, sat, and swiveled to face Carpenter.

"The lieutenant said you gave yourself up. Why?"

"I only went with that guy and his friends because they said they'd kill me if I didn't go. Besides, they were holding my sister hostage."

"You say this man was in command. How many troops does he have?"

"About twenty-five; most of them from the Harrison camp. I only saw five other outsiders with him, and four of them were in on the raid on the cave."

"The lieutenant said they got cooked. Is that so?"

Carpenter swallowed, "Yes sir."

"You don't seem very sure of that."

"Well, I…I can't be absolutely positive."

"No matter." The captain dismissed the possibly dead men with a wave of his hand. "If they didn't burn, we'll catch them at

Bruno." He stroked his chin. "Could he have had other men you didn't see?"

"Not with him, but he did send a radio message, night before last."

"To whom?"

"I don't know."

The captain quickly extracted all the worthwhile information Carpenter could give him, including the location of the cave and the condition of the men and women with him and their equipment. When he'd finished questioning Carpenter, Miller turned in his chair and studied Reynaud through narrowed eyes. "What's your name?"

"Reynaud Dechaine."

"Hmmm...hydromatic coon-ass, huh? You aren't from around here. Where?"

"Port Arthur, Texas, before I left to go to college."

"You're going to die a long way from home, boy." Watching Reynaud's face closely, he asked, "Been through Springfield lately?"

"A little over a week ago."

"What happened to the Colonel and Walter Davenport?"

"They're dead."

"I thought that might be the case. Did you do it?"

"No."

"But you know who did." It wasn't a question.

Reynaud could guess the Steel Fist still had agents inside Springfield and his naming Norton could cause the man's death. He clamped his jaws together and waited for the captain to shoot him.

Miller laughed again, and the sound was more chilling than his angry outbursts or even his cold attempts to sound courteous. Flicking the safety on the pistol, the captain carried it to his desk, dropped it in a drawer then returned with an item Reynaud didn't immediately recognize. Miller held it up and Rennie could see two rods projecting from it. Electricity leaped across the gap between the tips with a vicious crackle.

"You were going to tell me who you were working for," Miller coaxed.

"I don't need to work for anyone. I put in six months in a Russian prison camp. I learned to hate authoritarian motherfuckers on my own."

Miller thrust the stun gun at him and Reynaud tried to dodge, but the tips touched his left arm, then he was seized and shaken by a jolt that drove the breath from his lungs, and his heart seemed to explode.

He was vaguely aware of his surroundings before he could force his mind to think. He looked at the room blankly, his eyes seeing it but his mind not recognizing it. His body still twitched and his wrists hurt, then he realized his hands had been freed. From someplace impossibly far away, he heard a voice.

"Who sent you?"

Conditioning took over, and he heard his voice croak, "Dechaine, Reynaud, U.S. Air Force, first lieutenant, serial number five-three-five—"

Something struck him a stinging blow across the face, but with no real force. Shaking his head, he opened his eyes again to see a pair of boots.

"Get up," said the calm, ugly voice he now recognized as Miller's. He had to fight his own body to stumble to his feet. He was still unable to think clearly, and the strength seemed to have run out of his body.

Miller held a fly swatter and he again used it to slap Reynaud across the face. "Now, sit back down. You know it's impolite to leave your chair during our conversation." Again he was using that infuriating "courtesy."

"It's very interesting—as well as illogical—for General Meyer to use a chance-met Air Force officer, particularly when he has infantry of his own who're much better qualified for this kind of work. You're not working for Meyer, are you?"

"Not directly."

Miller again made the stun gun throw an arc. "Don't let's be clever. Carpenter tells me you have a nucleus of only five other men—"

"Carpenter doesn't know shit. How much do you think I trusted him? I think the bastard's a pathological liar. Stop and think about what he's told you. Would I drag someone I had to threaten along on a mission as important as trashing your gas dump?"

Miller's smile was more intimidating than his glare. "Oh,

believe me, I've considered all that. Do you think I trust him?" He laughed. "No, he sold you out, just as he'd sell us out, if it could be made profitable to him. I have faith in most of his answers, not because he's reliable, but because he's a coward in fear for his life." He faced Carpenter for a moment. "A fear which is not unwarranted, I might add."

Carpenter turned pale again and Reynaud hid a grin. At least the bastard wouldn't be allowed to walk away.

"But that brings us to you. You have information that might be useful to me, information Carpenter doesn't have. You still have to learn." He thrust the stun gun at Reynaud, who screamed before the lightning struck him again and he was able to feel a moment of agony before the blackness took him away again.

He heard voices and finally recognized one of them as his own. He had no idea what he'd been asked, nor what his answers had been. His body still twitched a bit but he managed to force his mouth shut. He had only a moment's rest before his face stung from another slap. He couldn't seem to focus his mind on the room before him or recognize the men in the room.

"How did you get out of the Russian prison camp?"

"We escaped."

"Who is 'we?'"

"Logan, the Deacon, Juho the Finn, Steve Villareal, Smyth-Davis, and I."

"And what did you do after you escaped?"

Reynaud finally realized where he was and who was questioning him, and realized Miller was trying to lead the questions to more current events. He answered the questions until the escapees had met the Reconstructionists in Poland. He still couldn't force his mind to work quickly enough to invent a plausible lie, so he lapsed into silence.

His face stung from another slap from the fly swatter. "Answer me!"

"What was the question?"

"Get up," Miller said. "You've been terribly inconsiderate, forcing me to discipline you. Do you want another touch of the stunner?"

"No!" Reynaud felt tears running down his face and realized his reserves were gone; he had nothing left with which to resist.

His emotions were beginning to do a trampoline act, totally out of his control. He struggled for what seemed hours to get his legs under him and lever himself up into the chair. Once in the chair, he slumped like so much jelly.

"You were explaining to me your connection to General Meyer and with the garrison in Fayetteville."

"I don't know anyone in Fayetteville."

"It was coincidence, then, that your radio message, sent the night before last, preceded the attack of the garrison at Fayetteville."

"It might've been relayed—or picked up."

"Interesting. Who could've relayed it?"

Reynaud paused and Miller thrust the stun gun at his face. "I understand it's especially painful if I hit you near the eye."

"No!" Clumsily, Reynaud raised an arm to fend off the stunner. "It was Baker."

"What's Baker's first name?"

"I never heard it."

"Why would he be interested in Arkansas? Surely, General Meyer has enough to do in southern Missouri."

"Baker was from here."

"Why should you care what happens here? And how did you know to contact Baker, or he, you?"

Reynaud's mind still refused to function and he couldn't seem to find a lie within reach. Miller's hand shot out again. Reynaud tried to duck and defend himself, but the stun gun touched his face and, again, white electric light exploded inside his head.

The interrogation room was cold. It was always cold. Questions were bellowed at him. He gave his name, rank, and serial number again. He could still remember the commandant's face only inches from his own. Days and nights without rest, scraps of food not fit for livestock, constant pain and fear, being forced to watch sick prisoners being beaten to death by the commandant, who used them to practice his martial arts skills.

"Who are you working for?"

His tongue and lips seemed to slur the sounds as he shaped them in the unfamiliar language. "The Reconstructionists. It was a network formed during and right after the war by a handful of young officers and some former civilian authorities. My orders came directly from Norton—" the name seemed to elude his tongue as it was wrenched out of shape by the other words. "—he wanted us to break the Steel Fist. We've destroyed their supply of poison gas—"

"Who's your immediate superior?"

Why was the commandant asking in English?

"I've just told you that. The Reconstructionists aren't really a group, just a network. We're volunteers who're trying to help reestablish local order so the country had time to heal—"

"Get him out of here. A night in the can will make him more responsive."

Strong arms hauled him up and dragged him away. By the time he was really aware of the world around him, he was outside. The weather was hot. Hot? It was never hot in that place on the Polish-Czech border at the edge of expanded Russia. Slowly, the scene around him began to register. He was in Arkansas, but he was also back in the camp where men were broken, tortured beyond endurance. Cicadas droned in the trees, as evening had fallen. His belly burned and ached with hunger, and his throat was so parched it seemed ready to crack from dryness.

Half-carried and half-dragged, he was hauled by the guards to a barrel lying on its side. They folded his legs so his knees were drawn up under his chin, then shoved him into the keg. When he was partially inside, they pressed his arms tightly against his body, then pushed him completely into the barrel and stood it on its end, so he was cramped inside, unable to stand, barely able to breathe.

A bucket of water was dumped on top of him and he managed to get a mouthful, but then he was left, still thirsty and crouched in water but unable to get any of it into his mouth.

The night was long and sweltering, and his already shaky sanity was strained by the nearness of water and his need for it. Even more maddening were the self-recriminations. He'd broken under questioning and told Miller everything. He was going to die here, and assassins would kill Norton, and another light of freedom would be extinguished. The Steel Fist would regroup, and their next attack might succeed.

~ * ~

"General Davenport—" The look on Captain Drummond's

face combined worry and wariness.

"Have you heard from my son or the Colonel yet?"

"No sir. But we also have other problems."

"I don't have time to cut through the sugar coating. Get to the point."

"Well, sir, first I got a report from Captain Miller in Harrison. Major Evans didn't immediately report a major raid."

"What does he call a major raid?"

"Harrison was attacked last night by a large force of elite troops, probably from Fort Leonard Wood. They destroyed the helicopter, a tank, and a number of other vehicles. They also killed sixty men or so and wounded about half that many. And they freed the prisoners."

"Damn Evans! Tell Miller I want Evans tried, convicted, vigorously interrogated, and hanged."

Drummond paused before he replied, "Captain Miller reports he has already arrested Major Evans for treason but the major didn't survive interrogation."

"What else?"

Drummond cleared his throat. "The raid on Harrison seems to have been timed to coincide with an attack on our forces around Fayetteville. We think that attack was by local forces but—"

"We're both too old to believe in coincidences," Davenport snapped. "Why wasn't Fayetteville gassed?"

"The plan was to hit them with gas dropped by the copter, but it was lost in the raid and we'll need another day or two to fit the OV-10 with equipment to use to deliver gas. In the meantime, the lab and most of our gas stockpile was destroyed by another attack, probably more elite forces from Springfield or Leonard Wood."

Drummond paused. "They caught two of the raiders when they tried to get away after blowing up the stockpile. According to Captain Miller, one of them claimed the Colonel and your son are dead."

Icy fury almost choked Davenport and he stared at his hands, surprised to see they weren't trembling from the emotion. When he could trust his voice, he said, "Tell Captain Miller that I personally want to interrogate his prisoners. Tell him I do *not* expect them to die during his questioning. Do I make myself clear?"

"Yessir."

"Excellent. Now get that message out immediately. Tell him I expect the prisoners to be sent in the next convoy."

As Drummond rushed out of his office, Davenport glared at the map.

Damn! He should have known things were moving too smoothly. And now disaster loomed.

He couldn't believe Walter was gone. In addition to being his son, he'd been the finest agent they'd had in the field. Walter might have inherited the entire organization. Flashes of the good times flooded his memories but he boxed them and stored them in his mental safe. He had no time for that now. Now he had to adjust to the change in circumstances.

If his son were indeed dead, he could step out of the shadows. He'd remained anonymous to avoid endangering Walter. Now it was personal, and he wanted his followers and his enemies to know it was Robert Davenport they dealt with.

For the present, he'd have to leave Miller in command in Harrison. The man was ambitious and a sadist, both desirable qualities in a tool but not in a commander. Right now, changes in leadership would undermine the order so necessary for success in Harrison and would be yet another disaster. He could eventually find another man to take over when a stable situation could allow a new commander to adjust to the men under him and perhaps even establish a cadre of loyal followers. Miller would then be promoted to some impressive but powerless position until an accident could be arranged.

Right now, the situation was becoming desperate and called for desperate measures. When the plane was able to start spraying the poison gas available, he'd start wiping out some of the small towns. This would provide easy victories, some booty, and cow the other locals.

~ * ~

Hasteen had taken cover when the plane strafed them, then the thing had dropped what the Deacon would call Hell on earth. Looking down the slope, he saw Mario scrambling up through the bushes.

"What about the others?" he asked.

"If they're lucky, they're on the other side of the fire," Mario said. "Keep moving. If they're dead, we can't help them. If they're alive, we'll meet them at Bruno."

Scowling at the flames, Hasteen raised a hand to protect his face from the fierce heat. It troubled him to abandon a friend, but what Mario had said made sense. At least the fire would slow the pursuit.

As they trotted across the next valley, he thought he heard gunfire far behind him. At first, he thought someone following them had blundered across a booby trap, but more shots rang out, along with automatic weapons fire. He broke stride and turned toward the distant sounds.

Mario caught up with him again. "Go on ahead," Hasteen said. "Someone back there is still alive. I'm going after them." As he spoke, the sound of gunfire stopped.

"Forget it," Mario said. "They're either dead or captured. If they've been captured, we'll spring them later. We have to get to the other group first, though."

When Hasteen still hesitated, Mario hissed, "Rennie took the tail position to cover us. Don't throw away what he gave us." Shooting Mario a glance, Hasteen turned and trotted after the Deacon.

They kept moving, Xuan's apparently tireless trot eating up distance, until they reached the highway, where the group closed up then, and darted across the road one at a time. Plunging into the woods on the other side, they rested in a tree-filled hollow. The Deacon's face was pale and the dressing around his head dripped blood. Mario noticed it and changed dressings, keeping the old bandages.

"Will you make it?" Hasteen asked.

"I feel about a quart low," Billy Joe said, with one of his rare flashes of humor, "but He will give me strength for the journey."

"If they took either Rennie or Carpenter alive, they'll probably send them to Mountain Home for interrogation by the leaders. People like that prefer to keep some of the dirty work for themselves, and they don't completely trust their subordinates," Mario said. "They'll be sending them by truck."

"Why not by air?" Hasteen asked.

"The only bird they've got big enough for the job and still be able to take off and land at the strip in Harrison is the Bronco,"

Mario replied. "I scoped it as it banked, and it's been converted to a single-seater. It looked like they'd used the second seat position for more ammo." He looked at Xuan. "We're making awfully good time."

"I brought us as close around Harrison as I dared. We've been paralleling the highway since Bellefonte. The junction's about four miles north of here."

"Very good. I want to link up with the other group as soon as I can. If they took Carpenter alive, I don't trust him to keep his mouth shut."

Hearing the rumble of heavy trucks, they scrambled up the embankment to where they could observe the highway from cover. A column of troop trucks rolled southward. "I knew it," Mario gritted, "Carpenter spilled his guts." He glanced at his watch. "A little after four. We leave here right away, and in the same order. Xuan, keep a sharp lookout for tracks of Logan's bunch. If we're lucky, we can catch them before sunset."

"Time to dump these," Hasteen said, as he tore the armbands off the uniform he wore and removed the helmet.

"Hang onto them until we find a safe place to lose them and the bandages. I don't want to leave too much of a trail."

Setting out again, they moved more slowly, as exhaustion turned their feet and legs to lead. They stopped again at six to rest and eat.

"Any sign of Logan's group?" Mario asked.

"We've been following their trail for the last two miles," Xuan said. "They're doing a fair job of hiding their tracks, but they've crushed some greenery. If the Steel Fist have any decent trackers, they'll be able to follow the trail."

Hasteen's lips twitched with a hint of a smile. "I think the Steel Fist would like to get ahead of us, but I don't think they're too eager to follow us. They might be afraid we've left a few items for them to remember us by."

Xuan finished chewing a piece of dried meat. "I've also found a few other signs of people moving through here. Most of it is old sign, but some's more recent."

"Steel Fist patrols, maybe?" Mario asked.

"They don't move like a patrol, or the Steel Fist. They don't leave that much sign, and they seem to know their way around the area," Xuan replied.

"Maybe we'll find help," Mario said.

"With His help, all things are possible," the Deacon observed.

"I'll take help where I can get it," Mario said. "Any idea how far behind them we are?"

"About two hours, maybe a little less."

"Stay alert for sentries. We don't want to be shot by our own people."

Xuan led the way again. The sun was setting when he heard the voice of the man named Ross. "Hold it."

Xuan halted. "It's us."

"Come forward, slow and easy, with your hands up."

Xuan cursed himself for not seeing the sentry first, but did as he was told. When he came within a few yards of Ross, the man relaxed. "Sorry," Ross said, "but we just got the word the Steel Fist has troops in the area. We were just gettin' ready to break camp."

Xuan waited with Ross until all four survivors had reached the lookout point, and together they walked down to the camp.

As soon as he saw them, Logan's delighted grin almost glowed in the dark then he noticed there were only four of them. "Where's Rennie?" he asked.

Mario told him about the pursuit and the capture of Carpenter and the possible capture of Reynaud. "Rennie was bringing up the end of the line. If they caught Carpenter, they'd have had to catch or kill Rennie first. We were trying to catch up to you to tell you to stay away from Bruno."

"We'd heard." Logan introduced them to Andy. "Sit down and get somethin' to eat."

Xuan had already helped himself to stew. "You seem to be in charge now, Logan. What do you want to do?"

"Get outta this trap and spring Rennie. Andy's offered to lead us outta here."

Xuan glanced at the rest of the group. No one seemed to want to argue, all were apparently determined to try to rescue the Cajun. "You should have someone provide a diversion. I'd like to have Mario with me, but you'll need him to set explosives—"

"Hell," Andy interjected, "my uncle Ben used to work on the highway. You give him a stick of dynamite and he could blow your hat off without mussin' your hair."

Looking up from his stew, Mario said, "If you don't need me, I'll tag along with Xuan. How many more do you want along?"

"Only a guide, someone familiar with the country."

"Take Ross," Logan said. "He knows the area. What're you plannin'?"

"We'll go south and try to make them think the whole group's gone that way. That should make it easier for you to ambush the convoy—if it hasn't left already."

"Good," Logan said, "but be careful. You're gonna hafta slip through their lines at night. Where and when do you wanna rendezvous with us?"

Ross joined the group around the fire. "Noel took over for me," he explained. "The best I could suggest is to meet in five days in Gassville."

"I know the place," Andy said. "They's a draw north of town, in a straight line north from the water tower. We'll meet you there, say, just after sundown, in five days."

Checking his canteens and the store of food he carried in his pack, Xuan added a few strips of dried mule meat and a handful of dried corn. "We'll try to get their attention near dawn." Finding ammunition, he reloaded a magazine. "Mario, bring some plastique and detonators."

"We can let you have two blocks of the stuff," Logan said. "Spend it wisely. We may need the rest of the boom stuff for the convoy. Wanna take a LAW? We liberated three of them at the junction. They were loaded for Kenworths."

Xuan shook his head. "The lighter we travel, the safer we'll be." Mario and Ross had checked weapons and packed supplies, and the three of them prepared to slip out of the camp.

"Take care," Logan said. "Don't get yourselves shot or captured. I'd hate to have to spend all my time getting buddies out of the pokey."

Xuan grinned, for the first time anyone could remember, then he and the others vanished into the night.

Logan stared after them then faced the local. "Andy, you're sure about the way out?"

"That's how I got here. It's an old creek bed overgrown enough you can't see it unless you know just where to look. It's still a little muddy from the last rain, but nothin' you can't handle."

After checking his equipment, Logan nodded to Hasteen and Billy Joe. "Good havin' you boys back. You wanna bring up the rear?"

Hasteen had found his carbine, checked the tube magazine and the chamber, and nodded.

"All right, Andy," Logan said. "let's see about gettin' outta here."

CHAPTER 9

By the time the line of fugitives had reached the highway, in the dark hours before dawn, Hasteen was laden with equipment like one of the mules and was supporting Noel, who'd wrenched a knee in a fall. The equipment had been carried by former prisoners who'd just begun to regain their stamina but weren't yet ready for almost twenty-four hours of continuous battle and flight.

The group trickled across the highway between two Steel Fist outposts and Andy led them northeast, to a hollow no more than six miles from the cave they'd abandoned. Eight more men were waiting in the hollow, two of them former prisoners of the Harrison camp.

After introductions all around, Logan said, "This ain't really a social call. We need to get to a good ambush site and set up shop."

The men stood. "We picked a spot about eight miles east of here," a barrel-chested man in rough work clothes said. "It's about two miles east of the Crooked Creek bridge. That piece of road's been clear for them, so far. We've never hit east of the bridge, so they may worry about fallin' rocks, but not about bein' hit."

"Sounds good. We'll take a look. Deak, Hasteen, are you up to this trip?"

"If you're not in too big a hurry," Hasteen said. "An hour's rest would be a big help."

Logan pondered a moment. "All right." He looked at the new men. "You all know where we're goin', right?" At their nods, he continued, "All right, you and the Deacon and the rest take an hour's break. I'll go with a coupla these fellas so I can plan the set-up and plant the charges. That's gonna take longer than anything else, anyway. The rest of these fellas can lead you to us. Travel as light as you can—better leave the machine guns behind—and bring only what you'll need for one helluva fight." Pulling on a backpack holding most of the group's explosives, he followed two locals into the woods.

Hasteen, relieved of his extra baggage, lay down with a sigh and permitted himself to doze. It seemed like only moments before one of the men said, "Time to go." Hasteen checked both Colts and the carbine, made sure his canteen was full, and chewed on an old biscuit and some dried meat. A dozen of the twenty members of Logan's group had also risen and were making their own preparations for the trip, with varying degrees of enthusiasm.

Noticing Noel hobbling around the camp, he shook his head. "You stay. Rest the leg. We'll want to divide up the group after the raid. That'll be soon enough for you to move."

Angie Carpenter was also packing a knapsack. "Are you sure you want in on this?" he asked. "It might be better to sit this one out."

"My brother may be in that convoy. I'm going."

Hasteen shrugged.

His indifference annoyed her. "Why shouldn't I go? You want to rescue your friend. Why should I care any less about my brother?"

"It depends. I want Rennie free because I know he'd do the same for me, or any other member of the group. It doesn't seem to me you can say the same for Adam Carpenter. It also seems to me he is less your brother than are the other men and women who came out of Harrison. He may be related to you by an accident of birth, but shared hardships and dangers either make us brothers or drive us apart. Did your time in Harrison make you kin with the others, or are you apart from them?"

Angie had no answer, but her brow furrowed before she walked away.

It might've been easier to travel on the highway, but it was far more dangerous, and Hasteen and the Deacon kept the group in heavy cover and were grateful there were no gyroplanes to observe the group crossing the river. The terrain on the other side of the river rose gradually, then the pitch steepened. The band crossed the highway then toiled up a much steeper slope.

One of Logan's scouts appeared in the brush ahead and led them upslope to where Logan sat, waiting.

"It's about time you boys and girls got here." He glanced at his watch. "I make it about ten o'clock. Accordin' to these fellas, convoys to the east usually run between eleven in the mornin' and two in the afternoon.

"I don't want anyone within sixty yards of that point," Logan indicated a place where naked rock reared forty feet above the road. On the opposite side of the road the mountain fell abruptly for almost fifty feet before leveling off and sloping to the floor of the hollow.

"Deacon, I want you to take out the second vehicle in the line. Shoot up the cab with rifle fire and, if the thing's a troop-carrier, put a grenade in the back of it." He raised his voice. "I want all the truck cabs taken out. We don't know which ones have radios, and we don't want 'em to send a message."

"What about Reynaud?" the Deacon asked.

"Sorry," Logan said, "but he's gonna hafta take his chances like the rest of us. He'd hafta do the same if it was one of us. This is the only chance we have to save him, but we also have the rest of the people and the mission to worry about.

"Hasteen, I want you over there." Logan pointed to a clump of brush. "I want you to provide top cover. If they got no air power along, then open up at targets of opportunity."

Looking over the group, he continued. "Another thing—I want everybody well hidden. If you have to, stay back in cover till you hear the first blast. I don't want this ambush lookin' like a Hollywood production, complete with lines of gun barrels stickin' out like pickets in a fence. You should also be hidden to anything in the air.

"Finally, I want you all to eject the top round in your weapons, make sure they're all loaded and charged and on 'safe.'" He led by example.

After checking his weapons again, Hasteen carefully crawled under the overhanging branches of the clump of shrubbery, and settled himself to wait.

~ * ~

Dawn had found Mario, Xuan and Ross south of the road leading to Bruno, in dense cover with a six-hundred-yard view of a military truck parked near the town of Verona, watching troops dismount the truck. Ross and Xuan watched through binoculars, while Mario steadied his rifle and peered through the scope.

Xuan noticed a man crouched with two others just to the left of the truck. As the man stood, Xuan observed he wore a pistol and carried no rifle. As if to confirm Xuan's suspicions, the man waved his arms at the troops from the truck, who dispersed and started toward the woods, their rifles at the ready.

"Just to the left of the truck," Xuan murmured. "The one with the pistol is management. Hit him."

Mario seemed to pause a moment, then the shot rang out and the man spun and fell. Instantly, all the others dropped or dashed for cover. Because of the distance and the heavy woods, the soldiers had no idea from where the shot had come. Mario had provided an interesting enough morning for the Steel Fist, Xuan decided, as he led the way into deeper cover.

~ * ~

The barrel was kicked onto its side, and Reynaud screamed at the pain to his cramped body. Two men in the blue uniforms, one of them carrying Reynaud's shotgun, dragged him out of the barrel. Captain Miller smiled down at him.

"Prisoners should have their exercise," Miller said. "We wouldn't want them becoming unhealthy. Get up."

Reynaud gritted his teeth to keep from screaming at the red-hot needles of returning circulation that peppered his body. He tried to move his arms and legs, and almost blacked out at the pain and weakness that overcame him.

"Now, now," Miller said, "no malingering. Help him up."

The guards hauled Reynaud to his feet then laughed as his cramped legs folded under him. Under Miller's urging, they kept dragging him up and letting him fall. Finally, enough circulation had returned and enough muscles could function so Reynaud was finally able to stand, although it was bent over, hands on knees.

"That's not exercise," Miller said, "I was thinking of a mile run. Start moving." He pointed down a tree-lined driveway.

At first, Reynaud could hardly shuffle, but gradually he was able to trot. The guards directed him down the drive to a former National Guard armory. By the time he'd arrived, sweat was leaving muddy runnels in the dust covering him, and he was panting through a parched throat.

Miller had been driven to the armory. As Reynaud was escorted, panting, into the vehicle bay, Miller sipped water from a ladle. Returning the ladle to the can, he gestured for Reynaud to drink. "We want you in good shape when you get to Mountain

Home. General Robert Davenport wants a conversation with you."

Reynaud was so thirsty he didn't even hear the name. His hands trembled as he drew the ladle out of the water and emptied it into his mouth. Knowing he'd vomit if he drank too much too soon, he rinsed his mouth and spat out the first mouthful, then sipped cautiously.

"Yes," Miller elaborated. "General Davenport will personally see to you. Walter Davenport was his only son. I'm sure it'll be touching meeting." Miller laughed. "You'll be wishing you were back here as my guest again. I'm afraid the General's views on hospitality are less enlightened than mine.

"You might also want to know we caught your group outside of Bruno. No more than five or six of them got away, and the mop-up detail should take care of them in the next hour or so."

Reynaud said nothing. Between Carpenter's treachery and his own breaking under "shock therapy," his group had no secrets left. The group was gone, Norton was as good as dead, everything was now an open book to the Steel Fist.

"You'll be leaving as soon as the rest of the convoy assembles," Miller said. "I'll leave you in the charge of these men," he gestured at the guards in blue uniforms. To the men, he said, "I'll have the other prisoner sent over. We've just got a few more questions for him." He studied Reynaud a long moment. "I think this one had better be handcuffed again."

The man with the bullpup shotgun leaned it against the wall, pulled a pair of handcuffs out of a leather pouch, and clasped them, painfully tight, on Reynaud's wrists. At least this time they'd cuffed his hands in front of him.

As Miller walked away, the man picked up the Mossberg and pointed it at Reynaud. "This's a right nice shotgun you had here, Caje. Why, I could sit right across the truck from you and still chop you in two with this thing and never need to worry about your getting too close." For a moment he stood admiring the weapon, then glanced back at Reynaud. "By the way, what was that shit you was talkin' to Cap'n Miller?"

"When?"

"Right after he gave you that third jolt. You started babblin' somethin'; sounded like German, or Russian, maybe."

Relief washed over Reynaud. To hide his feelings, he took

another ladle of water and sipped at it. He must've thought he was still in the Russ POW camp and answered Miller in Russian. He hadn't yet given everything away. There was still Carpenter to deal with, but suddenly things looked much less bleak than they had just a moment before. Hell, it was as good as an even-money bet Miller was lying about the group being wiped out.

"Well," the guard snapped, "what was it?"

"It was Russian, wasn't it?" The other guard pointed his AK at Reynaud. "Maybe this guy's a Russki spy."

"Get real." Contempt dripped from the first guard's voice.

"Yeah," Reynaud replied, "it was Russian. I'm the first wave of an invasion of paratroopers."

"Knock off the crap, Caje," the guard with the shotgun said. "We don't need no stand-up comics here." He found a case to sit on. "You can just stand there and watch 'em load that truck."

The other guard had also found a crate and sat down, leaving Reynaud to stand, with nothing to do but watch men in gray work clothes load one of the trucks with truck parts and some rough wooden boxes of small parts.

Just past the truck the men were loading, Reynaud could see another vehicle, which looked like a semi tractor stripped to its essentials and covered with armor plate. The trailer hitch had been covered with an armored box with a pair of .50s in a dual mount, and the short, thick tube of a heavy rocket launcher was mounted just above the cab.

"Like it, huh?" the guard with the shotgun asked. "Pity your friends got themselves wasted. It would'a been great to have them try to get you outta this. They'd make almost a full meal for 'The Thing,' there."

A car pulled up outside and another man in a blue uniform escorted Carpenter into the building. He pointed at his prisoner. "This 'en is yours, too," he said, and left. Reynaud observed that Carpenter looked none the worse for wear, and his hands were free.

Carpenter was careful to give Reynaud a wide berth and the guards didn't object when he found another crate to sit on, leaving Reynaud standing, waiting for the convoy to form.

A convoy of nine troop trucks finally arrived just before noon and five of them were immediately refueled for the trip to

Mountain Home. The troops from the Fayetteville front were marched away and their places were taken in the trucks by fresh troops. The new convoy pulled out of Harrison just after one in the afternoon, "The Thing" in the lead, followed by a troop truck. The cargo hauler was the third truck in the line. It was only half full of cargo, leaving plenty of room for Reynaud, Carpenter, and the two guards. The guard with the Mossberg sat facing Reynaud, with Carpenter opposite the Cajun and closer to the rear. The other guard sat several feet from Reynaud, facing Carpenter, but spending most of his time watching Reynaud.

As the string of trucks barreled through Bellefonte, Reynaud, looking out the back of the truck, saw the single bored guard had been replaced by a track and a troop truck. As they slowed for the junction of highways 62 and 65, Reynaud wondered how much damage he'd see, and how much had been cleared away. As they passed the place the radio hut had been he saw blackened timbers and the rusty corrugated roof, discolored by heat, lying on the ground. A truck and an APC were parked beside the wreckage, and more trucks rimmed the edge of the highway.

The convoy turned onto US 62 and Reynaud saw men crawling over the burned-out hulk of another track, and a tank had been moved into the position once held by the sandbag bunker. The impression Reynaud got was ants scurrying around to restore a damaged anthill.

For the next ten miles or so the guards were silent, and he could sense the tension in their tight jaws and in the way they sat and handled their weapons. More trucks were parked at the point nearest the cave they'd abandoned. Reynaud laughed.

"What's so damn funny?" demanded the guard across from him.

"Just figuring how many of you it's taking to run down a handful of people. Meyer's troops will just eat you alive."

"Shut the fuck up," the guard snarled, his fury tinged with fear.

Reynaud grinned at Carpenter. "Did I tell you I found your bikes and booby-trapped them? That ought to really thrill your new friends." Captain Miller wasn't the only one who could try to rattle an enemy with a handy lie.

"I said, shut up," the guard roared, rising to his feet and pointing the shotgun at Reynaud's chest.

The man was in a dangerous mood, near the snapping point, and the Cajun wondered if he hadn't pushed the frightened man too far. He sat quietly, waiting, and finally the guard sat down again.

The tension seemed to build then they crossed a bridge. After the truck had cleared the bridge, the anxiety seemed to leak out of the guards, and the one who'd threatened him grinned at him.

"Your friends lost their last chance. Now your ass is really ours."

The truck slowed and the engine labored as they started up a slope. Reynaud could see, through the back of the truck, that the road was flanked by a bare wall on one side and a drop on the other. He turned his head and stared at the crates.

"Did those things just shift?" he asked the guards. "I don't want to be crushed if this shit falls. Let me move closer to the back, will you?"

The guards laughed, and the one who'd been more silent and nervous found his voice. "What's the matter, tough guy? Afraid of a little luggage? Stay where you are. We're supposed to get you to Mountain Home alive, and I'd hate to hafta shoot you tryin' to make a jump for it."

Reynaud was trying to think of an answer, something that'd make them move him to the back of the bus, when they all heard the blast, followed immediately by a roar that was a mixture of rocks smashing into the road and metal being pounded by stone. The driver of the truck seemed to be standing on the brakes, and they could clearly hear the squeal of brakes and the tires skidding on the asphalt.

Reynaud braced himself for a long fall and a sudden stop then the vehicle slid to a halt. Both the guards had been shaken by the wild ride, and Reynaud flung himself at the nearer guard. Seeing him, the man swung up the shotgun.

Reynaud swung desperately at the gun's barrel, shoving it upward as the gun almost deafened him with its bellow. Reynaud and the guard struggled to their feet, Rennie trying to keep the guard between himself and the back of the truck. The guard started to pump the shotgun's action, and Reynaud slammed the chain of his cuffs against the fore pistol grip, driving the action shut again.

Reynaud knew the Mossberg had a quirk; it cocked the action

within less than an inch of travel of the forearm. If the action were only opened a fraction of an inch, then closed, it was locked forward on a dead round until the release was pressed or the trigger pulled. Reynaud could only hope the guard, having little experience with the bullpup, would try to fight the weapon, supposing the gun was jammed.

The guard had forgotten everything but to try to force the action open, knowing that to fail was to die. Reynaud could see the fixation in the other man's eyes. After slamming his knee into the guard's groin, he drove his handcuffs against the guard's fingers around the pistol grip. In pain, the guard lost his grip on the weapon. Reynaud grabbed the grip, pressing down on the grip safety and pulled the trigger, so the action was pumped open.

Realizing what Reynaud had done, the guard shoved down on the foregrip, struggling to hold the action open. Reynaud thrust the gun butt into the man's belly then twisted the weapon the other way, so the barrel hit the man's head with stunning force.

Releasing the shotgun, the guard began to fumble for his pistol, and Reynaud drove the weapon against the man's neck, hooking the foregrip over his shoulder and jerked back, slamming the action shut on a live round. A kick at the guard shoved him away and freed the foregrip then Reynaud shoved the muzzle up under the man's chin.

Everything seemed to happen in slow motion. Though he saw it for only an instant, Reynaud could read the entreaty in the man's wide eyes, and the certain knowledge of his doom.

Reynaud pulled the trigger. The shotgun roared and the man's face collapsed; his eyes popped out then sank inward, crossing. The entire top of his head was gone, and blood and brain was blown everywhere.

Dropping into a crouch, again using the body to help him work the pump action, Reynaud pointed the gun at where Carpenter and the other guard wrestled and rolled on the floor of the truck. The guard managed to get on top, then Carpenter surged upward and they rolled out the back of the truck, Carpenter falling on top of the guard. Hearing a short burst of fire, Reynaud began to scramble to his feet then, as a grenade hit the truck and shrapnel whistled past his head, he hugged the floor. Fortunately, the grenade landed in the front of the truck and the boxes and crates of spare parts took most of the blast and the lethal fragments.

While fighting for his life, Reynaud heard only the sounds closest to him, and only those sounds he needed to hear. Now, he became aware of the chatter of automatic rifles and the roar of grenades. Looking up, he saw the truck behind his was stopped and the windows had been shot out of the cab. The driver and the man beside him lay slumped and sprawled in the seat. Crawling to the back of the truck as quickly as his tormented body could move, he looked outside, but the guard lay dead on the pavement and Carpenter was already gone, the guard's rifle with him.

~ * ~

Logan heard the trucks before they were in sight, then gradually distinguished another noise, and one of the gyroplanes raced overhead, no more than forty feet above him. He froze, moving nothing but his eyes, as he watched the machine follow the curve of the highway below. Within less than a minute the gyroplane reappeared, returning to the convoy, and Logan worried the pilot might've seen something. Clinging tightly to the stunted tree in which he hid, he waited. The engine sounds became louder as the trucks approached then a lumbering war machine crawled into sight.

The thing rolling ahead seemed to confirm his fear that the ambushers had been seen, but the vehicle never slowed, and then a truck appeared. Logan hoped they'd used enough explosives. They'd assumed a Jeep or Humvee would be leading the parade again.

The third truck came into view, then the fourth. Logan decided to wait until the monster truck leading the convoy was even with the tin can he'd used to mark the spot where the dynamite had been planted. He could already see six trucks in the column, and the gyroplane slowly working its way up the file, and yet another truck appeared. The Steel Fist was ready for trouble. The semi cab reached the hidden charges, and Logan touched the bare ends of the wires together.

The blast and the roar of the rockslide came as one. The concussion buffeted the monster and the rocks blown loose by the explosion pounded into the side of the armor, then the thing was gone, shoved off the side of the mountain. He heard the crash as it smashed into the rocks below, and a great gout of flame and smoke rose into the air.

The trucks skidded as their drivers panicked and locked the brakes. The second truck was already slowing when it hit the slope of rubble on the highway. For a moment, it seemed to pause then slowly it rolled over and off the road, to follow the lead machine. Two or three men in camouflaged uniforms bailed out the back before it fell forty feet into the other truck. The third truck skidded to a stop, its front wheels just short of the stone blocking the road, and immediately its cab was peppered with bullet holes. Two men fell out of the back of the truck, struggling for a rifle. Logan wanted to shout to the Deacon to hold his fire on the truck, but the grenade had already been launched, and a red and gold blossom bloomed on the gray-green canvas tarp.

The fourth truck had the windshield shot away and the top of the cab was jagged metal. Troops tumbled out of the truck into a withering fire. Logan saw Billy Joe slam the action of his grenade launcher shut, then fire one of his few flechette rounds and four soldiers went down, screaming. Someone tossed a grenade into the truck and the tarp was blown away, and bodies were thrown over the side. One of the ambushers slumped, hit in the face by a bullet, and lay with his head and right arm dangling over the boulder he'd used for cover.

The fifth truck in the column had skidded badly when the driver locked the brakes and the left rear set of wheels had crashed through the guardrail and hung over forty feet of clear air. The cab had been holed and the body of the passenger lay beside the truck door. A few boxes still fell from the back of the truck. The truck behind that was blazing, and men in battle dress, some with their clothes on fire, were dashing from the truck. The last two troop carriers were also afire, and some former prisoners had slid down the slope, which was lower nearer the base of the mountain, and fighting the few troops to escape the fires.

Logan noticed the gyroplane must've been hit—he hadn't noticed it before, or seen it come down—but the pilot had set it down on the highway between the fourth and fifth trucks. The pilot still slumped in his seat, bloody from the waist down. Logan decided he'd better reach the machine before one of the Steel Fist tried to use it to escape. Turning, he dashed the sixty yards to the slope created by the explosion and saw Hasteen at the bottom of the bank of rubble, running toward the machine.

~ * ~

Hasteen had watched the gyroplane closely as it passed the first time and decided against trying a shot. If the thing had a radio, the ambush would be sprung on an empty trap. Better to catch it when and if it came back after the ambush had begun. When the gyroplane returned, headed back toward the convoy, he again held his fire, almost certain it'd return with the trucks.

When the convoy approached, he sighted on the whirlybug. The blast caused him to pull his first shot off, firing low and ahead. Stroking the lever, he'd corrected by the time the lever hit the disconnector. At his shot the gyroplane lurched in the air. Again he swung the lever through its arc and snapped off a third shot that, he was almost certain, missed. By then, blood was spurting from the pilot's upper leg and Hasteen guessed the bullet had hit an artery.

The plane's descent was less a landing than a barely-controlled fall, as it set down hard on the blacktop. Hasteen sprang to his feet and raced for the place where the explosion had created a slope down which he could scramble. Reaching the road in a shower of dust and gravel, he raced for the first truck, leapt onto the bumper, threw himself onto the hood, and made sure both driver and passenger were dead, then rolled off the hood and crept to the back of the truck. There he found a body lying face-down, the back of its shirt almost torn away by bullet holes, then someone dropped out of the truck bed.

Hasteen had drawn and cocked his revolver before he realized the bruised, hollow-eyed wreck was Reynaud. Letting the hammer down softly, he holstered the weapon.

"Rennie," he blurted, "you look like hell."

Reynaud had swung the shotgun toward Hasteen then relaxed as he recognized his friend. "Thanks a hell of a lot," Reynaud managed to croak. "You're ugly too." He pointed back along the line of stalled trucks. "I think Carpenter went that way."

Laying his carbine on the truck bed, Hasteen helped Reynaud sit. "You'll be all right. Just stay here."

"He talked," Reynaud said. "He told them about Bruno. Did

you all get out?"

"We figured he'd spill his guts," Hasteen said. "We're generally in better shape than you are. Just rest."

The gunfire slackened to an occasional rifle shot. Hasteen could see the corpse beside the next truck and the body of the driver, leaning half out of the driver's window, and he could smell the nauseating burnt-feathers odor of roasting human flesh. More corpses lay around the back of the burning truck. Keeping low, Hasteen sprinted toward the shallow ditch at the base of the cliff.

The heat from the burning truck made it hard to breathe, hard to see, then he was on the ground, crawling past it, nearing a truck squatting at the edge of the road, its rear end sticking through a broken guardrail and hanging over the edge of the cliff.

Four of the Steel Fist soldiers had reached the ditch and pressed themselves against the rock face as though trying to burrow into the stone. Hasteen shot the nearest man in the chest and the man behind him looked up, saw Hasteen, then spun away, his face a bloody three-eyed mask. A grenade fell between the other two and the bodies, riddled with shrapnel, were flung against the cliff face, where they left patches of blood. Hasteen reloaded the Colt as he crawled forward and shoved the cartridge cases into the mouths of the men he'd killed.

Rounding the curve of the hill he saw the gyroplane, its pilot sagging in his harness, and Carpenter, who must've crawled under the truck, made a dash for the machine. Rising to kneel on one knee and using a two-handed grip on his revolver, Hasteen aimed at the assault rifle Carpenter carried. The Colt made its thunder and the rifle clattered on the asphalt while Carpenter screamed and clutched his ruined right wrist.

Hasteen stood. The shooting had stopped, and he strode to where Carpenter was trying to wrap his belt around his right forearm. Carpenter saw him then spun, looking for the rifle he'd dropped.

"Forget it," Hasteen advised, and cocked the pistol.

"Just give me a chance," Carpenter begged. "I can fly out on that," he pointed at the gyroplane.

"I'll let you fly out of here," Hasteen said. "How much did you tell them?"

"Nothing. I didn't tell them anything."

"I'd hate to have a lie for my last words," Hasteen said. Raising the pistol, he pointed it at Carpenter's head. "That makes you a liar as well as a coward. You have no loyalty to anyone, not even your own sister."

"He told me she wouldn't be hurt," Carpenter said.

"And you believed it?" Hasteen spat. "You didn't care. You were ready to sell everyone out."

"And now you're lying?" Carpenter asked. "You said you'd let me fly outta here."

Holstering his Colt, Hasteen stepped closer to Carpenter. "I keep my word," he snapped, then snatched Carpenter's left arm and swung the man around. The backs of Carpenter's knees hit the guardrail and he screamed as he felt himself falling. The scream lasted until he hit the rocks, forty feet below.

Hasteen leaned out over the drop. "You forgot to flap your arms, you stupid redneck," he shouted down at the broken body below.

Hasteen spun at a sound behind him, his gun drawn, but he twirled it back into the holster as Logan, half-supporting Reynaud, walked to the gyroplane.

"God, I'm tempted to grab that bird," Logan said. "But it'd just attract unwelcome attention and, the first thing you know, there goes the neighborhood. Give me a hand with the Cajun here, will you? He looks like a runner-up in a corpse look-alike contest."

"I feel like it, too," Reynaud admitted. "Let's get the hell out of here. We've got a long trip to cover, and we don't know how quickly the Steel Fist can scramble their airpower."

"Awright, ever'body," Logan roared, "we got a quick shoppers' special. Round up all the guns and ammo you can make off with in one minute, then we gotta start humpin'."

Angie Carpenter walked toward them, seeming somehow lost, and she'd stopped to look at the face of each body she passed.

"Where's my brother? Do any of you know?"

"I think he got away," Hasteen said with a straight face.

Reynaud, standing behind Angie, glared at him. "I'm sorry. He got away before I did, but he ran into the crossfire. It looked to me like he never felt a thing…" He let his voice trail off as he seemed to be putting his foot in even deeper.

Angie started to sob, and he awkwardly put his arm around her.

Logan had been staring at the gyroplane with real regret, then he picked up the tail of the craft and trundled it around until the wheels were against the guardrail. With Hasteen helping, he raised the tail until the gyroplane, still carrying the body of the pilot, tumbled over the cliff and smashed on the rocks and wreckage below.

Carrying a spare rifle and a grenade launcher, Andy joined them. To Logan he said, "Your friend," with a nod at Reynaud, "ain't up to a long haul. My folks had a farm up on Little Sugar Orchard Creek. The place's only about three miles from here, about a mile north of a wide spot in the road called Pyatt. I can probably provide enough space for three or four of you, and if nobody's raided the pantry, I might even be able to feed you."

"Sounds good," Logan agreed. "We need to split up, anyway." The men and women who'd been in the raid began to straggle in, most of them carrying several weapons. "Okay," Logan shouted, "we're headed east. If anybody's got a good hideout, break for it and take as many people with you as you can—up to four. We'll meet again in four days outside of Gassville."

As they hurried down the road, away from the ambush, Logan moved to again help support Reynaud.

"Rennie, I want you and Hasteen to go with Andy. You still ain't movin' any too well, and you'll need a strong arm with you. I'm sendin' the Carpenter girl with you." He glanced at Angie, who'd fallen several paces behind. "You know anything about nursin'?"

"Nothing much beyond first aid."

"That oughta do it; I don't think anything is busted." He lowered his voice. "The kid's pretty shook up," he confided to Reynaud. "I want her to feel useful, to have somethin' to keep her mind off family, if you catch my drift."

Reynaud nodded.

"By the way," Logan said, "I forgot to tell you—it's damned nice to have you back. I was beginnin' to taste the cookin'. Now I know why you Cajuns spice everything up."

Reynaud managed a grin. "Everything tastes better with a little hot sauce on it."

"Yeah," Logan agreed. "I guess that stuff'd damn near make a fencepost edible." Looking sidelong at Reynaud, a predatory grin splitting his face, he murmured, "You'll have to tell me how it is on brown-eyed blondes."

"Careful, boy," Reynaud muttered, "you're treading on troubled water." He looked over the ragged column of men and women. "Where's Mario and Xuan? Didn't they make it out?"

Logan explained how they and Ross had gone south to draw off Steel Fist soldiers. "It seems to have worked, too," Logan added. "Apparently they're beefing up the convoys but we never saw any patrols."

"That ambush you threw just blew the game," Reynaud said. "I just hope they make it back north."

"With a little luck," Logan said, "I hope we can convince those Nazi bastards there's a lot more of us than there really are."

"Not likely. They've got a lot of good, current information on us." He paused to make sure no one but Hasteen and Logan could hear him. "Carpenter told them everything he knew. For what it's worth, the Steel Fist is afraid the Springfield garrison may drive south and the people in Fayetteville may be knocking on the side door. It sounded like they lost six or eight tanks there, and I couldn't guess how many APCs or troops."

"Sounds like the Steel Fist is starting to rust a mite," Logan observed. "It sounds to me like it's about time to go for the kill."

Reynaud nodded. "One other little tidbit of information—the character leading them now is a man named Davenport. Ring any bells?"

"Bells and whistles. Is he related to the creep Norton smoked in Springfield?"

"It's Walter's daddy. Old tyrants don't die, they just smell like it."

They were finally able to get off the road and, with Andy in the lead, Reynaud, Hasteen and Angie split from the rest of the party and headed northeast. They'd only gone another quarter mile when they heard the sound of aircraft engines. Moving deeper into the shadows of trees, they watched an elderly C-47 following the road. As soon as the plane was out of sight, they started moving again and were almost caught by the much less noisy Bronco. Hasteen watched the plane with baleful eyes.

"That's one sneaky buzzard," he said, "one of these days…"

For most of the afternoon they slipped from one patch of cover to the next as the aircraft worked a search pattern. Twice,

Reynaud got a good look at the Gooney Bird through Hasteen's field glasses. Two .50 barrels jutted from ports cut in the side of the fuselage, along with the squat, businesslike barrel of an automatic grenade launcher.

Once they saw the C-47 bank and heard the guns open up, saw tracers leaving smoky welts in the air, but after a single firing pass the plane continued its pattern. When they reached where the gunners had fired they found a rawboned old cow, dead, with massive bullet holes.

Andy crouched beside the carcass and drew his knife. "Waste not, want not," he said, and trimmed enough meat off a haunch to serve for a meal or two.

By the time they reached the farm, Reynaud was exhausted and dizzy with hunger, ready to eat the meat raw. Andy pointed out a pair of graves in the front yard, rough hand-made wooden crosses over mounds of dirt.

"Plague," he said. He cleared an area in a stand of trees while they all gathered firewood, then he built a fire and began to roast the meat. Handing Reynaud a rusty bucket, he pointed beyond the house. "Crick's about eighty yards that way. You can bathe and wash your clothes in the crick. Just be careful about water mocs and be sure to bring back a bucket of water to prime the pump."

After the bath, and wearing clean clothes again, Reynaud felt almost human, for the first time in what seemed years. Andy handed Angie some pulpy pieces of what he called "burn cactus," and had her smear the sap from it onto the burns Reynaud had taken, and a few scratches. The sticky goo actually seemed to take some of the sting out of the wounds. Reynaud sank back against a tree with a grateful sigh.

The meat was cooked and Andy emerged from the house with a jar of canned tomatoes. The sight and smell of the food almost overwhelmed Reynaud, but he was able to eat only a small cut of meat and a couple of the tomatoes as his shrunken stomach filled rapidly.

"I've checked the house out," Andy said. "No snakes or rats. There's a bed in the back room, and a kid's bed in the loft. You two look like you need the rest most."

Reynaud tried to protest he could sleep on the ground, but the words were slurred by weariness. Hasteen helped him to his feet, supported him into the house, and he was so exhausted he scarcely saw the inside of the building before Hasteen and Angie set him down on the bed.

The last thing he remembered was Angie leaning over him, tears brimming in her eyes. "Thank you for trying to lie," she said, and kissed him on the cheek. Then he seemed to fall down a deep, black well.

~ * ~

Once the group crossed Crooked Creek, it began to disperse, with locals each taking two or three of the party to a remote farm or a cave, and by the time they'd reached Noel and the others, only Logan, the Deacon, and one of the locals remained. Logan and the Deacon passed out what extra weapons and ammunition they carried.

"The spies in the skies are up," Logan informed them.

Dust rose from the road as trucks rumbled past, racing for the site of the ambush. "Pity we didn't have more dynamite and plastique," Logan said. "We could've made it a lot more entertaining for them, too."

"They'll start to search," Billy Joe said, "and they'll find the tracks on the riverbank. We can't stay here."

The local studied the party a moment, then said, "If we go north, we'll cross the river again, out of sight of the bridge, and, if you don't mind some hard hikin', we can reach Johnnie Creek by late tomorrow mornin'. It means pushin' on until last light today and startin' again at first light in the mornin', but they's a big old farmhouse and barn there."

Twice they had to stop and find heavier cover as at least one C-47 and the Bronco worked the area, but their route took them beyond the search area within a couple of hours. They managed to find a place where the river was almost fully hidden underneath trees, and crossed without attracting attention from the air. They stopped for dinner while it was still light, and the light of the fire was less obvious than it would've been after dusk, then pressed on and pitched a cold camp over a mile away.

Logan took the first turn at sentry duty with the local. For three hours he stared at the black trees picked out in silver moonlight. "How come you fellas never got around to hittin' the Steel

Fist before?" he asked.

The local, a farmer named Bood, had been nodding his way into a doze, but his head snapped up at the question. "We couldn't get organized. Every time we'd try to get a few men together, we'd either run out of supplies and have to split up again, or the Steel Fist fuckers'd hit us. They'd use them little helicopters to call in a nasty little twin-engined job they have, or they'd bring in a big mother-humper of a copter and drop a couple dozen troops on us. They had us out-gunned right from the start.

"It was real tough. If we tried to get together, the Fist fuckers'd hit us with an army, and if we didn't, we'd get raided by bandits. The best we could do alone was to catch a few of 'em alone and shoot one then get the hell outta there. It wasn't much, but it let 'em know how we felt."

"Do you have much trouble with bandits around here?"

"It ain't so bad, here. I've heard tell it's a lot worse around Little Rock and some other, bigger, places. Some of the bandits are just people who want somethin' to eat; others are real badmen. One 'a those is a worthless bastard name of Carpenter. He runs with a coupla real sonsabitches."

Logan kept his voice casual. "Was one'a them a big, ugly dude, and another one a sneaky little shit?"

"Damn right! You know about 'em?"

"You don't need to worry about any of them. They got generous and decided to give their all to Ma Nature. They oughta push out a bumper crop of daisies."

"Best thing them assholes could do," Bood muttered. "I hope them bastards hurt a lot and died slow."

"Well, Carpenter had a little time to reflect on his sins," Logan said. After sitting in silence for a while, "What're you gonna do after the Steel Fist is gone?"

"Ain't really thought that far ahead. Reckon I'll try farmin' again."

"You might think about settin' up a local government and a militia."

"Government, huh?" Bood spat. "I don't like anybody tellin' me I can't drink up my corn crop."

"That's why you wanta make it local," Logan replied. "Hell, government and laws aren't any good when they don't help people. That's all they're for—to sorta put oil between the wheel and the axle. Laws are only needed when people disagree, and then it just gives you an out to punchin' or shootin' the other guy. It's to limit disagreements. That's why you want a local government and a local militia. 'Cause the country's gonna fill up and grow again, and the only hope you have of keepin' what's yours is to have your own local government.

"Otherwise, some asshole from Little Rock or Springfield is gonna decide you need 'help' governin' yourselves, and they're gonna move in on you, outside laws, carpetbag, and all.

"And, in the meantime, you get groups like the Steel Fist, or bandits, who figure they can take what they want from people who aren't organized to defend themselves. Think about it."

Logan rose and shook the Deacon awake, then found a soft spot on the warm ground.

~ * ~

Leaving Verona far behind them, Mario, Xuan, and Ross stopped at noon to eat and rest. Before they moved on they built half a dozen campfires within yards of each other. They used dry wood, but built the fires in the open, so smoke might be seen by anyone very near, then set out for Freck's Lookout.

Ross fell into step beside Mario. "Do you really think we did any good, with just one shot fired?"

Mario reached back and patted his rifle's stock. "That one shot killed one officer, right in the middle of one of their patrols. Unless the locals are a lot better at this game than I think they are, they'll be sure it was outsiders, and we're the only game in town. If they're close enough to find the campfires, they should think we're the main party. We only have to play this game until this afternoon. They'll know they're on the wrong track when the convoy gets ambushed. Then, all we have to do is cover heaps of miles crawling with enemy troops to reach the rendezvous."

By later afternoon they were nearing Freck's Lookout when Xuan raised his hand to signal a halt, then slipped like a ghost between trees to stare at something on the forest floor. Mario and Ross, after peering through the trees and undergrowth and seeing nothing, joined him. Xuan pointed to a dead squirrel, dried blood around its mouth and nose.

"What's the problem?" Ross asked.

"No bullet hole," Xuan said. "It's still got a nut between its teeth. Looks like it was eating when it died. No warning, no marks, nothing."

"How long ago?" Mario snapped.

"From the blood, at least thirty minutes. Probably longer."

Mario let out a held breath. "Looks like it might've been gassed. How close is the Lookout?"

Ross waved a hand at the trees ahead of them. "Just about eight hundred yards past those trees."

Mario's face had gone cold and hard. "Don't expect to find any survivors. This was done by gas. Those bastards must've had enough stored at Mountain Home for a few small raids. They probably sprayed the place, and this was downwind. I just hope the other group doesn't find out they've got the Bronco rigged for this the hard way."

Ross suddenly felt cold. "Did anybody bring any gas masks?"

Xuan shook his head, then found a stick and prodded the squirrel's body. It was already rigid.

"It's been dead for over an hour, at least," Mario observed.

"Probably since this morning," Xuan corrected.

"We'd better shake this place," Ross muttered.

"The gas has dissipated," Mario said, "and they're not likely to gas this area again." He looked at Ross. "Any idea why they might've rubbed this place out?"

Ross shrugged. "Maybe they took fire from around here. Maybe they thought this is where we were headed. Maybe they just wanted to make the locals afraid to help us. Who knows, with those bastards?"

Xuan had crept to the fringe of trees and trained his binoculars upward. Ross and Mario joined him, carefully staying in the shadows of the trees. One of the Steel Fist troop trucks was parked near a cluster of four or five buildings near the top of a mountain and, through their field glasses, they could see a man in a wooden tower, binoculars to his eyes, scanning the countryside.

"Think you can make the shot?" Xuan asked.

Mario pursed his lips and considered the shot, as well as the likely results. "There's not enough cover for us to safely get much closer, much less take the place. There's quite a bit of it for them coming down. Do you want to make this a kiss-and-run or what?"

Xuan glared at the men above them. "I'd like to kill as many of them as we can. They must have gas masks. We need them."

Ross squinted up at the men and the truck. "It'd be a lot easier if we could wait until dark. And what if they have a radio?"

"They're not going to wait until dark," Mario said. "They're already gathering around the truck. And I don't see an antenna on the truck." He raised his rifle and laid down a camouflaged cloth where the muzzle would otherwise kick up dust. "It's decision time."

Ross licked his lips. "Let's go for it."

Mario took his time, murmuring softly to himself. "Uphill shots are a lot like downhill. The bullet doesn't drop as much as it would for a level shot at the same distance. The way the bushes are moving—or not moving, it's fairly still up there. Don't need to worry much about windage—" He interrupted his monologue with the shot.

The man in the tower dropped, although they couldn't tell whether he'd been hit or just ducked. The men around the truck froze for a moment, then scattered, dropping behind bushes or rocks.

For perhaps ten minutes, no one moved then a man with an M-60 climbed into the tower. Mario sighted carefully. "I think I've really got the range, this time." He squeezed off a shot and the gunner fell. The rifles on the mountain began to spew automatic fire and a few bullets whined into the trees around them.

"Better spread out," Mario said. "I think we're going to be here a while."

CHAPTER 10

"Time to split up and move," Mario said, and crawled twenty yards to a new position. Xuan had gone with him and found a vantage spot another ten yards beyond Mario, while Ross slipped into cover in the opposite direction.

The machine gun began to yammer, but most of the bullets went high. Mario grimaced, then relaxed. If this substitute gunner was representative of the quality of the men they were facing, they had a good chance to wipe out the whole group of them.

One of the soldiers had crept around the truck and slipped in through the passenger's door. Taking careful aim, Mario fired. A spot appeared on the driver's door. He'd worked the bolt while the rifle was still recoiling, and he ignored the sudden barrage of rifle and machine gun fire to put a round through the engine.

The troops above were enthusiastically wasting their ammunition. Most were simply firing, hoping a stray bullet would be lucky, then a single bullet hit near enough to spray rock chips into Mario's face. Ducking rapidly, he moved ten yards to his right.

Hidden behind the trunk of a tree, he opened the bolt and fed four more cartridges into the magazine. That single round hitting so near disturbed him, and he wondered if they had a counter-sniper team. When he looked up again, he did it without moving his own cover. Men were advancing down the mountain in a leapfrog maneuver, half of them moving from one spot of cover to the next while the others remained hidden, ready to provide covering fire, then advancing after the others had reached more secure positions from which to provide cover in their turn.

The nearest troops had reached a rock shelf, four hundred yards from the trees, when Mario spotted, higher, a man peering through binoculars. He hadn't seen the man reach the boulder, meaning the man wasn't playing leapfrog with the others. Using his own field glasses, Mario found, two or three yards to the right of the man with the binoculars, another man with a bolt-action rifle with a long telescopic sight. The counter-sniper lay on his side, his head turned toward the spotter.

Mario remembered how high to hold for the range and laid the vertical hair of his scope on the man's ear. He took a deep breath, then let half of it out, and waited to squeeze the shot between heartbeats. He was almost surprised by the report of his own rifle, and the counter-sniper's head snapped to the side, then the body slumped.

The machine gunner opened up again, holding the trigger down for a full ten seconds, and Mario cursed as a lucky round tore into the tree just above him, showering him with bark. Ducking again, he slithered toward a break in the line of bushes. Before he could reach the spot he'd chosen, a blast erupted in the bushes, showering him with dirt and small limbs. Xuan's .223 fired a single shot and more return fire raked the area.

~ * ~

Xuan had seen a puff of smoke as the grenade launcher was fired. Through his scope, he could see a man had an M-203 mounted under his M-16 rifle. The grenadier had shoved the launcher's action open to dump the empty case and shove in a fresh round. The range was about four hundred yards. Xuan sighted on the man's head and fired.

Return fire buzzed and whined around him. For a moment, he lost the man with the launcher. When he found him again, the grenadier was steadying his weapon. Xuan cursed himself for forgetting what Mario'd said about uphill shots. He tried to hold lower, but hurried the shot.

He saw a puff of rock dust behind the man with the launcher then ducked. The grenade fell short and showered him with clods of dirt and a spray of gravel, and rifle fire inched closer as half a dozen men emptied their magazines.

He was being pinned down, unable to prevent the grenadier from improving his aim. Far to the right, Ross fired a shot and drew most of the fire. Xuan searched with his scope until he found the man with the launcher again, who was wiping blood off his face, and several scratches were bleeding freely. At least Ross' shot had kicked some rock into his face and distracted him. Xuan lowered his aim and pressed the trigger again. The man's left arm jerked in a spastic twitch, and the grenade went well wide of the fringe of trees.

Again Xuan was forced to seek better cover and crawled a few yards to where a rock jutted from the ground. Once behind the stone, he looked for the man with the launcher, found him fumbling after his weapon, holding his left arm against his chest. Mario's rifle barked, and the grenadier bounced, then fell in a heap.

The troops had continued their advance, and Xuan snapped off a shot at one of them barely two hundred yards away. The man spun and screamed, then went down, still screaming.

Three hundred yards was about the maximum accurate range of the .223 round, and these soldiers were getting entirely too close.

Mario's rifle crashed again, and a man with a scoped rifle and a pair of binoculars hanging around his neck fell from a ledge and hit the cliff face twenty yards below, then slid, limp, down to the road winding its way around the mountain.

The machine gunner had finally fed another belt into the gun and began to fire short bursts, walking them from the bare stone into the trees.

The man Xuan had hit was still lying in the open, screaming, his arms wrapped around his belly, his legs kicking at the rock. Another soldier dashed out to help him and Xuan dropped the man with a bullet through the chest. The man shot in the chest lay dying silently, while the other man stopped screaming and lay moaning and sobbing. Xuan let the man live. The noise didn't bother him, and it was upsetting the other Steel Fist troops.

Ross caught another trooper dodging from one clump of cover to another and hit him with a short burst that made him jerk and dance before he fell.

The fire from the Steel Fist soldiers weakened as they lost some of their advantage in numbers and became aware they were starting to run low on ammunition. The machine gun had fallen silent again.

~ * ~

Taking careful aim, Mario placed a bullet within inches of the machine gun's muzzle. The gun chattered angrily, for almost a full seven seconds, spraying everything in general and hitting nothing in particular, then the belt of ammunition ran out and the gunner had to feed in another belt.

Suddenly, the truck at the top of the mountain started and

jerked forward. The man hit in the cab had recovered enough to try to escape. Cutting a bootlegger's turn, the truck disappeared from view around the curve of the mountain. Mario set himself to fire on the truck when it came back into sight, but when it reappeared it was already hurtling out of control. The driver's side fender screamed as it was torn away like paper by the rocks, the front wheel slammed against the mountainside then the vehicle rebounded and left the road.

It seemed to hang suspended in the air then it dropped. The engine was already on fire, and the truck fell like a comet, to crash again on the mountainside. A few shrubs helped to cushion it as it started to roll, then it hit, upside-down, on the next winding of the road. It started to roll again, then fell back onto the road, upside-down and burning.

Four men tried to rush the line of trees, and they all fell within the first thirty yards of their charge.

The mountain was silent, except for the crackling of the fire and the groaning of tortured, heated metal, and the remaining troops cowered in their cover, waiting.

Mario took a break. He wiped at his face then stared at the blood on his hand, and he finally remembered being sprayed with rock dust. Taking out his canteen, he drank deeply then replaced the flask in its cover.

"Are either of you fellows hurt?" he called out softly.

Ross crawled into view, a bloodstained cloth wrapped around the fingers of his left hand. "I lost my social finger. Other than that, I'm fine."

Xuan, like Mario, had scratches on his face and the shoulder of his shirt was torn, although there was no sign of blood.

"It's been amusing so far. Shall we end it?"

"What do you think, Ross?" Mario asked. "Every shot they pop off at us steepens the odds against us."

Ross looked up the mountain and wiped his mouth with the back of his hand. "It doesn't look like they're getting any help, and we've already killed over half of them. We're down here in the trees, and they're caught up there in the rocks. I hate leaving a job half-done."

"They may just wait for dark," Mario pointed out, "and try to slip away then. At this point, it looks like they'd rather just book out of here. They seem to have lost interest in trying to take us."

Xuan interrupted by shooting a man trying to work his way back up the mountain. Only a few shots were fired in reply.

Ross twisted the cloth tighter on his hand. "They've probably got medical supplies of some kind, which we could use, and we still haven't gotten any of those gas masks. If they slip out at night, we can strip a few of the nearer bodies and be far away by morning."

One of the soldiers raced from cover to crouch behind the body of the man Xuan had killed and began frantically pulling magazines from pouches. Mario's shot took off the top of his head.

"Yeah," Mario said, "I'd say some of them are getting low on ammo."

Ross licked his lips. "How many do you think are left?"

"No more than seven," Xuan replied. "Probably five."

Another half hour dragged by. "This is boring," Xuan snapped. "Do you think you can kill the machine gunner with a single shot?"

"If he gives me a shot, I think I think I can put one into him. At this range, I don't guarantee a head shot."

Xuan crawled about thirty yards from the other two then touched off two short bursts in the direction of a patch of cover. The machine gun popped off two rounds and jammed, and Mario shot the gunner as he opened the action, while Ross hit the man Xuan's gunfire had flushed.

Xuan replaced the magazine in the Armalite with a fresh one. "Now, no more than five."

"My turn to try it," Ross said, and steadied his rifle. The weapon made a sound like canvas being ripped and a stream of brass erupted from the bolt port. Dust billowed and ricochets whined off the rocks. The soldier jumped up, gun blazing. Mario's round took the man in the throat and he fell six feet to the next ledge down, leaving a smear of blood on the rocks.

"Held too low on that one," Mario said.

Ross reloaded. "Think there are any left?"

Xuan crept to the edge of the trees and studied the ground. "You know, I think I can make it to that rock by the ditch."

Mario frowned. "Bet you a cold beer you won't make it."

"Double or nothing on your being able to cover me," Xuan

replied. After waiting until the other two were braced and their rifles were pointed at the rocks above, he sprang to his feet and sprinted for the ditch, using the irregularities in the stone to throw himself from side to side.

Mario saw a muzzle winking light and put a round just above it, while Ross snapped a shot and cursed.

"I thought I got him, but he ducked back onto the ledge." He looked at the rock where Xuan lay. "You hit?"

Xuan moved the fingers of his left hand then flexed the hand at the wrist. It was painful, but he didn't think any bones had been broken. One bullet had smashed his wristwatch and torn it off his arm, while another round had drilled his left forearm. "Only a little, but one of those milkfaces owes me a new watch. We're still even, Mario. Did you get them?"

"There were only two left," Ross said. "At least, there were only two shooting at you. Mario got his, but I think I pulled my shot." He sighted on the edge of the shelf where he'd seen the man go down and fired single shots, trying to frighten the man out of cover. He stopped firing after the sixth shot, when he saw a line of blood begin to run down the rock. The trail of red zig-zagged down the stone and widened.

"My turn to try the water," Ross announced, and scrambled up and across the bare rock to where Xuan lay. The mountain remained silent.

"It seems to be all clear," Ross shouted back to Mario, "but why don't you stay back, just in case?" He examined Xuan's wound. "It looks like you could use a dressing. Are you carrying any med supplies?"

Xuan shook his head.

"I'll go see if any of them had anything we could use." Rising slowly, rifle tucked tight against his hip, he prowled toward the nearest bodies, those of the men Xuan had shot. The soldier who'd been gut-shot had been quiet for nearly half an hour.

As he approached, Ross could see the belly-wounded man was drawn up on his side in a fetal position, his right hand wrapped around his rifle's pistol grip, the M-16 lying facing Ross. The man's eyes were hidden by his helmet, tipped over his upper face and the side of his head, but a line of blood ran from the corner of his mouth to the rock. Ross stopped. Better to be sure.

He raised his M-16 to his shoulder.

At the same time, the wounded man's M-16 came to life, stammering out a burst. Recoil made the muzzle bounce and rise, and Ross felt a blow to his right thigh, another to his belly, and a third slammed his left arm up and away from his rifle's forearm. He jerked at the trigger and the man screamed again and rolled onto his back.

Xuan flinched at the sudden, unexpected gunfire and twisted to bring his rifle to bear, but Ross was between Xuan and the soldier. Rolling to his feet, Xuan raced to where Ross had fallen. A glance sufficed to assure him Ross had killed the soldier. His face burned with shame. Ross had been trying to help him, and had been shot by a man he'd wounded and forgotten.

Xuan knelt beside Ross, who was moaning and clutching at his belly.

"Take it easy," Xuan said. Ross was bleeding from three new wounds. The hit on the outside of the right thigh had probably missed the femur and the femoral artery. Another bullet had smashed his left upper arm and, from the way the arm lay, Xuan guessed the bone had been shattered. He gently pulled Ross' hand away from his belly and lifted his shirt, exposing a bullet hole an inch above the navel and two inches to the left.

Footsteps pounded on the rock behind him and Xuan spun, drawing his Automag then lowered the pistol as Mario dashed toward them. After glancing at the wounds, Mario gestured toward the dead soldiers.

"See if they've got any dressings."

"God, I'm thirsty," Ross gasped.

"You've got a belly wound," Mario said. He cut away the shirt sleeve and the pants leg to examine the wounds, then pulled out his canteen and gave Ross a drink.

"That bad, huh?"

Mario nodded. "I'm afraid so." He pulled the belt off the man Ross had killed and started to wrap it around Ross' arm, but Ross groaned and said, "Forget it. If I'm gonna check out, I'd rather not drag it out any longer." He stared down at the belly wound. "It hurts like a bitch. Just stay with me, will you? I hate to think of dying alone."

Xuan returned with dressings and a few pills. "This is all these two had."

Mario set the dressings aside then picked up Ross' head, resting it on his lap. "Think you can swallow a pill or two?"

Ross nodded, and Mario put two aspirin in his mouth and gave him another drink to wash them down. Ross sighed then shuddered, his lips turning blue.

"Get me the clothes off those two," Mario said, nodding at the bodies.

"One's got a blanket roll," Xuan said, and went to get it.

Ross' breathing was labored. Mario leaned closer. "What's your last name?"

Ross opened his eyes. "McCallister. Ross McCallister. You run into any McCallisters from Batesville or Charlotte, you tell 'em I died right, will you?"

"Consider it done," Mario said. Xuan returned and laid the blanket over Ross. "Want another drink?" Mario touched the canteen to Ross' lips. "Sorry it isn't good white lightning."

Ross' face knotted up as a spasm of pain seemed to roll over him, then relaxed. His breathing stopped.

Mario pulled the blanket up to cover Ross' face then tore open a capsule Xuan had given him, sprinkled its contents directly on the wound in Xuan's forearm, and bound a dressing around the arm.

"The price of gas masks just went up." He handed another capsule and an aspirin to Xuan. "Take these and call me in the morning."

Xuan swallowed the antibiotic and the aspirin with water then studied the area for loose stones. The sun had set before they'd finished the cairn.

After they'd buried Ross, they chewed dried meat and sipped water from their canteens. Mario had sat beside one of the corpses and, after he'd finished his meal, rummaged through the man's pouches, producing a gas mask and a spare filter.

"Be sure to take spare filters. Hydrogen cyanide gas fucks up filters. The Russians planned to hit the opposition with it first then follow up with a second dose of it, or with some other gas, when they could catch the other guy with clogged filters." He held up a couple of magazines he'd found in a belt pouch. "Can you use M-16 magazines in that rifle of yours?"

"Some of them." Xuan found a couple of plastic thirty-round magazines that fit his weapon, a good gas mask, and a pair of extra filters, as well as enough ammunition to more than replace what he'd used. He also crawled up and recovered the weapon with the M-203 grenade launcher and four rounds for it.

"Let's follow the road a couple of miles," Mario said, "then find some good cover. I don't think some people are going to appreciate our attempt to clean up the social environment."

~ * ~

When Reynaud woke, the sunlight streamed in dusty bars through a dingy window onto a wall from which discolored wallpaper hung in strips. From the few patches of original color left, Reynaud decided the aging had been an improvement. He realized then his hand was resting on his bare stomach under a musty patchwork quilt. Pulling off the cover, he found himself naked. The uniform he'd worn, all its insignias ripped off, hung on coat hangers, drying.

Moving slowly to favor his aching muscles, stiff from the punishment they'd taken in the last few days, he sat up. He turned, swinging his feet off the bed. Where was everybody? He started to reach for his clothes, then heard a sound at the door and grabbed for the quilt.

Angie's laugh was a silver sound. "You have a nice body," she said, leaning on the door frame, her arms crossed. She laughed again at the expression on his face. "Andy and Hasteen undressed you; I just washed your clothes again. Men get all the fun jobs."

Grinning sheepishly, he pulled the quilt around his waist. "I suppose it'd be too much to ask—for you to leave while I get my pants on."

"Well, if you want to be a prude about it…" She turned and walked out the door.

Reynaud rose and pulled on his pants. The bottoms of the legs were still wet, but it was a pleasure to be back in clean clothes. His Catholic boys' school upbringing had conditioned him, and he realized many of his inhibitions were foolish, but he still felt uncomfortable being buck-ass naked in front of a woman. Especially, he admitted to himself, when he really admired the woman.

"Andy said to tell you," Angie's voice drifted from outside, "you should treat the place like it was your own, and if you found anything you needed, take it and use it."

"Where is he? And where's Hasteen?"

"They said they were going scouting. Said they'd be back sometime tonight or early tomorrow."

He zipped up the pants. "You can come in, now," he said. "I may not be decent, but I'm partly dressed."

"Why don't you come out? I've got breakfast ready; I just have to warm it up."

"I'll be out in just a few," Reynaud shouted back. He'd noticed an old leather shaving kit. Rubbing his cheeks, he winced, as much from the feel of the beard he was growing as from the tenderness of his bruises. He opened the case and found an old straight-edge razor, a hone, a shaving cup with a disc of dried, yellow soap in it, a brush, and a small bottle. Opening the bottle, he took a breath of a scent from his childhood; witch-hazel. The kit also held a small shaving mirror with a hole in its top, and a strop.

He carried the kit out with him and Angie served him coffee and pan bread with sand plum preserves. He ate and drank slowly and carefully, savoring each morsel and sip. When he'd finished, he grinned at Angie.

"All I need now is brandy and a good cigar." He said. "You thanked me for something last night. What'd you mean?"

Angie looked away. When she answered, her voice was subdued. "About my brother. I'd heard things from some of the other people..." She poured herself a cup of coffee and sipped from it. "And I'd gotten to know some of your friends better; Hasteen, for instance. He still frightens me a little, but he's got more loyalty and integrity than almost anyone. I didn't know Adam's friends, but, to be honest, they bothered me; at least, the two who were killed. There seemed to be something—ugly— about them."

She sat, huddled over, holding her coffee cup in both hands, staring into the brown liquid. "I guess I'm kind of old-fashioned: I think you can learn a lot about somebody by the company he keeps. I heard a lot I didn't want to hear or believe, but sometimes the truth is bitter medicine."

"It doesn't matter, now," Reynaud said. "Whatever your brother did or didn't do is dead past. The question is: What do you want to do?"

"I want to live. I've been robbed of that, and I'll have to give it up again, maybe more than once, before this is all over, but I want to savor the taste of coffee and smell flowers again and just feel completely alive again. Is that selfish?"

Reynaud's grin was an awkward, uncertain thing. "No more than anyone else." He pointed to a kettle of warm water. "Could I have some of that? One of my selfish urges is to get this fur off my face."

She helped him dip out a panful of water and he found a nail driven into a tree trunk, on which he hung the mirror. He was almost shocked at his reflection. Most of the swelling in his face had gone down, although one eye still looked a little more slanted than it normally did, and most of the face he could see was still in ugly shades of purple and yellow. He wondered if he really wanted to see the rest of it, but he honed the razor, which was spotted with brown drops of rust, and which apparently hadn't been used since the plague days.

When he'd finally sharpened the razor to his satisfaction, he lathered his face and made the first tentative strokes. He glanced back at Angie, who'd been silent for so long he'd almost forgotten she was there, to see her watching intently. "What're you staring at?" he asked.

"Men make such strange faces when they're shaving." She demonstrated, exaggerating the facial contortions men made, and Reynaud found himself laughing. Laughter was a rare pleasure, one he enjoyed for a moment then he forced his face into a parody of sternness. "Do me a favor; don't break me up while I've got a razor this close to my face. The other guys tell me I'm already too ugly; I don't need a set of odd scars."

Angie smiled. "Sometimes you listen to your friends too much. I think you've got a very nice face. I thought so the first time I saw it, and I think so now."

"Careful," Reynaud said, "the swelling in the rest of my head just went down. I don't want to start any more of it for a while."

Shaving heavy beard off a face still bruised and tender took Reynaud what he considered far too long, but at last his face was bare but for the luxuriant moustache he favored. Gingerly splashing a little of the witch-hazel on, he looked at himself critically. His jaw looked as though he'd tried to break down doors with it, and there were other bruises along his ribs and on his back, where he'd been kicked and had tumbled down a bluff, but, apart from some soreness, he felt fit again.

Angie had gone then reappeared at the door of the cabin with his shotgun. "It's awfully hot," she said. "I thought we'd go for a swim." She handed him the shotgun. "You may need this for snakes."

Reynaud checked the weapon, trying to look very martial and professional, to hide the sudden attack of nervousness he felt, the feeling that a whole flock of butterflies had taken up residence somewhere under his ribcage, then followed Angie to the creek. The water was too clear and shallow for any attempt at concealment, and he found himself a little afraid and very excited.

Carefully, he searched the way they took to the river and the riverbanks for snakes then found a place to sit.

Angie laughed. "You're not going to just sit there and play guard, are you?" Sitting down on the riverbank, she stripped off a pair of boots at least four sizes too large. "Skinny-dipping is no fun alone." She unbuttoned her blouse and, despite a conscious attempt, Reynaud couldn't keep his eyes away as her hands flew down the row of buttons. Shrugging the coarse fabric off her shoulders, she hung the shirt on a low limb. Angie had a trim waist with what Reynaud thought were the most lovely breasts he'd ever seen.

Reynaud seemed to have a lump in his throat, one making it difficult to breathe then Angie fumbled with the belt. She got the buckle loose and the pants, several sizes too large and gathered at her waist, fell around her ankles. Angie's long, slender legs went all the way up to trim hips and a beautifully shaped ass.

Reynaud's voice sounded strange, even to him. "You know, 'pert' is the only word that comes to mind when I see that backside."

Angie turned partly around, displaying an almost flat belly and a triangle of dark pubic hair. "Hey, this is no free show," she said. "Shuck the clothes and come into the water." She waded into the river, which only came to her mid-calf. "What's the matter; don't you swim?"

He hid his embarrassment behind an impish grin. "Hey, I

only came for the view. Besides, that water looks damned cold."

Angie bent and scooped double handfuls of water at him. "You're going to take a bath or get a shower. Which'll it be?"

The water was shockingly cold against his bare chest. "All right," he said, "you win." Turning around, he doffed his pants then stared down at his crotch. "Gee, I must've bruised the hell out of that, too. You ought to see how it's all swollen."

"That's fine with me," she giggled. "But, that's what cold water's for—to reduce swelling." She stared at him openly as he turned around and stepped into the chilly water. "Still, it does seem a waste."

He waded into the stream. Angie had already sat in the water, and he did the same, having to suppress a squeal as the cold water hit his crotch. Angie leaned back and tilted her head back to wet her long, ash-blonde hair, then washed her face and chest. Reynaud copied her actions then she turned toward him. "Turn around and I'll wash your back." He presented his back to her and she carefully rubbed it down with clear water. Being naked with her was easier when he sat with his back to her.

When she'd finished, he turned to face her. "My turn now." She turned her back and he washed it then traced the very pale lines of a couple of fine scars running across her back. He wanted to say something, do something, to make her pain go away, but could think of nothing.

Angie turned her head. "You have very gentle hands. You're just full of surprises."

Reynaud's embarrassment returned and the only reply he could manage was another unsteady grin.

"Well," Angie said, "I guess that finishes things up here." She stood, retrieved her clothes, which she folded over her arm, picked up her boots, and strolled back to the cabin. Recovering his pants and the shotgun, Reynaud followed her.

Angie had set her clothes on the wreckage of a chair and pinched off the points of several leaves of the burn cactus. "Lie down on the bed," she said, "and I'll take care of those burns of yours." As he lay, face-down, on the bed, she said, "The proper name for this plant is *aloe vera*."

He could feel her applying the sap from the crushed leaves to the scabbed-over cut on the back of his calf and the scratches on his back. The cool, soft feel of the aloe was followed by a feather-light touch as she spread the sap with her fingertip, then another coolness as she blew gently on the moist sap to speed its drying. When she'd finished tending his back he rolled over. She seemed unaware of his erection as she tended the scratches and the burn on his face. He looked into her eyes as she applied the moisture to the burn on the cheek, and could almost feel her sympathetic pain radiated back to him.

"It doesn't bother me, now," he said.

"I've seen those marks before. I've heard they hurt a lot more than the cattle prods."

"It was…uncomfortable. Let's let it go at that."

Seeing her moist brown eyes and lush lips so near made the ache unendurable. His hands reached for her, stroked her back, and gently drew her down to him. Her lips were as soft and sweet as they looked. His tongue slid out and Angie opened her mouth to receive it, and her arms clutched at his with something like desperation.

Suddenly Angie stiffened and broke the kiss.

Reynaud, surprised, moved away from her.

"I'm sorry," Angie said. "I can't. In the prison camp—they used me—"

Reynaud stroked her hair. "That's all right. You don't have to do anything." He smiled at her, although he couldn't hide the ache showing in his eyes. "I know how you feel. Just remember, you're not alone. Anyone without power is used in one way or another." He held her close.

Angie's voice skated on the edge of tears. "I really wanted to—"

"I know; I did too." He grinned at her. "You'd understand better if you could see yourself. You're lovely. Will you at least stay here with me?"

She buried her face in the crook of his neck. "It feels good. I'd almost forgotten how good it can feel just to be close to someone." Her hands slid around his back until she was holding him tightly. "Thank you for understanding."

He tried a chuckle, but it didn't work very well. "I've been there, too."

"I heard something about some of you once having been in a

Russian prison camp. What was it like? I mean, if you can talk about it…"

"A lot like the one you were in. There's a sort of grim, drab similarity to places like that. They spoke Russian at the place I was, of course, and it was cold. God, it was cold. I think I would've traded almost anything for some of this heat, but then I imagine you'd have given a lot for some of our snow." He was silent for a long time, and his hand absently stroked her back, just feeling the smooth skin drawn over muscles and bones finer than porcelain.

"Does your family live around here?" Reynaud asked, then bit his tongue.

"Dad died of a heart attack about three years ago. Mom and my older brother, Ted, died of the plague." Her eyes welled with tears and he stroked her shoulder.

"You don't have to talk about anything that hurts."

She wiped away the tears, swallowed hard, and waited until her voice was steady. "Talking or not, it's past."

They lay together in an embrace that was more affection than passion then Angie asked, "What about your family?"

"Port Arthur took a nuke." It came out sounding more brutal than he'd intended. "I'm sorry. It's mostly scar tissue now. I don't know whether it was good or bad that Logan, the Deacon, and I all got the news at the same time. I think we were all pretty much prepared for it."

He stroked her hair and kissed the tip of her nose. "We're being entirely too serious. I could probably tell stories about Logan but not many are fit for mixed company."

Angie chuckled.

"Now that is a beautiful sound. I'd like to hear it more often."

"Does he actually believe he's related to the Lone Ranger and the Green Hornet?"

"You know, I really don't know. We all went a little crazy, each in our own way, in that prison camp. Maybe he flips a coin every day."

"Were you all in that place together?"

"No. We lost two on the way to Krakow, an Englishman in Krakow, and Steve in Texas. We met up with Hasteen in Texas and Mario and Xuan in Springfield."

"Losing them was like losing family, wasn't it?"

After a moment's thought he nodded. "Yeah, I think you could call it the brotherhood of shared dangers. You come to depend upon each other, and it's really intense. It really makes you understand other vets better. They might not have been in the same battles—hell, they might not even have been in the same war, but there's still a sense of camaraderie."

Angie kissed him on the forehead. "Maybe that's why I feel so attracted to you."

"Damn! And I thought it was because of my classic good looks, witty repartee, and dazzling conversation." He laughed.

"I like that sound, too. I don't remember hearing you laugh before." She leaned toward him and kissed him tenderly on the lips.

He returned the kiss and what had been gentle became passionate, and she responded in the same way.

His voice came out hoarse. "Are you really sure you want to do this?"

"I'm sure."

The emotion and the passion became the same.

~ * ~

Reynaud woke first and gently kissed her lips and eyelids, then started to draw his arm out from under her. She made a happy sound in her throat and snuggled closer.

Reynaud felt trapped. Angie was obviously happy with the closeness and, he admitted to himself, so was he, but the heat and his own sweat were oppressive. It was impossible for him to sleep again, so his free left hand began a gentle exploration that became more captivating than a trip back to the creek would've been.

Eventually, the moving fingers roused Angie and started again the foreplay leading to another coupling, this time with Angie atop him. His hips bucked, while her back arched, then she slowly and softly collapsed on him. His hands again caressed her back, her hair, the line of her cheekbones, and when they were basking in languid satisfaction he grinned at her. "Seems a shame to leave, when I'll just be trying to get back in again before we know it." He stroked her hair again. "I don't mean to scare you off, but I think I'm falling seriously in love with you."

She studied his face intently, as though to find a lurking smile to let her dismiss what he'd said as a joke, then she stroked his cheek—the one without the burn. "Are you sure you want to do that? Being close to me hasn't been very lucky for anyone, lately."

"It's been lucky for me," he replied. "I'm feeling alive again, for the first time in a very long time. I guess I'm being selfish, too, if that's what you were when you wanted to feel alive."

"Well," she said, with a slightly rueful smile, "I got my wish—I do feel completely alive again. In a way, it's a little scary. When you feel really alive, you start to worry about being hurt or dying."

"That's just because life's become worthwhile again." He was suddenly uncomfortable with the nakedness of the conversation, which was more revealing than his physical nudity. "Personally, I'd feel a lot livelier with another bath."

Angie withdrew from him then rolled off the bed. "That's one thing we can agree on." Gathering her clothes, she waited for Reynaud to find his pants and his shotgun, and together they walked back to the river. Judging by the sun, the day had aged into almost noon, and the cold water was like a blessing, washing away the heat and the sweat.

When they finally felt completely revived they stepped onto the bank and he watched her dress. It was, somehow, as exciting as watching her take her clothes off, and Angie was now, dressed, more exciting than she'd been before, simply because he's become so intimately familiar with the body beneath the bulky uniform. He pulled on his own pants and, arm in arm, they strolled back to the house.

"Do you want something to eat?" she asked.

Reynaud chuckled. "Yeah, but you're dressed now."

Angie smiled and said, "Maybe for dessert." From the pantry they chose a couple of dusty jars at random and took them outside. Reynaud primed the pump and drew water so sweet and clear it was a delicacy. One of the jars contained pickled okra and the other held peaches. They added a couple of sticks of dried meat and feasted.

Reynaud, for the first time he could remember since before the war, felt at peace. It was more than being happy and content; it was the return of a sense of fun that bubbled in him like champagne. He felt as though he were back in college and on a picnic. He ate and drank slowly, often looking at Angie to appreciate her beauty from different angles, enjoying each moment, storing each impression in a treasure-house in his mind.

"When did Hasteen and Andy say they'd be back?" he asked.

"Either late this evening or early in the morning."

"I really hate to waste the time," he said. "Would you care to go for a walk in the woods with me?"

"Aren't you supposed to be convalescing?"

"I'm afraid if I stay flat on my back, I'll be a lot more sore than if I get a little exercise."

They returned to the campsite early enough to cook dinner before the fire would stand out in the darkness, but neither Andy nor Hasteen had returned, and as darkness fell, they shared the bedroom downstairs, although they didn't get to sleep until after midnight.

Angie was preparing breakfast when Hasteen and Andy returned, two hours after dawn. Hasteen grinned at Reynaud. "You're looking better than you have in a while."

"Rest and good food agrees with me," Reynaud said, "but you're not looking so good. What's up?"

"We linked up with Logan yesterday and heard the news on the radio—"

"The radio?"

"Yeah, the Steel Fist has a working radio station out of Mountain Home. Anyway, Mario, Ross, and Xuan have a real problem."

"What kind of problem?"

"It could be a real fatal problem. The Steel Fist has sicced an elite squad on them, and it might get worse. They might just track them right to Gassville."

~ * ~

As soon as the sky had lightened enough to let them see their way, Mario and Xuan headed east, eating as they scrambled through rough country. They halted at midmorning, Mario often turning to stare at their back-trail.

Xuan removed his headband, wrung it out, and tied it around his brow again. "Something bothering you?"

Mario nodded. "I've got an uncomfortable feeling, and I've learned the hard way to pay attention to feelings like that. They're right too often to ignore. Do you know where we're going?"

"Roughly. Ross mentioned a place ahead called Ware's Chapel, or something like that. I gathered he was going to keep heading east until we ran into a big river, then follow that north to—"

"Shit!" Mario snatched up his binoculars and scanned the mountainside behind them. "I saw a flash. Somebody got sloppy. I'd bet anything somebody is using field glasses to try to find us, and the flash was from the lenses. It's a good thing we're going east. If we'd been headed the other way, they'd have had us before we'd seen them."

"Ambush?"

"Maybe, but it might be ticklish. If they're following our trail, they're pretty good. We don't know what else they might be good at."

"How far?"

"It's hard to say." Mario frowned. "I only saw the flash once. They're using cover I'd guess, about twelve hundred meters, but I could be off by two or three hundred meters either way. Anyway, we're too damned close. We'd better start moving but not making tracks."

"That won't be easy. If we stay in the trees, it's difficult to avoid leaving traces, and if we go to the rocks, they'll see us."

"We'd better break off our track. If we keep going due east, they're liable to try to get ahead of us or radio for a committee. I only like surprise parties when I'm the one doing the surprising."

Xuan turned his head as though sniffing their possible routes. "North or south?"

Mario hesitated. Going south would take Xuan and himself further away from the rendezvous point but going north would possibly endanger the rest of the group. "Let's go northeast for a couple of miles then break to the southeast."

Xuan was already on his feet and he began to trot northeast. Just before noon, Mario sighted a cross on the horizon and halted to train his binoculars on it.

"Looks like a church steeple. That may be Ware's Chapel. We'll turn southeast now, which should put us between those two mountains." He pointed to where a pair of mountains stood against the sky.

An hour and a half later, they faced the pair of mountains

and began to scale the northern slope of the southern mountain, but a little over halfway up they ran out of cover and confronted a stretch of bald stone extending for a little over fifty yards, and both up and down for nearly a quarter of a mile.

Mario studied the stone face. The rock was rugged enough to provide some cover. After checking to make sure his rifle was well secured, he dashed across to the first boulder offering safety. He'd just gained the boulder when a bullet hit the rock face behind him and whined away. He counted the time until he heard the rifle's report.

"He's shooting from about seven hundred yards back," Mario shouted to Xuan. "He's really pretty good. Let me get set before you make your move." He slipped to a position from which he could cover Xaun's run to cover.

Xuan was still ten feet away from the boulder when Mario saw a flash and snapped off a shot. Xuan dived behind the rock, his left shoulder bleeding from rock chips thrown by the near miss.

"He's getting the range," Xuan said. "Think you got him?"

"I don't think so, but he may be a little less eager to try it again." They crawled as far as the shelter of the boulder extended then Mario took up a firing position. "Do you want to be the little duck in the shooting gallery?"

Xuan twisted until he'd gathered his feet under him, then he sprang out of cover and, dodging as he ran, raced for the next boulder. Just before he ducked behind the rock he heard Mario's rifle crash and, two or three seconds later, a distant gunshot.

Mario sprinted toward him, staying as low as possible, and finally reached cover with his rifle held high to protect it. "I think I might've got him that time," Mario said. Another bullet spattered the rock just above them and Mario glanced sidelong at Xuan. "Or maybe I didn't." He studied the way before them. "That sniper is trying to pin us down long enough for his buddies to close in on us." He paused a moment. "The last time he fired, while you were running, he shot at me. If you feel like taking chances, I'm going to suggest we break our pattern and screw with his head. It's twenty yards from the trees here, and the next piece of cover is five yards away. Go for the cover, but as soon as you're able to, go ahead and make your break. I'm going to hold my fire to see if I can't coax him into showing himself."

"If you miss him, he's going to get a free shot at you when you move," Xuan observed.

Mario licked his lips. "Believe me, I've thought about that, but we have to keep moving. If they've got a machine gunner along, he's got to be getting close enough to start opening up on us, and then the excrement will really hit the oscillator."

"About how far?"

"He might open up just about any time, if he's got a tripod, but these guys are traveling fast and light. With a bipod or bracing it on a tree limb or some such, I'd say four hundred yards, max."

Xuan flipped up the sight for the grenade launcher on the M-16. "This thing will reach out half that far."

"Don't forget, they've almost certainly got launchers, too. If you want to play 'duelling grenades' with them, wait until we get off these rocks. If they get a chance to use all their toys on us, we won't need body bags—a damp blotter will do the job."

Xuan clutched the M-16 and raced for the next rock, ducking, even spinning, giving the sniper no good shots. He slipped behind the rock and, almost instantly, broke from the far side, still presenting only the most difficult possible target. A bullet caromed off the stone behind him and, seconds later, a second slug struck just in front of him.

"Got you now, you bastard," Mario breathed, and squeezed off his shot.

A grenade exploded forty yards short, and Mario took the time to sling his rifle, broke straight for the rock nearest him, then began to dodge as he made his final run into the trees. Bullets whined and buzzed around him, none coming very close then he heard the racket of the machine gun.

Xuan waited for him in the trees. "I'm tired of running. Let's kill them. We'll never have a better place."

Mario waited until he'd caught his breath. "All right, you go up, I'll go down. Remember, shots and grenades carry further when you're shooting at an angle." He looked back the way they'd come. "Watch out for some of this crowd taking the long way around. They may send riflemen ahead to secure the rock. And if you don't have to, don't shoot anything less than a man with a launcher or the machine gun."

"How many, do you think?"

"The sniper's history. They've still got a hogman, probably a launcher, maybe two, and at least three riflemen. Add a tracker or two. That should do it."

Xuan's only reply was to move up the slope where he could intercept a man coming around the bare rock or have a clear shot at troops trying to cross it, choosing a place under an overhang with a fallen tree to protect his front and his left flank. Using his binoculars, he watched Mario setting up behind a slight ridge of stone surrounded by a clump of trees.

Xuan unslung the Armalite and laid it across the log in front of him, taking care to make sure the scope didn't reflect sunlight back to the area around the rock field. A flicker of movement drew his attention to the trees at the far end of the rock. Moments later, a man stepped out of cover and Xuan dropped the field glasses to use the scope on his Armalite.

The man wore tiger-stripe camouflage instead of the usual U.S. Army pattern and a floppy-brimmed "boonie" hat. The rifle he carried was a bullpup design, making it as short as a submachine gun, and it had the flowing lines of something futuristic. The enemy darted along the way he and Mario had taken. From where Xuan lay, the man had almost no cover at all, but Xuan let the man reach the trees on his side without firing.

As soon as the first man concealed himself, a second soldier started across. He wore a different camouflage pattern and a helmet obscured by foliage. He carried one of the AK assault rifles. Xuan studied the area of brush the man had come from and, at first, saw nothing then he noticed a patch of dark green.

He simply stared at the spot before he realized it was a beret. Once he had part of the puzzle, he began to notice the shape in front of the man, its outline obscured. It had to be the machine gun. After swinging the rifle to the side, he found the gunner's position again with his naked eye, then set down the rifle, picked up the M-16 with the launcher, and sighted in.

A flash and a distant roar showed him the grenade had hit within a few feet of his target. The gun was flung out onto the rock and another man, a backpack radio strapped to his back, fell almost atop the gunner's body.

A grenade hit the overhang above him and Xuan tried to get

beneath the tree for cover. Because of the overhang, most of the shrapnel was blown away from him, but some slammed into the log and a shower of rock shards fell to the ground. Opening the launcher's action, he stuffed in another grenade, slammed the action shut then swung the barrel up again. A hail of gunfire hit all around him, forcing him to burrow for cover.

They had his position. All they had to do was keep firing, keep him down until one of them was close enough to toss a grenade, or even just walk up and execute him. For the first time, he realized he might die on this slope.

Another grenade hit only a few yards short of the dead tree and Xuan, even behind the tree, was stunned by the concussion. He began to crawl toward where some of the gnarled roots of the trunk had been torn from the ground, giving him better shelter.

After what seemed hours, he reached the roots and peered out. A man with an M-16 and a launcher ran from the last boulder of the field to the forest. Xuan pointed the M-16 he'd taken at the figure and fired but the man showed no sign of being hit. Swinging the muzzle after the running man, he squeezed the trigger again, but the weapon seemed dead in his hands. His left index finger groped for the launcher's trigger, and he winced as his arm cramped, then Mario's rifle spoke and the man spun, blood spurting out of his chest.

A puff of smoke and the sound of its odd report revealed where a second launcher had been fired and he lobbed his own grenade at the spot. In the glare of the blast, he could see a body flung forward, the weapon still in its hands.

Xuan dropped back behind the tree as bullets began to smack into the trunk or clip at the roots. The problem with most secure positions, he now realized, was that they were as hard to escape from as to attack. After yanking back the M-16's charging handle, he swung the barrel over the log, and squeezed the trigger. Again the rifle fired a single round and stopped.

Drawing the weapon back, he looked at the action then saw the ragged hole in the forearm where shrapnel had ripped through. The damned rifle was worthless, except as a clumsy repeater. Reloading the launcher, he heard Mario's rifle again. A body fell off the overhang and lay on the brush only feet from the log.

He had to be able to give cover to Mario, too, or the rest of this squad would outflank them. Bobbing up from behind the log, he fired the grenade at the edge of the stone field, where the first two soldiers went to ground, and heard a rifle being fired at him from uncomfortably near. He reloaded the launcher again and fired his last grenade in the direction of the sound of rifle fire, then dropped the all but useless weapon and scurried back to where he'd left his Armalite lying across the log.

It was gone. Looking around wildly, he found it at the base of the overhang. It'd apparently been hit by shrapnel and concussion from one of the near misses. The scope was shattered and the stock was bent at a strange angle from its attachment point at the rear of the receiver.

He heard the whisper of cloth against brush and twisted to see the man with the space-age rifle aiming it at him.

The man was hidden from Mario by a clump of trees, and Xuan was too far from the tree trunk to duck behind it for cover. The Armalite lay another four feet from him, well out of reach. Xuan rolled, clawing for his Automag, hoping he could stay alive long enough to kill the man who'd kill him.

A gout of blood sprang from the man's breast, then Xuan heard the sharp crack of a rifle. It was louder than a .223, not as sharp, nor as loud as Mario's magnum. The man spun, fell, lay twitching.

Xuan scrambled after the man's rifle, scooped it up, and ducked into the clump of trees. The bullpup rifle had a tinted plastic magazine, which was still over half full of cartridges, and a telescopic sight that doubled as part of the carrying handle. The gun was thicker and heavier than it looked at first glance, and he handled it with care, because it had no trigger guard. Instead, a section of plastic swept up from the bottom of the pistol grip to the bottom of the frame, making a loop to accommodate all the fingers of the shooting hand. The balance was butt-heavy, but not too awkward.

Chancing a look back at Mario's position, he noticed one of the squad behind and far to Mario's right. The trooper hadn't yet seen Mario, but was working his way slowly to the sniper's position. Xuan raised the unfamiliar rifle and sighted through the scope, finding the sight centered on a small circle rather than a crosshairs. Placing the circle on the soldier's back, just below the neck, he squeezed the trigger.

The rifle barked and the bullet hit low, below the bottom of the shoulder blades, and Xuan heard the man howl. Mario's rifle crashed again as he shot at something on the other side of the stone field, and Xuan put a second bullet into the wounded man's head, holding higher with the shot.

Keeping the rifle at his shoulder, Xuan stalked through the brush. The man he'd just killed hadn't looked like the second man across the rock. That left at least one of the squad still alive. He studied the way before him, being certain he was using the cover to his best advantage, and he stopped to watch and listen every step or so.

The rifle that wasn't Mario's crashed again, and the last Steel Fist soldier stumbled, stiff-legged, out of the trees, his rifle clattering as it fell from limp arms. The man staggered in a circle, staring with sightless, stunned eyes. Xuan raised his rifle but knew it would be a wasted shot. The man took a single, shambling step back in the direction of the trees then pitched forward onto his face.

Xuan hooked the sling of the rifle he carried over his neck, so it hung across his chest, ready for quick use.

"Don't git too comfortable," a rough voice grated. "I'll give you jist long enough to git what you need, then you 'n your buddy git your asses outta my woods."

Xuan scowled as he raised his hands. He'd been humiliated again, assuming the enemy of his enemy was his friend then disarming himself.

"You don't need to play cowboys," the voice said. "You jist take a breath wrong, an' this ol' thutty-thutty'll blow your guts to Little Rock."

"What's the matter?" Mario shouted.

Xuan slowly turned his head to the general area where Mario was hidden, but not near enough to give away his position. "The man who helped us isn't very friendly."

"I'd 'a killed you right off, but you was shootin' at them vermin," the voice said. "I don't cotton to strangers, but I really got no use for them weasels. You take what you need offen them bodies, then git, you an' your friend both."

Xuan lowered his hands, clutching at his left forearm, which was beginning to throb again, and returned to the overhang. Bending down, he picked up the battered Armalite. The buttstock came off in his hands. Storing the butt in his backpack, he slung the rifle over his shoulder. The man Mario had shot off the overhang lay like a bundle of rags. Xuan took the ammunition the man carried, along with a couple of hand grenades then picked up the M4 beside the body. "You want any of these guns?" he shouted to the voice in the shadows.

"Take 'em or break 'em," the voice shouted back.

After rendering the weapon safe, he smashed it on a rock, and did the same with the broken rifle and its launcher, for which he had no more grenades. The body whose rifle he'd taken had four more magazines, two of them fully loaded. He loaded one of the fresh magazines in the weapon, reloaded the magazines left with rounds from the M-16 magazines, which he discarded, then moved on to the body on the rocks. It still carried two canteens and a pack in which he found several MRE, military issue complete meals which were a vast improvement over the iron rations he and Mario carried. He took the pack and the canteens. The man also wore a pistol belt and revolver that looked familiar. If it wasn't the Cajun's, it was enough like it to make a set. He took the rig off the corpse, along with spare magazines for the rifle. When he added the AK to his load, he decided he'd just about reached the limit of the weight he could carry.

While Xuan stripped the last body, Mario shouted to the man still hidden in the forest. "We'd like nothing better than to be out of your territory, but where are we? And what's the quickest way to get to Gassville?"

"This mountain you're standin' on is Warrior Creek Mountain. T'other one is Hand Mountain. Ya jist keep goin' 'til you run inta the White River. It's a big 'un. Follow it north. You oughtta be able to find somebody else to bother for directions after that."

Xuan had taken the last body's rifle and ammunition, and he strode eastward, while Mario, staying in cover, followed. Two miles away from the ambush site, Mario stepped out of the trees and took some of the extra weapons and ammunition.

Looking over the weapons, he said, "Those clowns must've been some kind of special outfit. That, or they were damned well-equipped bandits."

"Bandits don't usually wear rank badges."

"An elite outfit, then." He glanced at the rifle Xuan wore across his chest. "You got a Steyr AUG there." He explained how the weapon was operated, then looked at the little black automatic carbine from the last body. "Valmet. M-82, I think. It's a bullpup AK design. It looks like these guys had weapons and choice of gear, not the standard issue stuff. Let's hope they don't have more where those came from." Making sure the extra ammunition he carried was well-secured, he pointed ahead. "We've got a river to find."

CHAPTER 11

Andy led Hasteen, Reynaud and Angie through the dim forest where, three times, they'd been challenged by sentries since they'd passed wide around the town of Summit. They found Logan, the Deacon, and almost half a dozen other men and women crouched around a carefully hidden campfire. After they'd made their greetings, someone handed them slices of ham and bits of cornbread on strips of bark for a plate, and cups of coffee laced with chicory.

Reynaud bit into a piece of cornbread, then found Logan in the gloom. "How'd you find out they had a radio station?"

"I found an old transistor radio in the raid at the junction. The other night, after I called Springfield, I was just fiddling around and turned the radio on. They were playing some gospel-type music that'd knock ticks off a dog then they had a 'news' spot. Turned out, some of the locals knew about the station too, and they just figured we already knew. Anyway, they run 'news' at six in the morning and seven and nine at night. During part of the day and all evening they run either gospel music that makes you want to convert to atheism or something that sounds like a cross between country-western and military marches. Kinda like Hail to the Chief being played on a threshing machine."

Reynaud glanced at his watch. "I guess Dr. Goebbels will strike up the band in about fifteen minutes. Did you hear anything else new and interesting?"

"Just rumors." Logan shoved another log into the fire with the toe of his boot. "There's supposed to be a lot of sniping and little raids around Harrison now. Some people think the Fayetteville crowd are still pissed at being attacked and are putting on a little heat of their own, others say it's people who were run out by the Steel Fist come back to collect some rent. Haven't heard anything on the radio that'd confirm it, though.

"The convoys have changed a lot, too," Logan went on. "According to some of the fellas, they used to run a lot of three-vehicle convoys all around the northeastern part of the state. Now, they never run less than six vehicles, and only between Harrison and Mountain Home. They also run a lot of patrols further out now. The convoys are heavy on troop trucks, and it looks like most of the gunnies are stayin' in Harrison. I don't know whether that means they're trying to re-start the poison gas production, or that Harrison is just the border they've decided they have to defend."

"They're scared," one of the locals said, "and they're just like rats; they're dangerous when they're cornered."

Logan poured himself another cup of coffee. "I don't like feelin' crowded, Rennie, and I don't like crowdin' you, but we gotta make the big push soon. These clowns are startin' to gas towns where they usta just collect 'taxes,' then send a clean-up squad to take everything they can use. Nobody wants to pull a little raid for fear the Steel Fist'll wipe out a couple-three towns as a reprisal. And the resistance is gettin' too big to keep hidden. It looks like we're gonna have anywhere from seventy to over a hundred people with us when we hit Mountain Home.

"That's good," Reynaud said, and leaned back, grateful for the dimness keeping his face hidden. Seventy or more people meant more firepower—and many more things that could go wrong. That many people would be harder to hide, would be more likely to make mistakes that'd spoil ambushes, and would be more likely to have spies. It also meant losses would go up in action. Logan was right: Reynaud was being forced into action by the situation. "About time for the 'news,' isn't it."

Everyone huddled closer as Logan snapped the radio on.

"Good evening, brothers and sisters, this is the Voice of Freedom." Whoever the announcer was, Reynaud thought, the bastard's voice could end an oil shortage.

"Late this afternoon, the First Rangers reported they'd be returning, having tracked down six vicious killers who'd been terrorizing communities from Verona to the area around Hand Mountain. Their spree of violence was ended in a short battle, in which two of the Rangers were reported to be lightly wounded."

Logan grinned. "He don't lie that well. If he's talkin' about Mario and the boys, he got the count wrong. Whattaya wanna bet we'll hear a different version tomorrow?"

"Maybe," Reynaud said, and waved Logan to silence.

"Bandit activity has become a minor problem around Harrison, but Captain Miller assures us his Soldiers of God have the situation well in hand, and he expects to report the bandits all dead or captured within the next two or three days."

"I guess the rumors about more guerrillas around Harrison are true," Hasteen said.

"Sabotage by the bandits has forced us to temporarily suspend production of fertilizer and insecticide for our farmers. We ask you all to be sparing in your use of fertilizer, and to turn in any unused insecticide to your electman."

"Sounds like they're tryin' to whip together more of the poison gas," Logan observed.

"Rumors persist about a new outbreak of plague, after the populations of two more villages of the un-chosen succumbed within a few hours. Electman Davenport has pronounced this outbreak of plague God's judgment, striking down those not of the Chosen."

"The lyin' sack 'a shit," one of the locals growled. "Them towns was gassed. God didn't have nothin' to do with it. More like the devil."

"Amen, brother," the Deacon chipped in.

"And now, brothers and sisters, I am honored to bring you Robert Davenport, the select of the elect, the head of the Chosen."

"Blessings and good evening, brothers and sisters," said a voice that made Reynaud's hackles rise. Glancing at Hasteen and Logan, he could see, even in the near-darkness, they also recognized the tones and rhythm of the voice. The voice of the father was so much like that of the son it was like listening to a ghost.

"…judgment of God has been passed against the defilers of the One True Way. I have been told by God Himself that these hard times are merely a test of our faith, a momentary darkness before the Chosen pass into the greater light of paradise on earth. God has told me, and our agricultural experts have assured me, the crops this year will produce a surplus. Some of that surplus will be offered, in Christian charity, to some of the unbelievers around us, another part will be traded to wealthy unbelievers to acquire for our people the few items not manufactured by our skilled workers—"

Logan snapped off the radio. "I can't listen to any more of that shit. Hell, I don't know why the announcer was bitchin' about a shortage of fertilizer; there was enough bullshit in that last speech to make all of west Texas the garden spot of the universe." He rose and kicked dirt onto the fire until it appeared to be out. "Well, Rennie, what do you think of finishin' this?"

"It's like motherhood: I'm in favor of it, I'm just not exactly sure how to go about it."

"You might have a better chance at motherhood," Logan said.

"First, how closely are you checking the recruits?"

"Pretty close. Anybody new has to be vouched for by at least two of the old hands. Anybody who can't pass that test is quietly and politely sent off to work mischief on his or her own."

"The best we can do is the best we can do," Reynaud said. "The second thing that comes to mind is we're going to need to hit at least three places at once." He held up three fingers. "First, there's the p-camp near Mountain Home—if there's anybody still alive there." He folded down his index finger. "Second, we need to secure Bull Shoals Dam. It's the source of all the electric power in Mountain Home and all the area around it. It could also be used to threaten anyone downriver of the dam. We need to remove that threat." He crooked his ring finger. "Third, we need to find out where their air force is operating from and take it out. We have to hit at night, and if we don't have the air force rubbed out, they'll blow us all away the next morning." He continued to hold his middle finger up. "And that's what I think of the Steel Fist." He closed his hand into a fist. "Any ideas about how we can accomplish any of the above?"

"Yeah," Logan said. "The planes are supposed to be usin' Lahar Field, just to the southwest of Mountain Home, and sometimes, as an auxiliary airstrip, Marian County Regional Airport. If we hit Lahar Field at night, we should catch the planes bedded down."

"That's fine, but do you know the lay of the land, or the defenses?"

"Not really. I've heard they have some kind of observation post at the airfield, but I'm not sure just what they've got there. Somebody said they thought the Steel Fist had pulled the infra-red and starlight gear out of some tanks and are usin' that."

"The stuff in the old M-48s was pretty primitive," Reynaud said, hoping no one would contradict him.

One of the locals spat into the darkness. "I got some bad

news for you, boy. I was in the guard, and at least one batch was upgraded. They got starlight for some of the machines that makes midnight just like high noon. You can go lookin' for the OP, but don't get too close for a real good look, or we'll hafta notify your next of kin."

Reynaud was struck by a sudden thought. "How many vets have we got here, Logan?"

"Most've these guys are. Not too many of 'em saw combat, but we've gotta whole lotta people who put in two years or more. There's even a half dozen or so, like Ross, who shook loose of Fort Len Wood."

"Have we got any artillerymen?"

The local spoke up again. "Give me a few hours, I could probably find you a decent gun crew, maybe two."

"Do it." Reynaud stared into the darkness by his feet. "Logan, you and Hasteen and I are taking a little trip tomorrow. We'll need a couple of guides, people who know their way around Mountain Home and the region around it. I don't like the idea of going in on an attack cold. I want to see what I'm going to hit."

"I'm going too," Angie said.

Reynaud put his arm around her. "Better not. I'd spend all my time worrying about you. It might take the edge off."

"What makes you think I'm better qualified to worry?" she demanded.

Sensing he was fighting a losing battle, Reynaud gave her a quick hug. "All right, but be packed light and ready to go as soon as there's light to see by." He thought for a moment. "Something else. Is there any way to catch Mario and the others? I'd rather they didn't go on to Gassville. I'm afraid there's going to be too many people there as it is, and the Steel Fist might catch that large a crowd.

"I think I might be able to find 'em," another local said. "They'll probably be followin' White River north. Where do you want us to move 'em?"

"That's the next problem," Reynaud said. "From the maps I've seen, White River's about two hundred yards wide. Getting across a river that size is going to be a neat trick. Getting a lot of people across it without being caught is going to be nearly impossible."

"It's tough," the same man who'd offered to find Mario and

his team said, "but not nearly impossible. The first thing to do is find the best place to cross. The only bridges in the area are the dam itself, and the bridge at Cotter. You can bet your ass them home-grown Nazis are gonna have a garrison in Cotter that's loaded for bear. The best place to get across has gotta be where the Litha River branches off of White River, north of Bayless Island. Any further south, and they'll spot your sign from a radio tower."

"How about it, Bood? You know the area well enough to get us across there?"

"Might be able to get, say, half a dozen people across there, especially if we use something like a log to mask what we're doin'. I probably know the area on the other side a' the river as well as anybody. With Orrin, I think I can get you around and back."

As they went to bedrolls in the woods, Logan handed Reynaud a web pistol belt with a .45 automatic in an old leather holster. "I know you prefer something with a little more heft than a nine mike-mike. By the way, you never worried about me."

"Because you're ugly. Thanks for the pistol. I'd been feeling about half-naked."

Reynaud bedded down beside Angie. As much as he wanted her, the presence of so many men around them brought all their inhibitions back in a rush. Instead, they slept together, wrapped in an embrace.

They were on their way into the stronghold of the Steel Fist by first light, and late afternoon found them across White River, deep in enemy territory.

~ * ~

Davenport set down the transcriptions of the latest report from Captain Miller in Harrison. Either the man was a total idiot or he thought Davenport was. The man had put a roseate glow on everything, but the fact remained a large convoy had been lost to ambushers, along with the prisoners.

And the mess just kept getting deeper. They'd lost the trails of several groups. The men were losing their nerve, not pursuing aggressively enough. They were so afraid of being shot at they'd lost their morale.

The most motivated, their ranger team, had been out of contact for over a day, which did not bode well. They were an elite team and any group large enough to wipe them out had to have a lot of troops and heavy firepower.

Some of his troops complained about not using enough gas. They had too little of it left to do more than one or two raids. Even if they'd had enough, simply spraying it wholesale with the hope of killing the enemy would be stupid. The attackers were too dispersed for him to gas more than a handful and the most likely areas to catch them were too close to their own forces. The Steel Fist had too few gas masks to issue them to everyone.

He'd put what he had to spare to better use; wiping out a few small towns. The loss of a few civilians had little direct military value but it had cut down on the random small attacks. Anyone inclined to try a little sniping or sabotage would think long and hard when they knew their families would be caught in reprisals.

Still, it was only a stopgap tactic. He knew something was building—he could feel it, could almost smell it.

He supposed Rutledge expected him to play Hitler in the bunker.

Easy for Rutledge to hide and give the orders. Davenport had an escape plan and it seemed an excellent time to put it into action. If Arkansas fell, he could find enough excuses to avoid liquidation and live to fight another day. If Colonel Seiler managed to actually defeat the enemy, he could return as a conquering hero. He must cut his losses and take what victories he could.

~ * ~

Reynaud approached Mario and Xuan, his hand extended. "Good to see you again. Where's Ross?"

"He's dead," Mario said. He shook the proffered hand, then gave Reynaud a bottle of clear liquid, from which he'd just taken a drink. "We were just toasting him. Have a drink."

Reynaud accepted the bottle, held his breath while he took a drink of white mule, then held his breath for as long as he could. When he finally drew in a deep breath, it was to cough. "Jeez, don't these guys take the corn off the cob first? Sorry to hear about Ross. Logan said he was a good man."

"He died well," Xuan said, shaking Reynaud's hand. For the first time, Reynaud noticed the bandage around Xuan's left forearm and the ugly bruise on his left wrist. Xuan noticed Reynaud gazing at the dressings. "They're only an inconvenience," he rasped. "They're healing."

"Do you think you'd be able to use a weapon with either hand?"

"I can."

"Good, because I have a job for you, and you're about the only one who can do it. Mario, I have a different job for you, and it's going to be tough. I want you to lead the attack on the dam. If you get there before dark you can recon it, and I can give you seven men for help. That's all we have gas masks for."

"We've got three masks, and twice as many extra filters," Mario said.

"Very good," Reynaud said. "I'll find you three more men. The only good news is we don't expect you to take and hold the dam, just keep the troops there from blowing it up or wrecking the power generating equipment. I want you to take the masks because they might have some kind of gas bombs there for defense. We'll try to get reinforcements to you as soon as we can, but it'll probably take a day or so. Are you willing to tackle it?"

"I'm willing to try. Can we hit them from both ends of the dam?"

"I wish we could, but the eastern end is on a hook of land that's too easy to defend against infiltration. It looks like it might be a last-stand choice for them; a handful of troops there could hold off a larger force as long as their supplies hold out."

"Okay," Mario said, "wish me luck."

"That's about the best I can do," Reynaud replied.

Before Mario and the men with him were out of sight, Reynaud faced Xuan and the two locals who remained.

"Let's get this show on the road." He helped waterproof the dressing on Xuan's forearm, then they crossed the river, using a log for concealment. One of the locals stayed behind to hide their trail out of the river, while the rest of the group pressed on.

"The job I have in mind for you—" Reynaud said, "do you remember that suit we got in Springfield? The anti-infrared, with starlight camo?"

"Yes."

"If you think you can handle it, you'll need to hit one of the observation posts the Steel Fist has outside the airfield. It's like a foundation of their defense system. There are two OPs by the airfield, just to the west of the base. One's northeast of the field, the other southwest of it. East of the airfield are open fields of crops all the way to the prison camp, then more fields to the edge of town. The crops are less than waist-high, so cover is damned limited."

"How are you going to get to the camp to hit it?"

"The hard way. We're going to have to send people way around the base to get into the fields and they're going to have to crawl a couple of miles to get into position around the camp. They'll probably have left before we get back to our base camp. They'll push off as soon as it's dark enough to move safely.

"The rest of us will hit Lahar Field. As soon as we've got it anywhere near secured, we grab what vehicles we can, and about half the strike force will hit the p-camp."

"It sounds complicated."

"A lot more complicated than I'm comfortable with, but the Steel Fist didn't lay out their installations with our convenience in mind. There are a few things going for us; there's no fence around the airfield, although they planted a few landmines, most of them in places where the OP coverage is limited. They also planted some in the woods nearest the OPs. We've cleared paths through that patch.

"The p-camp has a fence and, outside it, a vehicle trench, and its only opening is at the gate. Besides the guard towers like the ones at Harrison, it's also got a guard station right over the one entrance to the camp. We'll have to knock that out before we can get trucks into the place, otherwise they'll shoot our trucks to pieces before we can even get close to the gate."

"How about armor?"

"No tanks, either place, but two APCs at the airfield, and two more at the p-camp. They have artillery at the airfield, and we've got one good gun crew, and one that can get by. The artillery may be what saves our asses, if we can grab it."

They halted to rest in a glen, and Reynaud changed the dressing on Xuan's wound, which had begun to bleed again. To Reynaud, the wound appeared to be clean, but he would've felt better if there were a doctor to take a look at it. "Are you sure you can operate with that?" he asked.

Xuan flexed his left hand a few times. "It's a little stiff, but I can manage."

"They're supposed to have a med station at the airfield, sort of a rough medevac station, and a clinic in Mountain Home. It'd be nice to get our people patched up." He finished rebinding the bullet hole then remembered another problem. "You got the Walther back from Hasteen, right?"

Xuan patted the shirt at his waist.

"How much ammo you got for it?"

"Twenty rounds."

"Good. Remember to take Logan's Makarov, too. Your part of the mission is the trickiest. I want you to take out the observation post quietly. You've got to take it out to let the rest of us in."

Xuan only nodded.

They reached the rest of the group as the sun was going down behind the western mountains. Logan and even the Deacon broke into broad smiles when they saw Xuan, and Logan, when Reynaud reminded him, handed over the suppressed Makarov.

"The shells in the magazine are the last ones I've got. Invest them wisely."

"Where's Hasteen?" Reynaud asked.

"He went for one more recon," Logan replied. "And we've got bad news; one of the C-47s took off about an hour and a half ago and hasn't gotten back yet. Looks like they put it down somewhere else—probably Marian County Regional."

"Damn!" Reynaud slapped the buttstock of his shotgun. "That gunship can hurt us bad. Any ideas what to do about it?"

"Yeah," Logan said, "the same idea I had earlier. Look, I've been in the back seat of a Bronco—I know how the thing works. Once I'm airborne, I'll go get the gun-toting gooney bird. Either I'll nail it on the ground at Marian, or I'll pull an intercept."

"You're just itching to play 'Steve Canyon.' I don't remember a hell of a lot about Broncos, but it seems to me they have a warm-up time that's going to leave you vulnerable for several minutes."

"You just do your jobs," Logan retorted, "and I'll be fine."

Reynaud handed Xuan a couple of strips of dried meat, then started on his own dinner. "Noel," he said, "you try to capture the personnel carrier parked by the control tower. The Deacon thinks we have to wipe out the C-47 at the end of the airstrip. If he doesn't knock it out, rake it with your fifty-cal. Clobber either the cockpit or an engine. Your major job, though, is to haul the second ape crew to the APC parked by the artillery. You've got to hit the artie battery and rub out their gun crews. It's not going to be easy: it looks like they've dug in and built their barracks underground next to the gun emplacements.

"Logan, you and Billy Joe have to take out the barracks at the end of the airstrip. Deak, I want that gunship aced. If you can get a grenade into the open bays, you might be able to set off the ammo inside it."

"His hand will guide me," Billy Joe intoned.

"I hope so. Your next job, if you get the chance, is to knock out the control tower radio antenna. Hasteen and I are going after the motor pool barracks at the south center of the base. Bood, you back us up and grab the trucks. Use one of them to get our gun crews to the artillery, and the rest of them to move people to the p-camp.

"Cal, you're the reserve. If things go well, be ready to hop a truck for a quick ride to the p-camp. If anything goes wrong, be ready to back up any of the teams going in."

Finally he faced Xuan. "You're the one who starts the party. You're the only one of us who can wear the suit and who we can count on to waste the OP crew fast. We suspect they check the OPs regularly to make sure the crews are alert, and we're guessing they probably call on the hour, maybe on the half-hour, so you've got to hit the place just after three A.M. If you can manage it without alerting base security, we'll try to keep the lid on until 03:00. If someone gets caught moving into position, the balloon goes up with the first shots fired."

~ * ~

While Reynaud hadn't said it, Xuan realized the success of the raid was mostly his responsibility. If he didn't secure the observation post silently, no one would be able to reach their positions for any other part of the assault, and they'd face an alert enemy in strong defensive positions. The OP could probably be taken, but at a high price in men and a prohibitive price in time.

"Let me see the observation post."

Hasteen's voice came from the darkness. "I'll lead the way."

Without a word spoken by either man, Xuan followed Hasteen to where they could see the bunker at the top of a knoll, limned by moonlight and the lights from the airfield. The woods in which they hid had been cut back a good two hundred yards from the bunker, a featureless block of concrete. Even with his binoculars, Xuan could see only two openings in the side of the bunker facing them. One was a sensor array near the top, and a wide slot, probably for a machine gun firing port. The periscope gear on top of the bunker moved regularly as the men inside seemed to be scanning the woods. Xuan studied the bunker for several minutes, then tapped Hasteen's arm as a signal to withdraw.

Still silent, Hasteen led the way back to where Reynaud talked in undertones with Logan and the Deacon.

"I think I can do it," Xuan said.

"When do you want to jump off?" Reynaud asked.

"If you want me to make the kills just after three, I'd better move out at two."

Reynaud peered at his watch. "That's about four hours away."

~ * ~

Xuan tried always to wear a stoic mask, but waiting for action rubbed at his nerves, and he found himself checking the pistols for the eighth or ninth time. Both were off safety, the hammers down, rounds chambered. The suit would be hot, he knew, since it trapped body heat, and so he drank two canteens of water and relieved himself just before it was time to don the suit.

Hasteen helped Xuan into the suit. As soon as Xuan had drawn the zipper closed, Hasteen patted him lightly on the shoulder.

"Good luck."

Xuan was surprised by the words. His hand stopped, still clutching the zipper then he said, "Good luck to you. Tell them I'll show a light in the gun port when I have the bunker secured."

Almost immediately, Xuan was hot inside the suit. It reminded him of the purification lodge on the reservation, or the sauna in France. After securing the suit's hood, he taped three lockpicks onto his left arm. Hasteen slipped a watch onto Xuan's right wrist then covered the band and most of the watch with dark tape.

With a pistol in either hand, Xuan crept to the edge of the woods and slipped into the grass that, had he been standing, wouldn't have reached much past his ankle. He'd noted a runnel dug by rainwater running down the knoll, but knew it was just the sort of cover that'd be trapped.

His world narrowed to the two hundred yards he had to cover in an hour, and the cluster of lenses atop the bunker. He'd decided to creep toward the bunker at an angle, and he moved only when the periscope head swung away from him. The task became more difficult when the lenses of the suit's hood fogged up from his exhaled breath.

What had been an inconvenience became a torment. Sweat ran down his back in streams, and gathered in the front of the suit, so it felt as though he were crawling through a stagnant puddle. His left arm began to burn, as the bandage became soaked with sweat, and the salt stung his wound worse than the bullet had when he was shot, and more sweat ran into his eyes, stinging and blurring his vision.

The world narrowed even more, so it became just the lenses on the bunker and the yard or two in front of him. It seemed all his energy was being drained with his moisture. He licked dry lips with a tongue that felt like a wad of blotting paper, and when he reached what he thought was the halfway mark and glanced at his watch, it showed he'd taken forty minutes to reach where he lay.

For a moment he had to restrain himself. If he took too long to reach the bunker, the attack would be rushed and more of the people with him would die, but if he were shot down before he took the bunker the assault would fare even worse. He froze as the glass eye atop the bunker swung toward him then he crawled frantically as they turned away. The sensors seemed to have picked up something, perhaps a rabbit. By the time the lenses had swung back in his direction he'd covered half the distance, and was only thirty yards from the bunker.

The nearer he came to the bunker, the more certain he became the machine gun port had some sort of curtain in it, and he thought he saw a sliver of dim red light at one corner of the port. Again he slipped back into alternately lying motionless and wriggling forward until he was within five yards of the bunker's concrete wall. The next time the sensors swung away from him, he pulled himself near enough to be sheltered from the lenses by the bunker itself. He looked again at his watch: 2:57.

Crawling to the bunker wall, he rolled onto his back, carefully laid down the Makarov, and tugged the hood off the suit, then unzipped the suit itself, aware of the faintest of clicks as he pulled down the zipper with weak, trembling fingers. The night air hit his body like a bucket of ice water, and he had to force himself to stifle a gasp and keep his breathing steady and silent. After he'd opened the suit enough, he began to crawl out like a butterfly emerging from its cocoon.

After freeing himself of the suit, he twisted the lockpicks out of the tape and put them into his mouth, then crawled around the corner of the bunker to where concrete steps led down to a landing and the door of the bunker, and pressed his ear against the door.

He heard voices, one of them overlaid with static, and he waited until the bunker was silent again before he slipped into the square of deeper darkness of the doorway and carefully tried the latch.

The door was unlocked. Taking the lockpicks from his mouth, he slid them into his belt, then, the Walther riding in the hip pocket of his pants, he pressed the latch and slowly swung the door open.

The interior of the bunker was lit by a dim, red light. Whether it was some faint sound, the breeze from the door, or even the smell of his sweat, the machine gunner spun to face the door. Xuan swung his right hand up and shot the soldier twice in the chest while drawing the PPK with his left hand. The gunner staggered a half-step back and groped at the breech of the machine gun and Xuan, afraid the man would catch the gun's trigger, pointed the pistol at the man's head and fired. The Makarov's bullet made a hole connecting the man's eyebrows.

The observer ducked from under the periscope, saw Xuan, and opened his mouth to scream. Xuan snapped up the Walther and shot the soldier through the open mouth, but almost pulled the shot, as the wound in his forearm stung with the sudden movement. Sidestepping, he swung the Makarov to bear on the man and shot him again, just under the right eye.

A muffled grunt came from along the wall to Xuan's right. When he turned toward the sound he saw two cots. One man lay motionless, but the other had sat up and fumbled at the holster hanging from a peg above the bunk. Xuan's first shot hit him in the back of the head, splashing blood that looked almost yellow in the red light. Stepping to the side of the second cot, Xuan put the muzzle of the Walther's suppressor no more than an inch from the sleeping man's head. He pulled the trigger, placing the round just behind the man's ear. The body thrashed violently enough to roll off the cot.

Xuan sprang for the door and closed it, hoping no one at the base had noticed it open then he found a flashlight, pulled the curtain from the gun port, and flashed the light toward the ceiling, so it could be seen from the woods but not from the base.

While he waited for the other men to arrive, he checked the machine gun, an MG-3 on a pintle mount. Pulling the pin from the mount to free the gun, he hauled it to the door. In the dim light of the bunker, it was difficult to find the light switch, but he finally found the chain and tugged it, throwing the inside of the bunker into darkness then groped his way back to the door.

When Xuan opened the door, he saw the clumps of men stealing past. Suddenly, Hasteen was there, holding out the Steyr and Xuan's shoulder holster with the Automag. He took the machine gun from Xuan and handed it to a man rushing by then helped Xuan into his gear.

"Rest awhile. You've earned it."

Xuan's legs still felt weak, but the cool night air was reviving him. "I'll just follow you to the motor pool."

Four men rushed down the stairs to the bunker, jostling Hasteen and Xuan out of their way as they set up the .50 Browning in the doorway, its tripod holding the gun just high enough for the barrel to clear the top step.

Walking rapidly, Hasteen set out to find Reynaud, leaving Xuan to follow with the rest of the men.

~ * ~

Billy Joe and Logan had been some of the first men to move out when they saw the light in the gun port. The only lights on the field were those in the control tower and in the motor pool, where men still worked, but a motor pool door, open because of the stifling heat of the building, threw a long rectangle of light almost to the barracks that were their first target.

The raiders had decided that if other guards were posted among the buildings, the attackers would be more obvious if they tried to rush or creep, so those in the assault teams having to cross large, open area simply walked.

While he moved at an easy pace, Billy Joe kept his rifle at the ready and his eyes moved constantly, watching for any flicker of movement. Turning his head slightly, he saw Noel's group silently climbing into the tracked vehicle parked by the control tower. He and Logan had a little farther to walk than any of the other groups and he could guess Reynaud and Hasteen were already in the barracks that was their target, and men had taken positions around the motor pool.

Half a dozen paces to the right, Logan strode toward the squat building ahead, moving with a loose, flowing walk, looking as though he might be ready to start whistling some nonchalant tune.

Twenty paces from the barracks he noticed a sullen red glow, like the end of a cigarette, in the darkness and a voice said, "Hey, what's up?"

"First Corinthians, chapter fourteen, verse eight," Billy Joe replied.

CHAPTER 12

"Huh?"

"'For if the trumpet give an uncertain sound, who shall gird himself for the battle?'" He fired twice at the man whose face he could just see in the glow of the cigarette. The red glow dropped to the concrete and he heard the sound of the man's body falling, then Logan rushed past him, pulling a grenade from his pouch.

"'The fat's in the fire now.' Logan; verse one," Logan said, as he pulled open the door and tossed the grenade inside, then slammed the door shut again. The blast shook the frame building and blew the door off, and they could both hear screams and moans from the shack. Standing beside the doorframe, Logan had already pulled the pin of a second grenade, and tossed it in.

As soon as the rubble thrown by the second grenade had stopped falling, Logan sprang inside, his MAC chattering. He ducked out again almost instantly.

"It's cleared; go for the plane, but put your grenade into the cockpit."

"Reynaud said to fire into the hatch."

"You do that, and the blast is liable to take out the Bronco, too. They're too close together. Besides, there's no one to man the guns against us and we can use the firepower."

Billy Joe hesitated a moment, then aimed the launcher at the C-47's cockpit side window and fired. His grenade exploded on the roof, blowing a hole in the cabin roof and shattering all the glass in the cockpit. Billy Joe loaded another round and sent it after the first, saw the red and yellow petals of the explosion opening through the top and sides of the cockpit.

Noel's crew had started the personnel carrier and the gunner raked the control tower, shattering windows, and all but one light in the tower died. Billy Joe loaded another grenade and lobbed it into the tower. When the red-gold flash had disappeared the building was dark but for the flickering light of a small fire.

Reynaud had told him to destroy the antenna, but an antenna, even a radio, was useless to the Steel Fist without men to use them.

The firefight had suddenly left him alone. The fire in the control tower leapt fitfully a few times, then dimmed. The barracks was a smoking ruin, and Logan had dashed under the C-47 to the Bronco beyond. Billy Joe paused a moment, then loaded a flechette charge into the launcher and ran the hundred and fifty yards to the door at the base of the tower. Listening at the door, he heard nothing, kicked the door open to a dark, empty room. Staying outside the room, fumbling at the wall beside the door, he finally found the light switch and snapped it on.

He was surprised to find the light still worked. The tower's ground floor held four tables that looked as though they'd been plundered from a doctor's office, and one wall was dominated by a medicine cabinet. Seeing the stairs, he crept up them. Even in the stairwell, the smoke and the smell of burning flesh were so strong his eyes stung and he was forced back to the medevac station.

Taking a deep breath, he pounded upstairs to the control room. Two bodies lay sprawled on the floor, one of them burning, the other with a massive hole in his chest and gashed almost to unrecognizability. The gashed corpse lay several feet from a shattered radar screen. The air was a little clearer here, as the breeze sweeping through the shattered windows swirled most of the smoke away. He stumbled to a box on the wall, almost tripping over a third body, and hauled out a fire extinguisher, then sprayed foam over the burning equipment and the corpse still on fire. Finally, the dim, flickering lights died and the room was dark and silent, except for the hiss of the extinguisher and the pinging of hot metal.

As soon as he was sure the fire was indeed dead, he snatched up his rifle and made his way downstairs and into the blessedly clean night air.

Trucks in the motor pool were roaring to life and one of them, loaded with men, sped across the field to where the artillery, invisible in the darkness, pointed long barrels into the air. As tired as he was, the Deacon still forced himself into a trot toward the lights of the motor pool.

The only gunfire he still heard around the field came from the gun pits. Just as he reached the door of the motor pool, he heard a series of rifle shots, then several machine guns opened up at once, firing for just over a second, and the rifle fire stopped.

He joined a crowd of men climbing aboard one of the trucks and, within, moments, the truck moved out. The machine pulled out into the night then something exploded beside the vehicle. The truck swayed like a door caught in a high wind, threatening to overturn, and men and women screamed as shrapnel slammed into the truck and its passengers. The vehicle lurched, then the engine died and it jerked to a stop.

~ * ~

Reynaud strode toward the barracks he'd assigned to Hasteen and himself, Angie and Bood at their heels. He swung wide to avoid the light from the motor pool, from which he could hear voices and the clatter of tools. Hasteen, who'd stayed behind at the bunker, was suddenly beside him, moving almost soundlessly across the coarse grass. When he looked back at the motor pool, he saw dark figures creeping around the building, taking attack positions.

They approached the barracks and Reynaud knew it was still at least ten minutes before the attack was set to begin, but it'd be best to take commanding positions immediately. He knew someone would be seen or heard, and the assault could stall and die.

Hasteen tried the door of the barracks and it opened easily. Reynaud signaled for Angie and Bood to approach then leaned forward.

"Hasteen and I'll go in," he said, his voice low and urgent. "You stay here and cover us from attack from outside. Only come in if Hasteen or I call for you. And get down. There'll be a lot of unclaimed lead flying in just a few minutes."

Hasteen had already slipped into the building, and Reynaud joined him. With the door open, there was just enough light to see two rows of cots and a dark rectangle on the back wall that might be a gun rack.

"You know," Reynaud murmured, "they look so innocent asleep, it seems a shame to pop them—in their sleep."

He could almost see Hasteen nod in the darkness. "It wouldn't seem sporting."

"The Deacon wouldn't like it, either," Reynaud said, "sending a soul to Hell that hadn't had a chance to make its peace with God."

"Any ideas?" Hasteen inquired.

"Isn't that a stand-up locker over there, against the wall?"

While Hasteen made his way to the locker, Reynaud groped around for the light switch until he found it by the door.

No sooner had he located the switch than he heard rifle shots from the other barracks. He flicked the switch on and Hasteen shoved the locker over to crash on the floor. Men sprang out of bed or rolled to the floor, and the room resembled a madhouse.

"Awright, assholes," Reynaud shouted, "this is your wake-up call." One of the men, still dazed by sleep, had rolled off the side of his cot and scrambled to his feet when Reynaud's blast caught him full in the chest. He was hurled across the cot and fell against another man clad only in underwear.

By the time Reynaud had pumped the Mossberg's action, Hasteen had killed six men, dropped his revolver, and drawn his left-hand Colt. One man had reached the rack and was groping for a rifle when Reynaud's shotgun bellowed again, throwing the man against the wall. For a moment the corpse stood, propped against the wall, staring down at the ragged wound that'd blown away his heart, then his eyes rolled up and he fell.

Men spun and fell and, even over the roar of the guns, Reynaud heard the screaming. It seemed to be the death-cry of a giant, wrung from a single great throat, but became weaker as man after man died. The sound drove Reynaud into a frenzy until all he wanted to do was end the screaming.

As he started to pump the action of the Mossberg, Reynaud saw another of the troops snatch one of the M-16s from the wall rack, and he knew he couldn't close the action and fire before the man triggered a burst that would chop him in two, then the soldier was flung backward, a small black hole over his left eye. The body hit the rack with arms outspread, and most of the weapons fell with him.

Catching movement at the edge of his vision as he spun, Reynaud saw a man crawling under the cots. He pointed and fired and the man jerked up, taking the cot with him, then dropped, and the cot collapsed over him.

The room was empty but for Hasteen and himself, and a number of corpses. Reynaud counted fourteen cots and, after a little digging, the same number of bodies.

Hasteen emptied the dead cases from the cylinder of the Colt he held and reloaded it, then picked up the other revolver and performed the same operations with it. For a moment he stared down at the cartridge cases in his hand then tossed them onto the heap of bodies.

"Sorry, boys, no time for formalities. You'll have to sort them out for yourselves."

"Bood," Reynaud called out, "we could use your help in here."

Bood appeared in the door, and his eyes widened as he saw the bodies. "Here," Reynaud said, handing him some of the M-16s from the floor, "you and Angie haul these over to the motor pool. The prisoners will need to be armed."

He heard the "thump" of grenades and the sharper sounds of rifle fire, but the noises stopped almost as soon as he was aware of them. Digging more rifles out, he handed them to Angie, then he and Hasteen took the remaining weapons and strode to the motor pool, where the lights still blazed.

One of the men met him at the garage door. "They've got three trucks in here being worked on, but they's a buncha trucks and pickups out back in runnin' order." As the man shouted at him, a truck from the back drove through the building, men crowded into the back. "That's the assault team and gun crews," the man explained, as they watched the machine bound across the field to the gun emplacements. "We also found a radio, back in the corner. I don't think anybody here had a chance to get off an SOS."

"The Steel Fist may be dumb," Reynaud said, "but they're not deaf. By now, they know in Mountain Home we've hit this place and they aren't so dumb they can't figure out we've taken it."

Another truck pulled into the garage from the truck park behind the building, and men and women clambered into it. Reynaud noticed the Deacon among the last to climb into the truck before it pulled out. More of the people bound for the prison camp had just climbed into the third truck when they all heard the shriek of an incoming mortar round. Those who could do so hit the floor, and the people in the truck cowered against the sides. Seventy yards away, the round exploded beside the other truck, and bodies in the bed of the truck were tossed around like toys.

The truck chugged forward a few more feet then stopped,

and those unwounded or only lightly wounded bailed out the back of the vehicle. By the time Reynaud had regained his feet, the Deacon had dashed into the garage.

The Deacon scanned the group until he saw Reynaud, then waved to him and shouted, "There's a medevac center in the control tower." He had to repeat the information before Reynaud was able to hear him over the voices raised in panic.

"Angie, you and Bood grab a pickup and try to get the worst hurt to the control tower." He turned, trotted back to the corner, to the radio, grabbed the mike, and squeezed the send key. "Noel, do you read me? Over."

Hearing only static, he prepared to send another pickup to the gun pits when Noel finally responded. "Noel here, Rennie."

Another mortar round struck somewhere farther away. "Noel, we need the tracks to take care of those mortars—they'll murder the trucks. Over."

"We've got to leave one ape here to take care of holdouts, but I'll be right with you. Over."

"Do you need any more troops over there? Over?"

"Negatory. We'll just leave a track to make them keep their heads down. Over."

Another mortar round passed overhead and hit somewhere west. The Deacon caught at Reynaud's arm. "The C-47 still has its weapons, including the automatic grenade launchers," he shouted. "Could we mount them in the gun rings on the trucks?"

"Just a minute," Reynaud said to the Deacon, then thumbed the mike. "We're going to arm some trucks. Hold up for us until I signal you we're ready. Over."

"Affirmative," Noel replied, "but be snappy about it. If you take too long, there won't be anything left to rescue."

"Out," Reynaud said then spun to see the trucks in the garage. Three of them were parked nose-to-tail, the first two ready to pull out. "God bless your insubordinate ass." He pointed to the first truck in the line. "Get to the driver and tell him to make it to the plane and we'll strip the weapons from it. I'll be in the next truck."

Reynaud stopped by the third truck long enough to tell the driver to follow the others to the C-47, then hurried to the second truck. The launchers and the .50 guns in the gunship could make all the difference between success and failure in the assault on the p-camp. He was halfway to the truck when a blast shook the building and the lights momentarily dimmed.

The enemy mortar crew were probably firing blind, without coordinates, and with no one to direct their fire, but they were using heavy mortars and their haphazard fire was bound to hit something important if they were given long enough. Perhaps he should've tried to contact the gun crew with the radio, but if they had coordinates for the mortars, they'd fire on it as soon as they could. Without coordinates, they'd be more dangerous to the prisoners than to the mortar crew.

The truck was already moving when he sprang onto the driver's step plate. "Follow the other truck," he shouted, and hung on desperately as the driver gunned the engine and the truck bounded across the uneven field to the gunship.

While they hurried to pull the weapons out of the plane and install them in the gun rings or on the pillar mounts on the trucks, half a dozen more mortar rounds burst around the field, one of them within yards of the plane. A man screamed and fell from the cargo door, holding the stump of a left arm.

After leaving a man and a woman to tend the wounded men and get them to the medevac station, Reynaud waved at the others to move out. An APC clattered to a halt beside the trucks and the gunner shouted.

"You ready?"

"Are you? Have you got armor-piercing in that gun?" Reynaud roared back.

"No can do," the gunner replied. "Plain hardball and tracer was all they had in this thing."

Reynaud cursed to himself then shouted, "Be alert for ambushes. We don't know how many apes they have left, and they may have them on the road. Let's roll."

~ * ~

Logan had climbed into the Bronco and found, on the seat, a helmet, with what looked like an oxygen mask. Dropping into the seat, he pulled on the helmet then followed the hose with his gaze to a unit bolted to the instrument panel. The unit looked like a filtration unit from a gas mask, with a simple cut-off. He turned the switch to bypass the filter and secured the mask to his face.

While he strapped himself into the parachute and safety harness, he reviewed what he remembered about the Bronco, then noticed a handle, crudely mounted on the left console, had also been added, and he guessed it was for releasing the poison gas.

He armed the ejection seat, flicked on the engine master switch, set the condition levers at the "fuel shut-off" setting and the power control levers at "flight idle," then hit the start switch.

The engines were almost noiseless, most of the sound coming from the prop blades, which made a strange, deep purring noise, like large electric fans. He advanced the condition levers to "normal flight," and watched the engine temperature gauges.

He reversed the props, making sure the prop locks had been removed, closed and locked the canopy, and made sure all trims were set on zero. The engines were slow to warm up. He set the condition levers at the take-off and land mode and, standing on the brakes, slowly advanced the throttles, having to guess how much fuel to feed the engines, which weren't yet fully warmed.

Glancing up from the engine temp gauges, he saw muzzle flashes from the other end of the field and felt something strike the plane. This had to be the crew of the other lookout post. At the range they were firing, they were unlikely to hit anything, but the unlikely had already happened once, and he suddenly remembered the plane was loaded with poison gas and a single round in one very wrong area could wipe out him and most of the raiders.

Releasing the brakes, he swung the nose slightly to center the muzzle flashes in the sight reflected on his windshield. He stroked the fire button with his thumb, holding it down for only a second or so, but the four M-60s in the stub wing mounted on the bottom of the fuselage stuttered. He hit first one brake, then the other, to spray the gunfire over a wider area, and the muzzle flashes stopped winking at him.

It's time to go, he decided. The engine temperatures seemed to have finally stabilized. Using the steerable nosewheel, he moved the machine off the hardstand and onto the runway. Something heavy exploded behind him, and he advanced the throttles again and the plane rolled across the strip. It came unstuck slower than he'd expected, and he guessed the spray gear had screwed up the machine's flight characteristics.

Finding the gear latch handle, he punched it up and, ten

seconds later, heard the gear lock shut with a solid sound. He was flying again! While not as responsive as the fighters he'd flown, the Bronco was still maneuverable but steady, and could be flown with a light touch, the mark of a thoroughbred, and the view from the cockpit was superb. Banking, he turned the plane west, heading for where he guessed Marion Regional Airport should be. Navigating by guess and by God, he was afraid he'd gone too far north or south when he saw the ribbon of airstrip and two bushel baskets of blue flame that were the engine exhausts of the C-47.

Night strafing was dangerous work, and pilots tended to concentrate on their targets too much, sometimes flying right into them. Realizing he mustn't lose too much altitude, he flew wide around the field, catching the C-47 on the strip as it taxied. He caressed the firing button and saw by the tracers his rounds were falling short of the right engine. Making a slight correction, he fired again, the guns vibrating the ship slightly as they chattered.

He was sure he'd hit the engine, but the gunship continued to rush along the runway. He tried another burst, shifting his aim to put the rounds in the fuselage, but he was forced to pull up to avoid the trees at the end of the field.

Once the gunship lumbered into the air, he had to be certain it went down, and a good pilot and a good gunner could make that difficult and hazardous to his health. Banking, he swung the Bronco wide around. The C-47 was airborne, but the flames from the right engine were longer, and they were no longer blue.

He suddenly realized this gunship would be his fifth kill; it'd make him an ace, but he immediately put the thought away. Getting that gunship was far more important than just a number on a tally.

One of the gunners opened fire. The muzzle flashes looked like fifty-five-gallon barrels of flame, and tracers looking like blazing tennis balls arched after the Bronco.

Afraid to maneuver the Bronco too violently because of the spray gear, he swung the Bronco around in the classic tail-chase and climbed. As he approached, the bigger plane began to bank, and he knew the pilot was trying to let one of the gunners get another burst at him. Advancing the throttles to full power, he pointed the sight between and just ahead of the engines, and punched out a three-second burst.

He watched the tracers plunging into the cockpit. The gunship banked hard left and the right-side gunner fired a long burst falling wide to Logan's right. He side-slipped left, sliding behind the C-47's tail. The left wing continued to drop until the plane's wings were vertical, and the ship rapidly lost altitude.

Logan hauled back on the stick and climbed, then banked to watch the gunship fall. The C-47 was rolling onto its back, and the plane was almost completely inverted when it hit the side of a mountain. A huge ball of flame shot upward, and Logan had to swing hard left to avoid it.

"That's five," he shouted into the throat mike. "If anybody's listening, Logan Reid just became an ace!"

The whole combat had taken less than three minutes, and Logan had taken off only five minutes before. Now that he'd really cleared the air, he had a chance to help someone else. Mario, he knew, had been given a big job and a small force to do it with.

Heading east, Logan easily found White River and followed it north.

~ * ~

Dusk had fallen by the time Mario and the men with him had reached the dam, which was an impressive structure. A quick recon was enough to locate a guard post, a sandbag bunker just off the highway and using the bank of the river for a measure of cover. Any entrance to the dam from this side of the river would have to be beyond the guard post. The dam itself was well-lit but the woods on both banks were left in darkness.

Mario and his group could do nothing until much nearer the time of attack, so he withdrew his men into the heavy woods beside the highway and let them rest and eat cold rations. After the MREs he and Xuan had "liberated" from the Steel Fist troops, the dried mule meat and hardtack was more a challenge than a meal to be grateful for.

Of the men with him, a mountaineer named Phil seemed the most competent. Mario called him over then said, "Wake me at one o'clock. I'd prefer to be up for an hour before we have to move into position. Wake me immediately if there are any alarms or they start moving heavy stuff through here." He lay down on the grass and was, within moments, asleep.

~ * ~

When Phil shook him awake, four hours later, he was instantly and completely alert. He ate and drank again, then showed the men how to check their gas masks and led them on a final weapons check. One of the men carried the old M-79 grenade launcher. "Know how to use that?" Mario asked.

"I carried a 203 for five months at Len Wood."

"That means you know how to carry it. How well do you hit what you aim at?"

"I do all right."

"Good. You stay with me."

They were able to move along the highway relatively freely. Any traps would be in the woods or in the ditches, and all the lights were concentrated on the dam itself. He left most of the men nearly a hundred yards from the guard post. At fifty yards, he became conscious of the noise the grenadier beside him was making. Leaving the man behind him to cover him, or to advance if he called, he crawled alone to within twenty-five yards of the post. He guessed it was after three in the morning when he took a position, but had no idea how much after the hour. He'd taken cover behind a clump of weeds that had sprung up through a crack at the edge of the pavement and waited, watching the red glows of two cigarettes. One of the smokers apparently finished his cigarette and the glaring point of light arched up and to the river. The silence became oppressive then his nerves twitched as the quiet was shattered by a crackle of static and a voice, muffled by transmission, shouted.

"Red alert! Red alert!"

From the instant the radio crackled, Mario had marked his target and sighted on the base of the machine gunner's nose. He squeezed the trigger and had worked the bolt before the rifle stopped recoiling. The other soldier in the bunker was paralyzed by the shock of seeing his companion's head explode. Mario fired the second shot no more than three seconds after the first and, after the bellow of the gun, the outpost was silent, then static erupted over the radio again.

"Come in Coyote, this is Base. Are you there? Come in Coyote?"

Lunging to his feet, he dashed to the bunker. Both guards were dead, and there was no sign of other Steel Fist troops. The radio still sputtered and demanded a response, so he caught up the mike from the ground, set down his rifle, then drew his .45 auto pistol and fired it inches from the microphone while holding the transmit button down.

"Grenadier," he shouted, "we need a pass-key to the door over here."

The grenadier sprinted forward then carefully made his way down the bank. "This thing needs at least a twenty-five-yard running start for the grenade to arm itself." As the grenadier drew aim on the heavy door, Mario drew on his gas mask.

The launcher recoiled and the door disappeared in an explosion. When the dust cleared, the door lay beside the dark rectangle of the opening. Mario waved and shouted for the grenadier to get back up to the highway, then pointed east.

"Keep a sharp eye on the highway," he shouted, his voice muffled by the mask. "They may try to rush us or, if they can, send a team along the side of the dam. Try to keep them at least two hundred yards away."

Almost before the men with him deployed, they heard the whine of a truck speeding toward them, its headlights blacked out but for a narrow strip across each light. Mario aimed for between the lights and, at what he judged to be four hundred yards, fired. The darkness around him strobed with muzzle flashes and he was almost deafened by the staccato chatter of assault rifles on full auto.

Rounds bounced off the truck's armor or slammed into some chink in its steel hide. Mario's bullet had smashed through the plating in the front and torn a hole in the radiator, so steam rolled from under the hood. The front of the truck was silhouetted by the flash of a grenade as it exploded in the truck's bed. The truck veered then rolled in a shower of sparks, crashed against the concrete railing, and lay burning. The only movement on top of the dam was the leaping of flames.

Mario returned to the bunker. If he were going to dig into a tunnel after rats, he needed other tools. Fumbling around in the darkness until he found a flashlight, he checked the equipment in the bunker. Besides the M-60, the gunner's only weapon had been a pistol but the loader had a Thompson submachine gun. It looked like a newly manufactured gun, but appeared to be a short-barreled full-automatic version.

The weapon had a fifty-round drum attached, and the loader's body bore a magazine pouch with four thirty-round stick magazines. Laying his rifle in the corner of the bunker, he took the web gear from the corpse, drew it on, then pulled back the Thompson's bolt. It was definitely full-auto, firing from the open bolt instead of the closed bolt. He was willing to trade the loss in accuracy for the greater firepower.

While he'd prefer having the best possible man for back-up, Phil and the grenadier were needed to defend this end of the dam. He pointed to two men with M-16s and one man with a shotgun.

"You three, follow me."

One of the men abruptly pointed across the dam, and the rapid, heavy purring of the Bronco's engines and props became louder.

"Secure your gas masks," Mario shouted then the plane swept overhead. A cloud had followed the machine over halfway across the dam. The plane climbed almost vertically then came back, passing low over them. As the prop sounds receded, they heard the machine guns open fire then all the sounds died for a few seconds.

The Bronco came in again, this time coming from upriver, and as it passed the dam it performed a victory roll.

"The crazy bastard did it," Mario said to himself then waved again to the three men he'd chosen and they darted toward the doorway to the dam's interior.

~ * ~

The convoy of trucks stayed, as much as possible, on the shoulders of the highway and fifty yards or more behind the APC, which remained running in the left side ditch. Without warning, a .50 on the right side of the road flashed and throbbed. The APC gunner fired back, but the burst was cut short as the Steel First gunner corrected his aim, and the big slugs tore into the armor around the gun.

The automatic grenade launcher on Reynaud's truck thumped out a reply and a string of explosions walked to the enemy APC, then the vehicle was hidden by the blasts. The man on the "thumper" continued to lob grenades for another three or four seconds, and Reynaud heard something heavy fall into the field to his right. As soon as he'd stopped firing, the man at the launcher detached the empty ammo box, threw it off the side of the road, and reloaded.

The truck crept forward until it drew abreast of the stopped APC, and a man climbed into the gun ring.

"The gunner's dead. I just got promoted."

"All right," Reynaud shouted, "take the lead and go like hell."

His last word was lost in the roar of an explosion in the field that showered them with dirt and wheat stubble. The mortar crew had changed the range and were now probing for them.

The track roared up out of the ditch, past the burning Steel Fist machine and clattered down the highway. Reynaud was almost jerked off his feet as the truck rushed after it. After a slight rise, the road dipped, and, as they topped the crest, they looked down on one of the circles of Hell. Fires and muzzle flashes provided the only light. The guard station across the top of the gate was a wreck, but a few flashes there warned them a man was still there, alive and resisting. Four of the six guard towers had been demolished, and one was burning, as was the other enemy APC, twenty yards inside the gate. A few points of fire in the field around the compound showed some of the attackers were alive and fighting, but each shot from the fields drew bursts of machine gun fire from the surviving two towers.

A plume of fire leapt up from the mortar pit, like a fireworks display and Reynaud could see that once the APC and the trucks were inside the gate, they'd be safe from mortar fire. He took all this in at the split-second his truck cleared the crest, then they rushed toward the gate.

The man at the launcher opened up on the mortar pit then the truck was rocked by an explosion and he glanced back to see the truck following them, its front end in ruins, swerve into the ditch.

One of the barrages of grenades fired by the launcher must've struck near enough to the pit to teach the mortar crew the better part of valor. At the same time, he and half a dozen other men fired at the surviving guard over the gate. The APC, engine roaring and tracks clattering, burst through the gate, weaved past the first ruined guard tower, then tore down a section of chain-link fence between the prison compound and the rest of the camp.

The truck followed the ape through the gate then skidded to a stop fifty feet from the mortar pit, and the man at the launcher swung the weapon around and touched off a short burst at one of the two active guard towers. When the flashes and the dust cleared, only splintered upright poles remained.

Reynaud sprang over the side of the truck and raced for the mortar pit, the butt of his shotgun tight against his shoulder. A gun barrel swung up over the sandbags and Reynaud blasted at it, heard a scream. A bullet buzzed by him and he pumped the Mossberg, then leapt onto the sandbags and rolled, kicking his feet over first. Dropping about five feet into the pit, he heard a pistol shot and a muzzle flashed above him. Firing back, he heard a body fall.

A small patch of light showed where someone had dropped a flashlight. Grabbing it up and holding it at arm's length, he examined the pit. One man had been almost decapitated by the grenade that'd silenced the mortar, while another had shrapnel wounds to the chest. He was dead or dying.

Pumping the shotgun, Reynaud shot the wounded man in the head. The other two corpses in the pit had been wounded by shrapnel, but he'd shot one in the head, leaving only the bottom of the man's face, and the other had caught his shotgun blast in the upper chest.

He switched off the flashlight and, for a moment, simply sagged against the wall. Outside he heard a hellish cacophony of gunfire and explosions, shouts, screams, moans, and curses. At the moment, he just wanted the precarious safety and peace of the now-quiet pit then he shoved himself up and, hoping no one would mistake him for the enemy, looked over the sandbags.

The last guard tower was a shambles, and sand still dribbled from the ruptured bags. The gunners on the vehicles pounded the buildings from which the Steel Fist soldiers still fired. Ragged prisoners flooded into the administration side of the compound, some carrying weapons taken from the dead, others armed only with poles or clubs pulled from the rubble.

Through this Hell strode the Deacon, shouting, "'Think not I am come to send peace on earth. I come not to send peace but a sword.' Matthew, chapter ten, verse thirty-four." Silhouetted by fires and explosions, striding through the maelstrom, sometimes firing short bursts from the FN or launching a grenade, the Deacon looked like a demon sent from Hell to collect lost souls, then he began to bellow "The Battle Hymn of the Republic."

Reynaud stood, transfixed by the sight of the Deacon, and he began to believe that God did, indeed, protect children and madmen.

Xuan had been in the truck hit by the mortar round but Reynaud saw him running along the side of a building. Stopping by a window, he tossed a grenade inside and, as he turned his head from the blast, Reynaud saw Xuan had a gash on the left side of his face that laid the cheekbone bare. A flash and roar marked the explosion of the grenade, and Xuan waited for a moment for the smoke and dust to clear, then another explosion blew away pieces of the wall and hurled Xuan to the ground.

Reynaud flung himself up, onto the sandbags, then tumbled to his feet and ran to where Xuan lay to bend over the little man. "Can you get up?"

Xuan shook his head to clear it, started to rise then coughed at the smoke. For a split-second, the little man's face twisted in agony before his features settled into a bland mask.

"Don't move," Reynaud said. "Don't try to bullshit me. Stay down. That's an order. Where are you hit?"

Xuan slowly crawled closer to the wall, his eyes as dark and shiny—and almost as expressionless—as black beads.

"On the side. Back. Down by my elbow."

Studying Xuan's face, Reynaud couldn't see bleeding from nose or mouth; no assurance he didn't have internal injuries, but it was the only thing the Cajun knew to look for.

"Stay put. You've paid your dues."

Reynaud glanced about. Gunfire came from the other side of the building they leaned against. If the attack flushed the men inside, they'd probably rush out the door only a few feet away, but if he fired at them, Xuan might be hurt by any return fire. The mortar pit was a good twenty yards away, while a stack of lumber lay only half that distance from him, and it was almost directly opposite the door.

"Stay here and be quiet," he said to Xuan then ran for the

woodpile.

Two paces from cover, Reynaud heard a burst of gunfire from the doorway and a searing pain shot through his knee. His leg folded under him, spilling him onto the ground.

CHAPTER 13

Stepping out the door, the Steel Fist soldier corrected his rifle for another burst at Reynaud. Xuan pointed his Steyr at the trooper and pulled the trigger fully to the rear. The Steyr chattered and the trooper jerked and twitched as the .223 bullets hemstitched him from waist to throat, then he spun, slammed against the door frame, and dropped back inside the building.

~ * ~

Appearing at the corner of the building, Hasteen took in the situation at a glance, and rushed the door. He hurtled over the body in the doorway and almost ran into another soldier. With his left arm, he deflected the barrel of the M-16 and shot the trooper in the belly. Pushing the body away, he fanned two shots at a bulky figure in the hallway then dropped to the floor as a man fell and another man, standing behind the first, swept the hallway at waist level with a submachine gun. A single shot fired up into the soldier's lower chest threw him back against the wall.

Hasteen crawled along the hallway then rolled into the middle of the door at the end of the corridor. The only sounds he heard were gunshots from outside the building and the sounds of bullets ripping through walls, gouging furniture, and smashing office machines.

"Cease fire," Hasteen shouted, then, as the gunfire subsided, rose to his feet and crept back the way he'd come. Attackers kicked in the doors at the front of the building and prowled through the place room by room, guns ready.

Hasteen smelled something burning then noticed his point-blank shot at the first man had set the man's uniform to smoldering. Pausing only to reload and drop cartridge cases into the mouths of the three men he'd killed, he made his way to the back of the building, where he shouted.

"This is Hasteen. I'm coming out."

Xuan still lay beside the wall. Hasteen knelt beside him.

"The fight's over here. Can you get up?"

~ 234 ~

Xuan nodded and kept his face impassive as he worked his way to his feet, but Hasteen noticed the sweat covering his face.

"Are you bleeding anyplace but that gash on your face?"

Xuan shook his head then nodded to where Reynaud lay. "You'd better see to him. I heard him moaning. I saw him go down, but I don't know how badly he's hit."

"I'll check. Can you make it to the truck?"

Xuan nodded again then both men looked up at a sound like a freight train hurtling across the sky. Since the firing in the compound had finally died away, they were able to hear their artillery lobbing shells into Mountain Home.

"Get to the truck," Hasteen said. "They'll take you to the aid station at the airfield."

Hasteen watched Xuan hobble to the truck, then trotted to where Reynaud had fallen. The Cajun lay on his back, rocking back and forth. Hasteen caught him by the shoulders.

"How bad are you hit?"

"I don't know," Reynaud muttered through clenched teeth. "It's my right knee. I can't feel my lower leg or foot. I think they're still there."

"It looks, from here, like it's still attached," Hasteen said, and whipped a Bowie knife from a sheath at the back of his belt. After using the huge blade to carefully cut away the pants leg from above the knee down, he put the knife away. Gently, he pulled the cloth away from the wound. "It's not bleeding too badly, but it doesn't look good, either. It caught you right in the joint, about an inch or so back of the kneecap." He looked again at the bullet holes. "Looks like it was clean in and clean out. I don't think you'll lose the leg, but you've probably done your last deep knee-bend."

Bracing himself, Hasteen said, "Get ready. I'm going to pick you up and carry you to the truck."

~ * ~

Reynaud managed to smother a scream into a grunt. He'd felt the bones of the joint grating together, and the burning pain was so intense he almost fainted, then Hasteen was carrying him. He had to grit his teeth to keep from crying out at the agony, but was able to take the trip to the truck without screaming.

Hasteen deposited him carefully in the back of the truck, and

Reynaud looked up to see Xuan standing above him. The wiry little man was standing very stiffly, as though each movement would be painful. Reynaud caught at the front of Hasteen's shirt.

"Hasteen, get someone on the radio to Mountain Home. Tell them the Arkansas militia demands their immediate surrender."

"Nice bluff. What if they don't fold?"

"Then tell the artillery to try to level Mountain Home and have the rest of the people dig in for a long, nasty war."

~ * ~

Logan, flying at an altitude of two thousand feet, followed the White River until he saw the lights along the top of Bull Shoals Dam. Another light winked into existence, a large red and yellow glare and he guessed something was burning on the highway running along the top of the dam. The eastern bank, to his right, would be enemy territory, with Mario's team somewhere on the western bank.

Banking the plane, he pulled it into a wide, climbing turn to approach the Steel Fist defenses from behind.

It was time to start breathing through a filter, he decided. Reaching out, he twisted the valve on the breathing gear then took the Bronco up and over the mountains. As soon as he'd cleared the mountains he cut the throttle to cruise and dived to within a hundred feet of the ground, then shoved the gas release handle forward.

Nothing seemed different in the plane's responses, but he knew he was now trailing a cloud of death. Racing low over the highway, he spotted a group of men carrying cases and bags of what must be explosives, and he overflew them, still spreading the poison gas in his wake.

Approaching a burning truck on the edge of the highway, he yanked back on the gas release, opened the throttle to full power, and pulled the stick back into his belly. The Bronco shot upward like a fireball from a Roman candle, and he whipped it around in a hard, fast turn, then put the nose down to come at the highway from the west.

The explosives and writhing bodies lay strewn on top of the dam, but one man, wearing swimming trunks and SCUBA gear, was running back to the eastern end of the dam. Throttling back,

Logan took aim at the running figure.

"Run, you bastard," he murmured, "you'll just…die…tired." His thumb pressed the firing stud and the four M-60s in the winglets vibrated the ship. He watched the tracers lancing out, hitting the running man or bouncing off the pavement around him. The body jerked and danced, almost invisible in a spray of blood, then it crumpled.

He pulled up—he'd almost flown into the dam—and gained altitude, then sprayed a full five seconds of machine gun fire into the buildings at the eastern end of the dam. As he banked away, he looked back and was disappointed not to see more fires breaking out.

Swinging the Bronco wide, he advanced the throttles as he came in low enough over the lake to stir the moonlit water into ripples. Clearing the dam by a comfortable margin, he heeled the plane over into a barrel roll.

As soon as the wings were level again he put the machine into a steady climb and followed the river back south. He'd done all he could to help Mario and company. Now, he decided, he'd better make it back and find out how the rest of the crowd was doing. Humming "Born to Be Wild," he looked around the cockpit.

Down by the gas filter he found a compartment containing spare filters in sealed bags. Opening one of the bags, he put a fresh filter in his breathing gear. The Steel Fist base at Cotter could effectively cut the highway in two at the bridge, and they might have the manpower to make an assault on the airfield.

Another thing he found was the switch for the radio. Snapping it on, he felt as though he'd fallen into the middle of a mob scene. The airwaves were alive with warnings, threats, and requests and demands for assistance. Sighting the bridge, he swung wide right to cross the river above the bridge and along the highway. As he passed over the bridge he shoved the handle for the spray gear and dropped to just above the deck. As soon as he'd made his pass, he climbed and circled once. Most of the cloud had dissipated by the time he looked back, but he could see the breeze carrying the gas southeast.

One of the voices on the radio managed to scream, "We've been gassed," then there was one less voice.

Finding the highway again, he followed it back to the airfield, making sure the gas release lever was shut. Over the airfield, he banked and looked down. The only signs of action were several trucks pulling up to the control tower then he could see the flash of one of the 155 guns. The airstrip had been hit by two mortar rounds and the blacktop had been badly cratered. Bringing a strange bird in on that strip, or trying to put it down on the remains of the highway could be a very interesting job, but he doubted he'd stay alive long enough to make it a career.

Another voice, louder than most of the babble he could hear on the radio, asked, "Logan, is that you?"

"Hell no," Logan boomed into his mike, "this is Hazel the witch." He cackled into the mike. "I'm just trying to work some kinks out of my new broomstick. You were expecting maybe the Avon lady?"

Another voice took over the nearest radio. "Logan, this is Hasteen. We think they're trying to run troops from Mountain Home. Our gunners have been shelling the place, and we have coordinates for the highway, but we need somebody to correct the fire."

"Jeez," Logan growled. "I just made 'ace'—that's five kills—all the fingers on one hand, for those of you who're slow at math, and now you want me to do FAC work. That's 'forward air controller' for those not into military jargon. This is demeaning. This is humiliating. Does this mean I also have to take a cut in pay and give back my key to the little boys' room?"

Logan could hear Hasteen's sigh and could almost see him roll his eyes. "Just do it, will you?"

"I'm on my way." He followed the highway to the prison camp. Some buildings were still burning, but he could see no muzzle flashes. Changing filters in his breathing gear again, he banked to keep an eye on the road. Perhaps a quarter mile beyond the p-camp he saw men setting up weapons in the fields flanking the highway.

Only seconds later, he clearly saw Mountain Home. Fires raged and vehicles, their headlights dimmed, rushed in every direction, although a line formed on the road to the camp. Logan knew he should stand off, out of range of most of their guns, and call in longs and shorts, but hauling around poison gas was making him increasingly nervous, and here was a perfect place to dump what he had left.

Shoving the nose down, he opened the gas release. As the Deacon would say, "'Tis more blessed to give than to receive." Machine guns sent up probing lines of tracers after him as he swept over the column, then he climbed enough to clear the buildings ahead. He weaved a pattern over the town, using the rooftops for cover.

Pulling up, he turned and looked back, saw no vapor cloud in his wake. Breaking away from the town, he came back across the highway ahead of the relief column.

"All right, fire for effect."

A flower of light spread across the highway six hundred yards short of the column. "Correct six hundred out," he called. For almost half an hour he called corrections to the gunners, until the column had been shattered and the western fringe of Mountain Home had been reduced to rubble.

He heard a new voice through his headphone.

"We surrender. Cease fire. Repeat, we surrender, cease fire."

"Will that do it for you guys?" Logan inquired of the tower.

"We'll hold fire. We want a delegation from Mountain Home to come to the control tower at Lahar Field. You're to come in a single car or pickup. Over."

"Affirmative. Our delegation will be in a car with its headlights on bright. We'll be there as soon as we can get a car through the rubble. Out."

Heading back to the airfield, Logan circled once. He'd come to love this little bird that had given him back his wings, but trying to bring it down on a pot-holed highway, without lights, or on an airstrip chewed up by mortar fire, was just too risky. He might've tried it anyway, but he was very conscious of the poison gas tank and the spray gear. If residue remained in the tanks, an accident might release it, and friends and allies would pay the price.

He switched off the radio. "Sorry, baby, but I'm gonna hafta cut you loose." He turned northeast. If he were going to have to bail out, he was going to allow himself to enjoy the last few minutes he had with this stallion. He wanted to be far enough from the airfield and the p-camp that nobody else would be hurt if anything went wrong. Opening the throttle, he threw the agile little machine up into a loop, then up again, into a hammerhead turn.

Logan put the plane through its paces, using up as much fuel as he could burn while keeping the props from torquing out.

When he'd finally used up all but the last of the fuel, he turned back to the airfield. Bailing out was bad enough, without having a long walk afterward. The plane bucked a bit as he jettisoned the canopy. Approaching the field at six hundred feet, he pointed the machine in the direction of Cotter. "Wonder where they hid the time-clock in this thing?" he muttered to himself. "Well, time to punch out." He fired the ejector seat and was shot upward with bone-jarring force.

At the top of the arc he cleared the seat and hoped it would trip the parachute. Nothing happened then the parachute jerked hard at his harness. He pulled off the helmet and dropped it, then watched the Bronco for as long as he could see it. As the plane disappeared in the darkness of near dawn, he looked down, searching for a place to land.

~ * ~

Mario stood with his back against the wall of the dam, the Thompson held across his chest. Behind him stood one of the men with an M-16, while the other stood behind the shotgunner on the other side of the door.

"What kinds of loads have you got in that thing?" he asked the man with the shotgun.

"Number six shot. Is that too light?"

"Not for where we're going." Mario swung the Thompson to his hip and crept through the doorway, keeping his back to the wall. The section of corridor he faced was long and dark, and it appeared empty, but he could see light ahead.

He dropped to the floor, hoping if the corridor contained any tripwires, they'd be visible against the distant light, but saw nothing.

Rising again, and keeping his back against the wall, he began to sidestep down the corridor, being sure to put his feet down flat.

The shotgunner followed him, staying against the opposite wall. Trying to be as noiseless as possible, Mario was annoyed by the wheezing of his breath in the gas mask. The damned thing cut his vision down to what was just in front of him. Peripheral vision was gone, and the noise of his own breathing could easily hide other sounds, sounds he needed to hear.

An open door at the end of the corridor led to the generator room. Approaching the door with caution, he risked a quick look inside. Massive machines, divided by narrow walkways, made the room a maze.

Signaling for the shotgunner to cover him, Mario stepped out into the light. Still crab-walking, he followed a walkway around one of the machines. He crept to each corner and sprang out, weapon ready, being careful to watch for men above him as well as hidden in the machinery.

At the second corner he found a corpse lying doubled over, a pool of blood on the floor, and the dead man's face covered with blood.

He'd lost track of time, couldn't remember when Logan had gassed the place, but he knew the gas would dissipate slower in a closed space, and particularly one lower than most of the surrounding area. His nose began to itch, and sweat ran into his eyes. Shaking his head to clear the sweat from his eyes, he continued to prowl ahead.

A few paces past the corpse he found a simple bomb, set to explode in another twenty minutes. He pulled the positive wire loose then laid the bomb on a generator housing.

He began to feel like a Jonah, trapped in the belly of a whale of steel and concrete.

A few paces more and he'd reached another corner. Hearing nothing but his own breathing, he jumped out, gun leveled—and jumped back again as a man wearing a gas mask and armed with a shotgun fired at him. He clearly heard pellets whistle past him and hit the wall beyond.

"Hey, asshole," Mario shouted, his voice muffled by the gas mask, "it's me, your fearless leader."

"Sorry," said another muffled voice.

"I'm not going to stay fearless very damned long at this clip. You clowns scare the hell out of me." Looking back, he saw one of the men with an M-16 following him. To the shotgunner he shouted, "You guys find anything?"

"No. You?"

"A corpse and a bomb. We've got to clear this area fast. You take this side and I'll take the other." He moved back so he and the shotgunner would be walking parallel to each other, with the banks of generators between them. Halfway to the next corner, he found another bomb. After pulling the wire, he crept to the next corner, holding his breath.

Springing around the corner, he found himself almost face-to-face with a man wearing a gas mask and carrying a pistol. The Thompson pounded and bucked in his hands. The man snapped off a single pistol shot and Mario felt something like a hot needle hit his lower left side. His own burst had flung the man backward into the other aisle, where a shotgun blast tore a hole out of the body's waist.

Mario ducked back into his aisle just as he heard another shotgun. A pellet tore across his scalp and another hit his right shoulder but glanced off. The blast had come from above and he could guess he'd been hit by ricochets.

He gestured to the rifleman with him to find a way up the machine they hid behind, then stepped out of cover to fire a long burst at the top of the machine from which the blast had come. Over the chatter of the Thompson he could hear bullets striking metal and whining away.

Ducking back behind the generator housing, he pulled the drum from the Tommy to replace it with one of the stick magazines. From above, he heard the rattle of an M-16, and he sprang forward to the next machine, pressing himself against the housing.

Another short burst from the M-16 was followed by the sound of something heavy falling to the floor. He sidestepped along the housing as quickly as possible without making unnecessary noise. As he approached the corner, a shotgun barrel was thrust out and began to swing toward him. He dropped to the floor, biting back a groan at the pain in his side. The shotgun boomed, sending a spray of pellets above him. He could see only the shotgun and the shooter's hands. Rolling out into the aisle, he fired a two-second burst at the housing beyond the corner. A couple of bullets buzzed back in his direction, but most of them ricocheted against the other side of the housing.

Hearing a muffled scream, he clambered to his feet, wondering where the hell the others were. He was preparing to jump out and finish off the man he'd shot when he heard a shotgun blast, then another. After taking an extra moment to load a fresh magazine, he jumped into the space between the housings.

His own shotgunner prowled along the walkway, gun ready then Mario noticed the two bodies. One of them had apparently been wounded by the rifleman and another had a gaping hole in his right upper chest. Both had been hit in the waist by shotgun blasts.

The man he'd hit was dead or dying, but the other man moaned and tried to reach the shotgun he'd dropped. Mario kicked the gun away then bent over the man.

"How many of you are in here?"

"Go fuck yourself," the man rasped.

Mario reached out and gripped the filter of the man's gas mask. "I don't have time to waste on small talk or witty repartee. How many more of you are there?"

"We're all that's left," the soldier wheezed.

"Very good. How many bombs did you have?"

When the man hesitated, Mario wriggled the mask a little. "You won't care when the bombs go off. The first thing that'll happen when I take this off is you'll smell bitter almonds, then you'll start to bleed from your nose and mouth as you strangle. Finally, you'll go into convulsions. I don't know whether you'll be alive to feel them or not."

"We planted six bombs."

"Where?"

The man paused, holding his breath, then grunted, apparently fighting off a wave of pain. "Two of them were planted back where you were. Johnny had one with him when he climbed on top of the housing. There's one right over there, under the edge of the housing. The other two are planted on the first and second housings from the east entrance."

Mario stood. The rifleman had jumped from one housing to the other and now stood above him.

"There's a bomb up there somewhere. Find it." He strode to the housing and groped along the bottom edge until he found another bomb. Pulling it out, he disarmed it.

"I've got the one up here," the rifleman shouted.

"Hand it down—carefully." Mario started to reach for it then winced as the wound in his side stung again. The shotgunner reached for the charge, then held it out to Mario, who pulled the wire.

The rifleman jumped down and Mario gestured to him. "You, go back and bring about half the team. Tell them to double-time it." To the other two, he said, "Get to the east end and find those bombs. When you get ahold of them, yank the wire off the positive end of the battery."

As the men hurried to their tasks, he opened his shirt and looked down at the hole in his side. The wound itself wasn't serious, a straight through and through hole in the fatty tissue just above the hipbone, but it was bleeding enthusiastically. His fingers trembled as he took out dressings for the holes and held them in place with a strip of gauze he wrapped twice around his waist and tied off.

He bent over the wounded man again. "How many troops are left at the east end of the dam?" When he heard no answer he reached for the mask again then realized he no longer heard the panting sounds of breathing through the filter. He tore off the mask and a glance was enough to tell him the man had no more answers.

Although weakened by the loss of blood, Mario struggled to his feet then trudged after the men he'd sent to find and disarm the last two bombs. The shotgunner had neutralized one charge, but they'd failed to find the other. Mario approached them slowly —he felt exhausted, and it was hard to draw the deep breaths he desperately needed through the mask.

"Look under the edge of the housing," he croaked, afraid that if he bent down to look for it he wouldn't be able to rise again.

He heard the pounding of feet as their reinforcements hurried toward them, then the shotgunner found the last bomb, pulled it out into the open, and pulled the wire, with only two or three minutes left on the timer.

"We need to get outside," Mario told them. "If we stay here, they can try to dig us out with explosives in any of a dozen ways, and if we stay bunched up near the door to repel an attack, they only have to lob in a grenade or two to wipe most of us out. We've got to get outside and disperse."

He led the way into the darkness. His breathing had become so labored it cost him almost as much effort as running a mile normally would. It seemed to take forever to reach the door then they were outside. Reaching up, he pulled the mask from his face, breathing in cool, sweet air.

The night was quiet. Finding a comfortable place sheltered by the bank, he fumbled for his canteen. Noticing his clumsiness, the shotgunner handed over his own canteen. Mario took a long drink of water then leaned back against the bank, and the darkness deepened.

~ * ~

Reynaud stared down at his swollen knee and the crude splint on his leg. His leg hurt like a bitch, and the stitches closing the incision through which the doctor from Mountain Home had removed bone splinters and cartilage, itched as though they were packed with maggots. Cheerful bedside manner hadn't been the doctor's strong suit. Reynaud would be in a cast for about three months, and the leg would always be stiff, as the mending bones fused. Angie suggested that time spent in bed wouldn't be wasted, although, at the moment, she was assisting the doctor and the paramedic in attending the worst wounded in the control tower.

The losses had been high: Between the raiders and the people in the p-camp, they'd lost over thirty dead killed immediately, and half that many had died in the day after the fighting ended. Most of the rest of the injuries were light, but they had eight or ten people maimed, as badly as Reynaud or worse. It was no consolation the Steel Fist had lost even more. Antibiotics were running low, and most of the Demoral and morphine had been used up. Reynaud was alternating aspirin and moonshine.

Logan limped into the makeshift infirmary. He'd sprained an ankle, coming down in a field.

"Hi, Caje! Got some good news for you! Mario lost some blood, but he's eatin' and drinkin' and restin' good. He should be here tomorrow."

"That is good news. How many did his group lose?"

"He was the worst hit."

"That's very good news. Not that Mario got himself shot, but that his group didn't lose anyone. How about the rest of our team? Xuan was looking a little green around the gills, and I haven't seen him since they took us off the truck."

"He took a gash that oughta give him a real sinister look when it scars over, and he broke two ribs. They didn't do any internal damage, as far as the doc can tell. They taped him up like a racehorse and told him not to laugh or cough for a while, but he don't do much of either, so he's gettin' by. Hasteen and the Deacon came through the whole thing without a nick. The Deacon's calmed down some."

"I'm glad to hear that. He scared the hell out of me in the fighting."

"He'd probably be proud of that," Logan observed. "If he can't preach the hell outta you, he'll get at it some other way." His face sobered. "I think the stress of the firefights gives him flash-backs to the camp, or something like that. At least he always shoots the right people."

"So far—but I get the feeling he's a ticking bomb."

Logan grinned again. "I'm just an old Air Force boy who believes it's better for us to have the bomb than for them to have it." He studied Reynaud's face. "You got a burr under your saddle. What's the trouble?"

Reynaud stared down at the stitches in his knee. "What're you and the rest of the gang going to do now?"

"Hell, I don't know. I suspect Norton might have a few ideas about that when he gets here. Oh, did I tell you? Davenport got away."

"I got that feeling. He knows if he'd stuck around, he'd wind up decorating a tree."

"Yeah. Too bad about Miller."

Sitting up abruptly, Reynaud winced. "What about Miller? Did he get away too?"

"No, but you won't get a chance to put a rope around his red neck: he suicided. Some ex-sergeant is the ranking leader in Harrison. The Steel Fist in Harrison gave up right after the people in Mountain Home threw in the towel. According to the ex-sergeant, Miller and the other officers all ate their pistols. He's willing to turn over the bodies. I'm willing to bet a lot of them killed themselves by walking in front of automatic weapons."

"To hell with it. Tell him to bury his own garbage."

"That's what I told 'im. But you're dancin' around the prob-lem. You still haven't said what's eatin' you."

The left side of Reynaud's mouth twitched into a crooked half-grin. "That's the only dancing I'll be doing. I'm pulling out. The doc says I'm down for a good three months. The knee won't work anymore—you make any 'Chester Good' jokes and I'm coming off this bunk to tear you a new asshole—so…" He stared at his knee again. "Anyhow, the old 'go ahead and saw off my shattered leg with a rusty bayonet' crap is getting awfully old. And so am I. Too damned old to spend my life playing caped crusader. I want a life—a real one, and I want it here. There's a lot I can accomplish here; things that need to be done. And I want to get married, settle down, even raise some kids."

Logan shifted on the chair, as though he'd have risen and paced if his ankle hadn't been so sore. "Jeez, Rennie, are you sure you wanna do that? Stickin' your leg in fronta that bullet really cancelled your dance card, so I can see you gettin' outta the guns and drums stuff, but marriage? Hell, Rennie, most women'd marry a dildo if they could get it to mow the lawn for them."

In spite of himself, Reynaud laughed. "My, you're bitter. Laura Wessel must've gotten to you a lot more than I thought."

"Doesn't have a damn thing to do with it," Logan snapped.

"Right. Anyway, I've made up my mind. If Angie will have me—"

Logan grinned. "I think she already has."

Suddenly a bearlike shape loomed in the doorway, and Norton strode into the former garage. Glancing around the building, he spotted Logan and Reynaud then found a chair, which he carried over and set down beside Reynaud's cot. Parking himself in the chair, he shook hands with both of them. "Damned glad to see you boys again." He looked down at Reynaud's wounded knee. "Sorry to hear you got shot up. You interested in that job I mentioned?"

Reynaud nodded. "If the offer's still open. I seem to have fucked up in planning, and we lost a lot of people."

"You did alright," Norton said soothingly. "From what I've heard, you stayed flexible and you got the job done. I don't think anybody could've done much better."

"What job?" Logan interjected.

"Same as mine," Norton said, "but here in Arkansas." He looked at Reynaud. "You got your work cut out for you. You got a lot of Steel Fist goons still around. What're you going to do about that?"

"If any of them had anything to do with mistreating prisoners or if they gave orders to use poison gas, we'll put them on trial. We'll need to set up courts. A lot of people in the Steel Fist just want order, something we all need, anyway."

"Sounds kinda rough and ready," Norton observed.

"A lot of it will have to be 'buck and saw,'" Reynaud replied. "Hell, a lot of what we'll do is going to have to be trial and error and on-the-job training, but we've got good land and a lot of good people. We can try to deal with the people running Fayetteville. Between their reactor—maybe we can get that going again—and the hydroelectric plant at Bull Shoals, we'll have the raw electric power we need to start rebuilding."

A man entered with a cooler and Norton waved him over.

"That's my back-up ice chest," Norton explained. He opened the top and handed a cool bottle to Reynaud and another to Logan, then produced a churchkey. "Home brew, but it's pretty good stuff. Rennie, it sounds like you've been putting your thinking time to good use. You might even be able to make alliances with the eastern part of the state. They've got another reactor in Russellville, too. Hell, you might even be able to do something about the mess in Little Rock."

"How about us grunts?" Logan asked.

"Well, for right now, I think Rennie could use a little extra help and, from what I've heard, some of you boys could use the time to heal up before you go back into the line, say about two weeks to a month. Unless you want to settle down, too."

Logan held up his hands. "These ain't built to go around plow handles. These hands belong wrapped around a joystick, and I'm not talkin' about playin' 'pup tent' with a stroke book."

"You might like the next job you're slated for, then."

"Whatta ya got in mind?"

"Get ready to click your heels together, Toto, you're going back to Kansas, a place called Wichita. It used to call itself 'The Air Capitol of the World.' We've got a couple agents there—Tom and Bert—who think something big's brewing. We'd like you to go take a look."

Logan clapped his hands together and rubbed them vigorously. "I'm ready to go now."

"Not yet. Things are still pretty tentative. We'll need a little time to get information you need so you don't go in blind."

Hasteen, Xuan, and the Deacon all entered the building. Norton broke out more bottles of homemade beer and handed them around, and kept for himself the bottle the Deacon had declined.

"Well, boys, Rennie is staying here in Arkansas. Anybody else want out?"

Hasteen looked at Reynaud, then at Logan. "Rennie can take care of himself, but Logan needs somebody to look after him. I guess I'm elected."

Norton took a long swallow of beer. "How about you, McCluskey?"

"It's my calling to be a staff to smite the unrighteous."

"You'll get lots of chances for that," Norton said. "Davenport's trail led northwest, and that's where you're going next. Xuan?"

The little man's face was lopsided from the swelling around the gash, which had taken fourteen stitches to close. "I'll go."

"We'd better get out of here," Norton said, "before the doctor throws us out." He stood. "I'll leave you the beer, Rennie." He hesitated. "I think you'll do right well. Hell, someday you may be governor of the state."

"Don't threaten me," Reynaud said. As the group turned to go, Reynaud struggled to a more comfortable position. "Hey, Deak, do you do weddings?"

"God makes marriages," the Deacon said. "I only speak His words."

"I'll talk to you about it later," Reynaud said, and sank back onto the cot.

~ * ~

As the men filed out the door, Hasteen glanced at Xuan. Something had changed about him, something deeper than torn skin or broken bones. "It'll be good to work with you again."

"Bare is the back without brother to watch it," Xuan said, and Hasteen understood the lack of expression in face or voice added emphasis to the words. Xuan had found men he could trust, men who'd risk their own lives for him, and Hasteen knew the man's isolation had been tempered with a sense of kinship.

As they walked away from the infirmary, they saw Angie go in the door.

~ * ~

Reynaud knew he'd miss the others. He'd even miss the excitement, spiced with panic, of the battles. Even the times of boredom or deprivation would be forgotten or wrapped in a golden glow of nostalgia then he saw Angie walking toward him, and the only thing he felt was contentment. It'd been a long trip, but he'd come home.

ABOUT THE AUTHOR

Rob Jackson is the *nom de guerre* used by James K Burk for the Recon 9 series. It's not that Burk isn't proud of the Recon 9 books but is just to let his fantasy and science fiction readers know these books have a different vibe.

Burk is fascinated by history, especially military history, and weapons. He also felt all too often action/adventure novels are bad-rapped, some of them by people who reach their action limit reading Jane Austin.

He likes creating characters you love or hate or hate to love or maybe love to hate but who you won't forget.

ALSO AVAILABLE IN THE RECON 9 SERIES

The Long Way Home –

A handful of men escape a Russian POW camp and make their way to Poland to alert whatever governments are left that the Russians are planning a strike simply called Operation A. They discover a world that has changed, devastated by plague and war, but where some groups are struggling to rebuild civilization while others continue to serve dead ideologies.

The group becomes "Recon Nine" and sets out to track down the higher command from the prison camp who are instrumental in Operation A.

Despite the bleakness of the surroundings, THE LONG WAY HOME is filled with action, surprises, and even some humor.

Operation Annihilation –

Recon 9, a group formed by veteran Air Force pilots who'd escaped a Russian POW camp faces a world devastated by plague, a desultory world war, and a widespread civic collapse.

Recon 9 follows a trail of bodies across Texas, discovering that west Texas put the wild in the wild west.

To catch the Russian agent they have to deal with bandit gangs, groups of homicidal maniacs, and military holdouts.

The agent is carrying out a program called Operation A or Operation Alpha.

To them, it seems to be: OPERATION ANNIHILATION.

OTHER WOLFSINGER PUBLICATIONS BOOKS BY JAMES K BURK

The Twelve –

Valtierra, a city-state, is governed by archetypes. Every two years they choose twelve men and women to wear the masks and to become the Wise Old Man, the Fool, the Mother, the Harlot, the Warrior, and the rest of the council.

But now Valtierra faces hunger, decay, and an enemy on their border. When the need for leadership is greatest, one mask is worn by a foreigner and one mask hides a traitor.

High Rage –

Scarface, on his way back to a clan stronghold after assassinating a legate, meets and falls in love with a woman even more ruthless than he. To win her, he must reunite an empire and create a kingdom. His only allies are his wits, his sword, and the power in his scars—black marks like the taloned fingerprints of a demon.

To achieve his goals, he must deal with old enemies, gods of dubious worth, and his own family—who may be the most dangerous of all.

Taking Hope -

The power he once held depleted, Scarface has found contentment as Morgan. No longer seeking power or building kingdoms, he is happy with his current life.

However, when what he most loves is threatened, Morgan must again become Scarface to correct past mistakes. He must defeat a king and a god. Knowing one god can only be beaten by another, he seeks an alliance, but what price will be demanded?

With only a few allies, one of them mad with rage, and the

power in his scars returned, he must confront old enemies, including one who knows his deepest secret and greatest weakness. Will he be able to lay to rest his past, defeat his enemies and return to the life he has made for himself. Or will he lose everything and everyone he has come to truly care about?

MORE BOOKS FROM WOLFSINGER PUBLICATIONS

Crisis in Big-G City – S.D. Matley

Olympus, Inc., is locked in battle with climate change!

Athena's Secret Ops program steps in when bad boy and technological genius Hermes can't come up with a carbon-curbing solution. Undercover agents Cleo Petra and Pan are deployed in the mortal world to vanquish the notorious East brothers, chthonic fossil fuel magnates who pass as human and eat humans, too…

Two-month-old Pablo, the one-quarter chthonic infant son of two fathers formerly known as P.B., employs his extraordinary abilities of adult speech and intellect in pursuit of climate justice!

Meanwhile, David Bernstein, whose hot romance with Cleo Petra meets a rocky end, recovers the memory of his century-old love affair with a beautiful Spanish nurse. He time travels to 1918 to find her and encounters love, loss, and the City of Mount Olympus—a dark and sinister place where every inhabitant lives in fear of volatile and destructive Zeus!

David's birth father and Hera's former fling, Saul Crispin, is outed as a mortal made immortal. Will Hera's high crime of granting Saul eternal life land her before a jury of her peers for judgment?

And what of baby-crazy Queen of the Underworld, Persephone, pregnant at last but not by Hades?

Intrigue, espionage, crimes of passion, secret babies and looming existential threats—everywhere you look there's a Crisis in Big-G City!

Tree of Bones – Book Two: A Familiar's Tale
 - Verna McKinnon

Two Curses

A curse of Darkness… Deep within the Thill forest, stands a tree made of human bones, crowned in black leaves and red thorns.

A curse of Light... Beneath the Wastelands of Skarros, a crystal imprisons a dark, immortal queen.

The Sorceress, Runa, is tormented by horrific images of this tree of bones in a distant, lifeless forest. Even as the visions debilitate her, Mellypip, her beloved familiar, also experiences these sinister dreams, bound by the same dream seer magic as his mistress. The tree of bones summons Runa, and she must risk madness and death as obsession drives her on. What she finds reveals a devastating truth.

Koll the Sorcerer awaits trial for his crimes. His familiar, Xabral, searches for allies to free him. Driven by his own dreams of dark prophecy, Koll seeks to free Obsydia, the Bloodstone Queen, from her prison. Determined to let nothing stop him, Koll will commit any evil to achieve his goal.

Runa and Mellypip's newest journey reveals truths behind ancient secrets, as Koll's obsessive hunt for a fallen queen threatens to doom the world forever. Runa and Koll, bound by opposing magical destinies of Light and Dark, will ultimately face frightening revelations and unimagined consequences.

Gate of Souls – Book One: A Familiar's Tale
- Verna McKinnon

Familiars.
Magical animal companions of sorcerers.
Keepers of spells and secrets.
Most important, devoted friends for life.

When one such familiar, Mellypip, bonds with the young sorceress Runa, he shares in the wonders of magic. Together, Mellypip and Runa train under the tutelage of Runa's grandfather, Cathal, and his cantankerous mountain owl familiar, Belwyn. But secrets and spells do not make for good sorcery. Old friends begin to vanish even as enemies from Cathal's past return, threatening to reveal the truth of Runa's parents; a truth from which Cathal must protect his granddaughter at any cost. When Cathal is kidnapped, Runa and Mellypip rush against time to save their family and friends from dark sorcery that will not only destroy them, but shatter the Gate of Souls and release demonic creatures of The Otherworld into the mortal realms.

The Seven Exalted Orders – Deby Fredericks

Arkanost has Seven Exalted Orders. No more, no less. When a magus goes renegade in a far-off province, the Mage Lords demand something be done.

Ryamon is bitter and frustrated. He longs to be a Fire magus; as a Stone magus, he's miserable. If he can bring the rogue back, he has a chance—his last chance—to fulfill his dream.

It's a great plan—until he actually meets Valdira.

Tails from the Front Lines 2: The Thin Blue Line
– edited by Carol Hightshoe

Come meet some of the four-legged members of Law Enforcement who also serve and protect.

Here our authors will introduce you to the brave K9 officers who serve alongside their human partners. They are their eyes, ears, noses and sometimes when necessary they are their shield, protecting others.

Proceeds from this anthology will be donated to the El Paso County (Colorado) Sheriff's Office K9 program in memory of K9 Jinx who was killed in the line of duty on April 11, 2022.

Ring of Fire – edited by Dana Bell

Enter the Ring of Fire, as unpredictable as the land masses shaking a city and volcanoes erupting covering the landscape. Could there be other reasons for these events? Or could these rings be more than a geological location.

They may be dragons playing tricks
or magic portals opened to mysterious realms
or sacrificing the best work of a lifetime.
Perhaps a rescue during a forest fire
or an attempt to raise the dead
or even while attending a high school reunion.

Journeys are taken to far off lands, another world, and through caves, each with their own unique twist.

Each tale presents a new idea on what the Ring of Fire could be. It is more than what many have been led to believe. Pull up a chair and warm yourself by our fires—just don't let yourself get burned.

Coyote – Charles Combee

While camping in a remote canyon in Utah Jim accidently sees an ancient rite taking place with a coyote like creature presiding over it. Now this creature wants Jim dead.

Audrey and her family go hiking in Utah and are attacked by this creature. Audrey is the only survivor, but she is pulled into a strange world of darkness and glass. She is 'rescued' by Jim, but is still linked to the creature, whose hold on her will end in her death unless Jim can find a way to break that link.

In his dreams, or are they ancient memories, Jim begins to learn more about Coyote as well as the magics that previously bound him. But those dreams end without teaching him the full magics. Can he find a way to free Audrey and stop Coyote from once again terrorizing humankind?

Believing is Seeing – Joanna Michal Hoyt

What we believe shapes what we see. Sometimes the stories we tell free us. Sometimes they trap us.

Some people see things their neighbors can't or won't see. Are they inspired? Delusional? Who decides?

As the faithful people of her village cry out for their god's help in disaster, a young peasant woman faces the terrifying possibility that she may be that god.

A time-traveling Jewish refugee visits 21st-century churches and confronts almost unrecognizable versions of himself.

Three troubled people make the dangerous visit to The Library where the maddening stories lodged inside them can be removed—on certain demanding conditions.

Having been warned away from the vacant lot which is said to house a portal to Hell, the new girl in town naturally goes to investigate.

Early in the grid collapse—or apocalypse?—a Christian lesbian farm couple paint "WELCOME" on their barn and await visitors.

An old man in the Terran diaspora enlists in a crusade to save humanity and belatedly wonders if he's on the wrong side.

Step inside these stories and see what you believe—but don't believe everything you see.

Out of the Darkness – edited by Carol Hightshoe

Mental Health issues have long been stigmatized, with those facing them pushed into the shadows, often unable to deal with the darkness they find themselves trapped in.

In this collection, stories explore many types of darkness—Suicidal Ideation, Death from Suicide, Survivor's Guilt, PTSD, Chronic Pain, Chronic Illness, Depression, Death of a Loved One, Secrets, Bullying, and other forms of darkness are explored. Some related to mental health issues and some not, but all of them offer very human perspectives. As in real life, some stories have happy endings and sadly others don't.

We offer these stories of darkness without judgement, but with hope and compassion. Some roads should never have to be traveled—but we understand that for many they are being traveled alone.

Proceeds from sales of Out of the Darkness will be donated to the American Foundation for Suicide Prevention—or more information on AFSP please visit their website at: afsp.org.

Never Cheat a Witch – edited by Carol Hightshoe

Magical curses. Arcane revenge. Being transformed into a frog. Things evil witches do to mere mortals who cross their path. But, what if there is more to the story…

Deals made with a witch are magically binding and can bring dire consequences to those who even think about breaking them.

Whether they are seeking revenge for wrongs done to them, helping others or simply trying to live their lives—it is NEVER wise to try and cheat a witch.

Open your spell book and join our authors as they relate tales of witches and mortals. From classic fantasy witches to modern day witches and even the legendary Baba Yaga. Good and Evil as well as every shade of gray in between.

And, yes—there is a prince who is turned into a frog.

Blood Bride – Belle Blukat

Dr. Bertram Hoel had ignored all women he'd met until being introduced to Cira Landon at his first Science Fiction convention. Knowing he should ignore the attraction, he still takes the dangerous step to begin a relationship, aware that by doing so he is placing her life in peril.

Cira Landon wrote tales of vampire lovers unaware the handsome scientist she'd just met actually was one. Drawn to him, she finds her life threatened by an old enemy who would do anything to exact his revenge, including kidnapping her and selling her on the black market for rare blood types.

With no other options, Dr. Hoel is forced to appeal to the Elders for assistance, hoping rescue does not come too late for Cira and knowing if she is found, there is but one ancient tradition that may save her life.

Return of the Black Witch – M.R. Williamson

One should not expect to slap the hand of an old crone and expect to walk away without at least a limp. The old witch Ethrel Ibenus is up to her tricks again and this time they've turned deadly. But where did her spirit go after Professor Martin shot her with his wee pistol?

Now, all are looking for the crone's familiar, Seleene. But the big timber wolf cannot be found. The search for the spirit of Ibenus now begins in earnest. Will Entwhistle and her Dwarves be able to help? Perhaps the Green Witch Pereen will be able to use a crystal derived from one of the Witch's own spells will do the trick. Fearing failure, Entwhistle improvises a plan 'C', the use of a mythical creature once thought to be long dead.

Time Capsules – edited by Carol Hightshoe

Time Capsules—history and mystery—a gift or a message from the past to the future.

Messages that can easily be misunderstood.

What were the reasons for passing along a pair of pink, fuzzy handcuffs?

A glass vial containing a perfect dandelion puff?

A Japanese Katana?

A red and blue scarf?

A wooden spoon?

What magic do these items contain? What stories do they tell?

From the past to the future. Mysteries and meanings abound within these pages, as well as reminders of the things people find precious. What will you find?

US/THEM – edited by Carol Hightshoe

US/THEM – THEM/US

Fear of the Other breeds hatred of the Other

They aren't like us—so they must be bad...inferior... dangerous...

Humans are by nature social animals, but we tend to bond with other humans with whom we have something in common: beliefs, experiences, likes and dislikes, etc.

With the expansion of humans across the planet, it seems that, even as our numbers grow, we find ways to whittle our groups into ever narrower, specialized, and exclusive blocks. We target the Other for the most minor differences and interpret everything from THEM as an insult or an attack.

Within these pages you will witness hatred, intolerance and fanaticism as well as love, understanding and acceptance. Most of all, I, and the authors, hope you discover stories that will cause you to pause and think before condemning someone as being THEM and not US.

And more – check out our books at
www.wolfsingerpubs.com